JACK DUNCAN

IS

THE DEADLIEST CAST MEMBER

SEASON ONE

KELLY RYAN JOHNS

Author's Note

Deadliest Cast Member is a tribute to the brave men and women of our Armed Forces who dedicate their lives to ensuring our freedom. Your sacrifices will not be forgotten, and without you, places like Disneyland would not exist. This extends to our military, police, intelligence community, first responders, and anyone else who risks their life to save others. It's also a tribute to ALL Disney Cast Members past and present including Mr. Iger, Mr. Lasseter, Mr. Kalogridis, and Mr. Colglazier for keeping Walt's dream alive at Disneyland and for doing an excellent job of making the Resort a magical place for us to enjoy. Your hard work brings joy to millions of people around the world.

This is a work of fiction. However, I've integrated an abundance of real-life Disneyland history, tips, and trivia into each Episode, based on hundreds of hours of exhaustive research. Certain aspects regarding security, schematics and characters are purely fictional. Several Disney Cast Members reviewed this book for accuracy.

Thank you to everyone who loyally followed the release of each Episode and provided positive feedback through our interactive online form. Your comments inspired me, and I don't know if I would've finished the Series if it weren't for your encouraging words. Many wrote saying that *Deadliest Cast Member* made them feel as if they were in the Park, and that it opened up a whole new world to them as they discovered things during their visits to Disneyland that were mentioned in the book. Messages from readers around the world came in thanking me for allowing them to relive memories at Disneyland through this story. Parents told me this book ignited their children's desire to read and learn. One reader said she loved the way real history was infused into the plot. Several active duty members of our military stationed overseas said that this story kept them going while they were missing home.

I originally envisioned *Deadliest Cast Member* as a "thriller at Disneyland," however once I dug deep into the history of the "Gentleman Pirate" Jean Lafitte, and I read his memoirs—I realized this story could be so much more. If you've ever seen the sunken brick archway in front of the Haunted Mansion on the River esplanade and wondered what it was, you'll find out in the pages to come. I think this story will cause you to look at New Orleans Square, and Disneyland, in a whole new way.

I studied everything I could get my hands on about Walt Disney, I watched him talk for hours on YouTube, analyzing the inflections of his voice, and the way he captivated audiences with his soothing mild-mannered tone. I tried to make the scenes with Walt special for true Disney fans, giving them a rare chance to experience private moments with him so they could fully appreciate his genius.

I was in awe when I watched Walt explain his vision of EPCOT, with the climate-controlled bubble and the underground transportation system—I realized that Walt was far ahead of everybody from his era. I knew that if anyone would be capable of creating something that was out of this world, it would be him. I wondered—if Walt was speaking publicly about an elaborate city with an actual bubble surrounding it to control weather—what else could he have been working on that no one knew about?

This question made me dig deeper into the phenomenon of Disneyland, and its creator. I wanted to examine the brilliant mind of Walt Disney—the greatest innovator of our time, and uncover "secret" projects that he could have been working on. How did he have the vision to pull something off as grandiose as Disneyland? How did it continue to flourish after all of these years?

I wanted to weave Disney history and facts—along with US history—into a fictional story so people could learn interesting things about the Parks. I spent hundreds of hours over two years researching underground tunnels, the dark water system, Walt's Apartment, Club 33, New Orleans Square, and Walt's peculiar fascination with Lafitte. I purchased Lafitte's Memoirs and read them cover to cover trying to figure out a connection between him and Walt. Why did Walt make him a central figure of New Orleans Square?

I wrote *Deadliest Cast Member* using "Episodes," which are similar to television episodes. Most have cliffhangers and other things you'd expect to see in an action packed TV show.

This story will take you on a journey through time allowing you to experience Disneyland throughout several different decades. Have coffee with Walt Disney in his 1959 Fire Station Apartment on Main Street, and then eat a lobster sandwich with Walt and Admiral Fowler at Maurie's Lobster House on Fowler's Harbor. Witness a fairy-tale love story set on the romantic Skyway in 1994. Travel to 1966 to see the opening of New Orleans Square, and hear some of Walt's last words before his death in December of 1966. The "time travel" storytelling aspect permitted me to show the magnificence of Disneyland through the years, which will hopefully trigger fond memories from your past.

I've included the extended version of this author's note at the end of the book, which includes the dedication, my Disneyland story, and my gratitude to everyone who has helped make this Series possible.

I hope you enjoy this crazy ride through Disneyland history!

Kelly Johns
Founder of MouseWait.com
www.DeadliestCastMember.com

Like *Deadliest Cast Member* on Facebook for real-time updates and behind the scenes info!

Go to www.DeadliestCastMember.com to join our Priority Email List and to get notifications via Facebook and Google+!

First Edition

JACK DUNCAN

IS

THE DEADLIEST CAST MEMBER

SEASON ONE

EPISODE ONE

"If I could live for fifteen more years, I would surpass everything I've done over the past forty-five years."
WALT DISNEY

ONE

August 6, 2010
El Capitan Presidential Suite
Grand Californian Hotel
Disneyland Resort

"Mr. Duncan," said a voice through Jack's earpiece, "you should be seeing a live feed from Tom Sawyer Island on your screen now."

Jack squinted his eyes and slightly lowered his head to focus on two military-grade 17-inch Macbook Pros along with two iPads that occupied the cream-colored wood coffee table. He shifted his eyes back and forth as the devices blinked through a series of color video feeds, with real-time streaming data on the right side.

"No one has any weapons?" Jack asked the officer through his earpiece.

"No sir, but The System has linked them—the suspicious thing is they're acting as if they don't know each other."

After what happened in 2005, Jack spent millions of dollars of his own fortune improving *The System*—the most advanced large-scale security network in the world. He put all of his energy into rebuilding and improving the security system his dad built in 1955, when Disneyland opened.

He leaned back, stroking his chin as he analyzed the situation. He gazed through the impressive twenty-foot wall of glass in front of him overlooking Disney California Adventure Park. Twenty-four narrow panes infused with themed stained glass art joined to create a one-of-a-kind majestic glass mural —a constant reminder of how lucky he was to live in the middle of the most famous theme park in the world.

The voice came through Jack's earpiece again.

"Sir, we have approximately one hundred additional alerts at the front gate via our facial recognition system—these people have some type of affiliation with the ones on the Island."

Jack got to his feet and rubbed the back of his neck. He paced the hardwood floors of the 1987 square foot El Capitan Presidential Suite living room—a Craftsman-style residence patterned after the Arts and Crafts movement of the early 1900s.

At 6 foot, 2 inches tall, Jack had maintained his physique from his days with the storied SEAL Team Six (DEVGRU). Always well dressed, his black hair complemented his hardened face. Hundreds of successful missions earned him several Bronze and Silver stars for acts of valor—which took an extensive toll on his body. Jack had more confirmed kills than anyone who'd ever worn the gold trident. His body endured extreme torment during his Team Six years, which caused him long-term physical pain.

Jack didn't bother to ask how these people were related because he knew the man giving him the info wouldn't know that yet. *The System* used custom facial recognition software to match CIA, FBI, Homeland Security, Disney, and several other databases to detect real-time threats. It quickly determined various levels of connectivity; everything from where they went to school, political affiliations, criminal records, and other details. As people were linked, dedicated cameras generated a continuous live feed of their actions while on Disney property.

"A hundred alerts, are you sure about this?" Jack asked knowing this was an excessive amount.

"Yes, sir. Maybe more." The voice said.

"Are all these people heading to the Island?" Jack asked.

"It appears that way, sir, although not all at the same time."

"Okay, make sure we have an undercover team in place." Jack studied the data to try to figure out what was going on. None of these people had a record other than minor drug use from decades ago. Tom Sawyer Island had always been a security concern because of its location and the advantage it could give someone trying to take over or sabotage the Park.

Jack looked up at the dramatic twenty-foot raised ceiling of the El Capitan Suite living room. His mind moved towards the worst-case scenario as he clenched his fists. *We haven't had any other alerts, no other signals that would support a large-scale event like this?*

His mind flashed to Nikolai Grusov's malicious face, the man who had taken so much from him, the man who had haunted him for all of these years and still caused him to awake violently at night with feelings of rage and revenge. Just the thought of Nikolai changed Jack's entire demeanor—feelings of pure hate pushed adrenaline throughout his body.

His attention shifted to Andy and Grace. He switched his iPad to its default view of his kids. Jack always had a real-time view of them on at least one of his devices. It eased his mind to be able to watch their every move; after everything he'd seen and done in his life, it was the only way he could be apart from them.

Above all, he wanted his kids to be safe and happy after what had happened in 2005. He wanted to make good on his promise to live at Disneyland. Jack had been all over the world for most of his career, and in this season of his life, he wanted to stay in one place—the *one* place that made his kids happy.

Jack's mind jumped back to 2005, realizing that this situation was oddly similar to the events that preceded the attack. His heart rate increased, and his palms were sweaty. That fateful day made Jack Duncan an unlikely international celebrity, which was something he never wanted. He saved thousands of innocent lives—but paid a heavy price.

He pulled his iPhone out of his pocket and flipped to another screen giving him a different perspective of the situation. This was no ordinary iPhone—none of his Apple products were normal. They were all modified, military-grade devices. This iPhone had a screen that was larger than the civilian version, and it was custom curved to fit his hand. Jack had helped Apple on various security related projects over the years. Steve Jobs was notoriously difficult to impress and get along with, but he was fascinated with Jack and intrigued with his mental toughness. Jack had been to Steve's house several times. He was like a kid at Christmas when he visited since Jobs always had a new toy for him to play with.

"Sir, we have a problem," said the voice in Jack's ear.

TWO

August 6, 2010
The Pool
Grand Californian Hotel

Grace screamed as she slid down the Redwood themed water slide into the eighty-degree water. The stream of water from the slide forced her small ten-year-old body towards the exit ladder—giggling the entire way. It didn't matter how many times she'd been down that slide; she loved it all the same.

Grace had been taught to appreciate and admire all of the little details around her. The pool was perfectly themed to match the rest of the Grand Californian and California Adventure. She learned from her dad that most of the structures in the pool area were based on the Gamble House in Pasadena, which is said to be the best example of Arts and Crafts architecture popular at the turn of the century. Behind the water slide, sections of the Redwood Creek Challenge rope bridges were visible, surrounded by seventy-foot redwood trees. The massive Mickey's Fun Wheel loomed in the background. She loved this pool because it made her feel as if she was inside California Adventure.

Grace and Andy rarely had to say good-bye to Disneyland. They spent most of the year at the Resort, and they knew it like the back of their hand. They could live anywhere in the world, but there was no place they'd rather be —nothing else brought them this much joy.

Grace looked over at Max, and waved as she went for another ride down the slide.

Max Parker stood across from the slide dressed in black. Hired to be the ultimate bodyguard, Max never took his eyes off the kids. His head scanned side-to-side tracking everyone in the area through his black sunglasses as if he was protecting the First Family. At 6 foot 5 inches and 275 pounds, he stood out in the Disney crowd.

Max resembled a brick wall. He and Jack had known each other for years, serving side by side on many missions as SEALs all over the world. Max had also been good enough to make it to Team Six.

He stood by the pool with his thick arms crossed as he heard a familiar voice in his earpiece.

"Max, I need you to bring the kids up to the suite."

It was Jack.

THREE

August 6, 2010
El Capitan Presidential Suite
Grand Californian Hotel
Disneyland Resort

Jack headed for the balcony of the El Capitan Presidential Suite as he studied the real-time streaming data on his device. The clean scent of the Grand Californian hotel, a result of the meticulous daily housekeeping, calmed his senses. He walked by the magnificent light colored stone fireplace in the living room as he approached the balcony doors.

A refreshing, California breeze made its way into the living room. Patriotic music rang out from Condor Flats—a "Land" in California Adventure themed after an airfield in tribute to California's pilots and engineers from the 1940s to 1960s. Songs from *The American President, The Right Stuff*, and other inspiring movie soundtracks played day and night. The faint sounds of joy and laughter from the people below added depth to the rich ambiance. The smell of freshly popped popcorn and the scent of mature redwood trees lingered in the air as the swooshing sound of the iconic Monorail resonated from below. The lovely aroma from the wood fired oven inside the Napa Rose, located six floors directly under him, added yet another layer of elegance to the pristine environment.

The balcony was therapeutic for Jack. He loved watching the sunrise from this unique vantage point. It calmed his nerves watching the crowds meandering through the Park while basking in the refreshing view of Grizzly River Run and the mighty man-made waterfalls that resembled the white water rapids of Klamath. He had a choice between an ocean view from his house in Newport Beach and this view, and most of the year this view won the contest hands down.

Andy and Grace barreled through the front door of the suite with their friends followed by Max, Kim, and Tony. Their laughter and excitement echoed throughout the enormous living room.

The kids headed for the balcony, where they hung out to get a pulse on what was happening inside the Park. It made them feel as if they were still inside the gates.

"Hey Dad, let's go to Storytellers!" Grace said.

"Not yet sweetheart, I have to handle a few things first and then we'll go when I get back."

Jack motioned to Max, Kim, and Tony to follow him into the living room.

He addressed his most loyal employees in a quiet tone so the kids wouldn't hear. "Something is going down in Disneyland right now, and I need to head over there and take care of it."

All three looked concerned, but Jack did this sort of thing frequently—he was undoubtedly over cautious.

Jack had personally dealt with and exterminated the worst terrorists in history. He had the uncanny ability to look directly into the eyes of the most horrific human beings on the planet and cause them to be thoroughly intimidated and scared.

"I need you guys to lock this place down and be on high alert."

"Sure Jack, is everything okay?" Tony asked. Tony was shorter than Jack. As a former CIA agent with years of experience in everything from top-secret extraction missions to personal protection, his physical strength wasn't his primary asset—although he could certainly hold his own in a battle. Tony had the ability to analyze and figure out almost any situation with speed and acuity. He had protected the President of the United States during his tenure with the Secret Service.

"I don't know," Jack said, "but I'm going to find out."

Kim smiled at Jack. She had a way of comforting the kids, and her unrivaled close quarter combat skills eased Jack's mind because no one had a chance at getting to the kids when she was around. She was the best in her class with years of experience in protecting high value targets when she was with the FBI—instrumental in several raids and investigations that helped put a large number of terrorists behind bars. She'd put a bullet in your head without even thinking about it—even the most hardened terrorists were afraid of her when she entered the room.

"Don't worry Jack, we'll take care of things here," Kim said.

"Okay," Jack continued in a low voice, "have the team in Newport watch everything in the local area, including the airspace above, and put the 24-hour team on high alert."

"Yes, sir," Max said.

Jack followed Max to the front door. Max took up his position outside the door as Jack headed for the Cast Member elevator and the underground tunnel leading into Disneyland.

FOUR

August 6, 2010
Tom Sawyer Island
Disneyland Park

Jack entered Disneyland from backstage through two swinging doors next to the bathrooms in New Orleans Square. Whipping around the corner, he headed for the wooden rafts on the Rivers of America that shuttled people to Tom Sawyer Island.

It was another perfect day at Disneyland; 75 degrees, clear skies with only a few small clouds, low humidity, and the sun illuminated the Rivers of America like a Thomas Kinkade painting.

Robert Conroy, head of security at the Disneyland Resort spoke to Jack through his earpiece. "Jack, another group of people are almost to the Island now. They're going to be hard to recognize, but it's clear they're related to the people on the Island."

"I'm heading straight for the Island. I've been watching the multi-person feed of the main suspects, and they don't seem to be doing anything out of the ordinary."

Conroy paused for a moment. "Jack, it looks like there are more of them on the Mark Twain right now."

Jack glanced up at the Mark Twain Riverboat—the authentic steam powered paddlewheel riverboat that takes guests on a fourteen-minute tour around Tom Sawyer Island. It was a stark white boat resembling the nineteenth century riverboats that carried people and cargo up the Mississippi River.

Jack anxiously looked at the simultaneous real-time video feed on his device that displayed twenty small squares on each page. He could track the activity of everyone involved. He kept scrolling, trying to figure out what they were doing, looking for the smallest clue. He knew they were converging on the Island for a reason and that *The System* rarely generated false positives, not with this many people involved. Stepping carefully on to the raft, Jack made sure to not make eye contact with anyone. He was frequently spotted in the Park by people wanting a picture or an autograph—but he couldn't have any distractions right now.

Jack put on a pair of modified Google glasses. He scanned the Island, the River, and everything around him. Sergey Brin and Larry Page, founders of Google, gave him a prototype of the magic glasses they'd been working on dubbed "Project Glass". Jack modified them to work with *The System*, and they became an integral part of his protective arsenal because he could immediately identify people just by looking through the glasses. No one could tell what he was doing—they looked like normal sunglasses.

Jack scanned the area, compiling real-time facial recognition assessments. His entire team was equipped with Glass, which enabled them to broadcast their positions with live video feeds. These feeds could be assembled so that everyone could view the situation from different vantage points—*The System* determined relevancy, giving the team the information they needed, when they needed it.

Jack scanned the people on the raft and spotted several people who were related to the others in question. As the raft approached the Island, more were flagged. He glanced to his right as the Mark Twain passed by and over half the boat was deemed related. The old-style wooden raft decelerated as it approached the dock with the smell of exhaust wafting through the air. Waiting to be last to exit, Jack inconspicuously followed the people in question.

FIVE

Jack spoke softly to the undercover team, "Agents on the Island, report your position."

"This is Team Four, we're circling the Island now from the back side."

Jack glanced down at his iPhone and saw their current position via the live streaming feed. He swiped to an aerial view of the Island via the "Raven" which was a remote controlled flying camera that gave them instant information from above.

"Okay, keep moving and discreetly follow them. I'm tailing another group that just got off the raft."

"Jack, I'm going to close down the rafts and I'm thinking of evacuating the Park, too." Conroy's voice escalated through Jack's earpiece.

"Close the rafts but don't evacuate. *The System* has detected nothing in terms of weapons, not even pepper spray. I'm not sure what this is, but at this point we don't need to evacuate."

"Okay Jack, but I'm worried about this, weapons or not, something is wrong," Conroy was a seasoned professional and exceptionally good at his job, but Jack felt he worried too much.

"Don't worry, I'll handle this," Jack said as he followed the suspects down the dirt path around the Island. They weren't talking to each other, just walking with their heads down looking at their phones.

"Sir, this is Team Four leader. Two of the men have made it to the top of Lafitte's Tavern at the front of the Island."

Jack looked down at his iPhone as the video feed shifted to isolate the view. *The System* was not detecting any weapons or explosive devices.

"Sir, we've instructed them to get down from the building, but they're not cooperating. Do we have permission to engage?"

Most of the Disneyland security force dress in plain clothes. There could be thousands of undercover agents in the Park at any given time, and they're able to cover a lot of ground and intervene quickly.

"No, stand down. I'll be there in a minute. Do NOT draw weapons. They are unarmed, and there's no trace of any kind of explosive device."

The group Jack was tailing started to run, implying their involvement in the situation. He took off after them.

"STOP RIGHT THERE!" Jack yelled as he passed them.

They stopped in their tracks. They had a look of shock on their faces when they realized who it was.

Jack arrived at the front of the Island and saw two men on top of Lafitte's Tavern. The "Tavern" is the focal point for the Rivers of America. It's front and center on the Island and is visible to everyone in New Orleans Square and

Frontierland. The Team Four leader shouted commands at them as the men clumsily pulled a hefty cloth-like object out of a backpack. They fumbled with it, and barely managed to get the large flag out of their pack.

Jack put his hand on his weapon under his jacket. He realized they were trying to unroll a flag of some sort. He watched as it unfolded down the front of the building. At the same time, the Mark Twain came around the bend and the people on board broke out in an uproar, cheering as loud as they could. Hundreds of people on the Island began to cheer as well.

Jack took his hand off his weapon and looked down at his phone for the date.

The moment he realized it was August 6, 2010 he knew what this was all about.

SIX

"Rob, today is August 6—the 40th anniversary of Yippie Day."

The two guys on top of the building triumphantly raised their hands as they held the "Yippie" flag aloft. They reveled in the cheers from the crowd.

"Get off the building, NOW!" Jack roared at the two men. Their eyes widened when they realized who it was. They sheepishly made their way down.

They had planned for a massive photo op on Tom Sawyer Island to commemorate the anniversary.

"Well Jack, I guess we didn't need full riot gear for this one." Conroy said with a sigh of relief referring to the 1970 event when Anaheim PD entered the Park in full riot gear to stop the "Yippies."

The leader of Team Four interjected, "Sir, I don't think we would've needed the riot gear with Mr. Duncan here."

The guys were always a little star struck when they got the chance to work with Jack. They were all aware of his heroics in 2005, and his legendary career.

Jack smiled and nodded at the guys from Team Four. He wasn't happy about having to lock down the kids for nothing, but he was relieved that this wasn't a serious threat.

SEVEN

Jack put his head down and walked at a brisk pace through New Orleans Square, heading for the Cast Member exit. He wanted to get back to the Grand Californian quickly.

Everything was vivid in New Orleans Square: the flowers, the trees, and the vibrant colors emanating from thousands of purposely placed details.

He glanced up and noticed the French Market. He slowed down for a moment to take in the beauty around him. His dad always told him that there was something special about this area; a place where you could truly experience the magic of being immersed in a storybook world. Mature, meticulously maintained trees, most over fifty years old, provided shade and character to the Land.

The sound of the Disneyland Limited Railroad filled the air—it reminded him of the stories his dad told about Walt Disney's affinity for trains. The trains were a symbol of opportunity and adventure. The railways of his time made it possible for him to travel the country to follow his dreams. The train he boarded in his small hometown in Missouri, transported him to a 1920s Buena Vista Street in Hollywood—a place with endless possibilities.

Most of all, New Orleans Square reminded Jack of his one true love.

The enchanted environment, mixed with the sweet sounds of the Royal Street Bachelors playing their classic New Orleans Jazz, the smell of food being prepared at the French Market, and the whistle from the train coming into the station triggered something in Jack's mind that made him stop in his tracks.

1994
Disneyland Park
"Love in New Orleans Square"

It was another perfect Southern California day in New Orleans Square. Although Disneyland opened to terrible one hundred degree heat in 1955, the weather in Anaheim was rarely that hot.

The Royal Street Bachelors set the perfect mood for Walt Disney's utopian version of New Orleans. Romance lingered in the air because of the storybook atmosphere, the view of the water, sounds of people having fun, the aroma of food being prepared, and the escape from everyday life that New Orleans Square offered.

The Bachelors were on the small French Market outdoor stage, and their soothing Jazz added a rich layer of ambiance to the nineteenth century theme.

The squeaky-clean Disneyland Limited Railroad arrived at the New Orleans Square station, with the classic sound of the train coming to a stop followed by the call of the conductor.

The clatter of Morse code reciting Walt's opening day speech was in the background, along with the sound of people with their families eating together and heading towards their next adventure.

The French Market outdoor dining area was full of people. Several thick green canvas sections covered the area creating a serene, shaded place to relax. People enjoyed French-style cuisine with a stunning view of the River. It was the perfect place to sit and enjoy coffee while listening to live Jazz. Just around the corner, only feet from the train station, guests ordered the famous Mint Juleps with freshly cooked fritters.

Any seat on the veranda provided a fantastic view of the brilliant Rivers of America.

Jack had been here thousands of times, but each time he stopped to admire the lush green trees, the detailed landscaping with fresh flowers that appeared to be refreshed every few days, the magnificent Haunted Mansion, and the breathtaking Rivers of America.

He was at the Park in between deployments to decompress and relax. Usually he'd meet his dad or other friends, but today he was alone.

Walking leisurely through New Orleans Square, he perused the security plans his dad wanted him to review. Both he and his dad had the same passion for strategic security, so Stan would share with Jack what was happening at the Park, and they always worked on things together. It was their way of bonding.

Head down, Jack passed the French Market. He looked up to make sure he wasn't going to run into anyone, and glanced to his right at the table just past the small exit gate under the French Market sign.

Everything began to move in slow motion.

The sound of the crowd faded.

Everything blurred except for a blonde beauty sitting alone, reading a book. She had incredible, long hair with deep blue eyes and full lips. He instantly recognized she was a genuine, natural beauty—not a flashy 'look at me' type of girl.

Looking up from her book, she locked eyes with Jack for a brief second and time stood still.

Jack felt something he'd never felt before. It was more than just physical attraction; it was much different—something he couldn't explain.

She looked back down at her book.

Stan always told Jack that there was one person who he was destined to be with. Jack believed this when he was a kid, but as he grew up and was exposed to plenty of beautiful women who were shallow, selfish, and disloyal, he became skeptical. But this was different—when he locked eyes with her, it was significant—a life-changing event.

He continued to stare at her after she looked back down at her book, and then he caught himself gazing too long. He looked forward, and kept walking. He thought to himself about what his dad said, and wondered if this was one of those 'once in a lifetime' situations he'd told him about.

Jack rarely hit on women. As a SEAL, women were always pursuing him and his teammates.

He stopped walking, and looked up to the sky.

This is crazy. What am I doing?

Turning around, he could see her from behind, sitting and reading her book. Her long, thick blonde hair spread out evenly on her black blouse, and the contrast between the two was marvelous. He moved closer and then stopped.

I don't even know what to say? This is stupid, I'm not going to do this.

Jack paused, and his life flashed before his eyes. He was in his late twenties and still hadn't settled down. He was in empty relationships with women he could not trust and who didn't care for him. He was at the top of his game, but what was that doing for him? He was ultimately lonely and didn't have anyone to share his life with.

I've done harder things than this, I might as well just try and see what happens.

Following the same method he used to jump out of airplanes into dark, cold water, he stopped thinking about it— and just did it—he traced his steps and stood directly in front of her.

It was hard to explain her reserved beauty. It was natural, and she wasn't trying to be pretty, she wasn't trying to dress a certain way to be noticed. The way her hair cascaded over her face as she read her book was a showstopper.

She didn't look up. After a few moments Jack finally said, "Um, excuse me."

She seemed surprised to see the same guy she'd locked eyes with earlier standing right in front of her. Her eyes sparkled as she flashed a cute, embarrassed smile, at Jack.

"Hi," she said with a confused look.

Jack was at a loss for words.

"Um, I was wondering where you got that book." Nodding toward the book in her hand, he continued, "I've read all of Walt's biographies and I've never seen that one."

He mentally kicked himself the instant the words came out of his mouth.

She closed the book while keeping her place, glancing at the cover and then looking back up at Jack, "I got it on Main Street. This is the only one I haven't read yet."

Jack's heart dropped, not only was she beautiful, but she was a huge Disney fan like he was. He hoped she was there by herself.

"Really," Jack continued with a skeptical look on his face, "you've read *all* of Walt's biographies?"

With her eyebrow raised, she looked at him as if to say *you don't believe me?*

Jack realized how it sounded, shook his head, and rephrased the question.

"No, I meant I've never met anyone—well except my dad—who's read all of Walt's biographies."

"What's your dad's name?"

Why is she asking for my dad's name?

She smiled and clarified, "I would like to talk to anyone who's read all of Walt's biographies," she put the book down on the table and leaned forward, "because Walt is one of the most fascinating innovators of all time and Disneyland is the legacy he left behind to show us the depth of his imagination—to inspire us to do great things in our own lives."

Is this really happening to me right now? Someone who thinks exactly like me when it comes to Walt and Disneyland? Someone who just happens to be beautiful and apparently single?

"So, what's his name?" she smiled as she had this big, muscular, clean-cut military-looking guy flustered.

"Umm, it's Stan Duncan," Jack, who never divulged unnecessary information, even during brutal interrogations, was seemingly under a spell.

Her mouth dropped, and her eyebrows scrunched a bit, "You mean *the* Stan Duncan, as in Walt's closest advisor from the 1950s?"

Oh my, she is a legitimate Disney fan. Jack continued to be in awe of this woman.

"Yes, that's him."

"Are you kidding me?" perking up, she asked, "Your dad is Stan Duncan? The man who advised Walt on almost everything and the one who developed the entire security system for the Park?"

Jack smiled, "Yes, that's him." This had to be one of those moments his dad told him about. He couldn't believe this was happening.

He prepared to ask her if she was by herself and if she wanted to get a cup of coffee—when he noticed a tall man, around his size, approaching the table.

"Hey Kate," the man said to her as he scanned at Jack with a confused look.

She stood up with an excited smile on her face and gave the man a loving hug. It was like someone unplugged the Royal Street Bachelors bringing the jazz to a screeching halt, the background sound of the crowd got louder, and the slow motion movie scene came to a disappointing end—this guy thoroughly ruined the moment.

"Bobby," she said to the tall guy, "this guy's dad is Stan Duncan—*the* Stan Duncan, as in Walt's closest advisor!"

The man looked over at Jack, "Really? Well, it's nice to meet you!"

Jack gave the man a courtesy half smile and shook his hand.

"This is my brother Bobby," she said with a smile, "he's a huge Disney fan like me."

Jack felt a wave of relief roll over him.

"And I'm Kathleen," she extended her hand to Jack as her long hair blew across her face. Her smile was exhilarating. Her light golden tan emphasized her hypnotic blue eyes. She was the perfect California girl.

Jack was the *last* person to believe in love at first sight. He thought it was stupid and that it couldn't happen.

Maybe this time he was wrong.

EIGHT

August 6, 2010
El Capitan Presidential Suite
Grand Californian Hotel

Jack approached the doorway of room 6329, the El Capitan Presidential Suite, where Max was standing guard. Max opened the light colored thick wood double doors, and they entered through a small foyer with decorative stained glass on each side. The foyer made it difficult to see the inside of the suite from the sixth floor hallway—it set the room back several feet. It created an effect similar to the tunnels near Disneyland's main gate—where the grandeur of Town Square and Main Street are hidden until you emerge from under the passageway.

The El Capitan Suite living room was similar to a luxurious penthouse suite. The entire room was lined with rich wood borders and light cream-colored wallpaper that complimented the inset wood floors and large throw rugs throughout the suite.

Jack headed for the wide balcony that was accessible from several different doors along the width of the suite. He admired the sweeping view of California Adventure, the picturesque redwoods, the Soarin' Over California building, and Condor Flats. The walkway below resembled an old road leading guests from Condor Flats to Grizzly River Run and then on to Paradise Pier. The Aptos Blue Redwood Trees were scattered across the "Land" fitting perfectly into the landscape. These coastal trees magically flourished at Disneyland, despite the dry Southern California weather.

Millions of gallons of water rushed through the Grizzly River Run attraction. The sound of the water was calming. The beautiful rockwork, the glistening water, and the rich greenery gave the feeling of being in a mountain lodge. The final drop of Grizzly River Run, where guests plunged down a large waterfall, exuded the fun and excitement of California Adventure.

"Everything okay, sir?" Max asked.

Jack smiled with his signature half-smile, "Yeah, everything's fine now."

Grace spotted Jack on the balcony, and she ran out to give him a big hug.

"Yay, you're back," she said, "let's go to Storytellers!"

"You got it Gracie, let's go."

Tony and Kim stood in front of the wall of glass overlooking the massive oversized balcony. Jack flashed a quick smile to them as he came in the door.

"Let's go eat."

"Hey guys," Jack said to the kids as his eyes lit up, "the Depps are coming in tomorrow afternoon, so we need to pack our stuff and move to another room. I think you'll like where we're going—but it's a surprise. I'll tell you later." Jack wasn't known for showing much emotion, but his face was always animated and expressive when talking to the kids.

Andy and Grace jumped up and down with excitement.

"Can we hang out with Mr. Depp and the kids tomorrow, Dad?" Andy asked. He was a huge *Pirates of the Caribbean* fan; so hanging out with the real Captain Jack Sparrow was always a thrill for him. Johnny Depp usually talked like Captain Jack for Andy while on the Pirates of the Caribbean attraction because he knew he was a big fan.

Jack became close friends with Johnny in 2005 when Jack saved the Resort. Johnny and his family were at the Grand Californian that week, and they were just a few of the thousands of lives Jack saved that day.

Jack's phone rang; it was Luke, "Jack, do you have a minute? I found something you need to hear about."

"Luke, I'm heading to dinner with the kids right now, can we talk later?"

At twenty-seven years old, Luke was one of the most brilliant technological minds in the world. He was a lead tech at Google for many years before Jack tripled his salary to get him on board. Larry and Sergey were not happy about it, but they didn't argue with Jack.

"Actually Jack, I think you need to hear this," Luke continued, "I ran detailed profiles on everyone involved in that 'Yippie' anniversary thing today. They all had relatively clean records and were harmless—except I found one person on the Island who appears to be totally unrelated to the group, with a distant connection to—" Luke paused.

Jack stopped what he was doing and headed for the private office next to the living room. He knew Luke would not waste his time unless it was important.

"It seems he has a distant connection to the Grusov family."

Jack stopped dead in his tracks and pressed his phone hard to his ear when he heard the Grusov name, "What kind of connection?" Jack clamped his teeth together and dropped his voice.

"Nothing criminal from what I can find, he's totally clean, but I was surprised to find this connection. I'm going to look into this further. As we speak, I'm compiling the full video feed of him throughout the Park today so we can review every second of it."

Jack grabbed the back of his neck instinctively, and his vision blurred. Hearing the Grusov name was enough to send him in to a rage-filled frenzy. This was not only a threat to the Resort, but a personal threat to Jack's family. He was normally a patient man with the discipline of a Team Six Navy SEAL, but when it came to Nikolai Grusov, he could snap at any moment, and turn into a dangerous assassin.

NINE

August 6, 2010
Storytellers Cafe
Grand Californian Hotel

What should have been a fun time with the kids at their favorite place to eat turned into Jack being preoccupied, silent, and constantly looking at his phone. He impulsively and erratically scanned every person in the restaurant with a determined, disturbed look on his face.

Jack enjoyed Storytellers Cafe because of the warm and inviting atmosphere that allowed him to relax and unwind. It took two minutes to get there from the El Capitan Suite via the elevators located next to the Napa Rose. It was central to most of their activities; directly across from the pool, and approximately one hundred feet from the California Adventure Grand Californian entrance. It was one of those places that became a tradition for Jack and the kids, a place that felt like home, with warm and cozy fireplaces, rich wood panels, light green tile and carpet, and dark wood chairs and tables with intricate inset designs. Light green trees, mountains, silhouettes of cowboys leading horses, and metal cut outs depicting early American life were carefully infused into the walls. Exquisite early nineteenth century replica lanterns hung from the ceiling, which produced warm amber lighting that made the kids feel as if they were eating in an enchanted cottage.

When it came to food, Jack loved the Napa Rose because the level of cuisine was unmatched throughout the Resort. But when the kids could pick, they liked the simpler food of Storytellers Cafe and the relaxed atmosphere. Andy and Grace talked back and forth with their friends as they devoured their food. The buffet was their favorite because they could load up on whatever their hearts desired. Whether it was the hand carved, juicy turkey breast, or the homemade Charred Nebraska Corn Chowder with rotisserie chicken and bacon. They always looked forward to dessert, which was a third of the entire buffet display. The bread pudding was their favorite because it tasted like gourmet French toast.

At the Resort, Cast Members are like one big family, and they'd practically adopted Grace and Andy as their own.

Grace walked to the right side of the buffet behind the plates and smiled at the lady in charge of the ice cream. The CM looked fondly at her and gave Grace three towering scoops of rich chocolate ice cream along with a mountain of whipped cream and rainbow sprinkles. The ice cream was not officially on the menu, but the CMs always made sure Grace got some just the way she liked it.

Grace's bright eyes revealed her excitement. The sight of the cool and creamy mountain of chocolate thrilled her.

"Thank you!" She said smiling, and headed back to the table.

Jack looked at his watch, then at his phone, and continued to scan the room. He habitually scanned rooms, but tonight, it was noticeably excessive.

They sat together at a large table near one of the tall fireplaces. Max looked over at Kim and Tony—they were concerned about Jack.

Two Disney security CMs stood near the front and side entrances of the restaurant keeping an overall eye on things.

"Max," said Jack, "I need to run back up to the suite to check on something. Can you bring the kids straight up after they're done—we're not going in the Parks tonight."

"Yes, sir."

Jack headed back up to the El Capitan Suite.

TEN

"Max," Tony said, "you can head up early if you want. Kim and I will take the kids back up to the suite."

"Thanks Tony, but Jack gave me orders."

Tony liked and respected Max—and feared his overwhelming strength—but he was too 'by the book' in his opinion.

Tony turned to Kim, "Something is definitely wrong with Jack tonight."

Kim nodded, "Seemed like whatever happened at the Park today was resolved though, not sure why he's acting this way."

Tony and Kim were attracted to each other, but as high-level professionals they wouldn't let anything interfere with their main responsibilities. Working for Jack was a dream job, which not only paid more than any job they'd held before, but it also gave them a once in a lifetime opportunity to work for a man they believed in.

"Hey, so how's your mom doing?" Tony asked.

"Oh," Kim hesitated as she always did when they started talking about personal matters, "she's doing good, thanks for asking. She had another fall yesterday, but it seems like she's okay."

"If you ever need my help over there, let me know. My brothers are in construction, and they can help with her house."

"Thanks Tony, she'll be okay though. She's tough," Kim said half-heartedly.

Tony kept track of things happening in Kim's life because he was genuinely interested in her well-being. Kim kept her personal life discreet—Tony still hadn't met her mother even though they'd been working together for a long time.

"Max, what are you doing this weekend?" Tony asked.

"Not sure yet, but I'm probably heading down to San Diego to meet up with some of my old Team Six buddies."

Max had expressed his concern to Tony several times about his "relationship" with Kim. He strongly believed in zero distractions—with no compromise. His years with Team Six taught him extreme discipline and mental toughness. He didn't have time for games, and never lost focus of his priorities—especially his main one—protecting Jack, Andy, and Grace.

"Well, I'm definitely hanging out if Johnny Depp is coming into town tomorrow. I don't want to miss protecting Captain Jack again!" Kim said as she grinned at Tony.

Tony didn't reciprocate the smile. He wasn't fond of her frequent comments about her adoration for celebrities. Her beauty was intoxicating though, and put him under a spell.

ELEVEN

August 6, 2010
El Capitan Presidential Suite
Grand Californian Hotel

Jack was tempted to drive to his headquarters in Newport Beach to figure out the suspect's connection to the Grusov family, but he knew that Luke was a lot faster at getting to the bottom of these types of things, so he tried to be as patient as he could. Luke had virtually unlimited resources at his disposal; the best software and data analysts in the world, along with cutting-edge equipment.

Jack opened the windows of the suite and let the fresh Orange County night air creep in along with the different aromas and background sounds emanating from California Adventure. He headed to the dining room located behind the fireplace on the far left side of the suite. He sat in front of the 27-inch iMac on the table, which already had *The System* running on it. It opened to Jack's main dashboard after confirming his identity through its facial recognition software.

Jack flipped rapidly through headshot profiles populating in real-time—then he came to an abrupt stop. Squinting with focused disgust, he pressed his lips together as he gazed at a picture of a distinguished, older Russian man, with a well-dressed edge to him.

It was Nikolai Grusov. Jack looked at Nikolai's image with thoughts of revenge and hate coursing through his veins.

Next to his image was the word DECEASED, stamped in red.

Jack's phone buzzed. It was Monica, his personal assistant and secretary.

"Good evening, Jack," said Monica in her usual upbeat voice. She was the most positive person he knew.

"Hello Monica."

"Mr. Depp's assistant called to see if you wanted to meet them for dinner tomorrow night at the Club." Monica referred to the famous private Club 33 as 'The Club'.

"Yes, we are definitely a go on that."

"Also Mr. Iger is going to be at the Park tomorrow, and he wanted to stop in and say hi at some point."

"Sure."

"And then Director Sullivan, head of the Secret Service wants about an hour of your time to discuss a security issue."

"Okay, no problem."

"Oh and one last thing, Jack," Monica hesitated, "Melissa White called and she wanted to talk to you about something. She wasn't really clear about—"

Jack cut her off mid-sentence, "Tell her that I'm not interested," Jack said without hesitation.

Melissa had been pursuing Jack since their college days. She wouldn't give up. Jack was not interested in her or anyone. As far as he was concerned, he would never be interested in another woman again.

Jack hung up the phone and looked back at the image of Nikolai Grusov.

His phone buzzed again. It was Luke, and he answered immediately.

"What did you find out?"

"Jack, I looked through everything, and it appears that this guy is an American citizen who was an exchange student in Russia for four years. At that time, he was in contact and worked for a distant cousin of Grusov who, from what I can tell, has no relation to anything Grusov did in the past." Luke said.

"You're sure of that?"

"I'm still digging," Luke never made any generalized assumptions with Jack. "I'm going through the footage from today. We don't have much of him, but it seems like it was a normal family day at Disneyland."

Hearing this eased Jack's tension and anxiety because it seemed as if there was no direct or recent involvement with the Grusovs.

"Other than a recent bankruptcy proceeding, during which he lost his house, there's nothing else on his record." Luke continued, "He was taking an abnormal amount of pictures with his phone on Tom Sawyer Island—at one point it looked like he might have accidentally dropped something down a drainage grill near the rope bridge."

"What do you mean *accidentally*?"

"Well, he was with one of his kids and it looked like she dropped something and he couldn't get it back."

"Okay, send me that video. I want to look at it for myself, and send me everything else you have on him."

"Will do, Jack."

TWELVE

1994
The Skyway
Disneyland Park

Kate had a smile like a super model. Jack liked her because she was reserved, and not flashy—she was the kind of girl he could spend the rest of his life with.

Jack wasn't on "the hunt" for a spouse. He was going on his tenth year as a SEAL, being one of the youngest ever to make it through BUD/S when he was eighteen. He figured he'd be in the game for many more years because he couldn't get enough of the action.

Kate worked in the front office of Disney's new hockey franchise, the Mighty Ducks of Anaheim.

It took several weeks of calling to get Kate on the phone. They agreed to meet at the French Market in New Orleans Square. Kate was fascinated with Disney history, and she loved hearing Jack's stories about Walt Disney and his dad.

"So, I take it you're a big hockey fan?" Jack asked.

Kate smiled, "I love it. I've been a hockey fan since I was a little girl, so this is a dream job for me."

They both hit it off right away, and talked as if they'd been friends for years. They were total opposites. Kate was nice, pretty, confident, witty, and she had an intoxicating laugh that Jack loved. She was so different from anyone he'd ever met before.

"How long have you been coming to the Park?" Jack asked her.

"I was five the first time I came here, and I immediately fell in love with it. My parents would bring us first thing in the morning, and we would stay until it closed. I could never get enough of this place. After that, they tried their best to bring us back every year, and we looked forward to that day for months when we knew we were going."

"And how about now? Are you here a lot now that you're all grown up?"

"At least once a month. I love it because this is where I can relax and reflect on things." She glanced to her right at the Rivers of America. The gentle breeze lifted some of her long hair into the air, and the way the light reflected off the water and lit up her deep blue eyes was breathtaking.

Time stood still for Jack as he looked into her eyes, intrigued with how they seemed to glow—her face was radiant. Her eyes were mesmerizing and full of life—genuine, just like her smile. Jack was taken aback by her beauty and sincerity, and felt a connection to her that seemed almost supernatural.

Right then, as crazy as it sounds, he knew he would spend the rest of his life with her. He felt butterflies in his stomach (Jack rarely got butterflies, even on his first late night HALO jump as a SEAL). His heart was softening, and he was beginning to open up to the potential of falling in love, something he thought would never happen.

"Hey, how about we ride the Skyway?" Jack asked, "I think they're going to close it down in November, unfortunately."

"What? Why?" Kate asked.

"It's too expensive to upgrade for safety reasons and people keep throwing things, spitting, and things like that."

"That's so sad. I love the Skyway."

They walked up the staircase to the Swiss-style Skyway Station in Fantasyland behind the Casey Jr. Circus Train. As they were helped into the gondola, it rocked back and forth as the thick cables above them pulled it out of the station.

Once they were airborne, they could see the miniature world of Storybook Land and Dumbo on the left. King Arthur's Carrousel was on the right. Incoming Skyway cars approached as Jack and Kate headed for the middle of the Matterhorn. In the distance, they could see it's a small world and Sleeping Beauty Castle.

It was an awkward moment; they didn't know each other well, so they sat side by side with their arms on their lap. Jack wanted to put his arm around her but thought it was too fast, and it might make things weird.

They passed over the Mad Tea Party on their left as they approached the two large oval holes that allowed them to journey through the middle of the Matterhorn. It became darker while moving through the Matterhorn, a romantic part of the ride for some, and they could see the roller coaster tracks on each side. A hulking white Yeti snow monster emerged from the darkness as screams from people riding the first tubular steel continuous track roller coaster echoed through the hollow mountain. The light eradicated the darkness as they exited the heart of the Matterhorn and the large waterfall crashed to the bottom of the right side of the mountain. The sun was setting behind them beaming spectacular orange-reddish rays of light throughout the Park.

Kate looked to her right and smiled at Jack.

"What a great sunset," Jack said, "I love the Park at this time of day."

"So do I," she said, "I love the way it casts a different light on everything, and it turns this place into more of a fairy-tale than it already is. It's my favorite time of the day, I could come here every day at this time to see this."

This was a special moment. They hadn't known each other for long, but the romantic nature of Disneyland, the storybook setting, the sunset, the mutual love and respect for the Park, and the natural physical attraction caused them to develop a unique bond.

As they continued their journey in the Skyway gondola, they entered Tomorrowland. They saw the submarines on the left pushing through the crystal clear water in the lagoon; the Autopia cars raced around their windy tracks, and in the distance they could see the PeopleMover—as it slowly shuttled people through the Land of the future.

Their Skyway gondola slowed down a bit and coasted into the Tomorrowland station. The gondola rocked back and forth as a CM grabbed it and opened the door. Jack exited first and held Kate's hand as she stepped out. She bashfully smiled. Jack smiled back and then glanced toward the ground as her well-manicured feet touched the cement of the Tomorrowland station.

They met each other more and more at the Park, and each time they had moments like this where they would connect a little bit deeper. Both looked forward to each trip with child-like anticipation, although they didn't reveal that to each other.

It was almost as if they were made for each other.

THIRTEEN

August 7, 2010
The Dream Suite
Disneyland Park

"How long do we get to stay this time, Dad?" Andy asked.

"I don't know Andy, maybe three or four days?"

Jack liked the strategic location of the 2200 square foot Dream Suite because it allowed him to swiftly get anywhere in the Park. His dad designed several back entrances to the suite, some are hidden allowing him to slip backstage in an instant. Secret doorways lead to the Club 33 Kitchen for quick Club access. From there, they can easily access the Blue Bayou, and there's a shortcut leading to the Pirates of the Caribbean.

This luxury suite was originally conceived as an apartment for Walt and Roy Disney, something that would be near Club 33 where they could entertain sponsors and make deals. It was special to Jack because it was Stan who originally proposed the idea of a larger suite tucked further back in the Park. At Stan's suggestion, Walt decided to build a bigger place to entertain VIPs since his apartment above the Fire Station was much too small. They called it the "Royal Suite".

Their original plan was to make it so that they could easily access everything in New Orleans Square from the Dream Suite. Walt wanted to be able to take his guests through the back of the Dream Suite to Club 33 for dinner, and then after that to an adjacent Jazz club.

New Orleans Square was the ideal location for a luxury apartment. It had a delightful view of the majestic Rivers of America; it was directly on top of Pirates of the Caribbean, and it was in the heart of the magical version of New Orleans that Walt created. There were several underground facilities in New Orleans Square for Cast Members, and the Dream Suite had access to most of them.

Jack's goal was to spend more time with the kids over the next three days since he'd been working too much.

The kids entered the Dream Suite from the backside of the living room, and they squealed with joy as they were set to be in their favorite place for several days.

Jack looked around the living room—an enchanting design achievement that was intended to look like a New Orleans parlor. The design was directly adapted from the Dorothea Redmond sketches drawn in the sixties. Hand painted murals of European castles covered the walls—the same castles that inspired Walt—a glass chandelier made in Turkey was designed to match the fabric used in the living room, a magical fireplace with animated sparks resembled the fireworks over Sleeping Beauty Castle, and a full size carousel horse added to the ambiance of the room.

The kids darted over to the room with their favorite train set, and other Walt Disney inspired relics. A replica of the Disneyland Railroad steam train sat in an enclosed glass case. The kids hit the "Goodnight Kiss" switch on the wall and the train left its glass case and went for a grand circle trip around the edge of the room.

Grace's eyes lit up as she watched the train pass the collectibles placed along the way—they came to life as the train passed by—the Mark Twain replica lit up, the Sailing Ship Columbia, as well as other miniaturized items from Disneyland.

They opened the balcony doors and felt the subtle Southern California breeze sweeping off the Rivers of America. They could hear the crowds below, and the enticing fragrances of New Orleans Square drifted up into their room.

They loved the Grand Californian, but there was no hotel that compared to this; they were staying at the most sought after place in the entire Resort.

Jack's phone buzzed; it was Luke.

"Jack, I'm sending the video feed I told you about from Tom Sawyer Island. It should be on your phone right now."

Jack put Luke on speaker and immediately switched over to the video feed. He squinted his eyes and held the screen closer to get a better look, but the video was pixelated. He could see what appeared to be the man with the mysterious link to the Grusovs. Standing next to him was possibly his wife, and then a young girl who was maybe eight years old. The little girl was looking down at the ground; the man was looking left to right, and the woman was glued to her phone and seemed to be clueless about the entire situation. He watched the little girl drop something down one of the drainage holes that was covered with a small metal grill. When that happened, the man reacted as if the girl lost something valuable. The mom didn't react, but the girl was obviously distraught, and the man was too, or at least he appeared that way.

"Did they go to lost and found?" Jack asked Luke.

"No, there is no record of them going to lost and found or anywhere in the Park to try to retrieve what they lost," Luke explained, "but I've already had people scan that area and we weren't able to find anything."

"Also," Luke continued, "I dug deep into their background and they are as clean as a whistle, with no other flags. I know it sounds weird, but the link to Grusov is totally random."

"Maybe so, but we still need to look into this. Flag him and his family. I want to know if they come back and if they ever contact guest services about losing something."

"You got it, Jack."

FOURTEEN

August 7, 2010
Club 33
Disneyland Park

"You look like a princess Gracie!" Kim said as she looked at her in the mirror. "You could be a face character when you grow up."

"I don't think Jack will go for that, Kim." Tony said smiling.

Jack knelt down and gazed into Grace's big blue eyes. It was like looking into Kate's eyes. He stroked her naturally curly blonde hair, and smiled at her as his eyes brightened with pure joy—a rare, warm expression from Jack reserved only for his kids. "Gracie, you look beautiful—just like your mom."

Gracie smiled, but it quickly faded as she felt a wave of sadness come over her.

"It's okay baby, don't be sad. We're going to have fun tonight."

Grace tried to reverse her frown. Jack was taken aback at how closely she resembled Kate and how she'd taken on so many of her mannerisms.

Jack looked over at Andy, "Looking sharp tonight, Andrew."

"Thanks, Dad."

Jack looked up at Max, Kim, and Tony and they were ready to go. Max led the way through one of the back doors of the Dream Suite that took them through the kitchen and into the Club 33 Trophy Room. The kids preferred taking the famous French lift to the Trophy room through the normal green door on Royal Street, but Jack normally utilized the back entrances when staying in the Dream Suite.

"Jack!" Johnny Depp stood up, shook Jack's hand and gave him a hug.

"Johnny, how've you been?" Jack embraced him.

"I've been good," said Depp as he looked down at Andy and Grace with a big smile, "and how about you two? How are you guys doing?"

"We've been good Mr. Depp," said Andy smiling. Johnny was one of his favorite actors of all-time, especially as Captain Jack Sparrow.

They went to sit down as Jack greeted Vanessa and their two kids. Andy and Grace ran over to the kids and started to catch up on things—they were excited to see each other.

"Jack, I wanted to thank you for helping me with the security setup at my house in France and on my island—I could've never pulled it off without you."

"Oh, don't worry about it. I was glad to help."

"Dinner is on me tonight, Jack. Thank you for everything you always do for us," said Johnny as he raised his glass to Jack.

"Well, thank you Johnny. We really appreciate that," Jack said as he sat down at the long Trophy Room table, "we have something for you tonight, as well. We're in the Dream Suite, and we're going to take you through the Park after it closes."

Johnny looked at his kids, "Well, that sounds like fun guys! We get a tour of Disneyland from the man who knows it better than anyone else!"

Their eyes lit up—they loved being around Jack because he was a real Navy SEAL. They were accustomed to being around Hollywood actors most of the time, so it was a treat for them to hang out with a legendary military hero like Jack.

"Johnny, I think you remember Max, Tony, and Kim."

"Yes, I do, and it's wonderful seeing you again," Johnny said shaking each of their hands. He looked back at Jack, "I always feel like I'm the President or something with you guys around."

They laughed. It was fun for the crew to be around Johnny, especially Kim who was star-struck in a major way. She held his hand and smiled for at least three times longer than everyone else; it became awkward, but Johnny was familiar with women acting weird around him.

A tall, rough-looking man walked by the entrance of the Trophy Room and peeked around Max who was standing guard. The man was clearly inebriated as he tried to get a glimpse of who had closed down the Trophy Room.

"Oh," the man said loudly, "that's why the Trophy Room is closed tonight. We were going to have a party here, and apparently we got bumped by someone more important," he slurred his words.

Max dipped his colossal head down as if to say "*are you serious?*" Then he looked the man square in the eyes and said, "Sir, I think you better just move along."

The intoxicated man became more agitated. He was almost as tall as Max, but around seventy-five pounds lighter. He appeared to be sizing Max up for a fight, which would've been a monumental mistake.

"Who do you think you are?" the man said to Max, his voice rising in volume with each word. Jack looked over from the table to see what was going on and then glanced back at Depp. It would take an army of trained professionals to take Max down, so one disgruntled civilian wasn't a threat to them.

Two Disney security CMs came up behind the man along with a well-dressed manager and told him nicely that he needed to exit the Club.

The man came to his senses and changed his attitude—he continued to slur his words, "I'm sorry, no offense. Look, my dad pays a lot of money to be a member of the Club, and it just makes me mad when celebrities come in here and bump us from our spots."

Max glared at him with a stone cold stare—he didn't even blink. He couldn't care less what his problem was or what he had to say. He wanted him to head out, or he was going to knock him out.

"Look," the man persisted, "can I just get a picture with them? If I can do that, everything will be cool. Can they at least do that for me?"

Max took a step forward and leaned into the man getting within two inches of face, "I suggest you move along if you know what's good for you."

Max's intimidating demeanor startled the man, and he stepped back, "Look, *Pirates* is my favorite movie of all time. They took the room we reserved three months ago for a birthday party, so can I please just get ONE picture with Johnny Depp?"

The general manager of Club 33 approached the man and diffused the situation, escorting him downstairs.

"Andy and Grace," Johnny said smiling, "I brought you a little gift—something I think you'll like very much." Halfway through the sentence Johnny changed his accent to Captain Jack's, which put a huge smile on Andy and Grace's face.

"What is it, Mr. Depp?" Grace asked as she bounced up and down in her chair. She loved surprises.

"They're special gold coins that we used in *The Curse of the Black Pearl*."

Both of the kids shrieked with joy.

Johnny smiled at the kids and then glanced up grinning at Jack. Johnny always paid special attention to Andy and Grace because of all they'd been through.

Andy listened to Johnny tell stories about the things they did while making the *Pirates* movies, the first Pirates Premiere they had at Disneyland, and how Imagineers made the Captain Jack animatronics inside the Pirates of the Caribbean attraction.

They finished dessert, and Johnny stood up, "How about we all ride Pirates together?"

The kids jumped up and yelled with contagious excitement.

Jack leaned over and instructed Tony to take them to the Cast Member entrance of the Pirates of the Caribbean loading dock so they could avoid the fiasco that would ensue if people saw Johnny anywhere near the attraction.

"I can't believe I'm going on Pirates with the real Captain Jack," Kim whispered to Tony who smiled at her, semi-amused, and semi-irritated.

FIFTEEN

August 7, 2010
Pirates of the Caribbean
Disneyland Park

They headed down through the Cast Member entrance to the back of the Pirates loading dock known as Lafitte's Landing. The CM in charge of filling the boats caught a glimpse of Johnny Depp with Jack Duncan and let several empty boats pass through the line, reserving one just for them. Grace stepped on to the edge of the boat, and one of her yellow shoes slipped into the murky water that always had a distinct musty smell to it. Max, Tony, and Kim tried to retrieve it, but they couldn't grab it.

A few people noticed Johnny in the boat, which created a buzz in the queue. Flashes popped from all directions and the noise level of the crowd increased. The boat was dispatched, and they started to move.

Max, with his long arms and giant hands, tried to reach Grace's shoe again with the help of Tony and Kim. Suddenly the boat came to an abrupt stop due to technical difficulties. The man from Club 33, who appeared to be even more intoxicated at this point, emerged from the crowd with his camera and moved towards the boat. It looked as if he was trying to pull something out of his right pocket. Jack was the only one who noticed him as the others were still trying to retrieve Grace's shoe.

The boat jerked again and regained its forward momentum towards the awe-inspiring Louisiana bayou scene. The man ran for the boat. As the end of the boat cleared the dock, the man leapt towards the back of the vessel.

Jack stood up, grabbed the man in mid air with both hands, and pinned him to the back of the boat with a huge bang. Everyone's head turned at the same time—shocked at what they just witnessed.

The drunken man was flat on his back with a stunned look on his face as he stared up at Jack.

Immediately Max, Tony, and Kim helped subdue the man, even though the job was already done.

Johnny Depp's kids were thrilled at the chance to see Jack Duncan in action on their favorite attraction—the man they'd imitated so often in video games.

Max escorted the man off the boat as the rest of the group continued their journey through the world famous dark ride. The boat gently moved through the tranquil bayou scene with fireflies on the left complimented by peaceful nature sounds. A soft strumming banjo playing "Oh! Susanna" set the mood for the nighttime southern plantation backyard dinner party on the right—

the Blue Bayou restaurant. An old man rocked back and forth on his porch signaling the calm before the storm.

The kids screamed at the top of their lungs as they slid down the first drop beginning the descent underground. After the shorter second drop, they floated through the underground caverns home to the eerie skeletal remains of a few unlucky pirates and their loot.

The gloomy sound of a voice chanting "Dead Men Tell No Tales" rang throughout the attraction along with the slower, somber version of the Pirates of the Caribbean attraction theme song. Everyone was quiet as they admired the underground waterfalls while feeling the humidity of the cavern.

"Do you see that dark skull on the headboard of that bed?" Jack pointed over to his left to show Johnny's kids. "That's a real skull—the only real one in the entire attraction."

Johnny's kids got a kick out of that spooky skull and chattered back and forth with Andy and Grace about it.

Johnny tapped Andy on the shoulder, "Andy, do you recognize the Aztec chest over there?" Johnny pointed to the treasure chest in the corner of the final treasure room as they headed for a dark tunnel.

Andy looked over to where Johnny was pointing and got excited, "Ohhh that's the chest from *The Curse of the Black Pearl*!"

"You are correct, my friend," Johnny smiled and sat back in the boat as they journeyed towards the dramatic battle scene.

Davy Jones appeared on a curtain of mist saying, "If you be brave or fool enough to face a pirate's curse, proceed."

Andy fired back at Davy Jones, "You are no match for Captain Jack Sparrow!"

The kids cheered as Johnny smiled and playfully ruffled Andy's hair.

The theme song from the movie majestically echoed throughout as their boat slowly passed through the middle of a battle between Captain Barbosa and a Caribbean fortress on the right. Barbosa stood on the deck of the massive Wicked Wench pirate ship as explosions propelled water high into the air. The kids felt the "cannonballs" blowing past their faces.

Johnny turned to Jack, "This is probably my favorite scene, I love the music and the grand scale of this set."

Jack nodded in agreement, "I agree, Walt would've been proud of this."

They approached the village of Puerto Dorado. Pirates trying to get the mayor to divulge the location of the treasure were dunking him in the water. The first animatronic Captain Jack appeared hiding behind some dresses.

Andy looked over his shoulder at Johnny and smiled, "There you are Mr. Depp!"

Johnny smiled and put his hand on Andy's shoulder, "It's insane how that looks just like Captain Jack, hey?"

Their boat crawled through the underground pirate world as the infamous "Pooped Pirate" appeared, waving his treasure map and bragging about how Captain Jack Sparrow would never see it. Another Captain Jack animatronic, from his hiding place in a barrel, peered over the shoulder of the "Pooped Pirate".

"At least he calls me by my proper name," Johnny exclaimed using his Captain Jack Sparrow voice.

"Yes, he called you Captain!" Andy played along with a big smile on his face.

They approached the scene featuring the shootout between the drunken pirates and the captain of a ship inside a highly explosive ammunition warehouse. The pirates sang the theme song of the attraction in unison—"Yo Ho, Yo Ho, A Pirate's Life for Me."

Their boat drifted through the gunfight scene as they began the ascent up the waterfall taking them back to ground level. On the left, the final Captain Jack Sparrow animatronic appeared sitting on a throne in a room full of treasure.

"This is my favorite part!" Andy exclaimed looking back at a smiling Johnny Depp.

Jack smiled at Andy—it made him so happy to see him like this. Jack whipped his head to the left and noticed something unusual behind Jack Sparrow's throne.

He pulled out his iPhone, and with two quick strokes the entire ride came to a halt. They were in a holding pattern at the bottom of the steep waterfall with the treasure room on their left. Jack jumped out of the boat and into the treasure room. He ducked into a hidden door at the back of the room, and he was gone.

Kim and Tony looked at each other and then back at Johnny Depp. They were confused along with everyone else, but Jack did things like this all the time, always on alert for things that were out of the ordinary.

Tony put his finger to his earpiece as he received a transmission from Jack. He nodded as he received his orders.

"It's okay everyone," Tony looked back and reassured everyone, "Jack is just checking something out, we're going to hold here for a few minutes."

Johnny stood up in the boat, "Well I think this is the perfect time for me and my friends to explore the treasure room!"

Andy and the rest of the kids clapped with sheer joy. Kim looked more excited than the kids, but she tried her best to conceal her pleasure. Johnny stood next to the Jack Sparrow animatronic and smiled at the kids, "So what do you guys think? Is this Captain Jack, or what?"

"Mr. Depp," Andy said, "can we take a picture with you next to Captain Jack?"

"Well, sure you can, mate," Johnny used his Captain Jack voice for them, and everyone cheered. Kim rapidly clapped her hands and then caught herself. She jumped to her feet and offered to take the picture.

"Andy, what's your favorite Captain Jack line?" Johnny asked.

"Your final line in the first movie!"

"Okay, Kim, can you get this on film for me?"

"Sure, Mr. Depp, I would be glad to do that!" Kim said as she flashed a look of exhilaration at Tony, who rolled his eyes.

Johnny stood next to his animatronic, waited for a pause and dramatically recited the final lines from *The Curse of the Black Pearl*:

"Now, bring me that horizon. And really bad eggs. *Drink up me hearties. Yo ho*!"

Kim giggled like a schoolgirl as the kids screamed with excitement. Even Tony clapped as it was a rare moment for anyone who was a fan of the movies. "Mr. Depp," Kim said, "is there any way I can get a picture with you really quick for my mom, she's your biggest fan!"

"Sure Kim, step into the treasure room." Johnny said while still in character.

Kim put her arm around Johnny, and they both smiled as Tony reluctantly took the picture. Kim got back into the boat and couldn't hide her glee. "You're just lucky Max wasn't here to see that," Tony said.

Jack emerged from the hidden door in the treasure room surprised to see everyone out of the boat.

"Dad," Andy exclaimed, "I got a picture with Mr. Depp right here in the treasure room and he said my favorite line from the movie!"

Jack smiled and thanked Johnny as they made their way back to the boat.

"Everything okay, Jack?" Tony whispered.

Jack whispered back, "Yeah I thought I saw someone open that door—no one should be using it during regular hours—but everything is fine."

Andy hugged Jack, "Thanks Dad, this is the best time I've ever had on Pirates!"

Jack hugged him and gave him a kiss on the top of his head. He reactivated the ride from his iPhone, and their boat jerked back into motion.

SIXTEEN

August 7, 2010
New Orleans Square
Disneyland Park
"Lafitte"

Johnny, Vanessa, and their kids strolled along the esplanade of the Rivers of America with Jack, Andy, and Grace. Max, Kim, Tony, and two officers from the Disney Security team followed close behind.

Jack stopped in front of a large ship's anchor that looked as if it was from the 1800s.

"There's an interesting story about this anchor," Jack explained as everyone stopped to listen, "it was installed on opening day in 1955, and even though it has been moved throughout the Park, it's remained in the same basic area. The plaque has always had the same message on it."

Lafitte's Anchor: Said to be from a pirate ship commanded by Jean Lafitte in the battle of New Orleans January 8, 1815. It is also said that Lafitte's privateering ships left a wake of blood from the mainland to Barataria Bay. But don't believe everything you read.

"Lafitte," Johnny lit up with an intriguing grin on his face.

Jack grinned at Johnny because he knew Lafitte would pique his interest.

"My dad talked a lot about Walt's fascination with Lafitte and American history over the years. Lafitte was in New Orleans before it was part of the United States. He was a legendary figure of sorts being a pirate and a smuggler, yet the 7th President of the United States, Andrew Jackson, considered him a hero and a patriot. When Walt and his team were designing New Orleans Square, it was natural to set the Land during that same time period—with the Pirates of the Caribbean attraction in the middle of a nineteenth century New Orleans. When Walt discovered how fascinating this real life pirate Lafitte was, he decided he would be the perfect central figure for New Orleans Square. He was a pirate with compassion, a patriot that had a cause greater than himself, and possessed unrivaled maritime combat skills which were necessary to defeat the ferocious British army."

"But Jack, when you look around, Lafitte isn't exactly plastered all over New Orleans Square."

"True. Imagineers tried to rekindle the legend of Lafitte several years ago. He was written into the back story of the Haunted Mansion called 'The Beginning of Gracey Manor' where they created the story of Captain Ambrose Gracey, the man who built the Haunted Mansion that overlooks the river on the outskirts of New Orleans. Gracey built secret passages and tunnels connecting the house with the graveyard and the riverfront. Also, it was rumored that Gracey had a peculiar relationship with the pirate Jean Lafitte and that he 'sometimes returned to the docks with more than he started with.' They said that the secret passages provided a means of escape during attacks from pirates, thieves, and the British Army in the war of 1812."

The Depps and others were fascinated with how Walt and his Imagineers weaved so much history into the fabric of the Park.

Jack walked them further down the River esplanade and stopped at a small crypt in the wall in front of the Haunted Mansion facing the River.

The "crypt" was an odd archway lined with red bricks. The center of the archway was sealed with bricks and simulated sloppy mortar, the same type of bricks used in nineteenth century New Orleans buildings.

"This crypt has the numbers 1764 above it, which is supposedly 200 years from the birth date of an Imagineer who worked on the project," said Jack.

"What project?" Vanessa asked.

"It was the plan to unite Pirates, Haunted Mansion, and Tom Sawyer Island to create a central theme based on Lafitte. They wanted to create an underground tunnel that took guests from the Haunted Mansion under the Rivers of America, to Pirate's Lair on the Island. The Island was the perfect "Barataria" and Pirates of the Caribbean was clearly set during the time of Lafitte. The Haunted Mansion "Gracey Manor legend" introduced the thought of secret passages and tunnels linking the house to the riverfront. These tunnels were used in the Battle of New Orleans. These backstories linked the three attractions."

Kim was visibly excited, and she was so entrenched in the conversation that she blurted out, "Some people say there really is a tunnel under the River —a secret tunnel."

Johnny looked over his shoulder, surprised at Kim's statement. This piqued his interest even more.

"Is that true, Jack?"

Jack smiled and looked at Kim, "No, that's an urban legend. A few Imagineers tried to make it happen several years ago, but it never came to pass. This crypt is a reminder of the project that never happened."

"But Jack," Johnny said, "are you saying the idea to unify the three attractions was something a few Imagineers tried to create at a later date?"

"It seems that way. Modern Imagineers attempted to bring this to fruition long after Walt's death. They probably started with the anchor and the references to Lafitte in various places in New Orleans Square. They invented the Gracey Manor legend along with other things in an effort to connect the dots."

"Wow," Johnny paused, "it almost seems like Walt had all of this planned from the very beginning." Johnny wasn't doubting what Jack said, just thinking out loud, "Walt was extremely intentional about everything he did. Why would he incorporate Lafitte into the Park from the beginning, build Tom Sawyer Island, and set the Mansion on the River if he had no plans of unifying them?"

Jack paused and looked at Johnny, "Good point, I guess the idea could've originated with Walt."

"Or maybe not," Johnny said, "I guess the Mansion, and even Pirates didn't open until after Walt died."

"Another interesting thing," Jack continued, "in 2007 Imagineers installed Pirate's Lair on Tom Sawyer Island which was largely due to the success of a certain movie franchise." Jack looked in Johnny's direction and grinned.

"In Mark Twain's books, he talked about an island called Jackson's Island —a fictional place where Tom and Huck visited and found traces of pirates." Jack turned to his right and showed them a bulletin board in front of the rafts that shuttle people to Tom Sawyer Island. An old fashioned newspaper created by Imagineers was sealed in the glass, telling the story of Tom and Huck and their visit to Jackson's Island, which was allegedly Lafitte's headquarters. The paper read, *There are those who say the gentleman pirate of New Orleans, Jean Lafitte, once made this island his headquarters.*

"This is an obvious attempt to make a connection between Lafitte and Tom Sawyer Island," Jack said, putting the pieces of the puzzle together for the group.

Jack paused as everyone looked out over the River, wondering if there truly was a secret underground tunnel.

"What an amazing place, huh?" Johnny said. "It's like a living museum."

Jack half-smiled at Johnny.

"I don't know about you Jack, but I would pay a lot of money to find out if there's really a tunnel under that river."

SEVENTEEN

1994
Disneyland Park
Jack and Kate

"Your dad gave Walt the idea to build the Royal Suite, didn't he?" Kate asked as they walked in front of Pirates of the Caribbean in New Orleans Square.

"Yeah, my dad was a bit on the paranoid side, always thinking of security issues and strategic locations, so he talked Walt into building a larger apartment in New Orleans Square."

"Oh, so that's where you get it from." Kate said quickly with a smile.

"Get what from?" Jack grinned at her wondering what she'd say next.

"Being paranoid—strategic locations—everything like that."

Jack smirked as he sipped his drink.

Jack and Kate met every Saturday night to watch the swing dancing at the Carnation Plaza Gardens. They didn't dance, they just watched the old married couples have fun week after week. Most of the same dancers were there each time, and it was fun to watch them and listen to Big Band music.

Jack and Kate already had a special place in their heart for Disneyland, but it was becoming a memorable place for them as a couple, and they were developing more than just a friendship.

Jack had a desire to learn everything about her; what she was thinking, what she liked, and her dreams. Kate felt the same way; she was interested in Jack as a person, and his well-being. This was foreign to Jack.

He constantly thought about things he could get for her—anything that would make her happy.

"Oh," Jack said as they walked, "I have something for you."

"You do?" Kate smiled, her face lit up as it always did, her blue eyes sparkled while her lips formed the perfect smile. Each time he saw her, Jack discovered another one of Kate's features that revealed more of her beauty.

He opened a plastic Disneyland bag that exposed a stuffed Dumbo doll and a CD of the movie soundtrack.

"Oh, thank you, I love it!" Kate gave him a hug.

Jack remembered her favorite classic Disney movie was *Dumbo* and her favorite song was "Baby Mine". Her dream as a little girl was to grow up, get married, have kids, and drive them around in a mini-van. She always wanted to be a mom, although she didn't tell Jack that just yet. She didn't want him to think she was suggesting they get married, or move too fast with anything.

"It has my favorite song on here, too," she said as she glanced at the CD and smiled.

"Oh, another thing that you're going to like—I got us all-access passes to be the first to try out the new Indiana Jones attraction. Do you want to go on Friday with me?"

"Yes!" Kate had been waiting a long time for Indiana Jones to open.

Jack remembered his dad telling him that Disneyland was the perfect place to take someone you're falling in love with. The way the Park is illuminated at night, the sounds, the smell of fresh brewed coffee, and the excitement of the attractions transport you to another world.

They never went on many attractions—they didn't need to. The ambiance of the Park was enough, listening to the charming background music that matched each Land as they walked through, the live bands, the smell of the famous fried chicken from the Plaza Inn, and the rag time piano player at Coke Corner. They could never get enough of it and on some nights they talked on Main Street hours after the Park closed.

"How about we get coffee at the French Market and watch Fantasmic on the veranda?"

Kate loved coffee. It was one of her favorite things to drink, especially Disneyland coffee. Fantasmic! was her favorite show—a relatively new production that utilized the Rivers of America for everything from fireworks to water screens, and included the Mark Twain, Columbia, and a bevy of Disney characters.

They sipped coffee together on the French Market veranda, overlooking the River where Fantasmic! was getting ready to start.

A live band played sweet Dixieland Jazz on one of the floating Tom Sawyer Island rafts. As the band floated around the front of the River, their live music played through the speakers positioned along the esplanade of the Rivers of America. It was a big New Orleans-style party as thousands gathered for the main event.

Kate looked uneasy. She lowered her head, and then glanced up at Jack.

"Jack," she paused as Jack looked into her eyes, "there's something I need to tell you."

EIGHTEEN

August 8, 2010
Dream Suite
Disneyland Park

Robert Conroy radioed one of the Disney security CMs assigned to Jack. The guard pressed his finger to his earpiece.

He stepped toward Jack, "Sir, Mr. Ruddy would like you to call him."

Jack looked at the guard and frowned. Brett Ruddy was the number two person in charge at the Disneyland Resort under the president of Disneyland. Jack constantly butted heads with him. Ruddy didn't like him, and was vocal about it, disagreeing with almost everything Jack did. Ruddy was the only one at TDA (Team Disney Anaheim) who didn't like having Jack on property.

Jack reluctantly pulled his iPhone out of his pocket to call Ruddy.

"Jack," Ruddy didn't sound happy, "this is the second time in two days either you or one of your guys has had an altercation with someone in the Park."

"Good afternoon to you too, Brett." Jack said sarcastically, "It wasn't an altercation. The guy jumped at our boat, we had no choice."

Jack was firm with Ruddy, but not disrespectful.

"Jack, that's what you always say when things like this happen," Ruddy said, "every time something happens, it's either life or death or something like that. We can't have this kind of stuff happening at the Park for everyone to see. There's a video of it all over YouTube and Twitter, and it only shows the part where you slammed the guy on the boat. It'll probably be on the news tonight."

Jack looked at Tony and grinned. Tony already knew what this was about because Ruddy always called when something like this happened.

"I can make one call and make all of those videos disappear if you want, Brett," Jack smiled again towards Max, Tony, and Kim.

"No, it looks bad enough as it is, we don't need more problems. We need guidelines here, Jack. You guys can't just do whatever you want on property. Can we meet tomorrow?"

Jack hated meetings in general because he thought they were a complete waste of time—but he'd rather be interrogated by al-Qaeda instead of attending an excruciating, waste of time whining session with Ruddy. Ruddy was one of those guys who sucked the company dry with all of his pet projects. Instead of solving real problems, he targeted the good guys as a watchdog in an attempt to improve his image within the organization.

"Oh, Brett, tomorrow is not good," Jack squinted his eyes trying to think of a way out of this, "I tell you what, I'll have Monica get in touch with you tomorrow and we'll talk more about this."

Ruddy hung up on him.

"Well, I guess that means no meeting tomorrow!" Jack said, smiling.

"What did he do, threaten you again, Jack?" Tony said laughing. Not even Iger told Jack what to do, although Jack respected the CEO a great deal, but Ruddy made it his daily mission to make new rules for Jack.

"Yeah," said Jack, "he actually scares me, in a weird kind of way."

The kids came in from the balcony and Jack could tell they wanted to head into Disneyland.

"Okay guys, where do you want to go next?" Jack hoped they'd say they wanted to play in the Dream Suite, and then head into the Park towards sunset.

Grace looked at Jack with a smile that could get her anything she wanted, "Let's just walk around and have fun!"

This wasn't exactly what Jack wanted to do, but that didn't matter.

"That sounds like a great idea Gracie, let's move out." He motioned to Max, Kim and Tony, and everyone prepared to head downstairs through the back elevator.

"Can we just use the stairs this time?" Grace asked.

Jack hesitated but agreed. He could never say no to her. It was the same problem he had with Kate.

Going down the front stairs of the Dream Suite attracted a lot of attention, which is why they usually didn't do it. The majority of the queue for Pirates of the Caribbean had a front and center view of the staircase. Since the stairs were seldom used, it created a stir in line when anyone walked down them. Once people recognized Jack coming down the stairs it would create a frenzy.

"That's Jack Duncan!" An excited guest proclaimed as he pointed to Jack coming down the stairs.

Hundreds of smart phones redirected towards Jack and the kids as they walked down the stairs. Cheers from the crowd erupted as everyone realized who it was. The public regarded Jack as a hero. He had an emotional attachment to Disneyland and people were thankful to him for what he did in 2005 and what he continued to do for them at the Resort.

Jack looked up and waved to the crowd. He liked the attention and appreciation to a certain extent, most people would—although he wasn't fond of the attention it brought to his kids. Now, everyone at the Resort knew he was staying in the Dream Suite since the pictures would be posted on Twitter, Facebook, and MouseWait for the world to see.

"Thank you for your service Jack, we appreciate it!" A man said to Jack as he walked by. Jack nodded at him and smiled in acknowledgment.

Max and a few Disney Security CMs cleared the way while Tony and Kim stuck to the kids, shielding them from the cameras.

"Let's go to Big Thunder!" Grace exclaimed.

They walked through New Orleans Square, towards Frontierland, and around the River to the left until they reached the Big Thunder Mountain Railroad entrance. After Big Thunder, they went the back way to Fantasyland because Grace wanted to ride Casey Jr., Peter Pan, and a few other Fantasyland attractions.

As they entered Fantasyland from the backside of Big Thunder, Jack looked up to the left at the old Skyway entrance near the exit of Casey Jr.

He remembered his first trip on the retired attraction with Kate. He always stopped when he passed this relic from the past. The Fantasyland Skyway station was a symbol of his love for Kate. It was a place filled with so many happy memories from the past, a place where the love of his life began; holding hands they would walk up those steps and travel to Tomorrowland.

Now it was just an empty station. No more birds-eye views of Disneyland, no more trips through the middle of the Matterhorn, no more romantic journeys in the Skyway gondolas.

Jack frequently climbed the stairs of the extinct Skyway station, which is off limits to guests, and sat on the cool, deserted concrete reminiscing about the past. He felt closer to Kate in that old station, and it helped him manage his anger by reliving their good times at Disneyland.

After the kids rode Casey Jr., they headed through the Castle, and into The Hub where they decided that Space Mountain would be next. Tomorrowland is always congested, and since the word was out that Jack was walking through the Park and staying in the Dream Suite, there were lots of people taking pictures as they went by. Max diverted the group towards a Cast Member exit on Main Street that would take them to the backside of Space Mountain.

Grace saw the Little Red Wagon Corn Dog cart, which put a big smile on her face. She couldn't resist those corn dogs and begged Jack to get her one. Jack agreed and they all stopped at the Corn Dog Cart before going backstage.

Conroy's voice shot through Jack's earpiece like thunder, "Jack, head towards New Orleans Square right away."

Conroy had a history of overreacting, and Jack knew it, so he didn't jump to any conclusions.

"What's wrong, Rob?" Jack asked as he got ready to devour a famous Main Street corn dog.

"Standby, Jack..."

Jack looked at Max, "Why don't you guys go ahead, I'll meet you there."

"Yes sir," said Max.

Jack remembered something that Grace wanted from the little shop inside Sleeping Beauty Castle, so he headed that way. He got all the way to the Castle without anyone recognizing him, which was unusual.

"Jack," Conroy's urgent voice came through his earpiece again.

"It's Dmitri Komarov," Conroy said urgently, "He's heading towards New Orleans Square."

Jack dropped the bag full of goodies he'd just bought for Grace, and it landed with a huge crash as it hit the ground. Everyone in the shop jumped and turned to see what happened, but Jack was already bolting for the door.

NINETEEN

Jack blew past the Carnation Plaza Gardens, the iconic stage with the famous red and white old-style awnings that had been graced by so many renowned musicians throughout the years. He charged through the tunnel leading to the Rancho del Zocalo restaurant—a short cut to Big Thunder Mountain when you're coming from Sleeping Beauty Castle.

"Where is he?" He asked, putting his finger on his earpiece as he increased the speed of his fast-paced walk, trying not to run over guests.

"Jack, we just spotted him near the Stage Door Cafe, and he's headed towards New Orleans Square," Conroy said. "I've got guys headed that way from the Critter Country side."

"Send the live feed to my iPhone. I want to see exactly where he is," said Jack.

Making a sharp left, he walked down the esplanade on the River and glanced to his left to see if he could catch a glimpse of his prey. The live image of Dmitri appeared on his iPhone. The camera angles updated, following his every move.

"You're sure this is him, right?" Jack asked Conroy.

"Yes, Jack, The System returned a positive facial recognition match with the FBI database."

He kept a close eye on his phone as he zigzagged through the heavy crowd.

"Jack," said Conroy, "he just went into the bathroom by the New Orleans Square Train Station."

"Okay, who is there right now?"

"Smith and Pauly. They're outside waiting for him."

"I'm almost there. Do NOT let him out of your sight," Jack said.

"We don't have good video coverage in the bathrooms, but there's only one way out so he won't get away."

Racing down further, Jack made a left in front of the Haunted Mansion and headed towards the New Orleans Train Station. Smith stood in front of the bathroom.

"Where is he? Is he still in there?"

"Yes sir," said Smith.

"Stay here and block people from coming in so I can take him through this CM exit." He commanded as he motioned to the convenient back stage access to the left of the bathroom.

Walking through the themed bathroom doors, he scanned for Dmitri but didn't see him.

"Dmitri," Jack called out calmly. "I need to talk to you."

A guy who was washing his hands looked over at Jack and then to his friend and said under his breath, “Is that *Jack Duncan*?” His friend looked over and nodded as they both headed for the door.

Jack decided it was time to clear the area, “I’m sorry everyone, but we need to clear this restroom NOW. Everyone needs to exit immediately.”

Another guy looked up from the sink and was shocked to see Jack. Men exited the stalls, looking perplexed, and made their way out of the restroom.

Only one stall remained occupied.

“Dmitri, you need to come out of that stall now,” Jack said with a stern tone as he did a four-finger swipe on the screen of his iPhone to activate his scanner.

He scanned the stall, and there was no sign of any weapons or explosives. Jack doubted himself for a second; the last thing he wanted to do was to scare the life out of an innocent guest.

“Jack,” said the man in the stall with a thick Russian accent, “I have a message for you.”

“What are you talking about—a message? You need to come out here, now,” Jack drew his SIG Sauer P226, the weapon he carried as a SEAL, and was ready to kick in the stall door.

“Nikolai sends his regards,” said Dmitri in a purposely-slow Russian drawl.

Jack couldn’t believe what he’d just heard—he exploded through the stall door. It came off its hinges and landed on Dmitri who was sitting on the closed toilet. The door hit him with a thud and crashed to the floor.

In one motion, Jack thrust his left arm to Dmitri’s throat, lifted him off the toilet, and pinned him to the wall. He put his gun to Dmitri’s head with his right hand while holding him off the ground with his left.

Smith and Pauly heard the bang and ran into the bathroom. They could tell something was terribly wrong. They’d never seen Jack like this.

“What are you talking about?” yelled Jack who was visibly out of control.

Dmitri just grinned at Jack with his scruffy face. He looked as if he was just out of prison although he was dressed nice enough to blend in. It became harder for him to breathe yet he still smirked at Jack—Dmitri was clearly enjoying every minute of this.

“Nikolai is dead,” said Jack with a convincing glare. He could have pulled the trigger on Dmitry just for mentioning Nikolai’s name in this manner—it was a direct insult to Jack.

Dmitri struggled to speak because Jack still had him by the neck against the wall.

“Nikolai,” he strained to get the words out, but he wanted to deliver his message so that it would hit Jack like a dagger. “Nikolai is not dead.” He summoned all of his strength to look Jack directly in the eyes.

"Nikolai is ... *alive*."

Jack eyes bulged, and his mouth dropped. He let go of Dmitri's throat, and struck him in the head with his Sig P226. The blow threw Dmitri savagely against the wall and brought him crashing to the ground.

"Jack!" Smith yelled as he ran into the stall, "Sir? What are you doing?" The banging and crashing sounds were heard all the way out in the streets of New Orleans Square.

Jack was silent as he backed out of the stall. It felt like everything was spinning around him in slow motion. Thoughts of rage dominated his mind as he tried to figure out what was going on.

Nikolai could NOT be alive—Jack was sure of this—because *he was the one who killed him.*

"Search him," Jack told Smith.

Blood covered the stall.

Smith searched him, found his phone, and handed it to Jack.

He quickly hit the home button. The screen flickered.

Jack froze as he saw an older Russian man with a rough beard.

Blood rushed to his head as his face became red, his eyes fixed, and his jaw locked.

It was like seeing the devil face to face.

The smug and confident look on the man's face was repulsive, and it made Jack want to smash his skull in.

It was none other than Nikolai Grusov.

Jack could not believe what he was seeing.

The video started.

"Hello Jack, it has been a long time," Nikolai's voice echoed eerily out of the phone with a dense but clear Russian accent, his face looking right at the camera.

Jack was perplexed. It looked as if he was going to crush the iPhone in his hand.

"As you can see I'm very much alive, and I'm sure you are very surprised to see me." Nikolai grinned as he spoke. "I just want you to know that I am coming after you, I am coming after your pathetic park, and I will get revenge for what you and your father have done to me and my family. I will make YOU pay if it is the last thing I do."

Smith and Pauly listened and looked at Jack.

His eyes were glazed over.

He was breathing hard and becoming more and more unpredictable with each passing second.

Jack glanced at Smith and Pauly with a puzzled look and then grabbed

Dmitri by the back of his jacket; he was starting to come around. Jack yanked him off the ground in one motion—as if he was grabbing a stuffed animal off the floor. He holstered his gun, pushed Dmitri through the bathroom door, and diverted him through the swinging doors of the CM exit heading for the Control Center.

Jack was out of control.

TWENTY

August 8, 2010
Disneyland Security Control Center
Disneyland Park

Jack burst into the Control Center, the security hub of the Disneyland Resort, holding up Dmitri by the back of his shirt. The agents in the room turned to him wide-eyed.

"Put him in Room One NOW," Jack ordered.

Flat screen monitors covered the walls of this state of the art facility. Hundreds of simultaneous video feeds streamed from every square inch of the Disneyland Resort. It resembled something you'd see at CIA or FBI headquarters, but this was more advanced. It looked like a miniaturized version of NASA mission control—everything at the Resort was controlled and monitored from this building.

Conroy walked toward Jack, "Jack, what's going on? The guys said you almost killed him in the bathroom."

Jack ignored Conroy as he dialed Luke.

"Luke, analyze this video, and get back to me ASAP—I need to know if it's him."

"Yes Jack, I'm on it," said Luke.

"Robert," Jack looked at Conroy, "turn off the recording equipment in Room One. I don't want any trace of what I'm going to say or do to this guy—and don't let anyone in, no matter what happens."

"Jack," said Conroy who was visibly nervous, "keep in mind, you're on Disney property, please remember that—we're not in a war zone or an underground government building, we have to follow strict rules here."

Jack glared at Conroy, ignoring his obligatory message.

He headed for the holding room, ready to do anything to get the truth out of Dmitri.

Conroy trusted Jack's judgment, under normal circumstances, but this was too close to home for him. Jack's worst enemy was back from the dead—threatening to hunt him and his family down.

Jack walked down the hall with a look of deadly determination seared across his face. He was going to get to the bottom of this, no matter what the cost.

Jack's phone buzzed, it was Ruddy. Jack answered it and growled, "NOT NOW," and hung up.

Jack paused for a few minutes as he reached Room One to get himself under control. He could feel the hate and rage gushing through his body. He wanted to take it all out on Dmitri, but he knew he needed to extract information about Nikolai from him first.

He opened the door, and his face turned white.

Dmitri shook violently in his seat with foam coming from his mouth.

"NO—"

Jack darted for Dmitri and tried to pry his mouth open. He cleared his mouth with a few quick motions—but it was too late. The violent shaking stopped, and Dmitri's head dropped.

"CONROY," Jack yelled, "GET A MEDIC IN HERE, NOW."

It was too late—Dmitri was dead.

TWENTY-ONE

August 8, 2010
Dream Suite
Disneyland Park

Jack entered the Dream Suite from the backstage entrance, and the first person he saw was Max.

"Where are the kids?"

"They are locked down in their room with Tony and Kim. I didn't know what was wrong, so I locked them down in there."

Jack walked towards the master bedroom as Max radioed Tony through his headset.

"Hey guys, how are you doing?" Jack said to the kids in a calm voice.

"Hey Dad," Andy and Grace both said at the same time. "What's wrong? What happened?"

"Oh, nothing. Everything's okay now, and there's nothing for you guys to worry about. We had someone who was slightly dangerous in the Park, but we caught him and got him out of here so he couldn't cause any problems."

Tony glanced at Kim with a worried look and then back at Jack.

"You guys hang out in the suite for a little while, okay? I need to follow up with this, and then we can hang out later tonight—maybe we can head over to The Club again for dessert?"

"Okay Dad, we'll hang out here. We've been in the Park all day anyway."

Tony looked at Jack and asked him what happened in a low voice.

Jack was still noticeably shaken and in battle mode. He looked both ways and leaned into Tony. "Nikolai is alive," said Jack in a vivid whisper.

Tony turned white and was shocked. He squinted his eyes.

"WHAT?"

"Just don't let the kids out of your sight and escalate the protection until I find out what's going on. We're on high alert."

Tony nodded and looked at Kim nervously as they maintained their position in the kids' room.

Jack's phone buzzed. It was Luke.

"What did you find out?" Jack asked as he moved into his room and closed the door.

"Jack, from what I'm seeing so far, the man in the video genuinely appears to be Nikolai—but there are some subtle inconsistencies as well, so I can't say it's him for sure, but I'm still working on it."

"I'm positive it's him," said Jack, "everything about him, his words, his anger, the inflection of his voice… it's him."

"It can't be..." Luke hesitated, "it can't be possible."

Jack thought the same thing for a second, *how could he be alive? There's no way?*

"Luke, Dmitri committed suicide. It doesn't make sense if Nikolai is dead—he got caught and then killed himself before I could extract anything from him."

"Yeah but Jack, it could be a trick or maybe someone is trying to distract you. Also, I crosschecked all of Dmitri's activity in the last month. He's had no contact with anyone even remotely related to Nikolai's previous contacts."

"Okay, figure it out Luke, and in the meantime we're on high alert. I need you to escalate surveillance and send an extra Special Ops team over here for more protection. Monitor all surrounding activity in a twenty-mile radius. Bring the night crew into the office and put all of our resources on this. We need to get to the bottom of this, NOW."

"Yes sir."

The tone of Luke's voice signaled that he understood the significance of what they were dealing with.

They were at war.

Jack hung up and looked out the window into New Orleans Square, trying to make sense of all this—trying to figure out what to do next.

He was ready to kill anyone who was involved.

He dialed his dad next—the legendary Stan Duncan.

TWENTY-TWO

1959
Walt Disney's Private Apartment
Main Street USA
Disneyland Park

As head of security for Disneyland and Walt Disney's personal bodyguard, Stan Duncan was always with Walt. Stan designed the first version of *The System* in the Park and was the leading expert at the time for large-scale security operations.

Walt knew that Disneyland needed a robust security system to give people that special feeling of safety. Most amusement parks at the time did not charge admission so anyone could get in. Disneyland was one of the first places to charge admission, and Walt's critics thought he was crazy for doing so. Walt did what was necessary to keep his guests safe, and to keep them free from worry when they were inside his gates.

Stan had worked in several presidential administrations and was the most sought after security analyst of his time. He knew how to protect an entire area from danger. It was second nature to him, and he used all of the available technology at the time to accomplish this.

Stan was there during the rapid one year construction period of Disneyland, and he was able to install several security features, including tunnels, sensors, secret entrances, and more. He knew exactly where to put these things for maximum effectiveness. He walked the grounds with Walt and inserted security suggestions around Walt's ideas. Because of this, he grew particularly close to Walt, and they spent a lot of time together.

It had been four years since they opened Disneyland and things were going exceptionally well. The growth was phenomenal, even after the disastrous opening. People flocked to Disneyland from all over the world; celebrities, presidents, heads of state, dignitaries—everyone wanted to see Walt's magical creation. Walt's critics, who predicted the demise of Disneyland, had been wrong…again.

Stan sat at a table in Walt's apartment above the Fire Station as he talked with him about a few security enhancements. Walt methodically sipped his coffee as he tried to make sense of various diagrams on the table showing what Stan believed to be the greatest security vulnerabilities at the time. Walt traditionally had his favorite orange juice in the morning from the machine on Main Street, but today he opted for coffee with Stan.

The plans for New Orleans Square were in the works, and lots of preparations were necessary. The attendance at the Park was skyrocketing.

Every day they had more and more people on the property, which also meant an increased risk of something going wrong.

As Disneyland quickly became the symbol of the American Dream, it also became a larger target for threats.

Walt sat with his legs crossed on the small red couch with two rose-embroidered throw pillows. The fabric of the couch had a particular sheen to it, with a decorative design throughout. Perusing security diagrams was not Walt's favorite thing to do, evident by the look on his face, but he knew it had to be done.

Walt made a habit of turning the light on in the apartment window to let other CMs know he was in the Park. Even though the apartment was only around 500 square feet, Walt and Stan enjoyed starting their day there.

Stan never took his position for granted. He was extremely grateful and woke up each morning with a passion for his work. To sit with Walt Disney each morning inside his apartment on Main Street, while being an integral part of building the dream called Disneyland, was an honor. He knew he was at the beginning of something huge, and it was a pleasant change from his days with the CIA.

"Walt, I really think you need another place to stay in New Orleans Square, something set back from the main entrance where we can protect you and other VIPs easier. I like this apartment, but you need something bigger, and it needs to be deeper in the Park."

"I think you're right Stan, that's a good idea," said Walt, in his smooth, calming tone. Walt usually agreed with Stan, and they didn't argue much, only because he knew Stan had his best interest in mind at all times. Stan would take a bullet for Walt, and Walt knew it. He trusted him with his life, and he knew there was no hidden agenda behind his ideas.

Walt leaned back into the sofa, resting his coffee cup on the ornate table next to him. He slowed down his speech, which was what he did when he entered storytelling mode, "Isn't it so much fun to watch the Park expand like this Stan?" Walt gazed out the apartment window into Town Square.

Stan smiled and listened as the master visionary of his time was in full character. Walt talked with a soothing tone. He talked slowly, like a captivating storyteller around a campfire. Walt was the master storyteller of his time, and his unique voice mesmerized television audiences around the world. Walt launched Disneyland through a television special he narrated on ABC, which created a tremendous amount of buzz for the Park. No matter how many times Stan heard him talk about his vision and dreams, he was equally fascinated, and just like everyone else, he was under Walt's magical spell.

"It's like another world in here, and we have the opportunity to build something that people will enjoy for generations—with their kids *and* grandkids." Walt smiled because he knew they were making magic, and this is what he loved to do. Disneyland was an extension of his imagination. It was so much more fun than making movies. He often said that once a movie was in "the can" it was done—with Disneyland, it was never finished—he could keep expanding it so that it could withstand the test of time.

"We're transporting people to another world once they walk through those gates. And once they're inside, we're building a place where you can't see the outside world, a place that looks and feels like something out of a storybook. Parents can walk hand and hand with their kids down a turn of the century small town, and then just around the corner they are transported into Tomorrowland. They can go anywhere their hearts desire."

Walt leaned forward with enthusiasm, "We get to build this world and watch it grow! Disneyland will tell a story that will transcend generations; people will share their experiences here at the Park with future generations. It's the most exciting thing I have ever done, Stan."

The phone rang, and Stan answered it even though he wanted to keep listening to Walt, "Yes—okay put him through." On the other end was Los Angeles Chief of Police William Parker. "Hello Chief, what can I do for you?"

"Stan, I hope you are doing well," said Chief Parker, "General Zakharov, whom I am sure you are aware of, is requesting a security clearance for Soviet Premier Khrushchev—he wants to visit Disneyland when he's in Los Angeles."

Stan was silent for a few seconds and glanced at Walt. "I don't think that's a good idea, Chief. We're vulnerable right now due to the recent expansion. I don't think it's a good time."

Walt looked at Stan with an expression that said, *what's not a good idea?*

Stan caught this look from Walt and asked the Chief if he could call him back.

Stan looked at Walt, "That was Chief Parker. Khrushchev wants to come to the Park in three weeks."

"Khrushchev?" Walt asked in a surprised, confused tone, "He wants to come here?"

Walt loved it when dignitaries, celebrities, and political leaders wanted to visit Disneyland, but he was kind of torn on this one due to his disdain for communism. He thought he might somehow be endorsing communism by walking the Russian Premier through his Park.

Walt paused for a moment, "I think we should do it—I think it might be good for America; we can show them what the United States is all about that if you have a dream and you give your people the freedom to follow that dream, anything is possible."

"I agree, Walt, but we aren't ready for a high profile leader like this right now. We have too many potential security loopholes due to the expansion."

"We can figure it out, though," Walt continued. "We have the best security system in the country here—if anyone can protect him, you can." Walt's face lit up, "Besides, I want to show him one of the world's largest peacetime submarine fleets!"

"Okay, let me call a meeting with the heads of security and let's see what we can come up with—although I must reiterate that I don't think it's a good idea. We can tell them 'no' in a nice way without looking like we don't want him here."

Stan walked down the staircase and headed for Main Street to perform his regular checks. He took a deep breath, marveling at the magical world he was privileged to work in each day. He appreciated every square inch of the Park and was in awe each time he walked through the Lands.

Working at Disneyland was a dream.

Working with Walt Disney inspired his soul.

The brilliant Wurlitzer sign was illuminated at the start of Main Street, the red and white Carnation Fresh Milk and Ice Cream truck was parked outside of the Carnation Cafe, and he could smell the sweet aroma of pipe tobacco coming from the Fine Tobacco shop as the tall double-decker bus slowly approached him.

There was always a buzz in the air, especially on Main Street. Walt had created his own world, Cast Members were like family, and no one wanted to go home. Everyone hung out and talked after their shifts. Most CMs didn't even think of it as work.

Stan knew he could make this Khrushchev visit happen, but the bottom line was that he didn't want him in the Park.

He hated what Khrushchev stood for and more importantly he hated Stalin, and the atrocities he committed.

But there was something else…

JACK DUNCAN

IS

THE DEADLIEST CAST MEMBER

SEASON ONE

EPISODE TWO

ONE

August 8, 2010
Dream Suite
Disneyland Resort

Jack paced back and forth on the balcony of the Dream Suite as the sky transitioned from a clear blue, to a pinkish-orange. This particular sunset haunted Jack instead of leaving him in awe.

He pressed his iPhone to his ear waiting for someone at his dad's house to pick up.

No answer.

Jack turned to Max, who stayed close to him as he scanned the area, "Max, how long until the special ops team shows up?"

"Should be roughly another twenty minutes, sir." Max was 'in the zone' and ready for war.

"I need my helicopter in the parking lot as soon as possible."

"Yes, sir."

Jack's phone buzzed, the call was coming from his dad's house.

"Dad—"

"Um, hello Jack, this is Michael. I'm sorry; it's been a rough day over here. Unfortunately, your father has taken a turn for the worse. I was going to call, but—"

"Michael," Jack said urgently, "this is an emergency. I need to talk to him right now."

"Jack, you don't understand," said the nervous caretaker, "he's incoherent, he can't talk, and he's not responding to anything right now."

Jack's shoulders slumped with disappointment as he realized he could be losing his dad sooner than he'd thought.

"What do you mean *not responding*?"

Michael stuttered, he was always a little edgy when talking to Jack, "He can't talk Jack, he's been unconscious for most of the day and when he does wake up he tries to talk but can't." He paused, "It honestly doesn't look good, Jack."

Jack took the phone away from his ear and looked beyond the massive trees in New Orleans Square as if he was trying to summon help from above —nothing was going his way. He quickly pulled himself together, "Michael, please do whatever you can, this is more important than you know. I *must* talk to him. Get the best doctors to the house, NOW. I don't care what it takes, or how much money it costs, just get it done."

"Okay Jack, I'll do my best."

"No—don't do your best Michael—MAKE IT HAPPEN. Do you understand?" Jack snapped.

"Look, I'm sorry Michael," Jack realized he wasn't making things better by yelling at him, "but I really need to talk to him—this is a matter of life or death. I'm also sending an extra security team to you right now."

"Another team, Jack?"

"Yes. Don't worry, you're safe. Just focus on getting my dad better so he can talk."

"Yes, Jack. I'll call you with updates." Michael said.

"Thank you, Michael."

Jack put both of his hands on the railing of the Dream Suite balcony, gazed out across the River, and looked below at the people frolicking through New Orleans Square. His phone buzzed again. This time it was an unknown number.

"Mr. Duncan, this is Mike Bradley, the President's Chief of Staff. The President needs to talk to you immediately—this is an urgent matter."

Jack's heart stopped for a second as he made eye contact with Max. He'd received several calls like this from the President over the years, and it was rarely good news.

"Yes, sir," Jack said.

President Hayes took the call from the Oval Office with a quick confident tone, "Jack, it's been awhile. I hope you've been well."

"Actually, Mr. President, we're in a bit of a crisis here."

"Does this involve Nikolai Grusov?"

Jack was shocked that the President mentioned Nikolai.

"Yes, sir, Mr. President, it does."

"Jack, we have credible intelligence showing Grusov on US soil and that he's planning an attack on Disneyland. At first we thought this was a hoax, but it was confirmed today. Shortly after, we received news of the incident with Dmitry Komarov at your location, and this confirmed what we've been thinking."

Jack's vision clouded as he contemplated the reality of Nikolai being alive, and nearby. The thought of Nikolai being anywhere else but the grave elevated his pulse to a frightening level. Adrenaline rushed through his body as he thought of all the different ways he could kill Nikolai and make him suffer.

"Jack, I know this hits close to home for you, but I need you to lead this mission. I sincerely believe that you are the only one who can pull this off. An attack on Disneyland would be a catastrophic blow to the entire country as you already know."

"Mr. President, what kind of attack is he planning?"

"We're not sure, but our intelligence supports the theory that it could be a dirty bomb capable of leveling the Resort and a substantial portion of the surrounding area. The CIA has been digging, and it seems Grusov's associates have had recent involvement with al-Qaeda."

"Mr. President, how is this possible? How could he put together something of this magnitude undetected?"

"I wish I had an answer for you, Jack, but it doesn't matter right now. We need to stop Grusov at all cost. By my authority, you have the full resources of the United States government, and you can take whatever *legal* action necessary to stop this attack. It's imperative that you come through for me again, Jack."

"Yes, sir, Mr. President—I'll deliver Nikolai's head on a platter for you—I can guarantee you that—and all of his associates will be dead when I'm done with them. This bomb will not go off, you have my word, Mr. President."

"Okay Jack, I'm going to pretend like I didn't hear most of that. Remember, we need to play by the rules on this one. Please keep me updated."

The most powerful man in the world disconnected the call, and Jack immediately sprang into action.

"Max, we need to get the kids out of here NOW. Tell Tony and Kim to get to the helicopter immediately. Give the pilot orders for John Wayne airport and get my jet ready to fly to the Bay Area house."

"Yes, sir," Max said as he acted on Jack's directive. He'd overheard Jack's side of the call with the President and knew something was seriously wrong.

Conroy's voice came through Jack's earpiece, "Jack, I just got word your helicopter is landing in the parking lot. It's extremely busy here today, and we can't have it there for long."

"I'm sending my kids out there now," Jack said in a low, determined voice. "They'll be off the ground in twenty minutes."

Conroy hesitated with Jack on speakerphone in the Control Center with at least twenty people listening. He picked up the phone and spoke in a lower tone. "Is everything okay, Jack?"

"No, it's not okay. Nothing is okay. I'll brief you when I get there."

TWO

Tony and Kim rushed Andy and Grace into the living room of the Dream Suite, backpacks in hand, preparing them for immediate departure. Everyone looked flustered.

"Daddy, what's wrong? Why are we leaving?" Grace said with her bottom lip quivering.

"Gracie," Jack said as he bent down to look in her eyes, "there's a problem here—a threat—and I need to take care of it. But don't worry, everything will be okay."

Grace put her head down as a tear began to stream down her face. It brought back terrible memories of what happened in 2005.

"Dad," Andy said as his voice cracked out of fear, "are you sure everything is okay?"

Jack put his arms around Andy and Grace and squeezed them.

"Everything will be fine, you guys head out with Tony and Kim, and I'll get this sorted out. We'll be eating dessert at the Club again in no time!"

"Jack, we'll keep you updated on our progress," said Kim with a reassuring smile. Jack took comfort in the fact the kids had Tony and Kim to protect them. They were an impenetrable duo. As hard as it was to send the kids away, out of his sight and out of his reach, he knew they would be safer with them, far away from this threat.

Jack nodded, gave the kids one last hug, and they moved towards the rear Cast Member exit of the Dream Suite.

Jack reluctantly watched them go, and then forced his focus back to the situation at hand.

"Sir," Max said to Jack, "the special ops team is on site."

"Have them escort the kids to the helicopter."

Max nodded and issued commands through his earpiece.

"Who's on this team Max?"

"It's our best team; several former Team Six SEALs."

"Okay, good. Tell them to head to the Control Center after the kids are safely in the air. I need my full assault kit, body armor and everything."

Jack's phone buzzed again. It was Ruddy.

"Jack, I'm glad you finally decided to pick up your phone," Ruddy's whiny voice screeched through Jack's iPhone.

Jack cut him off, "Ruddy, listen to me very carefully. We're in a bad situation right now, and there's absolutely nothing you can do to help. Don't call me again—I will call you if I need you."

Jack abruptly hung up.

He put his finger to his earpiece to message Conroy, "Rob, we need to evacuate the Park, NOW. Don't ask questions, just do it."

Conroy's voice cracked, "Jack? Wait, what? Jack?"

"Just do it. You're taking orders from me now, don't ask questions, just do what I say. Get a hold of yourself—we're at war."

Jack moved to the Dream Suite balcony. He put his hands on the rails, trying to think as his mind raced through all of the possible scenarios. He saw moms and dads holding hands with their kids while they strolled through New Orleans Square. The Pirates of the Caribbean theme song cheerfully played directly below him. It was a fun day at Disneyland with no thought of danger for these innocent people. They were accustomed to being in the protective bubble of the Parks, they took their safety for granted—they had no idea of the potential disaster they were facing.

He involuntarily gripped the balcony rail tighter and tighter as he stood in front of the ornate 'W'. Everything was hitting him at the same time; the thought of losing his dad, being separated from his kids, thousands of lives in danger, and the uncontrollable feeling of hate running through him like an illegal drug. At the same time, his insatiable desire for revenge seemed to comfort and energize him.

His phone buzzed again from another unknown number, and he answered it immediately, "Duncan."

There was a pause on the other end; he heard scratchy sounds echoing in the background as if the call was coming from a remote area.

"Jack Duncan," the voice was low, rugged, and instantly recognizable to Jack. "Do you know who this is?"

The voice sliced through the phone like a dagger—Jack knew exactly who it was.

It was Nikolai Grusov.

THREE

"How do I know this is you?" Jack said in a low voice, knowing full well who it was. He immediately sent a message to Luke from his iPad telling him to trace the call.

"You most certainly recognize my voice. Don't play games with me Jack."

Every muscle in Jack's body contracted as he turned from the balcony and walked towards the living room of the Dream Suite. He pressed his phone hard against his ear so he wouldn't miss a word. He stared at the floor while a thick vein on his forehead became engorged. He had to keep Nikolai on the line long enough so Luke could pinpoint his location.

A message flashed on Jack's iPad—"few more minutes Jack, keep him on the line".

"No, I don't recognize your voice. I don't believe this is Nikolai because Nikolai Grusov is dead—rotting in hell."

Nikolai mocked Jack over the phone with a slow and deliberate chuckle designed to get under his skin and grate his nerves.

"That's what you thought wasn't it, Jack? I would think a military legend of your caliber would know how to finish off an enemy combatant—but I guess you aren't as good as everyone says or thinks. And I guess your precious 'system' isn't as good as you think, either."

Another message flashed across his iPad from Luke—"voice authenticated, calling from a secure line, still can't track it."

Jack ground his teeth and slammed his hand on the table in frustration with rage burning in his eyes.

"Nikolai, it doesn't matter what you do because I am going to hunt you down. *You will* suffer. You cannot even *comprehend* the physical pain I will inflict on you, and I'll keep you alive while it's happening to make your misery seem never-ending. You'll beg me to die, but I won't let you." Jack was losing it —he was morphing into another person.

Nikolai continued with a sadistic chuckle.

"I believe you, Jack. I really do, because I remember what you did to me right before you *thought* you killed me. Except something distracted you at the last minute. Do you remember what that was?"

Jack's rage switched into high gear.

His eyes bulged, and his heart forcefully pounded against his chest at an alarming rate.

"YOU took her from me," Jack roared and gasped for air while his hand shook uncontrollably, "and for that, I will hunt you down and take away everything that is important to you. I will get my revenge; justice will be served, and you will pay dearly for what you've done."

Nikolai laughed again and responded, "Jack, I have nothing to lose, I have no one left who is important to me. I'm not afraid to die, I've never been afraid to die. I just want to watch *you* suffer—that is all I want—and *you will suffer*. If you think losing Kate was bad, you just wait until you see what's next."

Jack's face turned a bright red as heat flashed throughout his body. He yelled back over the phone, "DON'T YOU EVER MENTION HER NAME AGAIN, OR—"

"Or what, Jack? What are you going to do to me? You are the one on the defensive right now. You have a park to save from a bloody disaster." Nikolai paused for a second, "You are *consumed* with your hate for me, aren't you Jack? Isn't that your problem? Your thirst for revenge? It controls your life, *doesn't it*?"

Jack seethed. His disgust for Nikolai increased by the second. It *was* consuming him and clouding his judgment. But it felt good, and his longing for revenge against Nikolai fueled his fire. Images randomly flashed through his mind. Kate's beautiful, innocent face. Nikolai's evil smile, Andy, Grace, and the innocent children in the Park. Jack struggled to maintain his composure; he needed to keep Nikolai on the line a little longer, but it was painful listening to his demonic voice.

"Let me tell you how this is going to work, Jack," Nikolai continued. "I have a dirty bomb that is ready to detonate on my command. It's somewhere in your Resort. If you try to evacuate the Park in any way, I will ignite it, and Disneyland, as you know it, will cease to exist."

"I don't believe you have a bomb here. There is no way you could've gotten it in here without us knowing. You're bluffing."

"Really, Jack? Why don't you take a look at your screen and I will show you what I mean."

Jack's face turned deathly pale as the screen on his iPad changed remotely, without him doing anything, to a live video feed—not even Luke could control Jack's screen. He saw the live view of the *Berm* that was continuously monitored by the Disney security team—giving them a privileged vantage point of the entire perimeter of the Resort. Jack's mouth dropped, and his eyes twitched as he came to the horrifying realization that Nikolai had control of *The System*.

FOUR

"You see, Jack," Nikolai said, becoming more confident and cocky, "your system is not as impenetrable as you think. An amateur might have a hard time with it, but not someone like me."

Jack's head spun as his world turned upside down.

Luke flashed a message across his screen—"Jack, don't know how this is happening, still can't trace the call, he's hacked into The System somehow."

Nikolai continued with his orders, "Oh, and when I say no evacuations, I MEAN EVERYONE—"

Jack's jaw dropped as sheer terror engulfed him.

The video feed on his iPad switched to a view of his helicopter in the parking lot.

It was as if a dull blade sliced through his heart—twisting side to side. His stomach clenched; he tried to breathe but couldn't, and he collapsed into the chair next to his iPad, hunched over with his hands holding his head.

Nikolai continued to chuckle with undertones from his deep Russian accent. "You'd better tell Tony and Kim to stay on the ground and bring your kids back to your suite, or that bomb is going off, Jack."

Jack clamped his teeth down so hard he could feel pain deep in his gums. He tried to figure a way out, but Nikolai had his back to the wall—torturing Jack without even being in the room.

"If I bring them back, you'll set off the bomb regardless," Jack said, trying to mask his unbearable pain.

"No, Jack. That isn't true. I won't set off the bomb if you follow my instructions and meet my demands."

"What demands?"

"Well, it's not money if that's what you're thinking. I already have enough of that from my new friends. I want you, Jack—and your dad—just the three of us so we can have a little chat."

"My dad is dying. I can't get him down here."

"I'm aware of your father's situation, and I also know you are *Jack Duncan* —and you can do whatever you want—I know you'll make it happen."

"Where?"

"I will let you know. In the meantime, no evacuations. Do precisely what I say, and no one will get hurt."

Jack glared at the live video feed of the helicopter carrying Andy and Grace as his chest pumped harder and harder, his heart rate soared—he was NOT going to call that helicopter back under any circumstance.

"Jack," Nikolai read his mind, "if I have a live video feed of your kids, do you actually think they are safe? You either do what I say, or I will blow your helicopter out of the sky. How would you like to watch that happen on your live video stream?"

Nikolai hung up.

Jack jumped up to roar back at Nikolai, but realized the call was disconnected. He overcame the overwhelming anguish of what he'd just seen —his face turned from despair to laser-focused determination.

He was ready to break all the rules to stop Nikolai.

Jack scrambled to get Tony on the phone.

"Tony shut the bird down and get it out of here. Bring the kids back to the Dream Suite."

"Jack?" Tony was confused, but he didn't ask questions. "We're headed back to you right now."

Jack dialed Luke. "Did you get his location?" Rivulets of sweat poured from his forehead as he rolled up his sleeves.

"No, Jack. I couldn't get it. It was a secure line, and I couldn't break it. I tried everything."

"Luke, find out how he hacked our system—NOW!"

"Yes, sir." Luke, normally extremely confident, was unsure of himself.

All Jack could think about was how he was going to cut Nikolai's fingers off one by one and make him suffer more than any human has ever suffered. But he had to get it together, Nikolai had the upper hand, and he was controlling Jack like a puppet.

He radioed Conroy. "Rob, cancel the evac, effective immediately. I repeat DO NOT EVACUATE—I'll explain shortly."

Rob was more confused than ever as he broke out in a cold sweat.

"I'm headed to the Control Center now. Assemble your entire team and get Anaheim PD in there, as well. I need our best people in that room when I get there, so make the calls."

Max overheard everything, and his face was white as a ghost. He looked uncharacteristically rattled as if someone whacked him over the head with a 2x4.

"Sir, I have your weapons in route with your full kit. Should I send everything to the Control Center?"

"No, bring them here," Jack gave Max that familiar look of super-human determination, the same type of scary look he had on the human trafficking mission. "I need you to come with me. Have the Special Ops team stay here and guard the kids with Kim and Tony."

FIVE

August 8, 2010
Disneyland Security Control Center
Disneyland Park

Jack burst into the Control Center dressed in black—armed with his full assault kit; ballistic chest plates, his Heckler & Koch MP7 with suppressor, a Heckler & Koch 416 assault rifle with a ten-inch barrel and suppressor; his P226 at one side, and his Sig P239 .40 caliber handgun at the other. His ballistic helmet was outfitted with the latest generation of night-vision goggles, a helmet mounted flashlight, and IR strobe.

Jack was ready for battle and was not taking any chances; he knew he needed to eliminate or apprehend anyone involved with this attack—and there were probably hostiles on site already.

Conroy, Anaheim PD, and other high-level operatives took a step back when they saw Jack come through the door in his assault kit. Most had idolized Jack growing up, and now he stood in front of them sporting the gear that had made him a legend.

They looked worried about the severity of the situation seeing Jack in full battle mode.

Ruddy was thoroughly intimidated; he'd never seen Jack like this. He came up to a little below Jack's chest, and had to look straight up to talk to him.

"Umm Jack, you can't go into the Park like this, we have 50,000 people here today."

Jack looked down at Ruddy and then over to everyone else standing at attention.

"Gentlemen, there is a bomb on the premises, and we need to find it—IMMEDIATELY."

Everyone looked back and forth at each other nervously. Ruddy was speechless for the first time in his life. Conroy had a blank look on his face and didn't know what to say. Nobody knew what to say, so they waited for Jack to continue as they processed this life-altering information.

"The President believes this to be a credible threat; they're sending the counterterrorism unit over here now."

Conroy blurted out, "Jack, why are we not evacuating?"

Jack paused and looked into the worried eyes in the room.

"Because—" Jack paused for a second because even *he* had a hard time believing this. "We're being held hostage—"

"Held hostage? By who?"

Chatter filled the room; they couldn't figure out how in the world they could be held hostage at Disneyland.

"Nikolai Grusov," Jack said with hate in his voice. "He's threatened to detonate the bomb if we attempt to evacuate the Park."

Dead silence swept across the room.

Everyone stared at Jack, hanging on his every word. They knew that their hope for survival depended on him. He was the only one who had a chance of getting them out of a predicament like this.

"And another thing," Jack paused again because he still couldn't believe it, "Nikolai has access to *The System*."

Conroy's mouth dropped again, "Jack, that's not possible, how—"

"I saw it with my own eyes, Rob. He has access. We're still not sure to what extent, but it doesn't look good. We have to stay on our toes because he could be seeing and hearing everything we're doing."

Silence and dismay swept the room. Ruddy was way out of his league at this point. He had no clue what to do under these conditions, and looked as if he was going to wet himself.

"Along with the counterterrorism unit, I have SEAL Team Six from Coronado en route right now. They're experts at finding and disarming bombs of this magnitude. The President is giving us full access to necessary resources, but it's up to us to find this bomb. We know the Park better than anyone, and we need to scour every square inch with everything we've got."

The group started to gain confidence in light of the devastating news—it was life or death. It was all about survival at this point as they quickly understood the threat.

"Failure is not an option, gentlemen. There are 50,000 civilians who could die today, not counting people in surrounding areas— unless we stop Nikolai."

Ruddy started to back out of the room, looking as if he was trying to slip out inconspicuously. Jack saw this, but he knew Ruddy wouldn't be much help anyway. He actually didn't care what he did at this point as long as he kept out of the way. Jack thought of a way to ensure that Ruddy would do just that.

"Ruddy," Jack said. "I need you to take the Park to Level 3, only allow hotel guests or readmissions in the Parks. Front gate CMs will be confused, but sell it to them. Make sure there are NO mass exits."

"Um, yeah, sure Jack. I'll get right on that. That's where I'll be if you need me, okay?" Ruddy nodded like a dashboard bobble-head as he backed out of the door, leaving Jack and the rest of the professionals to handle the situation.

Jack continued to speak to the group, "The local bomb squad should arrive before Team Six, so we need to identify the highest probability locations before they get here. We cannot create a panic, which means we have to keep this information to a limited number of people. But at the same time, we need a lot of bodies on the hunt; we need every canine on property checking every possible location. This search has to appear like a routine check; otherwise people will panic, and if there's a max exodus, Nikolai could think we're evacuating."

Jack continued to bark orders to get everyone going in the right direction.

"Oh and one more thing, you cannot call home. No one outside of this room can know the entirety of what I've just told you. Is that understood?"

Everyone nodded, although some were apprehensive because they lived nearby.

A muscle bound giant, who looked like a human tank, walked into the Control Center, and the entire room stared at him in awe. He was bigger than Max and built like a semi-truck. The man was dressed in all black with a full assault kit, similar to Jack's. He looked like *Thor* on steroids. People frequently mistook him for Chris Hemsworth due to his blonde hair, blue eyes, and well-developed physique. However, Kendall was a lot taller. Jack turned around and smiled.

"Kendall, am I glad to see you."

Kendall alternated with Max on Jack's personal protection detail. If Jack was the most feared SEAL in history, Kendall was number two—he was on Team Six with Jack, and they'd been friends since they were kids. Kendall saved Jack's life twice in combat situations. Jack hired Kendall as his personal bodyguard paying him almost a million per year plus perks.

"Wouldn't miss it for the world, Jack. I heard what happened, just let me know what you need me to do," Kendall said with a deep, booming voice that matched his enormous stature.

Jack's rage leveled out. He had everything on his side that he needed to win, which gave him a slight level of comfort. His hate for Nikolai fueled his fire along with the never-ending confidence he'd gained from prevailing against dozens of top al-Qaeda leaders. Mission after mission, Jack took out the hardest, and most feared terrorists to ever threaten the safety and security of the United States—this caused him to believe he could do anything.

Max and Kendall, the special ops team assigned to the kids, SEAL Team Six coming in from San Diego, and the CIA Counterterrorism unit were all at his command—he had the best people and tools in the world on his side. If this team couldn't stop the threat, no one could.

Kendall was a Godsend. Jack knew that with Kendall on his side, he could do anything.

Even with everything he had going for him, he still had a sinking feeling in his gut. What if they couldn't find the bomb in time? This would be the deadliest attack on US soil—in history. It would be the end of Disneyland.

Walt's dream would be destroyed. Even worse his kids would be gone, and there would be no reason for him to live.

SIX

August 8, 2010
Main Street, U.S.A.
Disneyland Park

"Conroy," Jack said, "I'm going underground to check all the tunnels. I need you to put the word out to CMs in the Park that we're doing routine training, and that's why we're in full gear. Cancel all Fantasmic shows and Fireworks for tonight."

Conroy nodded at Jack in agreement and jumped on the radio.

"Max and Kendall, you guys are with me."

In the background, they could hear the familiar voice of Disneyland, Bill Rogers as he announced the cancellation of the Fireworks show. Multitudes of guests sighed with disappointment.

Jack, Max, and Kendall headed for the door. A video surveillance officer stopped them, "Mr. Duncan, I just got an alert—the man you flagged from Tom Sawyer Island just walked through the front gate."

"WHAT? Send the feed to my phone."

Jack looked at Max and Kendall, "You two head underground and let me know what you find. I'm going after this guy."

"Sir," Max interrupted, "shouldn't one of us stay with you? It's our job to protect you."

"No, Max. We need to find this bomb, that's more important right now."

Jack removed his gear, knowing his full assault kit would not fare well with guests on Main Street.

Tony's voice came through Jack's ear bud, "Jack, we are safely in the Dream Suite, the full ops team is here, and I have the Raven flying above to monitor our location. Don't worry, the kids are okay."

"Thanks Tony. Stay put for now and stay vigilant. Use of deadly force is authorized to protect my kids."

"Roger that, Jack,"

Jack walked down Main Street from the Cast Member entrance near the Little Red Wagon Corn Dog cart in an effort to intercept the man as he entered the Park. His Google Glass was active, scanning everyone around him.

"Put on your Sunday Clothes" played throughout Main Street, U.S.A. as the lights from Coke Corner illuminated the end of the thoroughfare. The aroma of the fresh handcrafted candy at the Candy Palace was in the air as the Smellitzer pushed the sweet scent throughout the most famous street in the world. People were everywhere, leisurely walking and admiring the magic of

Main Street with its vivid lighting and flashing marquees.

Authentic gas lanterns flickered at the top of their lampposts on each side of the street. The Gibson Girl waffle machines cranked out freshly cooked waffle bowls. People lined up for mint and chip sundaes. Parents sat with their children and talked on the patio of the Carnation Cafe over hot chocolate. Moms and dads nestled side by side with their kids on the curb of Main Street as they listened to music, admired the peculiar second story windows, and mapped out their next adventure.

A buzz was in the air; people were happy and having fun—little did they know that tonight, Jack Duncan was their only hope of survival.

Seeing the splendor of Main Street at night, the care that Walt put into its design and all of the innocent bystanders enjoying it, amplified the urgency of the situation.

A young mom pushed a stroller directly in front of Jack. Her four-year-old boy had a giant smile on his face as he thrust his finger in the air, pointing at the flashing lights. Jack got a lump in his throat knowing this bomb would change thousands of lives forever. Innocent men, women, and children would be murdered in cold blood. He couldn't stop thinking of Andy and Grace. He would not lose them or let them be harmed—he would die before he let that happen.

Jack crossed the street in front the Magic Shop where Steve Martin's career got its start, scanning everyone as they walked by.

"Jack," said Conroy over his earpiece, "his name is Stephen Colby, his bio is on your device."

Jack's custom tactical iPhone wrist device was strapped horizontally to his arm with heavy-duty black straps. The screen was longer than a consumer iPhone, which gave him a much bigger viewing area. Jack quickly turned his forearm to get any view he needed. This tactical iPhone setup was particularly useful in pursuits.

He glanced down at the image of the man and then looked up at the thousands of people on Main Street, scanning side to side.

Hundreds of bright white lights illuminated the majestic Opera House as Jack approached it. The patriotic Great Moments with Mr. Lincoln show played inside. Park-wide audio controls were housed in there as well. As Jack scanned, he suddenly got a red alert in this glasses that outlined the body of a man in front of him. Next to the red outline, the text read "Stephen R. Colby" with supporting information underneath.

Jack walked up slowly behind the man and said in a low voice, "Mr. Colby, you need to come with me."

The man slowly turned around with a confused look on his face, "I'm sorry, is there a problem?"

Colby looked and sounded like any other American in the Park that night. Blonde hair, blue eyes, well dressed—he looked like a normal, everyday family man.

Jack didn't say another word; he grabbed his arm and abruptly shifted his direction. The man didn't resist. He was helpless against Jack's overwhelming strength. Jack moved him to the Cast Member entrance near the Opera House, the entrance to Liberty Street if Walt had his way decades ago.

Jack didn't know how many chances he would get to obtain information about the bomb. This might be it.

He knew one thing—he was going to latch on to this man like he was their only hope. Jack was positive that Colby's link to Grusov was no coincidence.

SEVEN

August 8, 2010
Dream Suite
Disneyland Park

Tony and Kim rushed back into the Dream Suite with Andy and Grace as Jack's Special Ops detail followed close behind. The team rapidly covered each exit of the suite. Several remained outside guarding the perimeter, two covered the balcony, one covered each stairway leading to the suite, and three moved to the roof. No one was getting into the Dream Suite with this team on duty.

Tony put the kids in the master bedroom with Kim and two more former SEALs as he headed for the living room with his phone to his ear.

"Tony, what are you doing?" Kim followed him out of the master bedroom. Tony stopped in his tracks and put his phone down to his side.

"Kim—it's my mom," Tony hesitated before he spoke again, "she lives less than a mile from here, I need to tell her to get out of town."

"Tony, you can't do that, Jack gave us orders, this can't get out, or it will put everyone in danger including the kids."

"I know Kim, but she won't tell anyone, no one will know." A flash of emotion gripped him as choked up.

"Tony, you know how these things work, one phone call could be detrimental to the entire operation. You know that. We have to do the right thing."

Tony avoided eye contact with Kim and seemed confused. He knew Kim was right, but he also knew she would do the same thing if her mom lived in the area.

Without any emotion, Tony agreed, "Okay, Kim. You're right."

Kim smiled at Tony as she locked eyes with him and put her hand on his arm, "Let's get back in the room with the kids. Jack has things under control, and everything will be fine."

Walking back into the master bedroom of the Dream Suite, they saw Grace on the bed crying with her small hands covering her face as Andy tried to comfort her. Kim walked over to the bed and put her arms around her.

"Gracie, honey, everything is going to be okay. Your dad is on this, and he will take care of whatever is wrong. In the meantime, you have us." Kim held Grace's pretty little face in both of her hands and wiped the tears from her eyes. "Come here, both of you." Kim said in a comforting voice, motioning to Andy.

Kim took Andy and Grace into her arms, and she hugged them tight. She never tried to be a replacement mom to the kids, but she was the closest thing they had to a mother because she was around them more than any other woman. Despite her rough history, Kim had a soft side for kids, and Jack treasured Kim's ability to comfort them. It was the type of consoling that only a woman could provide.

"Hey," Kim said as she looked both of them in the eyes, "how about this; once this is all over, we'll do a movie night in Downtown Disney, just the three of us, you guys pick the movie—as long as it's okay with your dad."

Grace smiled, and Andy did, too. They always looked forward to movie nights with Kim. She usually sat in between them and put her arms around them for most of the movie while they shared an extra-large tub of buttery movie popcorn.

The wall of "toughness" Kim put up was evident the moment you met her. Her assertiveness and her tough exterior kept people away—but she had a soft spot for Andy and Grace.

Tony looked to be in a daze and not thinking straight as he stared out the Dream Suite window into Adventureland. Kim noticed his phone sitting on the bed unattended, and she inched closer to it. She pulled her phone out, discreetly typed in a code, activated Tony's screen, and touched his phone with hers.

Kim looked back at the kids, "Hey, how about we talk about that story that always cheers you up—your favorite story about your mom and dad?"

The kids smiled thinking about the story that Jack had told them over and over again about how he and Kate had first met. Jack's face would light up whenever he retold this story, and he was uncharacteristically animated while telling it. He and Kate made it a point to tell the kids how they met, and Andy and Grace always got a kick out of it. The retelling of this event was fun for the entire family. The kids usually poked fun at their dad since the story was so mushy and sentimental.

Andy started the routine, trying to get Grace to laugh. "Well, my dad was walking in New Orleans Square like a big tough guy," Andy stood up and pushed his chest out doing his imitation of Jack, "he was looking down at something and then he looked up at a woman who was sitting on the edge of the French Market patio and said, WOW!"

Grace giggled, "He didn't say it like that, Andy!"

"Yes, he did," Andy continued in a silly tone, "so he kept walking, and he stopped, looked up into the air, and looked back at her and thought *what am I doing*?" Andy put his finger on his chin, adding his own comic flair to the story.

Grace decided she would pick up the story from there. Looking at Kim she said, "And then my mom looked up at daddy and smiled and it melted my dad's heart. My mom's heart dropped as she thought Daddy was so handsome and strong looking, but she didn't want him to think she was checking him out."

Andy cut in, mocking Jack's first line to Kate, "Duhhhh, is that a book about Walt Disney?"

Grace interrupted again, having fun with Andy, but wanting to set him straight, "Then my dad looked into her eyes and saw something magical—and my mom felt the same way."

Andy chimed in again, "So, like my dad always says, there is one person out there who you are destined to be with."

"And when you find her, you have to fight for her," said Grace smiling.

Kim grinned and briefly looked over at Tony.

Andy and Grace smiled realizing that even though their mom was gone, *no one*—no matter how evil they were, could take away the memories and stories that they kept inside.

Kim smiled at both of them, hugged them tight, and gently rubbed their backs. "See, even in a tough situation we can still have fun and be happy."

Tony grabbed his phone and exited the master bedroom. Kim was concerned as she watched him leave while gently biting her lip. She hoped he wasn't going to do what she thought he might do. She glanced down at her phone trusting that Tony would make the right decision—but the trace she put on Tony's phone confirmed the outgoing call to his mom.

Tony had directly disobeyed Jack's orders.

EIGHT

1959
Main Street, U.S.A.
Disneyland Park
Stan Duncan

Stan walked down Main Street towards the new Motorboat Cruise attraction in Fantasyland near the Matterhorn. Suddenly his mind flashed back to his best friend Mike Branum, from his days with the OSS. Stan still had occasional nightmares about what happened when he was an upper-level OSS operative. He never got over having to watch helplessly as his friend Mike suffered at the hands of the NKVD/KGB while tied up and unable to do anything to stop the torment. Even worse, having to tell Mike's wife what had happened. That event scarred Stan for life, and he was never the same again. His hatred for the Soviets, and especially the KGB, had festered inside of him and turned into a deep abhorrence for anyone associated with them.

Mike's death caused Stan to obsess over stopping the KGB, and he spent all of his time in pursuit of this until he met the love of his life, Genie, who persuaded him to retire from the CIA and join Walt Disney to help build Disneyland.

Stan never forgot what happened to Mike, and he sure wasn't going to let Khrushchev disgrace and defile Disneyland with his presence—at least not while he had any say in it. He had to find the right way to tell Walt, but he wanted to make sure he was acting in the best interest of Walt and the Park.

1959 was a momentous year for expansion—they went from 22 attractions on opening day four years ago, to 48. They had most recently opened the Matterhorn, The Submarine Voyage, and the Monorail. Vice President Nixon and his family were in attendance for the inauguration of the three attractions in June, and Stan had coordinated with the Secret Service to make sure everything was in order.

Jack Wrather, the original owner of the Disneyland Hotel allowed the Nixons to stay in his private suite. The Nixons were frequent visitors to the Park originally being from Yorba Linda. During their stay, Stan had to coordinate passage from the Disneyland Hotel to the Park, and everywhere else they went.

A gift from the Secret Service hung on his office wall featuring Stan and the Vice President's detail in front of the Monorail. It was a high honor for them to work with Stan. Next to that, was Stan's favorite picture of the Secret Service following Nixon on Autopia.

The day of the grand opening, the Nixon family had lunch in Walt's apartment before leading the procession down Main Street. They opened the Matterhorn and were the first to ride the Submarine Voyage. People retold the story for years about the Secret Service detail being left behind at the Monorail station while the Nixon family rode the entire track twice with Walt. They perpetuated the myth that the Secret Service was ready to jump on the outside of the Monorail as it went by due to their fear of being separated from the Vice President.

Stan was in the Monorail car with Walt and the Nixons—heavily armed, as usual. No one would have been able to get to the Nixons on the Monorail with Stan there, and the Secret Service knew this.

Stan reveled in the success of the Nixon family's visit to the Park—deep down he knew he could protect Khrushchev in the same way, but he didn't want to.

He arrived at the site of the Motorboat Cruise Lagoon and marveled at the brand new Monorail above, the towering Matterhorn attraction, and the expanded Autopia tracks. It was hard to believe Walt completed this large expansion even though Roy told him to hold off on it for a few years. After a few routine inspections, Stan headed back to his office and called Chief Parker.

"Chief," said Stan in his normal direct and confident tone, "I don't feel comfortable about this Khrushchev visit. We're not familiar with their security detail, and we have a lot of construction going on over here. I just don't think it's the right time."

"But Stan," the Chief said, "what am I going to tell him? Zakharov will be here in a week, and he wants to go over security arrangements. Khrushchev specifically asked to visit Disneyland, and he wants his family to see it."

"Just tell them that Anaheim is not in your jurisdiction and makes it hard for you to guarantee his protection. Not to mention, it's extremely difficult to guarantee his security due to the crowds we have here at the Park," said Stan.

"Yeah, but we've done motorcades for President Truman to Disneyland and other Soviet Dignitaries, they know this already," said the Chief. He wasn't buying Stan's excuses, "I can't just lie to them or make up stories. It'll be bad for public relations."

"Look," said Stan, "have Zakharov call me direct, and I will explain it to him."

Chief Parker agreed.

Stan hung up the phone and stroked his chin trying to think. He didn't know what he was going to tell the Russians. He knew Walt wanted him to make the visit happen, but it would be a publicity nightmare if something happened to a world leader at Disneyland—especially Khrushchev.

He picked up the phone to try to reach Walt in his Fire House Apartment.

Walt answered with his familiar, "Hello?"

"Walt, regarding Khrushchev—"

Walt politely cut him off, "Stan, I am with the guys from the network right now. Look, I trust your judgment. If you think it's too dangerous, then let's not do it—it's your call." Walt hung up and went back to his meeting.

Stan decided to grab some food at Aunt Jemima's Pancake House, where he ordered his favorite—The Golden Horseshoe Special, which came with four expertly prepared buttermilk pancakes. He always visited the Pancake House if he needed time to think and figure things out.

After lunch, he arrived back at his office with a call waiting for him. "Mr. Duncan," said Mary Jones, head of Disneyland Community Relations, who also served as a liaison to the State Department when foreign dignitaries wanted to visit the Park. "Nikolai Grusov is waiting on the line for you."

"Thank you Mary, you can put him through." Mary knew Stan's history with the Russians and appeared to be worried about how this whole thing would play out.

"Mr. Zakharov, thank you for waiting, this is—"

Nikolai cut him off, "This is not Major General Zakharov," he said in a thick Russian accent that brought back unpleasant memories for Stan, "this is Nikolai Grusov from the Soviet Security Police. Did your secretary not tell you my name?"

Stan was shocked at Grusov's tone—his first instinct was to blast him and go at him hard, but he paused for a few seconds to regain his composure.

"Sorry about that, Mr. Grusov. I think she did, but I got mixed up for a minute there. We've got a lot of stuff going on in the Park right now, so my mind is a little preoccupied at the moment. How can I help you?"

"Premier Khrushchev would like to visit your park while he's in Los Angeles, and I would like to make security arrangements with you. General Zakharov will be in town next week, and he would like to talk to your police chief to make final plans."

"Yes," said Stan, "I got a call from Chief Parker and I told him that I didn't think it was a good idea right now due to the amount of construction happening here at Disneyland. We just opened a few major attractions, and we're kind of spread thin security-wise right now."

"Look, Mr. Duncan, I am well aware of the strength of your security at Disneyland otherwise I would not recommend a visit by our Premier. You just had your Vice President in the Park, and I am well aware of the other high profile individuals you have hosted," said Grusov with a tone of disdain that Stan couldn't help but feel was directed at him personally.

Stan was heated due to Grusov's aggressive tone; his blood simmered, and his fight or flight reflexes kicked in. It usually took a lot to get him going, but when he reached the point of no return, it could get ugly fast. His history with the Soviets didn't help.

"Grusov," Stan said sternly, "I appreciate your trust in our security system and you are right, our system is quite strong—however as I mentioned, we're in a particularly vulnerable stage right now due to our expansion and it is hard to guarantee the Premier's safety in heavy crowds."

Grusov cut him off again, "Look Duncan, I already know your personal history and that's precisely why you do not want the Premier in your amusement park," Grusov continued, becoming more and more hostile, "do you think I take any pleasure in dealing with you knowing what you did to my comrades?"

"Listen Grusov," Stan's patience and politeness had reached the end of the line as he leaned forward in his chair with clenched fists, "you don't know what I went through in your country—nor do you know what your scum bag *comrades* did to me or my friends. If you were in my face talking like this you would already have a bullet in your head. So I suggest you take a step back. If you truly knew my history you would think twice before advancing on me like this."

With that, Stan hung up on Grusov, and immediately knew he'd made a mistake. He stepped over the line and let his anger potentially damage a fragile relationship.

Grusov heard the click of Stan hanging up on him, and he slowly chuckled. His loyalty over decades had put him in a powerful position within the Soviet hierarchy. His history in the KGB trenches, and fighting against the CIA left him with an undeniable hate for America and everything it stood for. While Khrushchev's goal was to be amicable to other governments, Grusov had a different agenda. He remembered reading about Walt's disdain towards communists back in the forties and hated Walt and his "American Dream" that he'd built in Anaheim. Furthermore, he knew Stan's record, and he was aware of the number of agents Stan had killed—sometimes violently—and other times through extreme measures in an effort to extract information.

Blueprints of Disneyland obtained by the KGB covered Nikolai's old wooden desk. Documents that were obtained during the initial construction in 1954. He analyzed the shockingly detailed plans to determine if it was safe for Khrushchev to visit. Grusov, due to his history of loyalty to the Communist Party, and being a hero in Russia for his military and KGB accomplishments, was allowed to work independently and wasn't questioned much.

He opened an old cabinet behind his desk, revealing a secret built-in wall safe. He quickly spun the dial, opened the safe, and pulled out a thick, sealed folder. He opened the folder and began to search through the top-secret documents. Backstage structures and pathways were meticulously drawn and outlined down to every last entry and exit. Stan was the only other person who had maps with this level of detail.

He thumbed through the stack of papers until he found what he was looking for. This map contained detailed drawings of the underground tunnel system at the Park. Each tunnel had exquisite detail and every entrance and exit was marked. Gas lines, electric lines—everything was documented.

He skimmed past the last document in the folder, and there was a picture of Walt and Stan together. Grusov gripped the picture in his hand and stared at it with a stone cold demeanor—full of hate and aggression towards everything they stood for. Grusov growled under his breath, like an animal, his nostrils flared, and he slightly bared his teeth as he worked himself into a frenzy. He threw the picture on his desk and slammed his fist down on it, creating a significant dent in the photo.

"You have crossed the line, again—Duncan," he snarled as he picked up the phone to call Chief Parker.

"Mr. Parker," said Grusov in an agitated tone, "Mr. Duncan has not only threatened me personally, but he is deliberately refusing to let the Premier into his Park."

The Chief interrupted and said, "Mr. Grusov, there must be some mis—"

"No, there is no misunderstanding," Grusov fired back. "You tell your people that we are not happy about this and next time you should be wiser about who you allow to deal with us. Mr. Duncan has damaged our relationship with his arrogance." With that, he hung up on the Chief.

Grusov was furious. It was his duty to break the bad news to Khrushchev, who had trusted him to make arrangements. The Soviet leader was not going to be happy.

Grusov glanced at a picture of his son on his desk. He picked up the old wooden frame and brought it closer to him as his thick bottom lip trembled. His hand shook, and his anger swelled as he remembered his only son. He knew time would never heal the daily pain he suffered for the loss of his boy. He couldn't erase the way he was brutally murdered from his memory. His pain was eternal and could never be quenched.

His only outlet was *revenge*.

NINE

August 8, 2010
Disneyland Security Control Center
Disneyland Park

Jack sat Colby down in Room Two of the Control Center and restrained his hands. Colby was sweating and shaking nervously after being forced off Main Street. His lips and mouth were dry.

"Look, Mr. Colby. I don't have a lot of time here. We've just received a significant threat, so if you know what's good for you, you'd better tell me everything you know, NOW."

Colby looked perplexed and confused. His chest heaved as he tried to catch his breath.

"Look, I don't know what you're talking about. Is it normal practice to interrogate innocent people at Disneyland?"

"I don't know, is it normal practice to pay $100 for a Park Hopper ticket only to come into Disneyland at night, without your family?"

"How do you know about my family?"

Jack played the video of Colby and his family on Tom Sawyer Island. The man watched with a dumbfounded look on his face. He was speechless.

"What dropped down that drain Colby?"

"Umm, it was my daughter's necklace."

"And you didn't even go to lost and found to retrieve it?"

"Well, I didn't know where to go—look I don't know what's going on here. I'm a normal guy who likes to come to Disneyland every once in a while. I live locally, and I just got a job nearby."

Jack bent over and looked the man squarely in the eyes—he was inches from Colby's nose, "I do not have time to play games—you have five-seconds to tell me how you know Nikolai Grusov or I'm going to start breaking your fingers one by one."

The man's face flashed from a confused look, to a look of sheer terror as he tried to free himself from the restraints.

"FOUR," Jack yelled in his face.

Colby shook uncontrollably, "I'm telling you the truth! I don't know what you are talking about—YOU'RE MAKING A MISTAKE!"

"THREE." Jack yelled louder as the man flinched in fear.

Conroy watched the feed from his office with a few Security CMs. He put his hands on his head with frightening anticipation, "*Please* tell me he is not serious," he said. The Security CMs were glued to the video screen with looks of horror on their faces.

Colby pleaded with Jack, "PLEASE, I have a family, I don't know what you are talking about!"

"TWO."

The man shook his head side-to-side, started crying and blubbering, as he begged Jack to stop.

"LAST CHANCE, COLBY."

The man squeezed his eyes shut. His chest heaved uncontrollably, and he tried in vain to squirm out of the restraints.

Jack yanked his right arm out of the restraint, and in one quick motion forced his index finger back until there was a horrifying CRACK.

"Why?" He screamed in agony at the top of his lungs. His other hand was still behind his back.

Conroy couldn't believe what he was seeing, "Oh dear Lord, I can't believe he just did that, get someone to Room Two and open that door." Everyone looked at each other—no one wanted to go in that room with Jack.

Jack looked at Colby dead in the eyes, "This time you have three-seconds to start giving me answers."

"NOOO—" The man's eyes were bulging out of his head, not knowing how to deal with the excruciating pain.

"PLEASE, STOP!"

"TWO." Jack yelled over him.

"I DON'T KNOW WHAT YOU ARE TALKING ABOUT!"

Jack grabbed the man's middle finger and snapped it.

CRACK

The man cocked his head back and let out another agonizing howl.

Jack whacked Colby across the face and knocked him out of his chair. The man hit the ground with a thud as he came crashing to the ground, and suddenly stopped screaming. His other arm was freed from the restraint.

Jack bent down to pick the man up off the ground.

Out of nowhere, the man summoned the power to throw an ultra-fast tiger claw strike with the base of his palm that landed squarely under Jack's chin.

Conroy's mouth dropped as he watched. He stumbled out of his chair and ran toward Room Two.

The blow caused Jack's head to snap back, and knocked him off balance. The speed of the strike caught him by surprise. Only a highly trained operative could've pulled off a move like this, especially with two of his fingers broken. After he landed the blow under Jack's chin, he quickly snatched Jack's Sig P226 from his side and pointed it directly at him.

Blood dripped from Colby's mouth. He smiled at Jack and began to apply pressure to the trigger of the P226. Suddenly, the man's voice totally changed and became deeper. He began to talk with a deep Russian accent, which was entirely different from the voice he used earlier.

"Could it be *this easy* to take out Jack Duncan?" he said in a thick Russian accent as he chuckled.

The door of Room Two flew open, and the man turned his head.

Jack swiftly landed a devastating kick to his chest; the man's head snapped back violently, and the gun flew out of his hand as he landed on his back. Jack pressed his knee in the man's chest to restrict his breathing as he pressed his alternate weapon, the Sig P239, directly to his forehead.

"This is your last chance. Where is the bomb? TELL ME NOW!" Jack roared.

"Okay, I will tell you, but let me sit up, I cannot breathe, I am suffocating," the man had problems getting his words out.

"Tell me or I *will* suffocate you, I will find the bomb whether you tell me or not. If you help me, I will let you live. I will also keep your family safe from Nikolai."

"Okay," the man was panicking and struggling to breathe, "it's…in…the… tunnel."

"Which tunnel? There are several tunnels here."

"It's—" the man was close to blacking out due to the lack of oxygen and unbearable pain, "it's…the…*hidden* tunnel."

His head dropped to the ground. He was unconscious.

TEN

1994
French Market
Jack and Kate

Jack looked at Kate with anticipation across the table as she paused. He thought it was too good to be true for her to say 'I love you' at this point. He was obviously in love with her.

Kate was quick and straightforward, and he always knew where he stood with her.

"Jack, I can't tell you how much fun I've had with you over the past few months. I've never felt like this before. I've never bonded with anyone like this. But—"

Oh no, I didn't see this coming, Jack thought.

"I'm just worried about falling for someone who is in your line of work. When you leave on deployments, there's a good chance you aren't coming back. I don't know if I can handle that."

Jack didn't know what to say. Everything was going great, and now this? He stared at her not knowing how to respond.

Kate continued, "I mean Jack, I know how it works. Protecting the United States comes first, and everything else is a distant second. I don't know if I can live like that. I'm just being honest with you."

"But Kate," Jack leaned forward and looked into Kate's deep blue eyes, "what if we were meant to be together? I know that sounds corny, but what if we didn't meet by accident—what if that day at the French Market was supposed to happen? What if we were designed to be together?" Jack's voice uncharacteristically cracked with emotion.

Kate couldn't resist Jack's romantic sentiment. She smiled and leaned forward.

"I know, Jack, I think about that all the time. I think about how every day is perfect with you. Our time here at the Parks is, for lack of a better term, magical, and all I want to do is spend time with you, but—"

"But?" Jack interrupted, "Kate, I feel the same way. I've never felt this way about anyone in my life. It's like we have a deep connection and we've known each other for years."

"I know Jack, but I'm just worried about getting deeper into this relationship when I know how this type of thing works."

"Yes, Kate, but anything can happen. What about living for today like you always say?"

"But Jack, I've seen my mom go through this," Kate hesitated, "I haven't told you this, but my dad was killed in action." Kate's head dropped and her shoulders slumped, "Watching my mom go through that was devastating, she was never the same, and she always made me promise I would not get involved with someone in special forces."

Jack moved back in his chair. He was shocked, and didn't know what to say. "Your dad? What did he do?"

"He was a green beret."

It started to make sense—Kate had lived in a spec ops family, and she knew the routine.

"Kate, I'm sorry to hear that," Jack said as he looked down at her nervous hands on the table. "So, you already know what it's like. I'm assuming you haven't told your mom about me yet."

Kate looked down at the table and then back up at Jack; her thick blonde hair framed her face, her sparkling blue eyes, her perfect hands, everything about her was flawless. Jack knew he'd never find anyone like her again.

"No Jack," she said, embarrassed, "I haven't told her. She is so protective over me, and this is the only thing she's ever asked of me when it comes to relationships."

"I understand, Kate. The thing is that I love getting the call. I can't get enough of the action and I feel that I was born to do this. To keep people safe. Each time we take out of a dirt bag child killer or a guy who has raped and pillaged hundreds of innocent people, it feels good to me, and it feels like the world instantly becomes a better place."

"I know, Jack." Kate said.

Although she wouldn't admit it, this side of Jack deeply excited her, and she was drawn to him because of it. But this trait that made her heart flutter was also a red flag because she knew she would eventually get hurt like her mom.

"Look," Kate put her slender hand on top of Jack's on the French Market table as a cool breeze slowly moved through New Orleans Square. "I don't expect you to change what you do or who you are just for me, please don't think that's what I'm trying to do. I would never want you to quit something you were called to do because of me."

Jack felt a pit in his stomach; he did everything right with Kate, but he was going to lose her.

"There's something else Jack," Kate hesitated again. "I've been offered a job with the NHL in New York. It's a top position, something I've been trying to get for years."

This was the nail in the coffin for Jack.

"You've already accepted it?" Jack asked.

Kate paused for a few seconds, "Yes Jack, I have. I'm leaving next week."

Jack's disappointment was hard to hide as he broke eye contact with Kate and shifted his focus to the people on the walkway in front of the French Market veranda. *How could I have let my guard down and become this attached so quickly? What a mistake.*

"Kate, I don't know what to say," Jack's demeanor changed as he synthetically erased his disappointed look and detached himself from the situation, "congratulations, you'll do great." Jack smiled at her and stood up at the table.

"Jack," Kate looked up at Jack, "can we still stay in touch and go to the Park when I'm in town?"

"I don't know, Kate. I just don't know how that would work. But definitely call me when you're in town. Look, my dad needs me in the Control Center right now. I told him I'd stop by before I left."

Kate looked unsure of herself, her smile wavered, and she struggled to find the right words. Jack was everything she'd ever wanted from the time she was a little girl. She was enamored by his strength, physically and mentally, she was attracted to his confidence, and how he was a gentleman.

Kate stood up and awkwardly hugged Jack. "Thank you Jack, thank you for the wonderful times we've had here, I will never forget them. And I will never forget you."

Jack half-heartedly hugged her back, realizing this was wrong. He quickly reverted to his usual negative outlook on relationships—telling himself that sometimes things just don't work out.

"Take care, Kate," Jack said as he held her hands briefly. He exited through the small gate on the French Market veranda, and he disappeared into the sea of people in New Orleans Square.

ELEVEN

August 8, 2010
Tomorrowland
Disneyland Park

Hidden tunnel? Jack thought as he stood over the unconscious Russian. Two Disney Security CMs tended to the man as Jack hurried out of the room towards the main Control Center hub. He radioed Max and Kendall.
"Have you found anything yet?"

"No, sir," Max answered back. "The team has been through most of the tunnels, and we haven't found a single trace of an explosive anywhere."

"Okay, keep looking," Jack said.

His mind raced back to the concept of a hidden tunnel.

He barked orders at Conroy. "Rob, I need Park schematics pulled. Lay them out on the conference table. We need to figure out what this guy is talking about."

Jack got on the phone with Luke, "Luke find out who this guy really is and this hidden tunnel he's talking about."

Two officers rolled out the blueprints of the Resort across the conference table in the main hub of the Control Center as Jack began to analyze them.

"There isn't a hidden tunnel, what was he talking about?" Jack said to himself out loud as he scanned the schematics of the entire Resort.

Conroy sheepishly said to Jack, "Well maybe you pushed him too hard, and he just lied about it?"

Jack looked up from the blueprints, and without a word he glared at him until Conroy broke eye contact. He looked back down and continued to scan, searching for anything that might give a clue about the hidden tunnel.

"Jack," Conroy said as a transmission came in through his earpiece, "all teams have reported back, and there's no trace of a bomb in the tunnels. The local bomb squad is running tests to confirm."

"This bomb could be anywhere in the Resort. We need to check every single structure on the property without making it obvious what we're doing, or we'll cause mass chaos."

Jack's mind raced; this was like finding a needle in a haystack. They didn't even know what kind of a bomb it was and how it could've made it through ALL of their sensors.

"Conroy, keep me updated. I'm going back into the Park. I want to know when this *Colby* guy wakes up."

Jack headed out of the Control Center and into the Park to find above-ground clues about where Nikolai could've strategically positioned a bomb.

He started near Pixie Hollow, located on the Tomorrowland side of The Hub —where one of the longest tunnels in the Park is located. Starting under the Matterhorn side of Pixie Hollow, the tunnel travels under the backside of Buzz Lightyear's Astro Blasters, and under the Tomorrowland Terrace food center. It continues to the stage where the musical acts perform, then angles slightly to the right, towards the Autopia side of Innoventions.

Jack walked slowly through the lighted waterfalls of Pixie Hollow looking for anything unusual and then went behind the Astro Blasters building towards Tomorrowland Terrace.

Luke's number flashed on Jack's tactical wrist device and the call routed to his earphone.

"Jack, I don't know the extent to which Nikolai has breached The System, however, this could be what has prevented us from detecting the bomb or any type of explosives—so we don't know what kind of arsenal he has hidden at the Resort right now."

Jack scanned the area as he walked towards the back of the stage where the 80z All Starz where playing "1999" by Prince. This stage is famous for rising above the ground at the start of a set, and lowering at the end—allowing the band to load their equipment and take breaks in the underground tunnel.

As the band finished their last song, the large, oval shaped stage lowered to its underground position. Jack jumped on the stage from behind where the drummer was. The band turned around, shocked to see Jack on stage with them as they descended.

"Hey guys," Jack said, "nothing to worry about, just doing some routine checks."

"Okay, Mr. Duncan," said the drummer. "Hey, can I get you to sign my drum kit?"

Jack didn't have time, but did it anyway to make it seem like everything was business as usual.

When the stage lowered, Jack backtracked his steps toward the Pixie Hollow side of the tunnel. He quickly got ahead of the band as they headed towards the break room and passed random CMs as he picked up speed through the tunnel. He passed Cast Members in full Storm Trooper gear along with Darth Vader and others as he scanned everything with his glasses.

Things looked normal—and there was no sign of explosives anywhere. He headed in the opposite direction, towards the Tomorrowland Terrace stage, where the tunnel shifted towards Innoventions. As he approached the underground access to the enormous Innoventions building, he noticed what appeared to be a CM in a Darth Maul costume from the Jedi Training Academy show. Jack noticed this person where the large motors and equipment for the building were located—the maintenance area for the gigantic circular building that was formerly America Sings.

Normally, CMs stay clear of this area due to the spooky ghost stories about the tragic, yet legendary accident in that building where a poor CM was crushed to death in the American Sings attraction as the building rotated to the next scene. It was rare to see someone in this particular area, especially in character.

Motors and loud machinery made it hard to hear, and it was dark and gloomy—a creepy place to be, even without the urban legend surrounding it.

Jack lowered his night vision goggles over his Google Glass and pursued the figure.

It was loud, warm, and humid. Jack drew his SIG Sauer P226 and kept it hidden by his side as he cleared each section. He walked slowly scanning side-to-side trying to get a glimpse of whoever it was. He turned the corner near a large piece of machinery that was making a loud cranking sound—it sounded as if it was malfunctioning.

CLANK

Out of nowhere, the man dressed as Darth Maul belted Jack on the back with a large metal pipe making a haunting hollow pinging sound, sending him reeling towards the ground.

His gun slid across the floor. Jack tried to reach for his SIG when the man, who was in full costume including the face paint, stepped on his wrist. He raised the large metal pipe high over his head and prepared to strike Jack on the back of the head.

The *pffft* sound of a suppressed gunshot sliced through the air.

Out of the darkness, Kendall and Max emerged with their guns drawn, scanning for any other hostiles. Kendall landed a perfect headshot on the perpetrator which killed him instantly. They ran to Jack to see if he was okay.

"Jack," Kendall put his big hand on his back.

Jack rolled over and could see the image of his best friend in the darkness, "Nice shot Kendall, but I wish you wouldn't have hit him in the head."

Jack got up of the ground with the help of Kendall. "We need to find out who this is—and send the bomb squad—the bomb must be here."

Max radioed the Control Center and listened for a response. "Jack, they're saying SEAL Team Six is on site and heading this way."

"Okay, that's good news," said Jack, who still hadn't recovered from the blow.

"Jack, I'm taking you upstairs," said Kendall. "Max, you stay here and wait for Team Six. Run this guy through The System to find out who he is."

"You got it."

"Also, have them close down Innoventions, Space Mountain, Pizza Port,

Captain EO, and Autopia. Try to keep people out of this immediate area—make it look like a power failure or something." Jack said.

"Jack," Conroy's voice shot through his earpiece, "we just found the guy you were questioning—dead in his holding cell. The same way Dmitri died."

"WHAT? Are you serious? How could you let this happen?"

"I'm sorry, Jack. We're trying to figure it out. He was restrained and in our custody the entire time, so I am not sure how this happened."

TWELVE

Jack headed up the cargo elevator to ground level with Kendall as he monitored the live feed of Andy and Grace from the tactical iPhone on his arm. *I have to find a way to get them out of here without Nikolai tracking them.*

He thought of sending them to one of the old bomb shelters on the property. During the Cuban Missile Crisis, Stan persuaded Walt to create a few fallout shelters in the Park in case of an unexpected war.

Jack hesitated because he didn't want to do anything to put Andy and Grace in more danger, knowing that Nikolai could be watching.

On his screen, Jack saw Tony and Kim with the kids in the dark, rich, Americana styled room with the miniature Disneyland Limited train circling the room. Jack spotted the special ops team in strategic positions around the suite.

"Kendall, let's walk around the perimeter of Innoventions to see if there's anything suspicious."

Kendall nodded, and they used the backstage entrance next to Space Mountain to enter the Park. The 80z All Starz were starting their next set, and the mood in Tomorrowland was festive as people hurried to get in line for Space Mountain. Lines formed outside the Captain EO Theater as the making of the film played on the monitors. People ate on the upper deck of Tomorrowland Terrace as others danced to renditions of their favorite songs from the eighties.

Suddenly, CMs began to clear people out of the Space Mountain queue, Innoventions, Captain EO, and Autopia, just as Jack ordered.

Jack and Kendall investigated everything around the perimeter of the massive Innoventions building; they also conducted a preliminary search inside but didn't find anything out of the ordinary.

"Jack this has to be it—under Innoventions would be the perfect place to hide a bomb that would cause significant damage," said Kendall.

"You're right, but the guy I interrogated said something about a hidden tunnel—this isn't hidden. It's a well-trafficked tunnel, and everyone knows about it."

"Sir," Max came through Jack's earpiece, "Team Six is here along with the local bomb squad and they are scanning the area as we speak."

"Okay, Max. Keep me updated."

Jack and Kendall stood near the Autopia Fastpass station on the far side of the Innoventions building.

"Jack, we've been through all known tunnels and have found nothing so far," said Kendall. "We've been in the basement under Pirates of the Caribbean and this Tomorrowland tunnel. We checked the CM museum behind Space

Mountain, and all of the other basement-type storage areas."

"He could've been lying to me," said Jack referring to Colby. "He could be sending us on a wild goose chase. We know this Park like the backs of our hands, and there's no *hidden tunnel* here?" Jack said as he looked at Kendall. "If only I could talk to my dad, he would have answers."

"Sir, Team Six and the bomb squad are showing no trace of explosives down here. I did get facial recognition on the guy Kendall shot. His name is Vladimir Izmaylovsky, a separatist from Chechnya with a background in caesium-137 explosives."

"That's not good, Max. That means there must be a dirty bomb somewhere in the Park."

"Jack," Kendall turned his massive frame towards Jack, lowering his head and widening his stance, "this has to mean that Nikolai has people on the inside helping with this. We have a traitor or traitors among us."

Jack suspected this already, but when Kendall said it, the stark reality of having people on the inside working against him, hit him like a ton of bricks. "You're right, Kendall."

"He's hacked into *The System* which is virtually impossible. He's impaired our vision, and he has people inside the Park, possibly in high places, helping him out."

Jack usually had absolute control of every aspect of the Resort; with a touch of a button everything was at his command, but now, it was all out of his grasp. He was the one being controlled, and he didn't like it. A sadistic lunatic was now calling the shots and thousands of lives were at stake, including his kids.

Jack looked out at Tomorrowland from Innoventions and saw Disney Security CMs inconspicuously walking their dogs trying to find any trace of an explosive device.

"Max," Jack called over the radio, "lead the bomb squad and Team Six to every tunnel and basement area at the Resort so we can check all underground possibilities."

"Yes, sir,"

"Kendall, let's head back to the Control Center to regroup."

THIRTEEN

August 8, 2010
Disneyland Security Control Center
Disneyland Park

"Conroy, how could you let this happen? We needed Colby alive."

"Jack, I don't know how it happened. We had him locked down, and the next thing we know, he's dead. We're trying to check the tape to see what happened, but some of the footage is corrupted."

Ruddy barged into the room heading straight for Jack.

"Jack, I need to talk to you, NOW."

"Look, Brett. I don't have the time to talk about procedures with you unless you want me to break your fingers too."

"No, Jack. I heard what he said about the hidden tunnel. That could be where the bomb is, and it could be why The System has not been able to detect it."

"Brett, there is no hidden tunnel."

"I know Jack, but my dad has been Marty Sklar's friend since they were kids in Jersey. They've talked about this before—and no one knows the Park like Sklar. He was there when it opened, and he knows every little detail. There's no greater student of Walt Disney. He's the one who wrote the script about Lafitte in that World of Color show that aired in the 50s. I think he might be able to help."

Jack studied Ruddy with great suspicion. Why would he be so helpful now when he was so eager to scurry away and hide earlier? Why would he stick around when he could have easily stayed hidden on the perimeter, where Jack had sent him earlier? Jack was apprehensive of everybody at this point—especially Ruddy.

Ruddy looked Jack in the eyes and handed him a sticky note. "Here's his home number. Call him and pick his brain. It could be our only hope right now."

Jack took the phone number from him, dialed it, and the phone rang.

A man answered in a low voice.

"Hello?"

"Mr. Sklar?"

"Yes, speaking."

"Mr. Sklar this is Jack Duncan. Excuse the intrusion but we're in a major crisis here at the Park."

"Jack? It has been a long time, what can I do for you?"

"Sir," Jack paused, realizing how crazy this was going to sound, "is there a tunnel under the Rivers of America?"

Sklar paused on the other side of the phone. "Jack, everyone knows that's an urban legend, there's no tunnel under the River."

"Mr. Sklar, if you know something, please tell me—thousands of lives are at stake."

"Jack what's wrong? What's going on?"

"Sir, you cannot tell anyone what I'm about to tell you. It's a matter of national security and 50,000 people could die if it gets out."

Sklar swallowed hard realizing this wasn't about Jack trying to settle a trivia bet with one of his rich friends. "Sure, Jack. I won't tell anyone," Sklar said quietly.

"Mr. Sklar, we have substantial reason to believe that there's a bomb somewhere in the Park and a Russian operative I just interrogated said that it's located in a 'hidden tunnel'. We've checked all known tunnels, and there is no trace of anything so far."

Sklar paused again; in shock and not knowing what to say. There was an awkward silence as Jack anxiously awaited an answer on the other end.

"Jack...*there is a tunnel*."

Jack was wide eyed and didn't know what to say.

"There's a tunnel under the Rivers of America," Sklar continued, "but that's about as much as I know about it. Walt kept everything under wraps so only he and your dad knew the exact location and details. I was sworn to secrecy, and it was one of Walt's final wishes that this tunnel be kept secret."

Jack was in shock, how could there be a tunnel under the River without him knowing about it?

"So it was Walt's idea to do this from the beginning?" Jack asked perplexed and still in disbelief.

"Yes, Jack. He based everything on Lafitte. That was the central theme. The Island, Pirates, and the Haunted Mansion; they were all a part of the plan. Remember, Walt is the one who designed Tom Sawyer Island, and he is the one who embedded clues about Lafitte throughout New Orleans Square."

"So where's the entrance? How do I get down there?"

"Jack, I honestly don't know. Not even Admiral Fowler knew the exact details. No one did. Some of us knew bits and pieces of what was being built, but it was well-hidden. During construction in '54, everything happened so fast it was confusing and easy to miss—and then during the New Orleans Square construction, everything was locked down and kept under wraps."

"So you're saying only my dad knows how to get in that tunnel?"

"Yes, he's the only living person that knows." Sklar said solemnly. "Where's your dad?"

Jack paused, "He's incoherent right now up in Northern California. He's dying."

"Oh, Jack. I'm so sorry to hear that," Sklar paused, "Walt kept this very secretive, so I am not sure how a terrorist organization would know the location of this tunnel."

"Well, Mr. Sklar, we're dealing with Nikolai Grusov. He's been watching this place since it was nothing but orange groves."

"Jack, Walt kept this tunnel hidden because he wanted the right person, picked by your dad, to continue his plans. A few people have tried to unify these attractions in recent years, but your dad shut it down behind the scenes."

"He did?"

"Yes. Walt left it up to your dad to find the right person to finish this part of the Park with the foundation he built. I believe that Walt hid something in that tunnel. I am not sure what, but Walt was working on so many things before he died, he was determined to create the ideal city, and was working on several other secret projects. There are probably treasures from Walt's imagination down there that would blow our minds. But it could be dangerous if they fall into the wrong hands."

This was too much for Jack to take in during this type of crisis.

"Sir, what's my best bet for finding the entrance to the tunnel? If I can find the entrance I can disarm the bomb."

"Just follow the legend of Lafitte. Find the remnants that have been left behind in the Haunted Mansion, on the Island, and inside of Pirates. Several people have been on the right track and have discovered some of the clues, but no one has totally figured it out."

"Mr. Sklar, I don't have time to go on a treasure hunt. I need to stop a bomb from going off that could level the Resort and a good deal of the city around it."

"I know Jack, but it's either that, or find a way to talk to your dad."

FOURTEEN

August 8, 2010
Dream Suite
Disneyland Park
SEAL Team Six

Jack was dumbfounded as he hung up the phone with Sklar and looked at Kendall.

"That's where it is, Kendall. It's under the River. That's why we haven't been able to detect it."

Kendall had a blank stare on his movie-star-like face; he remembered playing on Tom Sawyer Island with Jack as a kid. They knew every square inch of the Island having spent most of their childhood at the Park together. Disneyland was their playground, and every day was a new adventure for them. They had free rein in the Park. They rode the Matterhorn over and over again; the Skyway, Motorboats, Mission to Mars, PeopleMover, and more.

"But Jack," Kendall said, "even if there is a tunnel, how would Nikolai know about it and how would he access it without you knowing?"

"I don't know, but right now this our best lead. We need to find the entrance to this tunnel."

Jack froze, realizing Andy and Grace were still in the Dream Suite—he needed to get them out of there.

"Tony," Jack said through the secure com, "I need you to move the kids back to the El Capitan. Johnny is probably out of there by now, but if he isn't, take the kids to the McKinley Suite and lock it down."

"Okay, Jack. We're moving now." Tony, Kim, and Jack's special ops team moved the kids out of the Dream Suite.

Jack and Kendall left the Control Center and headed for New Orleans Square.

Jack radioed Max. "Max, get Team Six, and the bomb squad over to New Orleans Square. Meet me in the Dream Suite—and be discreet."

Jack paced along the edge of the Rivers of America, hoping that something would jar his mind and give him a clue to get him going in the right direction. Big Thunder Mountain Railroad glowed in the distance, enhancing the skyline with its prominent features. The moon cast a significant amount of light on the River and throughout New Orleans Square. Old-fashioned lanterns lined the paved edge of the River.

Jack fixated his gaze on the Island trying desperately to put the pieces together. He was running out of time.

Jack and Kendall entered the Dream Suite using the front stairs.

He got chills up his spine when he walked into the living room and saw the famed SEAL Team Six standing at attention.

A confident grin spanned his face as he was reunited with his brothers again, an elite group of the deadliest fighters in the world. They were family—and he couldn't be happier to see them right now.

Jack and Kendall embraced each man on the team.

Team Six consisted of the most highly trained and elusive individuals on the planet, capable of performing in any situation. Their mental toughness is second to none, and their ability to execute under pressure is beyond human. Dressed in black with strong posture, high chins, and solid eye contact, they waited for Jack's orders—full of confidence and determination.

Team Six exists outside of military protocol; they engage in black operations that are highly classified and outside of the boundaries of International law. You'll never see them coming, they are quick and effective.

Most of the men in the room were on the mission that rescued Richard Phillips, the captain of the container ship *Maersk Alabama* that was held hostage by three Somali pirates in 2009. This legendary mission ended with three simultaneous shots from the deck of the ship as it rocked up and down on the large ocean swells. The pirates held Phillips hostage in a lifeboat floating near the main vessel. Three shots from the SEALs hit all three pirates in the head at the same time while their lifeboat rocked back and forth.

Jack, Kendall, and Max were highly respected in the SEAL community, especially with Team Six. The active duty SEALs in the Dream Suite were thrilled to be in the same room with them. They lived for situations like this. Working with Jack, Kendall, and Max, the men whom they studied for so long, the ones who inspired them to become SEALs—was like a dream come true. The only thing better for them would be getting the call to assassinate Osama bin Laden.

"Gentleman, you're a sight for sore eyes. I know we can stop this threat—because together we can do anything. There's no one in the world who's better trained for this type of thing."

Jack paced back and forth in the living room of the Dream Suite as Team Six hung on his every word.

"The President knows we're his only hope—that we have the best chance of stopping Nikolai Grusov. We're confident that there's a dirty bomb on property, and it's up to us to find it. I've come to the conclusion that the bomb is located somewhere in a tunnel under the Rivers of America."

The SEALs were surprised to hear this as they looked back and forth at each other.

"The problem is that we don't know how to get in the tunnel. We need to find the entrance first, in the dark, without making it obvious that something is wrong. Then we need to get to the bomb and disarm it—or thousands of people could die. I don't need to remind you what a catastrophic blow this would be to the United States of America."

SEAL Team Six always got the call for threats beyond normal comprehension, but this was a mission unlike anything they'd ever seen before.

"I also want you to know that al-Qaeda is probably involved, according to the CIA," Jack continued, "and I know this hits home for all of us. We cannot let them win; we cannot give them the upper hand and let them attack us on our soil again. This will rattle the heart and soul of America—innocent women and children will die—it could be the worst hit in US history."

"Sir," the team leader spoke, "what are our rules of engagement?"

"I need to extract information from anyone involved. So I need hostiles alive."

"Is there anyone from the inside involved?"

"Yes, we believe so. You need to be prepared for resistance from armed combatants," said Jack, "but it will be very hard to identify them under these circumstances. The bottom line is this: the President has given me the ability to do whatever it takes to resolve this problem and I'll do everything in my power to make sure this bomb does not go off. I'm switching over to your closed-loop com gear since our in-house system has been compromised."

"Sir, where do we start?"

Jack paused and looked at Kendall. He didn't have an answer because he had no clue where to start.

"Head over to the Island and search everything. No guests should be there right now since it's closed and we canceled the Fantasmic show, so you can do a full sweep without any distractions."

"Yes, sir." The SEAL team exited the suite from the back and headed towards the rafts.

Jack, Kendall, and Max stood together as they tried to figure out where to start.

"Sklar said this secret tunnel was based on Lafitte, so we have to dig into history to figure out where the tunnel is located. It must be in the vicinity of the Haunted Mansion, but the question is where. The Mansion actually goes underground under the railroad tracks and outside of the Berm so there could be a tunnel attached to the underground structure."

"We also have to take Pirates into consideration, since most things are housed partially underground and there are several basement type areas in the attraction," Kendall said. "There could easily be a tunnel attached at some point there."

"Okay, Kendall. You know Pirates better than anyone, so head there. Max, you go to the Mansion, and I'm going underwater along the side of the River to see what I can find."

FIFTEEN

1994
Main Street, U.S.A.
Stan and Jack

Stan walked side-by-side down Main Street with his arm around Jack. He could tell Jack was down and wanted to cheer him up. Stan stopped as they passed the Gibson Girl Ice Cream Parlor, walked in, and ordered a whopping mint and chip waffle bowl ice cream sundae. Stan knew the way to Jack's heart.

"Son, you've made a big mistake."

"I don't think I have, Dad."

"From what you've told me, this girl is the one. It's like I've always told you, there's one person out there that you were destined to be with, and once you find her, do not let her go."

"Dad, that's a nice saying, but I'm telling you it's not true in every situation."

"Well, it was certainly true for your mom and I," Stan paused and reflected, "she was the perfect woman for me, everything about her, we were made to be together, and it was no coincidence that we met." Stan teared up as Jack put his hand on his shoulder.

"I know that was the case for you and mom."

"I wish you could've known her better Jack. If you could've seen us together you would understand what I'm talking about. She always knew what I needed, and she deeply cared for me. I put her first, and we had a marriage made in heaven. We had our fights and disagreements, but ultimately we knew we were together forever, and nothing could separate us."

Jack smiled at Stan's older face with its distinguished wrinkles. He wished he would've known his mom, but she died before he ever got the chance. He only knew her from the stories Stan told.

"It was so hard raising you without her because I didn't have the same insight that she had. She always knew the right thing to do, and was the perfect mother."

"Dad, you did great, you know that."

"I don't know son, there's no way I could've given you what she had to offer. But what could I do?"

Jack smiled at him as they continued their stroll down Main Street with their waffle bowls in hand.

"Look, Jack. If you don't think she's the one, then let her go." Stan stopped walking in the middle of Main Street in front of Coke Corner and looked Jack squarely in the eyes. "But, if you do think she's the one, then fight for her, give up your pride and your selfish desires and go after her. Don't let her go because you will regret it for the rest of your life."

Jack looked at Stan with nothing to say. Stan was right—Kate was the one. He gazed off into the distance at Sleeping Beauty Castle, with the Skyway gondolas cruising in the background. It reminded him of the times he and Kate had together.

"The thing is Jack, you are accustomed to always getting the prize. You think that your self-discipline and iron-will can get you anything you want. With brute force you've taken out the most evil people who've ever lived. But you can't take the same approach when it comes to someone like Kate. You have to submit to her, listen to her dreams, and understand where she's coming from."

Jack nodded in agreement even though he didn't entirely understand what Stan was talking about.

"But the thing you *are* familiar with, fighting, does apply in this situation," Stan smiled at Jack with a loving look, "so don't be a little *wimp*, and go after her—fight for her—don't give up."

Jack laughed as they walked past the gates of the Plaza Inn towards Tomorrowland, "You're calling *me* a wimp?" Jack playfully straight-armed Stan on the back of his shoulder, knocking him slightly off balance. This was how all of their at-home wrestling matches started.

SIXTEEN

1959
Fantasyland
Walt Disney and Stan Duncan

Walt Disney stood in front of the brand new Matterhorn with his hands on his hips, marveling at the towering man-made mountain as he and Stan looked up into the sky. Walt frequently closed his fists and put them above his hips, looking similar to Peter Pan.

"Can you believe this thing, Stan?" Walt was thrilled out of his mind with all of the new additions to the Park.

"It was just five years ago that everyone told us Disneyland was a horrible idea!"

Stan smiled at Walt because he knew he'd been through so much. The never-ending money struggles, and the mental fight against his critics who'd all said that Disneyland was a fantasy that could never be financially sustainable.

The Skyway gondolas traveled along their cables above them and voyaged through the middle of the Matterhorn. Walt and Stan walked towards Fantasyland as they talked, passing the Mad Tea Party, Dumbo, and the Chicken of the Sea Pirate Boat and Restaurant in the middle of Fantasyland. The Pirate Boat was humongous and had massive red and white striped sails, along with shiny black cannons popping out of the side. This large and colorful pirate ship was the focal point of Fantasyland. Kids walked through the ship and pretended they were on Captain Hook's Pirate ship. Tuna sandwiches could be ordered on board, tuna burgers, and hot tuna pies. Walt smiled as he admired the real-life replica of the boat from his *Peter Pan* masterpiece.

They walked through the Castle entrance and over the drawbridge leading to The Hub and Main Street. The Disneyland Band, who Walt had hired on opening day, played in front of the Castle as people formed a group in The Hub to watch them. Walt originally planned to have them play for only two weeks, but he loved their music and the excitement they created so much that he made them a permanent fixture at Disneyland.

A few kids spotted Walt and ran up to him for his autograph. "Mr. Disney!" A young boy grabbed his leg, "Can you please sign my autograph book?" The boy was thrilled to meet the famous movie-maker. "Thank you for building this place for us, it's so much fun!"

"Well, sure I can," said Walt with a smile as he bent down to talk to the boy.

Others noticed Walt and began to crowd him. He loved talking to kids, park guests, and CMs about the Park. He was famous for asking kids for their thoughts about Disneyland right on the spot. He wanted to know what they liked and didn't like.

Sometimes he scooped the ice cream himself on Main Street dressed in a striped jacket and straw hat asking people what their favorite Disneyland attraction was.

Stan noticed the size of the crowd increasing, so he stepped in and moved Walt towards the Carnation Plaza Gardens where the Firehouse Five Plus Two Dixieland Jazz Band was playing. The band consisted of several Disney animators including Ward Kimball, Frank Thomas, and others who never quit their day job, but loved to play jazz at Disneyland. Walt always got a kick out of watching his guys play, he encouraged creativity, and this was a positive outlet for his animators. Walt frequently worked the band into his TV specials.

Stan took Walt further to the right side of the stage near a Cast Member backstage exit.

"Hey, Walt," Stan said, "about this Khrushchev thing. I had a little run in with one of his guys the other day and I think I made him mad."

"Oh," Walt said. "How?"

"This guy, Grusov, got aggressive with me, said he knew about what I did to his people when I was with the CIA. I lost my temper, Walt, and I'm sorry about that."

Walt crossed his arms and put his hand on his chin to think, "Hmmm, well, is there anything we can do to smooth things over?"

"I will make it right, Walt, but I don't think Khrushchev is going to be happy about this whole thing. I honestly do believe that it's a significant security risk having him here. We can't protect him against an unknown threat in the crowd, there are just too many people here on any given day."

"You're right, Stan. Let's smooth it over and sell them on our concerns."

"Okay, Walt." Stan paused because he wanted to tell him something else. "Also, Walt. You're aware of my history with the Soviets, and you know that I despise their government, their leaders, and especially the KGB. I hate what they did to my friends. I am embarrassed to say that initially, that's why I didn't want Khrushchev here."

Walt listened with an empathetic look on his face.

"But, I really did stand back and look at the situation objectively, from a security standpoint. I consulted the security team, and I realized it would be too risky at this time. I just wanted to be open and transparent with you about this."

"Well, thank you Stan. I appreciate you being upfront with me. You know we've been together for a long time, and I trust you with everything. You've always given me the best advice and watched 'my six' as you would call it."

Stan grinned at Walt's use of special ops language. Walt Disney was a patriot and had great respect for those who served in the military. He actually forged his birth certificate so he could serve his country in World War I.

Walt stepped closer to Stan and talked under his breath, "Do you remember that tunnel we put under the River?"

"Sure, Walt," Stan said, surprised that he was bringing this up.

"Only you and I know my plans for that tunnel, and of course, I need you to keep it that way."

"Absolutely, Walt."

"I have big plans for this hidden tunnel. I want to connect Tom Sawyer Island with the Haunted Mansion, and tie everything into Pirates of the Caribbean while having the central theme centered on Jean Lafitte."

Stan's eyes lit up because he loved it when Walt mixed history and intrigue into the story of Disneyland.

"But I'm also using this tunnel to stash some of my pet projects. I have been working late every night coming up with so many exciting ideas for attractions, for new Lands, and new worlds. Beyond that though, I am designing things that will benefit society, things that will make cities better and more efficient. My designs and ideas could solve so many of the problems we have today, and problems of the future."

Stan was amazed to hear this. Walt was the greatest innovator of the century, and if anyone could come up with ingenious solutions to make the world a better place, he could.

"I just don't think I have much more time on this earth, Stan. So I want to get all of my ideas and concepts on paper for future generations. But I don't want these ideas to get into the wrong hands."

"Walt," Stan looked worried, "is everything okay with your health?"

"Oh, yes Stan. There's nothing to worry about. It's about as good as it can be."

Stan was semi-relieved, although Walt wasn't convincing about the state of his health.

Walt continued, "Roy and the investors get worried when they think I'm focused on things that don't make money. But I'm not about making money. Money is necessary, and I understand that, but what I'm really about is making the world better for the next generation, improving lives through technology, helping poor people, and improving our local cities."

Stan listened intently as Walt continued, "But if something happens to me Stan, you have to promise that the tunnel will not be used to unite the three attractions unless it is done the proper way. And, more importantly, that my ideas will not fall into the wrong hands."

"Sure, Walt."

"I'm serious. It has to be done in a particular way; otherwise it shouldn't be done at all."

Stan nodded in agreement, although he didn't totally grasp what Walt was talking about.

"Someday a leader will emerge in the company that will have a clear understanding of what my vision is for the Park, and when that leader emerges, I need you to give them access to what I am storing down there. It needs to be someone who is forward thinking, an innovator, who is also interested in improving our world, and will protect the dream."

This confused Stan. He always focused on the current moment, the right now—how to stop existing threats. Walt was someone who thought hundreds of years in the future.

"Oh, and one more thing Stan," Walt had a playful grin on his face. "My special agent status with the FBI has put me in a position where I have to divulge more information than I would like to Hoover."

Stan knew exactly what Walt was referring to and he didn't like Hoover's guys snooping around all the time.

"As you know, to maintain good relations with the FBI, I volunteered complete access to Disneyland for both official and recreational use, but they can NEVER find what's in that tunnel."

Stan agreed with Walt without pressing the issue any further.

"No one can find out what is down there except you and I. Once the FBI starts snooping around, we have to assume the Soviets are spying on them—and it would be absolutely devastating if the KGB found what's down there."

JACK DUNCAN

IS

EPISODE THREE

ONE

August 8, 2010
El Capitan Presidential Suite
Grand Californian Hotel

Tony gazed through the massive glass mural in the living room of the El Capitan Suite with an empty look on his face. He stroked his chin methodically with his index finger. Four men from the special ops team stood guard on the balcony; several more in the hallway near the elevators and a man covered each door leading into the suite. Andy and Grace were sprawled out on the bed in the master bedroom watching TV as Kim kept an eye on them. Several other men from Jack's spec ops team walked slowly through the massive suite—keeping constant watch on the premises.

Kim walked out of the master bedroom, through the private office and into the El Capitan living room. Her sleek, all-black outfit caught Tony's eye, but he quickly switched his gaze back to the window. The amber lighting made the suite cozy and inviting. The fireplace flickered on the left, vague sounds came from the crowd below, and the tantalizing aroma rising from the Napa Rose entered through the balcony doors.

On the surface, it was just another night at the Happiest Place on Earth.

"Tony," Kim said as she put her left arm on his shoulder, "I'm sorry about earlier, I was just doing my job."

Tony looked at Kim with a half smile, "I know. You were right. I let my emotions get the best of me."

"So you didn't make the call?" Kim asked.

"No," Tony answered quickly, "like I said, you were right, I wasn't thinking straight."

Kim squared up with Tony and moved closer to him than ever before. Tony detected light traces of her sweet perfume as he admired the contrast between her ice blue eyes and her jet-black hair.

"We've been doing this for a long time Tony and there is no one better at protecting the kids than you," Kim took both of Tony's hands in hers.

Tony looked down, surprised that she was holding his hands, "I know Kim, but I don't know how much longer I can do this. I feel like I'm living from one disaster to the next. I can never relax; I can't do anything without thinking about this job, my whole life has been in service to other people—I think I'm finished after this situation is resolved."

"Tony, what are you talking about, you could never be fulfilled sitting on a beach somewhere, you'd be bored out of your mind?"

"Maybe so, but it would be a nice change," Tony leaned into Kim and lowered his voice, "the other thing is that while I love Jack, his relentless desire for revenge is going to be the end of him. It affects him, he won't admit it, and it will eventually get us *all* in trouble."

Kim looked shocked, "Tony? There might be some truth to that, but Jack has always taken care of us, he wasn't the cause of things in the past, and he certainly isn't the cause of this threat?"

Tony pulled back, "No—I know that, I didn't mean it that way."

"Then how did you mean it?" Kim let go of Tony's hands abruptly.

"I don't know, I'm just confused right now, I need a break. I'm not sure if I want to do this anymore."

Kim flashed a reassuring smile, "How about after all of this is over we take a break and go somewhere for the weekend—no talk of work, or anything, just a break?"

Kim's proposal put a big smile on Tony's face. This was the first time Kim had ever suggested they do anything outside of work.

"That sounds great Kim," Tony said nonchalantly, masking his excitement.

Kim flashed her pretty smile at him and walked towards the master bedroom. She opened the doors to find Andy and Grace bored out of their mind watching old Mickey Mouse cartoons as two armed agents watched over them.

"Hey Kim," Andy said, "can we order some pizza?"

"Sure Andy, that sounds like a great idea, I'll have it delivered here. How are you doing Gracie?"

Grace half-smiled at Kim, an expression she inherited from Jack.

Kim walked around the corner of the master bedroom into the enormous twenty-foot long master bathroom. She walked to the far end and locked herself in.

She dialed Jack.

"Jack," Kim whispered, "I need to talk to you."

"Why? Is everything okay? I'm going into the River now."

"I intercepted a call that Tony made to his mom, warning her about the bomb."

Jack stopped in his tracks. "WHAT? After I gave everyone specific orders?"

"Yes, I told him not to do it, but he did it anyway. Then he lied to me about it."

"Okay this is not good, I don't need this right now. We have a mole or several moles here at the Park who are helping Nikolai, and I cannot take any chances."

"He also expressed some doubt regarding his job."

"What do you mean?"

"Nothing serious, but he's not all there right now, he is in a daze, he said he's tired, and that this could be the end for him. I don't think he's a threat, but I feel it's my duty to inform you."

"I cannot take any chances, I need you to detain him and take him to the Control Center so I can talk to him. I want him out of that suite NOW."

Kim froze and didn't know what to say, "Oh, wait, Jack. I don't think he needs to be locked up; I was just giving you this info so you were aware of the situation. I will keep an eye on things to make sure everything is okay."

"Kim—do what I said—NOW."

Jack cut out. Kim closed her eyes, rubbed her forehead, and took a deep breath. She opened the restroom door and walked through the long master bathroom. She exited the master bedroom and made sure the doors were locked. She stopped in the private office as she peered around the corner at Tony who was still gazing through the wall of glass.

She messaged the agent who was in the living room and quietly gave him the orders.

The agent looked confused but acted on the orders. He walked up behind Tony. The man drew his gun and spoke softly, "Sir, I need you to come with me."

Tony turned his body slowly to find a gun pointing directly at him. "Is this some kind of joke?"

"No, sir, I have orders from Mr. Duncan to have you taken to the Control Center."

Tony raised his voice, "FOR WHAT?"

"I'm not sure sir, please just put your hands on your head and cooperate so we can figure this out."

"I'm not putting my hands on my head, what are you talking about, what's going on?" Tony's entire body tensed up.

"Sir, I need you to put your hands on your head, NOW." The man extended his arms and aimed his gun at Tony's upper body.

Tony inconspicuously advanced towards the man, "I'm not going anywhere until someone tells me what is going on—I'm calling Jack." Tony reached for his phone.

"Tony," Kim approached him from the other side with her gun drawn. "Do what he says, this is a direct order from Jack."

Tony was stunned to see Kim pointing her gun at him. He tilted his head, dumbfounded, and squinted his eyes. He reluctantly raised his hands to his head.

"Kim?" Tony said, "What's this about?"

"Tony, just go with him to the Control Center and Jack will explain everything there—please, I don't want the kids to know about this, or be scared."

When Kim mentioned the kids, Tony's demeanor changed, and he reluctantly nodded in agreement. His eyebrows accentuated the disgusted look on his face as he glared at Kim. The agent searched him, confiscated his phone, and weapons.

Tony stared Kim down as he left the suite.

TWO

August 8, 2010
Rivers of America
Disneyland Park

Jack submerged into the 70 degree water of the Rivers of America—a cakewalk compared to the "toasty warm" 56 degree Pacific Ocean temperature near Coronado. During training exercises as a SEAL, he was required to tread water for more than six hours in frigid conditions.

He waded through the green colored water of the Rivers of America that's dyed for an opaque look. The dark water concealed tracks and other things on the shallow riverbed. Jack's night vision goggles gave him an enhanced perspective of the River's bottom.

If I can just find the entrance to this tunnel, I can stop the bomb.

He glanced at the tactical iPhone device strapped to his arm. The video feed of Andy and Grace reassured him momentarily. He saw Kim in the room with the Special Ops detail, and no sign of Tony.

Jack swam to the place where he thought the tunnel might be, in line with the Haunted Mansion and Tom Sawyer Island. He moved into the dry dock at Fowler's Harbor, he thought the tunnel would have to travel under there at some point.

"Jack, I'm headed to Pirates as we speak, I will report shortly with what I find," Kendall said through Jack's earpiece.

"Roger that Kendall, report your progress at regular intervals."

"Sir," Max's voice came through Jack's earpiece, "I'm at the Haunted Mansion, looking for clues."

The leader of SEAL Team Six reported next, "Sir, this is Team Six leader, we are on the Island, and we're starting with the drain where the item was dropped."

Jack waded slowly through the water using his high-powered helmet-mounted flashlight to examine the bottom and sides of the River looking for anything out of the ordinary.

"Jack," Luke said, "we've been crunching every possible scenario of where this entrance could be, and I think I found something."

"Go ahead Luke."

"The water from the Rivers of America is pumped from behind the Island and elevated fifteen feet behind the Storybook Canal. From there it goes underground to the old Motorboat Lagoon by the Matterhorn, which then flows through an underground channel to the area that surrounds the Castle. The water flows beneath the surface as it fills the ponds near the entrance of

Adventureland—ultimately ending up in the Jungle Cruise. From there, a colossal pipe leads the water under Tarzan's Treehouse where it feeds into the front of the Rivers of America."

"So you think the tunnels could be associated with the dark water system?"

"I'm not sure, but what's strange is that I've been getting reports from the undercover units that the water seems stagnant right now, it's not circulating like it usually does."

"That's a red flag."

"The pipe that brings the water underground from the Jungle Cruise to the Rivers of America is massive, I think you should check it out to see what you can find."

Jack changed directions and moved towards the front of the River to locate this pipe. He immediately noticed a large metal grate protecting an enormous water entrance. The water was not flowing into the River as it should. He reached back for his bolt cutters and a wrench.

"I found the opening to the pipe, and like you said there's no water flowing through it."

"Jack, water should be constantly flowing through this pipe, they rarely turn this system off."

After loosening a few of the large bolts holding the grate to the wall of the River, he gripped the heavy metal grill with both hands and pulled with all his strength.

It broke free. He aimed his light into the large pipe but couldn't see anything. It was too dark and deep.

He slowly swam into the pipe scanning in all directions for anything out of place. He kept moving through the pipe until he reached the end—he had entered the Jungle Cruise water system.

"Luke, I don't know what I'm looking for here, it's a giant pipe that connects the River and the Jungle Cruise, I'm not sure how this would relate to the tunnel under the River."

"Let me check, Jack. If The System was at full strength I'd be able to see what you're seeing, but I can't."

Jack's head slowly emerged from the rivers of the Jungle Cruise near the beginning by the Indiana Jones queue. A Jungle Cruise boat approached as its skipper cracked jokes about the people in line for Indiana Jones. The boat full of semi-amused guests chuckled.

Jack ducked his head underwater as he made his way back through the pipe.

He reached the Rivers of America water entrance and his head slammed into a metal object—something towards the top of the pipe. Startled, he looked up to find a thick circular wheel.

"Luke, it looks like there's an opening to this pipe from above."

Jack reached up and began to rotate the wheel, which turned without much effort.

"Standby Luke, I am going up through this hatch."

Jack popped his head up out of the hatch and found himself in a dry, dark room. He propped himself up with his hands to get out of the pipe. When his feet hit the ground, he removed his headgear so he could look around.

"Luke, there is a large room under here, I guess it could be a maintenance room, but there's nothing here to maintain."

"There's nothing in the schematics that show this room Jack, I can't find it anywhere."

Jack lit up portions of the large room with his light.

His heart stopped as the light revealed something he'd never seen before, "Luke, there's a large metal door surrounded by a brick archway on this wall."

"Jack—that must be it, that must be the entrance to the tunnel."

As he got closer, he realized the metal door was massive, there were no handles, or any other way to open it. He pushed on the door to see if it would budge—it wouldn't move a fraction of an inch even with his entire weight behind it. He ran his hands under the bottom of the door, all the way across, and then up the sides. He swiped his hand slowly across the middle of the door, and he felt something engraved in the metal. He flashed his light, revealing an ornate "D" embossed in the thick metal with a small circle under it, surrounded by a fancy border—this was Walt's trademark "D".

In shock, he directed his light approximately thirty feet to the left, and he saw another archway. To his right there was another one. He looked back in the direction of the Jungle Cruise and saw a third door.

"Luke, I need you to get someone down here who can get this door open. This is the entrance to the tunnel."

THREE

August 8, 2010
Pirates of the Caribbean
Disneyland Park

"Mr. Sklar, this is Kendall Shepherd, I'm at Pirates right now, do you have any suggestions about where I should start?" Kendall walked fast holding his phone to his ear.

"Kendall, it's hard to say because the attraction is so large, there's so much to cover in there."

"We've already checked all known basements and underground areas near the Cast Member cafe."

"Your best bet is to check anything that refers to Lafitte, and anything that would seem to link Pirates and the Haunted Mansion together."

"Isn't the throne that Captain Jack sits on also used in the Mansion or something like that?"

"Yes, the same chair is in the picture of Reginald in the Haunted Mansion, and it was also used by Ambrose Gracey in the Haunted Mansion movie."

"Okay, Jack mentioned seeing something odd in the treasure room the other day, I'll check it out."

Kendall took a shortcut through the Blue Bayou busboy room and crossed the brick bridge inside the Pirates of the Caribbean as guests in boats passed under him. He headed behind the shack where the old man rocks, and towards the control tower near Lafitte's Landing. He lowered the phone from his ear and motioned to the CM on duty, "Hey buddy, I need you to shut this place down until further notice."

The CM nodded at Kendall with a surprised look on his face. People were always astounded at the size of Kendall. Everyone there knew him, and he was a favorite among the female CMs.

Guests began to clear out as Kendall inspected the loading dock, he looked everywhere but couldn't find anything out of the ordinary. The only thing that had anything to do with Lafitte was the sign above the dock, so he got down on his hands and knees to inspect the wooden deck. He slid his palm across the wood to see if there were any signs of a hidden entrance. He headed back through the CM walkway behind the old shed to walk the attraction.

As he journeyed through the show building, music played in the background and everything functioned normally. He didn't find anything of interest until he reached the final treasure room with the Captain Jack animatronic sitting on the mysterious chair. He searched the small treasure room, and everything looked as it always did. He went to the back of the room and checked the hatch that led down to the storage basement that doubled as a small tool shed. He crawled down through the hatch into the pitch-black room. His flashlight lit the basement full of boxes and merchandise for the stores in New Orleans Square. He found the light switch and turned it on.

He scanned side-to-side as he crept through the rows of boxes. Everything was neatly organized, and nothing was out of line. He stopped when he saw a stack of mangled boxes at the end of one of the rows. They looked as if they were forced open and ripped to shreds. On the left, there was a large crowbar on the ground.

Kendall headed back towards the hatch. When he arrived, he had a ground level view of the back of the throne that Captain Jack was sitting on. He noticed the metal platform under the chair was slightly raised and propped up by a piece of wood on the right side.

Using both arms, he propped himself up to the treasure room. He positioned himself behind the chair and grabbed the steel plate on the bottom with both of his massive paws to see if he could raise it. At first it wouldn't budge, but as he applied more of his strength, the entire chair began to move forward until the back of the chair, and the Jack Sparrow animatronic were perpendicular to the ground.

A square hatch was revealed under the platform. Metal bars lined the side of the hatch, which descended at least twenty feet into the ground.

Kendall felt a surge of adventurous energy—just like when he and Jack were kids exploring the Park together.

He got exactly ten feet down the hatch, and the platform above him slammed shut hitting the piece of wood that kept it ajar. Kendall paused for a second and continued. He was always the risk taker. He tried to get Jack to do crazy things when they were kids because he knew he could always get them out of a bind. Almost supernaturally, he never failed to get Jack out of impossible situations.

Kendall's feet hit the ground of the mysterious underground hatch. He noticed a large door in front of him with a safe dial and a latch. He reached for the dial not knowing how he would figure out the combination. As he touched the dial, the metal door moved forward—it was already open.

He pushed through the door, and his eyes widened at the extent of the room—it was much more than just an underground basement.

He pressed on his ear bud to radio Jack—he only heard static. He grabbed his phone—no signal.

Dust and cobwebs were everywhere. It didn't look like anyone had been down there in years. He slowly moved ahead trying to figure out exactly where he was. He noticed that the humongous basement was themed similar to Pirates of the Caribbean—bricks lined the walls, and every detail matched the attraction above him.

A still, rough face appeared out of nowhere, and Kendall almost jumped out of his skin.

He jerked his head back, and examined the disturbing figure as he moved his light from its head to toes. The man's attire was similar to the Pirates of the Caribbean animatronics. He scanned side-to-side as several more pirate figures appeared. Kendall got chills as his tactical light illuminated the pirate's bodies. There were dozens of them, and they weren't animatronics, they were statues of some kind. As he continued to scan the underground chamber, he found more and more of these pirates and the room seemed to get bigger. Thick layers of dust covered the human-like figures as if they'd been sitting down there for decades untouched.

Suddenly it clicked, and Kendall realized what this was—these figures were from the Pirate Wax Museum concept Walt had originally planned to build underground. This was no tunnel—it was a walk-through attraction capable of holding hundreds of people.

He approached a small building towards the end of the large underground room. It had red colored bricks on the outside with sloppy mortar spread arbitrarily across sections of the walls. The window panes were made of dark wood panels, the roof angled upward and was also made with the same bricks. There was a chimney in the middle of the roof, and on each side there were two protruding windows made of wooden slats.

He moved around the building. On the right side, there was an old-style New Orleans street sign with an authentic looking nineteenth century lantern.

The sign read BOURBON ST.

Kendall noticed a small wooden sign on the right side of the building. He could reach it with his hands because of his height. He dusted off the old sign, and his mouth dropped when the engraved words appeared:

LAFITTE'S BLACKSMITH SHOP

He randomly flashed his light down a little further, and he noticed a large wall with a massive steel door at the end. It had an archway made of bricks—the same bricks used on the outside of this mysterious Lafitte's Blacksmith Shop.

He tried Jack again but couldn't get through. He reversed his direction to head back for the hatch.

BZZZZZZZZZ

The clicking electrical sound of multiple Tasers rang out as several metal darts penetrated Kendall's skin.

He dropped to his knees and lost control of his body.

FOUR

August 8, 2010
Dream Suite
Disneyland Park

"Jack, the CIA Counterterrorism agents are on site headed towards the Dream Suite, they need to talk to you," Conroy updated Jack from the Control Center.

"Okay, I'll be there in a few minutes."

"Sir, this is Team Six leader," Jack pressed his earpiece so he wouldn't miss a word, "we've confirmed an extremely small trace of caesium-137 coming deep from the drain. From what we can tell this drain system is deep and complex, we've already dug a portion of it up, and we're trying to get as far down as possible."

Jack's heart dropped through his stomach knowing the detection of caesium-137 confirmed the reality of a bomb.

"The small trace is probably due to the fact that the bomb is underground in the tunnel," Jack said.

"Yes, sir."

"We need to get through these tunnel doors somehow. We're running out of time."

"Yes, sir. I sent a few of the guys over to the underwater pipe location to see if we can blow the doors open."

"Be extremely careful with what you use, we don't know the potential side effects of an explosion since we've never been down there."

"Yes, sir. I'll keep you updated."

"Kendall," Jack tried to call him through their secure com. No answer. He switched over to Max, "Max, have you heard from Kendall?"

"No, sir, I haven't. And sir, I can't find anything out of the ordinary here at the Mansion."

"Keep looking Max, we're running out of time. Team Six just verified traces of caesium-137 under the Island—we're in trouble."

Max was silent for a moment, "Copy that, sir, I will not fail you."

Jack walked up the stairs to the Dream Suite as he took a quick look at the live feed of Andy and Grace coming from the El Capitan Suite. He entered the Dream Suite, and the elite CIA field agents stood at attention. This unit was comprised of the best anti-terrorism operatives in the country. They handled threats on a daily basis, and they knew how to perform under pressure.

"Gentlemen, I am glad to see you, I don't have a lot of time to explain, but there's a dirty bomb under the Rivers of America—and we have no clue where it is."

"Sir, Director Camden brought us up to speed on most of the events, he wants to talk to you right now." The agent positioned his device, pushed a button, and it generated a widescreen television-type image in midair. The screen flickered, and Director Camden's image came into focus.

"Jack, it's good to see your face, although not under these circumstances."

"Thank you sir, I'm glad your team is here."

"I've got some bad news, Jack. We've determined that because of the breach in your security system there are probably hundreds of hostiles on site who are coordinating simultaneous attacks."

Jack's mouth dropped, "Hundreds sir?"

"Yes, a small army. They are most likely armed and capable of mass casualties."

"I already have our full undercover team in combat mode; Team Six is here, and with your team we should have enough—"

"Jack—" the Director cut him off, "it gets worse."

Jack froze, thinking there was *no way* this could get any worse.

"There's someone else besides Nikolai involved. Someone that you know."

Jack paused with a heavy feeling in his stomach as he looked at the other agents in the Dream Suite living room.

"It's Khalid al-Haddad," the Director said with authority.

"WHAT? Are you sure about this? *He is here*?"

"Yes, Jack we're almost certain that he's on site as we speak, and he's in command of the army of terrorists. We suspect he's the mastermind behind all of this—Nikolai is just there to help him on the intelligence side of things."

Jack's chest heaved as he breathed deep; his eyes shifted back and forth as his jaw clamped down.

"How did the number two most wanted terrorist in the world get on US soil?"

"That's not relevant right now Jack, our first priority needs to be finding this bomb. But you'll certainly encounter resistance. I have more agents who'll be arriving in the next few minutes."

"Sir, I need every SEAL you can get a hold of and I need stealth Blackhawks standing by outside the Park waiting for my command."

"You got it Jack. I am monitoring the live feeds from your location through our secure channels, the same com that everyone else is on now. Make sure you're not using any of your own channels at this point." Director Camden paused, "Jack, the President is relying on you to stop this threat—the entire country is depending on you—don't let us down."

The live video conference ended, and the mid air screen disappeared. Jack felt as if someone kicked him in his solar plexus. Khalid played a role in 9/11, where Jack lost so many people who were close to him. He lost even more good friends in the aftermath—brave men and women who died in pursuit of al-Qaeda.

Jack knew if Khalid was involved, they were facing a much larger threat than anyone had previously suspected. With Nikolai's understanding of the Park and Khalid's stone cold determination to destroy the fabric of America, they could be unstoppable.

"Sir, where do you want us to go?" The CIA team leader asked.

Jack shook off the impact of the news and tried to regroup. "Our main priority right now is to find out how to get into this tunnel. I think I've found one of the entrances. If we can get inside, we can disarm this bomb."

"Yes, sir."

"Go to the Island, there are so many places that could lead to an entrance over there. I pulled some of Team Six from the Island to try to get these doors open at the base of the River."

"Yes, sir."

"Search every possible drainage pipe, cave, and whatever else you can find. Send another part of your team throughout the Park, and be covert about it, keep an eye out for anyone suspicious. If there are hundreds of terrorists on property, we should be able to find them—I need someone to interrogate—someone who can give me answers. I'll make them talk."

FIVE

August 8, 2010
Lafitte's Blacksmith Shop
Disneyland Park

"Sir this is Team Six leader, we've tried everything and cannot get these doors to budge."

Jack looked up at the ceiling of the Dream Suite. He knew that if Team Six couldn't get the doors open, no one could.

"The doors seem to be extremely thick, but we found something on the right side of the main door that appears to be a modern electronic panel. We noticed it when one of our small charges ignited, and a piece of the brick broke off."

"An electronic panel? Was it damaged by the blast?"

"It doesn't appear to be. I have one of the guys messing with the wiring to see if he can unlock it."

"Okay let me know. Also, Director Camden has informed me that Khalid al-Haddad is on property along with an army of hostiles, so make sure your team is ready to engage armed terrorists."

"Excuse me sir, did you say al-Haddad is here?"

"Yes, this situation is worse than we thought—we need get through these doors."

"Yes, sir."

Jack radioed Conroy next, "Rob, have you heard from Kendall at all? I have not been able to reach him?"

"No, Jack, I haven't been able to reach him either. He was talking to Sklar earlier, but I haven't heard from him since he shut down Pirates."

Jack knew something wasn't right. He moved toward a secret back door of the Dream Suite leading through an enclosed hallway on the side of the Club 33 kitchen. This hallway turned into a passageway leading him down to the bridge Kendall used to get to the Pirates control tower. The boats were in a holding pattern as Jack approached the CM in the tower.

"Have you seen Kendall?"

"Oh, yes Mr. Duncan, he told me to shut down the attraction, and then he began his walkthrough."

Jack walked through the CM pathway behind the old shack and continued through the attraction. There was no sign of Kendall anywhere. He walked the entire track until he arrived at the treasure room. He noticed the hatch to the storage basement was open, so he quickly went down to investigate.

The lights were on, but no sign of Kendall. He drew his SIG P236 and held it by his side as he cleared each row of boxes. He headed back to the hatch and started to climb to the treasure room when he realized the same thing Kendall did earlier—the metal plate under Captain Jack's platform propped open by a piece of wood.

Jack sprung up into the treasure room and used both hands to lift the metal plate. The plate itself was heavy, and it also had the full weight of the chair, the animatronic Jack Sparrow, and the treasure chest.

As the chair moved forward, Jack's mouth dropped when he saw the square hatch underneath the chair's platform. He flashed his light down the hatch to see how deep it was.

Without hesitation, he descended into the black abyss. The door of the hatch closed above him.

His feet hit the ground, and he noticed the metal door with the safe-looking dial was ajar. He went through the door and scanned the area for any trace of Kendall.

With his night vision goggles, he recognized the theme of the room. It matched Pirates of the Caribbean seamlessly.

A human figure appeared in front of him, and he extended his arms to shoot it. He realized the person didn't react to him, and moved closer.

He gazed into the face of the man and realized it was a character out of the Pirates attraction. He glanced to his right and noticed more pirate figures. *This looks like the Pirate Wax Museum.*

He tried to radio Max, but he couldn't get through.

He passed dozens of wax pirates as he proceeded. He could feel the dust floating through the air as he walked, the stale smell of the poorly ventilated room and countless cobwebs stuck to his face.

His jaw dropped as a mysterious brick building came into view—he'd seen this building before and instantly recognized it. This was a life size replica of Lafitte's Blacksmith Shop from the real Bourbon Street in New Orleans. He could not believe his eyes. He was in the middle of a lost attraction that had probably been hidden underground for over fifty years.

He slowly opened the creaky wooden door.

The lights inside the room flicked on—Jack saw Kendall gagged and bound to a chair.

He jumped into battle mode extending his arms to fire on the hostiles. He noticed three Middle Eastern terrorists holding Kendall and two female CMs at gunpoint.

The man who had a gun to Kendall's head spoke, "Jack Duncan, put down your weapon or all three of these people will die."

"Who are you?" Jack scowled.

The man laughed and spoke with an accent, "You are in no position to ask questions, PUT YOUR GUN DOWN NOW."

Kendall squirmed in his chair trying to break free, but he was in a weakened state from being hit with repeated Taser charges. The metal darts were still under the surface of his skin.

The man removed the gag from Kendall's mouth and yelled in his face, "You tell him to drop his gun now or these women die."

Kendall nodded as if he was going to comply and said, "Jack, don't do what they say, they are going to kill us anyway, just get out of here—don't let them take you."

The two female CMs cried uncontrollably with their hands tied behind their backs, and guns pointed at their heads.

"DUNCAN—drop your weapon or these women get their brains blown out."

Jack paused, loosened the grip on his gun, and unlocked his arms as he began to retreat, "Okay, wait."

"JACK. DON'T DO IT. TAKE THEM OUT—IT IS OUR ONLY CHANCE, MORE PEOPLE WILL DIE."

The screams from the women were deafening, the two hostiles yelled while shaking their arms aggressively.

Jack lowered his weapon slowly and put the palm of his left hand up signaling surrender.

He dipped his gun and relaxed his stance.

"DROP IT, DUNCAN!" The terrorist yelled.

With blinding speed, Jack returned his arms to the locked position.

BANG-BANG-BANG.

High pitched screaming, and the deafening sound of gunfire created pandemonium in the authentic all-brick Blacksmith Shop. Jack's arms remained fully extended as he squinted his eyes. The smell of gunpowder filled the air; blood was on the walls, and Jack's vision was blurry.

Kendall didn't make a sound, still bound to the chair, and the women screamed as they squirmed on the floor. Jack moved forward in hopes that the three hostiles were down, and no one else was hurt.

He visually identified one, two, and three—all three terrorists were down with headshots.

Jack holstered his gun and tended to the women to make sure they were okay, then untied Kendall.

"I was hoping you were going to do that, Jack."

Jack smiled at Kendall, "You would have done the same for me."

"Done what?" Kendall asked, "faked the surrender or hit all three in the head."

"Probably both, but I don't think you could've hit all three in the head like that."

Kendall chuckled as the tension released. "Ladies, everything is going to be okay, I am going to take you back upstairs. How did they get you down here?"

The women tried to talk, but they were hysterical and couldn't get the words out.

Kendall looked down at the three dead terrorists and turned to Jack, "And you're the one who scolded me for hitting Darth Maul in the head? We can't get any information from dead people, Jack—oh, and there's a solid metal door down a bit further. Can you believe this place?" Kendall headed back towards the door to the hatch leading up to the treasure room.

Jack searched the pockets of the hostiles to see if he could find any communication devices or anything that might identify them. Nothing. He glanced around the room in utter amazement; this replica of Lafitte's Blacksmith Shop was unbelievable. The furnishings inside the shop matched the outside. Old wood workbenches lined the edges of the blacksmith shop, with different artifacts presented in classic Disney fashion. This attraction was most likely designed by Walt himself.

Jean Lafitte memorabilia from the Battle of New Orleans hung near the entrance. A picture of Lafitte in his uniform and sword was on the wall. Newspaper clippings touting Lafitte's contribution to the historical Battle of New Orleans were framed and displayed on the wall along with a picture of Lafitte and Andrew Jackson.

To the right, another section of the shop featured a picture of Jean Lafitte with none other than an earlier version of Ambrose Gracey, the owner of the Haunted Mansion.

Next to that was another rendition of Lafitte's hideout on Tom Sawyer Island with a hand drawn painting of Fort Wilderness featuring General Andrew Jackson in full uniform.

In the center of the room, Lafitte's Memoirs were on display, containing the entire volume of his alleged autobiography.

Next to that was a drawing of the catacombs that would lead people on a dark journey under the River to Pirate's Lair. There was also a picture of Lafitte's Anchor, the same one that had been in the Park since opening day in 1955.

On the far right, there was a hand drawn pirate's treasure map, which appeared to be designed to show guests how to get the tunnel doors to open so they could continue their adventure underground. An inscribed 1764 was at the top of the map, and under that a depiction of Pirates, the Haunted Mansion, and the Island. Dotted lines connected the Haunted Mansion across the water to the middle of the Island, from Pirates to the middle of the Island, and then from Pirates to the Haunted Mansion. The tunnels appeared to form a triangle, and they joined the three attractions.

Jack walked out of the Blacksmith Shop, flashed his light into the darkness, and discovered another large metal door surrounded by a brick archway—the same design as the one he found near the front of the River. He inspected the door. It wouldn't budge, and he couldn't open it no matter what he tried.

He went back inside the shop towards the far right side of the room. This room was laid out like a map to show guests how to get to Pirates Lair.

1764? This is supposed to be 200 years from the birthday of Matt McKim?

He continued to search this section of the shop, but he couldn't find anything that led to more clues. It was as if the attraction was incomplete.

He went back to the Haunted Mansion section of the Blacksmith Shop to find more clues. He opened the center drawer of the desk and discovered more hand drawn maps. Jack thumbed through them and found a map showing the tunnel entrance at the Haunted Mansion. He brought the map closer to get a better look at where the entrance was located. He grabbed everything that he could from the Blacksmith Shop and headed upstairs to find Max.

SIX

August 8, 2010
Haunted Mansion
Disneyland Park

"Max, I'm heading your way, meet me by the hidden pet cemetery," Jack said as he exited Pirates of the Caribbean.

"I'm on my way."

Jack raced towards the Haunted Mansion as he thumbed through the maps he discovered in Lafitte's Blacksmith Shop. They seemed to point to a crypt of some kind in the pet cemetery area.

He headed for the Cast Member only gate on the Splash Mountain side of the Mansion and ran up the steps. He found Max searching through the grass and behind the headstones of the "deceased" Haunted Mansion pets.

"Sir, I don't know where there could be an entrance over here, it's all grass."

"This map shows it's right here somewhere," Jack illuminated the map with his light so Max could see. Max looked down at the map and then up at Jack with his mouth open in shock.

"It's a long story Max, but there's definitely a tunnel under here. I think these tunnels form a triangle. This one goes to the Island, then it angles towards Pirates, and then from Pirates it connects the Mansion."

They used their tactical lights to explore the dark area. The pet cemetery wasn't visible to guests unless they walked through the Cast Member only gate.

"1764 seems to be a central theme behind these tunnels so that would be our first clue."

Max got on top of a thick cement slab at the far end of the cemetery and started to look around. He bent over and scanned the impenetrable edges of the huge slab to see if there was anything out of the ordinary.

He froze as his light lit up a set of cryptic numbers:

1764

"Jack, I found it."

He rushed over as Max showed him the engraved 1764. It was in the same old-style design that he'd seen on the other entrances and the crypt along the River esplanade.

"Okay this must be it, let's try to lift it."

With both hands, they tried to dead lift the immense cement slab, but it wouldn't budge. Under the slab, they saw what looked like red bricks.

"Every entrance I've seen so far uses these same red bricks. Let's dig deeper."

Max ran to the Cast Member exit to get a shovel. He went through one of the landscaping sheds utilized by the CMs who work the nightshift keeping the topiaries immaculate. He came back, shovel in hand, and he started to dig out the area under the slab. Max used his astounding upper body strength to gut a two-foot deep section under the slab. He plunged the shovel into the dense ground with brute force over and over again.

CLANK

He hit an iron bar with the shovel. Jack jumped in and moved dirt out of the way with his hands. He found an iron handle set inside the red bricks. Jack pulled on the bar with everything he had, but he couldn't move it. Max bent down using his massive arms, and full body weight to pull alongside Jack.

The slab released, and began to rise. A small hatch appeared.

"This is it Max." Jack cast his light down the hatch revealing spider webs, dust, and dirt. "Let's go."

They descended into the deep hatch. Jack took a few steps, and plummeted towards the bottom, hitting the ground with a thump.

"Sir, are you okay?"

Jack groaned, "Yeah I'm okay, here grab my hand." Jack helped Max down the rest of the way.

They were in a perfectly square room. Dead ahead was another entrance —bricks were aligned to create an archway that surrounded a large, thick metal door. They looked around, and everything in the room matched the theme of the Haunted Mansion. Traces of smuggled loot and gold hinted at a pirate theme as well. Pictures on the wall depicted scenes from the Battle of New Orleans—skeletons and skulls were carefully positioned throughout. Several pictures that had gone missing from the Haunted Mansion in previous years were hanging on the wall. The famous "June" portrait from the Mansion was there.

"Max, this is the same exact thing I've seen at the other entrances—they all have these thick doors that can't be budged. Team Six already tried to blow one of them."

Max put his full weight into the door, and it wouldn't move a millimeter. He searched along the sides, and there was no way to get in.

"Team Six said they discovered a panel on the right side, some type of electronic device, but they haven't been able to crack it."

"Sir, should I get Mr. Sklar on the line?"

"Yeah, let me talk to him. There must be a way to open these doors. Whoever installed this tunnel network updated it recently with electronic opening mechanisms. Walt might have had the idea initially, but someone else put this system into place afterwards to protect the tunnels."

"Mr. Sklar, please hold for Jack Duncan." Max handed the phone to Jack.

"Mr. Sklar, I've found a few different entrances so far, but I cannot get these doors open."

"Doors, Jack?"

"Yes, I found an entrance under Pirates and the Mansion and they both have massive thick metal doors surrounded by a brick archway, but we cannot get them open."

"Jack, I've never seen or heard of entrances like that. What you're describing sounds similar to the crypt on the River esplanade?"

"It looks very similar to that—and the brick work and mortar is strikingly similar to Lafitte's Blacksmith Shop under Pirates."

"*Lafitte's Blacksmith Shop?*"

"Yes, a full size replica under Pirates, it looks like a walk through attraction leading to an underground tunnel."

"Jack, I am going to get a hold of Eddie Sotto. He knows more about this stuff than I do, he was in charge when the crypt on the River was installed, and he tried to unify these three attractions decades ago."

"Yes, sir please have him call me ASAP—we're running out of time. If I don't find a way to get into these doors soon, the Park as we know it will cease to exist."

SEVEN

Jack pulled a picture of Kate out of his chest pocket. His lips clamped together as he stared at her. Kate's thick and wavy blondish-brown hair cascaded over her face; her striking blue eyes and her incredible smile surged through the worn photo. To this day, her beauty still captivated him. The photo was taken near the Huntington Beach pier—the picturesque rays from the sun lit up her hair and face, giving her an angelic appearance.

His rage mounted, the only thing he could focus on was avenging her death. The two men he hated the most were within his reach. He could almost taste their blood—he envisioned the satisfaction of putting a bullet in their heads after making them physically and mentally suffer. His hunt for Nikolai and al-Haddad was impeding his ability to focus on the task at hand, but he couldn't help it.

1994

Jack walked through Disneyland—alone. He'd left a message every day for Kate, for over a week, with no return call. He pulled out his phone and dialed the first part of her number—then he stopped.

What am I doing? This makes me look desperate.

He walked towards Fowler's Harbor on the Rivers of America near the dry dock for the Mark Twain and Columbia. Eating always gave him a lift when he was depressed. He ordered one of his favorites from the charming little wooden waterside shack—popcorn shrimp with an addicting spicy orange sauce on the side.

He dipped the delicate, crunchy shrimp into the thick sauce. His mouth watered as the fried goodness of the shrimp combined with the tasty sauce struck the perfect culinary balance—making music inside his mouth. He looked out over the River, the water sparkled, the air was warm on his face, he smelled fresh popcorn, and the jazz music emanated through the well-hidden speakers.

Jack took a deep breath and started to feel better.

Well, I guess this wasn't meant to be.

Just as that thought crossed his mind, his phone rang. It was Kate.

"Hello," Jack answered in a dry, monotone voice.

"Jack, hey it's Kate, I'm sorry I haven't called you back, I've been so busy over here I can't even think straight."

"Oh no problem, look if this isn't a good time then we can talk later."

"No, it's okay, I have a few minutes, what's up?" Kate said.

Jack froze. *Should I tell her how I truly feel, put myself on the line again, and risk being rejected? Or should I just move on?*

"Oh, I remembered that you said you were coming home this weekend, and I just wanted to see if you wanted to meet up or something."

Kate was silent for a second and then she spoke, "Let me check Jack, I don't know what my mom has planned. I seriously want to go to the Park, and I've missed it so much. I didn't realize I was going to miss home like this."

"Sure, well, ask your mom and give me a call. It would be nice to see you."

"Look Jack, I am going to be honest with you," Jack's stomach dropped as he remembered the last time she shot straight with him. "I've had a few months to think, and it has been good for me, it's allowed me to distance myself from the fairy tale romance we had so I could step back and see the reality of this situation. I remembered what you said to me when I asked you if we could still meet up in the Park. You were right when you said you didn't know how that would work."

"Yeah but Kate, I was in shock and not thinking straight."

"No, I think you were talking from your gut, telling me the truth. And I agree with you, I don't know how it would work either, now that I think about it."

Jack turned to look at the French Market veranda where they first met and spent so much time together. Emotion swept over him, and he could hear his dad's voice saying that he needed to fight for her if she was the one. He switched gears and took control of the situation.

"Kate, listen to me, I've never met anyone like you in all of my life. You are beautiful, my heart drops when I see you and your smile brightens my entire day. I've thought about you every day since you've been gone and I realized I made a mistake on that day in New Orleans Square."

Kate was taken aback by what Jack said, "A mistake?"

"Yes, instead of getting up and walking away I should have told you how I really felt. About how I want to spend the rest of my life with you. That you are more valuable than my career and that *we can be great together*. We have something unique that could last forever. I should've told you that I'd choose you over my career any day, because if we are together, everything will be okay, no matter what I do or where we are."

Kate was silent on the other end.

She stuttered, "Jack, I don't know what to say..."

"Just say that you'll come back home and give us another chance, or I will go to New York and be with you there. It doesn't matter. I'm done with The Teams, I am ready to turn from my selfish self-centered life to a life focused on you."

It sounded as if Kate was sniffling in the background trying to regain her composure.

"Jack, I feel the same way about you, I haven't been able to stop thinking about you since I left. I miss home, but I mostly miss it because of you. I'm so lost out here."

Jack smiled as he looked out over the Rivers of America.

"But—"

His smile vanished.

"Jack this isn't going to work. I need to give my new job some time, I can't just quit. And I won't be responsible for you quitting the one thing that you love to do."

"But Kate—"

"Jack, please," Kate wept, "please, this is the best thing for us right now. Let's take some time and not make any rash decisions. If we're truly meant to be together, a few months or even years will not keep us apart."

"Years? Kate, if you feel the same way I feel about you then how can we be apart?"

"Jack—I do feel the same way, but you have to trust me. I'm sorry, but I have to go into a meeting right now, I will call you back later."

She hung up.

Jack lowered his phone from his ear, defeated.

EIGHT

August 8, 2010
Fowler's Harbor
Disneyland Park

"Jack, this is Eddie Sotto, Marty said you had an urgent matter to discuss?"

"Mr. Sotto, thank you for calling so fast, we're in a major crisis over here, and I need your help—I need to get inside these tunnels ASAP."

"Tunnels, Jack?"

"Yes, the one under the Rivers of America, there could be three or more."

"Jack, I don't know what you're talking about, there are no tunnels under the Rivers of America?"

"Sir, we're dealing with a major threat here, and I really need your help."

"Jack, at one time, I tried to unify the three attractions, but the project was shut down, it never happened."

"It did happen, I've already found an entrance to a tunnel under Pirates, under the Mansion, and in front of the River. The problem is that there is no way to get through the metal doors."

Sotto was silent on the other end.

"Jack, I don't know what to say? What about your dad? If anyone knows about this it would be him."

"He can't talk right now, he's very sick. You built the crypt in front of the Mansion right?"

"Yes, but that was a symbol of the project that never happened, it's not a real tunnel."

"Okay but the things I've seen follow the design of that crypt, so they are related somehow."

"Your dad gave me the detail sheets to follow for the design of that crypt."

Jack was confused.

"The only thing I do know about, which very few people know of, is the basement under Fowler's Harbor."

"Basement?"

"Yes, when the Admiral built the dry dock for the Mark Twain and Columbia, since there was so much concrete involved, he also built a basement under the River—or more like a bomb shelter."

"What?"

"Walt didn't want to spend the money on the expensive dry dock. When Fowler convinced Walt that it was necessary to maintain the two ships, he reluctantly agreed but commissioned him to build a bomb shelter under there as well. There's a door inside the Fowler's Inn building that's on the water, I don't know how to get in, but I am sure there's a basement down there."

"What about 1764? What is that? It's all over these entrances."

"That is 200 years from Matt McKim's birthday."

"But that makes no sense, I don't see why it would've have been printed on maps, etched on stone, and doorways if it was just related to someone's birthday."

"I don't know Jack. 1764 was in the plans your dad gave me, we just followed them. There was a rumor that circulated between us high-ranking Imagineers that Fowler supposedly kept things in that basement—secrets—a fallout plan in case of a disaster. I think that's probably some sort of a legend, but you never know. A few of us knew about the basement, but your dad sealed it. I think the door to the basement is locked with a code that only your dad knows."

"Okay I'm heading over there now, can you please standby?"

"Sure, Jack."

Jack walked across the way to Fowler's Harbor. Guests lined up for thick clam chowder served inside fresh baked sourdough bread bowls. He walked through the eating area on the wood pier walkway until he got to Fowler's Inn, which resembled a charming seaside establishment. He checked the door labeled Cast Members Only, and it was unlocked, so he walked in. The room was empty with a few boxes stacked in the corner. He searched the ground with his light to see if there was any sign of a hatch. He moved a few boxes out of the way and found a small rectangular outline in the floor. It had a latch on one end of it that was locked with a thick padlock. Jack pulled the bolt cutters from his assault kit and clipped the padlock.

He opened the hatch that revealed a stairway leading down into the ground. He quickly walked down the stairs and entered a small, dark room where he found another door—this one had an electric lock on it with illuminated numbers.

He tried to think of what his dad would've used for the password. He tried variations of 1955 because he knew Stan used that number a lot. Out of desperation he tried 1764. Nothing. He went back to different combinations of 1955, but none of them worked.

He remembered that Stan had used Genie's birthday for a lot of his passcodes, even though he warned him not to do that. He entered 71839—the lock clicked and the door opened.

He hit a switch on the wall that lit up the entire basement. The room was the length of the entire dry dock, wall-to-wall concrete capable of holding a hundred people or more.

The large shelter was empty except for at the end; there was an all-metal wall with a door that had a padlocked latch. Jack clipped the lock and opened the door. It was dark inside, and the room was chock full of filing cabinets. One of the cabinets was labeled "Fallout," and Jack immediately made a beeline for this one.

Inside the cabinet, he found an entire box labeled "Admiral Fowler" and he rustled through the papers inside. He found old documents that appeared to be in Fowler's own handwriting. Schematics of the Mark Twain, the Columbia, and the dry dock. There was an entire folder dedicated to the famous golden spike on the Castle floor in Fantasyland. He dug deeper and found diagrams of the Rivers of America, Tom Sawyer Island, the dark water system, and another diagram of the same triangle tunnel that he saw on the map from Lafitte's Blacksmith Shop. The triangle was exactly how it appeared on the maps, connecting Pirates, Haunted Mansion, and Tom Sawyer Island. He dug further, and found another map—this one had the same triangle diagram of the underground tunnels, but it also contained more lines, this was a map of not just one tunnel, but an entire network of tunnels under the Park.

If there are this many tunnels, the bomb could be anywhere.

Jack's heart sank as he realized the unlikelihood of finding the bomb.

He dug through the cabinet to see if there was anything else that would help. He found a file labeled LAFITTE. He rifled through the folder. It contained several pictures taken throughout the Park; a close-up of the golden spike, Fortune Red, the crypt on the River, the 1764 they found in the hidden pet cemetery, Lafitte's Blacksmith Shop, the Pirate Wax museum, the same metal doors that he'd seen, the green Griffith Park bench Walt sat on when he dreamed of Disneyland, and finally, there was a picture of Kurt Russell. He stopped to look at the picture of the famous actor and Disney Legend trying to figure out why his image would be in this folder.

NINE

1959
Fowler's Harbor
Disneyland Park

Walt Disney, Stan Duncan, and Joe Fowler stood on the edge of the Rivers of America admiring the dry dock that Joe built. They savored each bite of their lobster sandwiches from Maurie's Lobster House on Fowler's Harbor.

"You know what I call this, Stan?" Walt asked jokingly.

Stan grinned because he knew what Walt was going to say.

"Joe's Ditch."

Admiral Fowler laughed.

"The Admiral here persuaded me to spend a fortune on this huge piece of concrete," Walt continued, "I fought him on it, but he won and we ended up spending a ton of money—for what?"

"I was just looking out for you Walt. This had to be a legitimate dock, not a movie prop. You wanted real boats, so you needed a real dry dock to manage them."

"I'll let you go on this one Joe since you came through on so many other projects," Walt smiled as he elbowed him. "Why do you think I called it Fowler's Harbor and named this lobster house after your lovely wife?"

"Fowler's Inn turned out great Walt. It has an authentic feel to it."

The Fowler's Inn sign hung over a rustic seaside building on the dry dock overlooking the Rivers of America.

Joe and Walt became good friends over the years even though their relationship began on rocky ground.

Walt patted Joe on the shoulder, smiled at him, and took another bite of his lobster sandwich.

"I'm headed to Tomorrowland, I will see you two later." Joe said as he shook their hands.

Stan and Walt waved to "Can-do Joe" as he walked away. Walt gave this nickname to Joe Fowler because of his can-do attitude towards building Walt's impossible dreams.

"I'm so glad we built that huge shelter underneath, it's the perfect location, and it didn't cost much more since the main structure was already in progress," Walt said.

"Yes, it's a good sized area down there that can provide adequate protection during a disaster."

"Since no one really knows about it, I've been storing things down there—you know spreading things out—some things I put in the tunnel, other things are down there. Just so everything isn't in one place."

Stan nodded with a mouthful of sweet lobster chunks.

"Hey, let's go down there really quick I need to show you something."

"Sure, Walt."

They walked through the door of Fowler's Inn—Stan opened the secret hatch. When they got down into the shelter, it was mostly empty, except for a large metal wall towards the far end. Stan walked with Walt towards the metal wall and opened the lock on the door.

"I need to show you this just in case something ever happens to me, Stan." Walt said as he opened one of the filing cabinets, "Several years ago, I was approached by a man named John A. Lafitte. He was an odd sort of fellow, and he claimed to be the great-grandson of Jean Lafitte. At first, I didn't believe him. Then I had someone from the office investigate him, and it turned out he was in fact who he said he was."

Stan leaned forward with curiosity, knowing this was going to turn into one of Walt's wild stories.

"He needed money, so he asked if I wanted to buy Lafitte's memoirs. I've always been fascinated with pirates and American history as you know, and I knew a little about the legend of Lafitte. I had a historian friend of mine check out the memoirs, and he found them to be legitimate. I paid John his asking price, and I read the memoirs on the spot. It was the most intriguing thing I've ever read. This guy Lafitte was like a super-human pirate, he could do anything. He was an expert dueler, unstoppable at sea, intelligent, and willing to sacrifice his life for a greater cause—the Declaration of Independence. He referred to the Declaration as a 'sacred document.' He was also a gentleman, a philanthropist, a romantic, and tremendously wealthy."

Stan smiled, "So that's why you integrated him into the Park?"

"Exactly, but there's something else. In the memoirs, he talked about treasure that he dumped in various places along the coast; he buried valuables while being pursued by the Spaniards. I asked John what he knew of this, and he said that he'd searched for the treasure, but eventually ran out of resources and couldn't get anyone to finance the search."

"So naturally, you helped him."

"Yes I did, Stan. I put a few people on it and John helped as well—we found a fair amount of gold that rightfully went to John and his family, but I got to keep something worth more than gold."

Walt grabbed one of the cabinets and moved it away from the wall—revealing a secret wall safe. He pulled out a key from his pocket and unlocked the safe. He pulled out a folder full of pictures.

"In Lafitte's Memoirs, he mentioned that he dropped gold plates in the ocean when the Spaniards were pursuing him. John said these gold plates belonged to some of our founding fathers, and that Lafitte obtained them due to his relationship with Andrew Jackson. I figured he was exaggerating the value so that I would agree to give him more of the gold. But I had the plates checked out," Walt showed Stan the pictures, "and I think they are legitimate, I have been trying to break the code for years, but I haven't been able to do it. These gold plates are stored in the vault in the tunnel system. The wrong people cannot see these Stan, only someone who is loyal to us, someone who believes in our dream for this Park—and for EPCOT."

EPCOT was Walt's idea for the Experimental Prototype Community of Tomorrow, a complete futuristic planned self-sustaining city. He dreamed of building a real working city with both commercial and residential areas. A city that would showcase and explore new ideas for urban living. This would be the perfect city, a utopia, a city that would be a blueprint for the rest of the world—a city that would *change* the world.

"Not only are the plates worth a fortune by themselves, but the code engraved on them has infinite value. I think they hold the key to what I need to build the Progress City. I'm working as hard as I can to figure it out—if the wrong people find out they'll want me to sell them since we always need money over here. Worse yet, if the enemy or even our own government gets a hold of them it could be detrimental as well. If people find out that I have these plates, they'll come after them."

"Who knows about this Stan?"

"Just you and me."

Stan had a look of bewilderment on his face; he couldn't believe this revelation from Walt, it sounded like a movie pitch.

"I need you to take this torch and run with it, Stan, just in case something happens to me. I want you to continue my research, push EPCOT forward, and find a successor who can take over after you are unable to continue. Don't tell anyone about this until you think they are undoubtedly ready to continue the dream—not a moment before. There will be many people who you think you can trust, but they'll fail you—make sure their motives are pure, and that they don't have skeletons in their closet, or uncontrolled emotions that will inhibit their vision. You can never let this information fall into the wrong hands."

"Okay Walt, this is a lot to take in."

"I know, but we need to act fast, I'm on to something that will change the world, and I have to make sure my succession plan is in place. I don't want this information to go to waste, and I don't want it to be limited to my lifetime."

TEN

August 8, 2010
Rivers of America
Disneyland Park

Khalid al-Haddad stood at the edge of the Rivers of America. He was a handsome man thanks to his six-figure facelift—well dressed, and he looked like any other guest at the Park that night. He put both of his rough hands together as he looked out over the River. The same hands that had snuffed out thousands of innocent lives—people who begged him for mercy but were denied. Khalid knew not of mercy; he had one goal—to destroy America and everything it stood for. Killing innocent men, women, and children was a necessary part of his plan to devastate America.

He spoke through his earpiece with a refined Middle Eastern accent on a secure channel, "Nikolai, where are you."

"I am inside the park, by the Opera House."

"You need to get in place now, and make the call. We need Duncan to play into our hands."

"Khalid, I'm the one who got you this far, do NOT forget our deal."

"You do not take that tone with me Nikolai, I have one goal in mind, and you already know what that is."

Nikolai uncharacteristically backed down. "Yes, Khalid."

"You do as I command, Nikolai. My operative inside of their Control Center is exceptionally reliable and has given me better information than what you've given me."

"I don't know what you're talking about."

"Nikolai, if you want to die before you get a chance at your silly revenge, then keep lying to me, keep questioning me, I will slit your throat when you least expect it."

Nikolai was silent.

"I need you to make the call to Duncan. Do it now."

"Okay Khalid, but let's be clear, I will get you what you want, but you need to get me what I want. I want both Stan and Jack delivered to me so I can accomplish what I came here to do. You wouldn't have gotten this far without me, and you know that."

"I have already told you what you will get out of this, why do you find it necessary to question me? We have the father in our custody; he is on his way here as we speak. You just follow the plan, or like I said, you will die a horrible death. I have hundreds of men watching your every move."

"Understood."

Khalid filled his lungs with fresh Southern California summer air. It felt good. The smell of expensive food wandering through the air, the arrogant music, and the well-dressed infidels spending thousands of dollars to escape from reality confirmed his stereotype of the American heathens. They all deserved death in his opinion, and their deaths would bring the United States to its knees. This event would forever cause Americans to doubt their safety—it would put their government in his hands. He would finally finish what he set out to do on 9/11.

Soon, they will ALL be put out of their misery, he thought.

ELEVEN

August 8, 2010
Dream Suite
Disneyland Park

"Luke, I need you to get Kurt Russell on the line for me," said Jack.

"Yes, sir, hold on a second."

Jack walked back towards the Dream Suite to regroup and find answers.

"Jack, I can't get a hold of him, but I left a message with his assistant."

"Okay, I need Sklar and Sotto on the line for a conference."

"Standby."

He ran up the stairs of the Dream Suite. In the living room, he spread the pictures he obtained from the basement of Fowler's Harbor across the coffee table.

"Okay, Jack I have both gentlemen on the line for you."

"Mr. Sklar and Mr. Sotto, I found a folder in the basement under Fowler's Inn, and it appears to have clues related to these tunnels."

"Did you say tunnels Jack as in more than one?" Sklar asked.

"Yes, according to a map I found there is an entire network of tunnels so it could be impossible to find what we need down there. I've found entrances to these tunnels, but I cannot figure out how to get in."

"Jack," Sotto said, "what if your dad is the one who masterminded this tunnel system?"

Jack paused for a second and realized that Sotto could be right.

"That's a possibility, but why would he keep this from me, he tells me everything?" Jack examined the pictures on the table, "What would Fortune Red, the golden spike, and the park bench have to do with all of this? Also, there's a picture Kurt Russell in the folder."

"Kurt?" Sklar sounded shocked, "You know that Kurt's name was one of the last things that Walt Disney wrote down before he died."

"Yes, I'm waiting for Kurt to call me back, in the meantime I'm going to take a look at these other things to see if I can figure this out."

"Jack, Fortune Red holds a map designed by Sam McKim."

"You're right, Matt McKim's dad, I forgot about that. Okay, I'm heading over there now, I'll call you shortly." Jack disconnected and spoke to Luke, "I need you to cross check everything you can come up with, every possible link between Fortune Red, the spike, the bench, and Kurt Russell."

"Yes sir."

TWELVE

August 8, 2010
New Orleans Square
Disneyland Park

Jack ran down the stairs of the Dream Suite and made a sharp left for the Pieces of Eight store. He stopped at the small opening to the Royal Courtyard where the famous fortune-telling machine was located. Fortune Red looked as if he was taken right out of the Pirates of the Caribbean attraction, and he was remarkably similar to the wax pirates he saw underground. He examined the intricate map drawn by Sam McKim looking for any clues. He noticed the following words hand-drawn on the map.

Land here, don't be misled, watch out, follow signs, step over, Ignore Lesser Treasure—Your Fortune waits below.

He quickly threw a quarter into the machine and waited for the fortune to drop out of the bottom as *A Pirate's Life for Me* played in the background.

A small card dropped out of the machine that read:

FORTUNE RED has this to say: Ye sails yer ship with a steady helm and a weather eye out fer the luff o' the sails. Though lackin' in formal book learnin', 'tis with a will ye worked to develop a keen mind. Ye would leave no sail furled to help a mate in need, and the deeds o' yer generous nature sparkle like the twinklin' lights at Disneyland on a warm summer night. Devoted, ye be, to yer kin but b'lay! Ye may be generous to a fault. Mark well me words: Generosity consists less in givin' much, than in givin' wisely.

Jack stared into the eyes of Fortune Red as his mind flashed back to the time when Stan gave him the "lesser treasure" talk.

1994

Jack and Stan exited their Pirates of the Caribbean boat and stepped on to the wooden loading platform of Lafitte's Landing. Stan had his arm around Jack as they headed towards the exit to Royal Street.

"So you told her all of that, and she still turned you down?"

"Yeah can you believe that?"

"Well, Jack I still think she's the one. Great women don't come easy."

"Where do you get all these goofy sayings, Dad? You're full of these corny lines?"

Stan laughed as they walked past the Pieces of Eight store. They ducked into the Royal Courtyard and stood in front of Fortune Red—the famous pirate fortune-telling machine. Stan and Jack always stopped there after riding Pirates.

"Look closely at this map, Jack. Notice how it starts at the top with warning signs along the way like 'don't be misled', 'watch out', 'follow signs', then before you get to the treasure it says: '*ignore lesser treasure*.'"

Jack stared with a blank look on his face at the mesmerizing pirate inside the classic machine.

"This is true for life as well," Stan continued, "there are many obstacles we have to overcome to get to a worthwhile goal—a goal that matters. We can be easily misled, but if we follow the signs—which means to seek wisdom—and ignore the lesser treasure, we'll make it to the finish line."

"Okay."

"You don't get it, do you son? If something is worth fighting for then you need to see it through to the end no matter what gets in your way—don't be tempted to settle for *lesser treasure*. Don't give up the fight. You run the race to win, not to place."

Jack titled his head as he began to understand what Stan was saying, but it still sounded too cliché for him.

"This applies to everything Jack, there are so many times when we get tired and weary. Instead of seeing the situation through, we settle for the lesser treasure, and we miss out on the vast blessing that awaits us in the end."

"Yeah but Dad how do I know if she really is the one?"

"You will know because you'll think about her all the time, you'll get butterflies in your stomach and experience feelings you've never felt before. But it's so much more than just a feeling—you'll feel a sense of commitment. True love is not based on feelings. Feelings ebb and flow, love is a commitment to be with someone for the rest of your life, 'til death do you part. If that's the way you feel about Kate, then she *is* the one."

The reality of the situation hit Jack all at once. That *was* how he felt about her. Kate was the treasure he was looking for. He was going to throw in the towel because of his pride—he didn't want to fail, and he didn't want to face rejection.

"You know what Dad, sometimes you talk a lot of nonsense, and other times you make total sense!"

"Jack, I always make total sense, but sometimes you aren't smart enough to realize it." Stan whacked him on the shoulder.

"The only problem is that she's essentially told me to leave her alone. If I pursue her I'll seem like a stalker."

"Give her time and space, but don't give up." Stan showed Jack his ring finger. "Do you see this ring Jack? I will always wear this ring because your mom was my treasure, the one I was made for." Stan took off the ring and showed it to him. “This ring is a never ending circle, made of solid gold, it signifies our never ending love.”

“You have become such a weak, sappy mess in your old age, Dad.”

They both laughed and headed towards the Haunted Mansion.

THIRTEEN

Jack headed for the golden spike in the ground at the entrance of Sleeping Beauty Castle.

"Luke have you found anything yet?"

"No sir, not yet, but we're crunching a lot of data. You probably already know the history of the spike—people have claimed it's the geographical center of Disneyland when it was originally built. There's a general consensus that the spike was a survey marker keeping the Castle centered with Main Street, and not the center of Disneyland."

Jack stared down at the golden colored circular spike that was flat and even with the brick walkway of the castle. He got down and tried to press on the spike, and it wouldn't budge, he couldn't figure out how this could have anything to do with getting the doors open underground.

"This is where my mom and dad were married. Right here on the spike. They did it here because the circle represented their union and—wait, you know what, I totally forgot—Kurt Russell was their ring bearer."

"Ring bearer? He would have been around 13 years old at the time?"

"Yeah but it was a last minute thing. Only a few people were there, Walt, Lillian, and a few others. Kurt was there with a few of the Mouseketeers for an appearance, and they spontaneously made him the ring bearer."

"But Jack, I don't see how that would coincide with Kurt being the last thing that Walt wrote down."

Jack didn't understand it either, it was a tangled mess, and none of it made sense. He was good at breaking down doors and killing terrorists, but not solving riddles.

Jack headed down Main Street towards the Opera House where the park bench was on display. He walked in the Opera House to find the weather-beaten green colored wooden park bench that had a plaque on it:

The actual park bench from the Griffith Park merry-go-round in Los Angeles, where Walt Disney first dreamed of Disneyland.

Again, Jack didn't see how this was related to the doors. He got on his knees and ran his hands under the bench.

"Jack," Luke said, "I found an old picture of your parents sitting on this bench with Walt, it looks as if it was from their wedding day."

Jack's phone rang—it was from a blocked number.

"Yes," Jack answered.

"Jack, you are running out of time. Where is your father?" It was Nikolai.

Jack tensed up and moved to a quiet place to talk. "I don't know where he is—where are you Nikolai, let's meet, just you and me—I am the one you really want."

"I gave you specific instructions Jack, I honestly thought you would come through. It looks like I have no other choice but to level the park."

"TELL ME HOW TO GET INTO THESE TUNNELS NIKOLAI." Jack yelled as his temper flared.

"Why would I do that Jack? I bet it bothers you that no one ever told you about these tunnels. Especially your father, I thought he told you everything?"

Jack's chest violently heaved. He put his hand on the back of his neck to try to knead out the pain.

"I will call you in exactly one hour, and I will tell you where we will meet alone—and I mean alone and unarmed, if you bring any of your friends, the bomb goes off—don't forget, I am monitoring your every move."

Nikolai disconnected the call.

"Luke did you get that?"

"Standby Jack I think I got it this time—YES, hold on I am trying to find the loc—"

Luke stopped in the middle of his sentence. "Jack, the call came from—what appears to be…the middle of the Rivers of America—*as in under the water…*"

FOURTEEN

"Jack," Kendall said, "this isn't adding up, it's a trap."

"Well, of course it's a trap, but I have no other choice. They want me for some reason, and my dad and I need to give them what they want—otherwise the bomb will detonate."

"Yeah but I think they need you to open these doors, and they are trying to lure you down there for some reason."

"Kendall, the call came from under the Rivers of America, they are already inside the tunnels."

Kendall stopped to think—Jack was right.

"I cannot wait for this meeting, we need to get inside those doors and attack, that's our only chance. We have Team Six, and the CIA unit here, if we can get to the bomb we can disarm it."

"But Jack this could backfire on us, it could accelerate the detonation, it could cause them to panic and set it off prematurely. I honestly think you are better off just meeting with him to see what he wants. This whole thing can't just be about killing you, they want something more, and they need you to get it."

"Kendall," emotion swept over Jack's face as he looked up in the air, "I don't have to tell you what this man took from me, I think about him every night, I see him in my dreams. Even when I thought he was dead, I could not get him out of my mind, he escaped the punishment that he deserved. I need blood, Kendall, and I'm not embarrassed to say it. I must have the satisfaction of watching him die and making *sure* he is dead this time. Not to mention Khalid, after all of our brothers and sisters he's murdered. If I can take these two out, and I know I can, it will be a significant victory."

"A victory for who Jack? And at what cost?"

Jack was frustrated, he couldn't figure out why his best friend wasn't behind him.

"I'm just saying, you could be falling into their plan without knowing it." Kendall said. "If you force your way through these doors, you could be making things worse."

FIFTEEN

"Jack," said Luke through his earpiece, "I have a Melissa White on the phone for you, she says it's important."

"Melissa White? What could she possibly want right now, tell her I'm not available."

"Jack she said it's urgent, regarding the threat."

Jack reluctantly told him to put her through.

"Jack," Melissa greeted Jack with a soft, yet confident and provocative voice, "how have you been?"

"Melissa, I don't have time to talk right now, Luke said you have information regarding this threat?"

"Yes, Jack. I've been monitoring this situation over here at the CTSOB, the entire LAPD has been watching, and I have a strong feeling that someone is working against you from the inside."

Jack stopped in his tracks.

"Who?"

"I'm not sure, I've seen several weird outgoing connections from people on your team—specifically Tony."

Jack paused, and his heart stopped, "Who has he contacted?"

"It looks like his mom and a few other relatives, but the odd thing is that he's been trying to access a CIA terrorist database with forged credentials."

The thought of his own people conspiring against him was worse than Nikolai being in the Park. *There's no way Tony would ever be involved with something like this?*

"Jack," Melissa continued, "I wouldn't trust anyone right now, Nikolai and al-Haddad are both involved, they have more money and resources than you can imagine, and they can make almost anything happen."

Jack was silent.

"Look Jack, I know you think I've been after you for all these years, and you really don't trust me or want anything to do with me after what I did to you in college. To tell you the truth, I have been after you, I think we would be great together, and I want to earn your trust again. But regardless of our personal life, I am telling you facts that are relevant to your situation."

"I'm going to talk to Tony now to figure this out, I will call you back, please look into this further and keep me informed, I need to know exactly who's working against me." Jack paused and changed his tone, "Thanks Melissa."

"You're welcome Jack." Melissa said with a big smile on her face.

SIXTEEN

1994
Fantasyland
Disneyland Park

"Yeah Kendall, it has been almost nine weeks of calling, and nothing," Jack said as they walked along the parade route of the new Lion King Celebration Parade.

Kendall had never seen Jack like this.

"Well, Jack, don't you think it is time you got the hint?"

Jack laughed. "Yeah, I actually got the hint months ago, but my dad has his ways of making me over analyze things."

They walked over by the Fantasyland Theater where the Beauty and the Beast Live on Stage show was in progress. They stopped and watched from the outside for a few minutes as they finished their Main Street corn dogs. Jack gazed into the theater listening to the music.

"Do you want to go in and get a seat?" Kendall asked with a smile on his face as he nudged Jack.

Jack snapped out of it and kept walking. "I don't know Kendall, there's something about her, I really think she could be the one."

Kendall laughed, "Yeah but I don't think she feels the same way about you."

Jack was not amused.

"Look, Jack, I'm just giving you a hard time. If you think she is the one, then your dad is right, you need to fight for her. I just hate seeing you get all wrapped up with someone who might not want to be with you."

"This sounds like an episode of *Days of Our Lives*, Kendall."

"Yeah, it does, but that's your fault, you need to snap out of this funk you're in, buddy."

Jack's phone rang, it was Melissa White.

"Oh boy," Jack said sarcastically as he realized who it was. "Don't know if I should answer this or not." He paused for a second, and then decided to answer.

"Jack?" Melissa's voice was pleasing over the phone, but Jack knew she was bad news and untrustable.

"Hey Melissa, what's up?"

"Hey Jack, I'm at the Park right now and wanted to see if we could meet up?"

Jack paused, knowing his answer should be no. He looked at Kendall who was still partially making fun of him through his entertaining facial expressions.

"Sure, where do you want to meet?"

"How about Fantasyland?"

"I'll see you there."

"Well, that was quick, Jack." Kendall said.

Jack smirked at Kendall, and they walked towards Fantasyland.

Melissa looked similar to Kate, but not as pretty. She forced the issue by dressing provocative, and she lacked Kate's pure and natural beauty.

Melissa saw Jack and ran to give him a hug.

"Jack, it has been a long time!"

"Yes, it has."

"Hey Kendall!" She gave him a big hug too. "So what do you guys want to do?"

"Well, actually I need to meet my dad in a bit," said Jack.

"Maybe we can get something to eat?"

"I need to run, I'm meeting up with a few friends, it was good seeing you Melissa." Kendall said as he backed away.

She smiled at Kendall with a lingering gaze as he walked away. Jack always thought she had a thing for Kendall.

"Sure, let's eat."

"What if we eat here at the Village Haus and then hit the Skyway?"

Jack hesitated but agreed. They sat and ate as Melissa told him about what she'd been up to, talking about other guys, crazy things she'd done, and other nauseating details of her life.

"How long are you home for Jack?"

"Probably a week, unless we get a call."

"How about joining me on my parent's yacht this weekend in Newport?"

"Um, I don't know."

"Well, think about it, I guarantee you it will be a lot of fun!"

Jack half-heartedly smiled and sipped his drink. It didn't feel right being at the Park with her. They finished their meal and walked up the Fantasyland Skyway Station steps towards the loading area. The winding steps reminded him too much of Kate and the memorable times they had there. As they waited in line, Melissa leaned up against him and put her arm on his shoulder as if they were together. *Kate doesn't want to be with me anyway, I guess this is how things will be from now on. Shallow relationships with no attachments.*

He started to lighten up towards Melissa.

Jack glanced up to the other side of the station and saw his dad looking over paperwork with one of the leads. *Oh, great.* He didn't want his dad to see him with Melissa, so he looked down and avoided eye contact.

"Jack?" Stan snuck up behind them in typical stealth fashion.

"Oh, hey Dad," Stan was the last person Jack wanted to see right now.

"Hello Melissa, how've you been?"

"Oh I've been great Mr. Duncan, how about you?"

Stan looked into Jack's eyes, and Jack kept looking away. Jack knew what his dad was thinking, Stan spoke to him with his eyes—*don't you remember the talk we had Jack*?

All he could think about was how Stan loved to spoil his fun, and make him feel guilty about things.

"Jack after you're done, meet me at Fortune Red, there's something I want you to see." Stan flashed a deliberate look as Jack smirked back at him. "It was nice seeing you again Melissa."

Seeing his dad made him think about the conversation they had about "lesser treasure" and it hit him hard. He looked at Melissa from the side as she checked out other guys in line. He eyed the Skyway gondolas, and all he could think about was Kate's beautiful face. He glanced back at Melissa, and there was just something about her that turned him off—probably her lack of loyalty. He hated to admit when his dad was right, but this time he was dead on.

"Hey Melissa, I forgot, I need to take care of something on the other side of the Park, really quick. I'm sorry."

"Oh, okay Jack, are you coming back or—"

"Maybe…"

"Maybe?"

"Look, I'm sorry Melissa."

"No, it's okay, I get it Jack." Melissa's face turned from happy and playful, to mad and upset. She was accustomed to getting whatever she wanted, especially when it came to men. When things didn't go her way, her mood turned on a dime.

"I'll call you, okay?"

She just nodded at Jack with a disappointed look and recognized a guy she knew further ahead in line.

Jack walked down the cement stairs of the Fantasyland Skyway station, making a quick right, heading behind Big Thunder Mountain, which led him to the far end of the Rivers of America. His phone rang.

"Hey Jack, it's Dad, something came up, and I can't meet you over there, but I sure hope you're not on the Skyway right now."

"Dad, I don't know why I ever listen to you."

"You listen to me because you know I'm right."

"Ha! I don't know about that."

"I'm working on something special that I want you to see tomorrow. I just reserved a room for you at the Disneyland Hotel, check-in, get some sleep, and meet me at the Fantasyland Skyway station at sunrise."

"What are you working on?"

"I'll show you in the morning, don't be late."

Jack looked up at the buildings on Royal Street and tried to figure out what he was talking about. Relaxing for the rest of the day at the Park, knowing he had a room at the hotel, sounded like a good plan. He'd just returned from a brutal three-week mission in the Middle East that had drained him physically and mentally.

Jack walked by the French Market veranda, stopping to look at the exact table where Kate was when they first met. He remembered how stupefied he was when he saw her sitting there, how she talked like an angel, and looked spectacular. It was unlike anything he'd ever felt before.

I need to snap out of this and get back to reality, it's over, and I need to stop being a baby about it.

Jack ended up at the Disneyland Hotel a few hours later exhausted and depressed. He went to bed early.

He woke up early the next morning, jarred by a wake up call from the front desk. He was an early riser, but this last mission wiped him out, some nights they only got an hour of sleep, if that. He took the elevator down to the Disneyland Hotel lobby, and then stopped at the Monorail Cafe for a quick cup of coffee to go. This 50s style diner was one of his favorites. With a warm Styrofoam cup in hand, he crossed the street and walked through the Disneyland parking lot until he reached the front gate. It was closed since it was before 6 a.m. One of the security CMs recognized him and let him in the side gate.

Jack looked forward to walking through the Park in the morning when no one was there; everything was quiet and immaculate. The Main Street music played in the background, everything was peaceful and relaxing. It was still dark, but the sky was beginning to light up and turn blue as he strolled down the vacant Main Street, nodding at CMs who were getting the Park ready for guests. He walked straight for the Castle. The water around the Castle was like glass; everything still, no wind, the temperature was perfect, and the skies were clear. A beautiful sunrise was taking shape. As he passed through the Castle entrance, the inviting lights of King Arthur's Carrousel gleamed ahead of him—these lights always seemed to draw him into Fantasyland. It was an example of how Walt used tunnels to lure guests to different worlds.

Jack headed left towards Casey Jr. and the Skyway platform entrance. He climbed the winding stairs realizing no one was there, his dad was probably running late as usual. He reached the charming Swiss-style wooden station with fancy arches and decorative paintings on the outside. Rich wood covered the interior walls of the station that made it look like a Swiss mountain lodge.

Ornate wooden rails lined the platform. The station smelled of natural wood, and the tall trees surrounding it added a fresh mountain forest scent. This structure made you feel as if you were in the Swiss Alps. The gondolas were motionless along the cables while a few sat in the station.

He walked out on to the open edge where the gondolas entered and departed; it was a sheer drop-off from there. Jack looked down under his feet at the thick foliage, and beheld the brilliant view of the sun as it peeked over the horizon—the dazzling orange hue blended with the pale blue sky. The miniaturized landscaped green belts of Storybook Land came to life as they were painted with the sun's rays, the water in the canals glistened, the glossy polish of the Dumbo cars shined, and the Matterhorn blushed in the distance.

Maybe it's time that I retire and wake up here every day?

He sensed someone behind him.

He turned to find a glorious sight.

The sun accented her perfect features and made her thick and wavy blonde hair glow in the distance. Her blue eyes smoldered from the light of the sun, she slightly smiled, and her full lips and white teeth lit up her entire face. She walked towards Jack, and the gentle breeze drifting into the station tossed her hair like a supermodel. Jack walked towards her, slowly at first, then faster as they met in the middle. Jack lifted her off the ground with a huge hug.

It was Kate.

"How did you get here?"

"Jack, I've been stupid, I thought about what you said, and you're right. I can't stop thinking about you—I was made to be here, with you, not in New York pursuing an empty dream. You're what I've always wanted."

"Kate, I don't know what to say, I haven't been myself, and being here at Disneyland without you is empty, life without you is empty, I miss your smile, your eyes, and everything else about you."

As the sun rose further, it lit up the Fantasyland station. Jack and Kate gazed into each other's eyes as the incoming rays of sunlight poured in from their right. They kissed for the first time as the rich color of the sun created a storybook setting for two people who were made to be with each other.

They held hands and looked out over Walt's magnificent creation in awe of each other and the beauty of the Park at sunrise. The Casey Jr. trains glistened below; the enchanted Fantasyland buildings sparkled as the sun animated them in front of their eyes, and the colors of the large pine trees magically transformed.

Stan stood towards the back of the Fantasyland station with a big smile on his face. He was silent, and they didn't know he was there. He watched Jack and Kate from behind as they held hands and looked out over Fantasyland

and into Tomorrowland.

He pulled out an old wallet-sized picture of Genie from his chest pocket. He admired her beautiful face and smiled at her with a tear in his eye.

"Jack has found his true love, Genie," he whispered as he talked to the picture, "our boy has finally found 'the one' after all these years, sweetheart."

He quietly left the Fantasyland Station and journeyed down the enchanted stairs.

SEVENTEEN

August 8, 2010
Disneyland Security Control Center
Disneyland Park

Tony sat in a chair in Room Two of the Control Center, his door was locked from the outside, but he still had access to the device he snagged on the way into the room. He frantically tried to search the database that he'd hacked into.

BLAM

Jack blasted through the door with his chest bulging and body leaning forward.

"TONY." Jack yelled.

"Jack, I can explain."

"You directly disobeyed orders, you lied to Kim, and you are here with a device hacking into the CIA's database?"

"I know, but—"

"BUT WHAT TONY?" Jack slammed both of his hands on the table making a whopping crashing sound as the table jumped off the ground. He looked Tony dead in the eyes. "You look me in the eyes, Tony, and tell me that you're not involved with this."

Tony looked Jack directly in the eyes and confirmed, "Jack, I swear to you, I am not involved in this at all, I would never betray you."

Jack glared at him, shifting his eyes left to right, homing in on both of Tony's eyes. "I don't believe you."

Tony started to panic. "Jack, you have to believe me, there is no way I could be involved with this. Sure I screwed up and called my mom, but that was it."

"No, that wasn't it, you broke into a CIA database unauthorized. You've made several scrambled calls off property after I specifically ordered everyone to keep quiet." Jack grabbed Tony's arms and cuffed them behind the chair.

"You leave me no other choice Tony, you tell me the truth or I will force you to tell me—and you know I will not stop until I have the truth."

By the look on Tony's face, he knew Jack was not bluffing.

"Jack, no, please, you have to listen to me. I think there's a bigger plot here, something that everyone's missing."

"What are you talking about?"

"I think there's something more to this threat—more than just a bomb."

"That's it Tony, I am done talking, you're wasting my time." Jack rolled up his sleeves, and then suddenly—

WHOOOOSH—BANG

The entire room disintegrated as pieces of wood, insulation, drywall and other particles filled the air. A white cloud covered what was left of the foundation—pieces of the wall sliced through the room, thick splinters of wood turned into daggers, chunks of drywall and white dust filled the air.

The explosion launched Jack ten feet across the room, Tony landed face first on the ground after being blown out of his chair. Dust was everywhere as pieces of the rafters and steel plates dropped from the ceiling—everything went black.

Jack laid motionless—face first on the ground.

Tony squirmed in pain on the floor.

Screaming echoed throughout the Control Center.

Jack slowly lifted his head.

He figured the bomb must have been detonated—the entire Resort had probably been leveled.

He thought about Andy and Grace.

He tried to get up, but he couldn't.

His face hit the ground.

JACK DUNCAN

IS

THE DEADLIEST CAST MEMBER

SEASON ONE

EPISODE FOUR

ONE

1959
Fantasyland
Disneyland Park

Walt Disney stood at the bottom of the towering new Matterhorn Mountain, cocked his head back, and smiled as he looked towards the peak. The "snow capped" manmade mountain modeled after the famous landmark in the Swiss Alps looked magnificent against the deep blue California sky. Walt used forced perspective, the same concept he utilized to build Main Street, to give the attraction a larger than life appearance. The Matterhorn was the first tubular steel continuous track roller coaster in history, complete with glacier caverns and alpine grottos.

"Can you believe that we built this thing without shutting down the Skyway for a single day, Stan?"

Stan smiled at Walt's child-like excitement. He was like a little kid marveling at a backyard construction project. Stan's smile quickly faded because he didn't have good news for the boss.

"Walt," Stan said as Walt gazed into the sky with a big grin on his face, "I have some bad news. Khrushchev is extremely upset about what happened."

Walt lowered his head as he transitioned from a fantasy world, to the cold reality of the business side of things. "Well, we thought he would be Stan, this is no surprise."

"Yes, but it's worse than we thought. Spyros Skouras upset him today during a public appearance in LA and they got into an argument about capitalism. Khrushchev said Skouras' remarks were an attempt to heckle him during this trip. Then, his temper flared, and he said this about Disneyland," Stan handed Walt a piece of paper with the quote from the Soviet Premiere.

I would very much like to go and see Disneyland. But then, we cannot guarantee your security, they say. Then what must I do? Commit suicide? What is it? Is there an epidemic of cholera there or something? Or have gangsters taken hold of the place that can destroy me?

Walt looked up at Stan with his eyebrow raised. "Wow, he does sound pretty upset."

"Yes, apparently he took it extremely personal, and it even spurred talks about the arms race. Even worse, Nikolai Grusov just left a threatening message for me."

The concern on Walt's face grew as he listened. He knew this was not good for public relations, and potentially damaging to the fragile relationship between the two countries.

"Grusov confirmed Khrushchev's sentiments, and reiterated the fact that they would not soon forget this action. He said that he would retaliate against us in his own way."

"Oh, Stan, this is not good. Who is this Grusov? Why would he threaten us?"

"I'm not sure Walt, I'm trying to figure it out. Grusov is ex-NKVD/KGB and was active the same time I was with the OSS back in the 40s. He seems to know a lot about me."

"Okay, please do what you can. Call him back and smooth this over, we don't want problems with the Soviets, and we sure don't want this issue to escalate."

"Sure, Walt, I'm on it."

Walt walked towards Tomorrowland and Stan followed. "I'm making progress with the gold plates, Stan. However, I'm becoming suspicious that someone is watching me. I worry about the wrong people finding out about the tunnel, and what's down there."

"What if we move everything to another location?"

"No, that would be too dangerous, and nothing is more secure than what we built under the River. I can't put more money into creating another vault."

"Okay, I will increase security and watch for any suspicious activity."

"Thanks, Stan. Let me know how it goes with Grusov."

"Will do, Walt."

Stan headed back to his office to call Grusov as he racked his brain trying to figure out their connection. *Why was Grusov using this incident to make threats?*

He dialed Grusov, and he answered, "Mr. Duncan, I'm sure you've heard by now how our Premiere was disrespected on US soil." Grusov didn't waste any time getting to the point.

"Mr. Grusov—"

"Listen, Duncan, listen to me closely. I have more power than you know —I gave you a chance to make this right. To allow Khrushchev to visit your Park, and all you could do was threaten me."

"Yes, and I'm sorry about that," Stan said.

"Sorry is not good enough, Duncan. Khrushchev will not publicly say another word about this, but I'm going to make sure you and your boss pay for this."

"For what Grusov? We didn't approve the visit for security reasons—why would you threaten us for that?"

"There's much more to it than that, Duncan, and you know it. You hate our country and what we stand for—and your boss is a staunch anti-communist."

Stan was silent.

"If you think I don't know that your hate for us was part of your decision, then you're dumber than I thought," said Grusov.

Stan's blood pressure rose, and he struggled to maintain his composure. He knew he needed to find a way to smooth this over for Walt.

"Look, you're wrong about that Mr. Grusov, but let us make it up to you. On the Premier's next visit, we will make it right, and we'll be in a better position to protect him."

"There will not be a next time, Duncan. I've made it my personal mission to come after you and your park."

Stan raised his voice, "*Come after our Park*? Are you threatening to attack Disneyland? Are you kidding me?"

"This is not a threat, Duncan, this is a promise—I know more about your park than you think. Including the things you have hidden underground."

Stan's eyes widened, and his throat constricted.

"Oh, do I have your attention now? This has nothing to do with our government this is between me and you, my government would never approve or condone what I'm going to do."

"I still don't understand what this is all about, but I challenge you to come after me, you will lose—I will personally make sure of that. You have no idea what I am capable of."

"Oh, but I do, Duncan. I know exactly what you're capable of," Nikolai's voice cracked with anger—his Russian accent thickened. He glared at the picture of his son on his desk. "You don't remember, do you?"

"Remember what? I don't know what you're talking about."

"LET ME REFRESH YOUR MEMORY," Nikolai yelled as he slammed his fist on his desk, "in 1942, you interrogated a 19 year old NKVD agent, DO YOU REMEMBER THAT?"

"No, I don't remember most things that happened during that time, and you'd better lower your voice, Grusov."

"Think, Duncan, he was just a kid, 19 years old, and you tortured him, you knew you could easily manipulate him because he was a rookie agent, so you pushed him to the limit—until you pushed him too far—"

Stan's stomach dropped.

"Do you remember that young agent's last name?"

Stan was silent; his mind raced, and he couldn't speak.

"DO YOU DUNCAN? ANSWER ME. ANSWER ME NOW!"

The image of the young NKVD agent's face flashed through Stan's mind. At the time, there was an imminent threat on US soil—Stan had to extract information quickly from to stop the attack. He remembered the fear in the young man's face and the ID card that he identified him with. The last name of the agent hit Stan like a sledgehammer as it came to him. He put his hands on his forehead as sweat poured from his hairline.

"You killed my son Duncan, and you made him suffer. You will most certainly pay for this," there was a distant crackle on the line as the weight of his words sank in. "I have been watching you for a long time, and it's time for me to finally get my revenge."

Stan sunk into his chair. His head spun with a mixture of rage and regret. His chest tightened with pain, and it was hard to breathe.

Nikolai continued his tirade, "When my wife became ill, I watched her body deteriorate in front of my eyes, she was a beautiful woman, and her illness robbed her of everything she had. She never recovered from the death of our son, and depression ate away at her until she ceased to exist. As I held her shriveled hand on her deathbed, I could not believe how the loss of our son had killed her mentally and physically. We wept together, and I asked what I could do, how I could ease her pain. The last words she uttered, the thing she wanted more than her own life—was for me to avenge the death of our only son. The son that YOU took from us, Duncan."

Stan's eyes shifted side to side as he leaned over. Beads of sweat splattered on his mahogany desk.

"I will honor her wishes, if it's the last thing I do, I will give up everything to haunt you and your family for the rest of your life. It might take time, but I am a very patient man—I will wait for the right moment, and I will strike when you least expect it. I will devastate you, your family, and your despicable amusement park."

The line clicked, and the call disconnected.

TWO

August 8, 2010
Security Control Center
Disneyland Park

Thin rays of light pierced through the dusty darkness of the demolished Control Center. Thick white powder created a fog of debris that made it hurt to breathe. Jack's face was on the floor.

"Jack—" Kendall recognized Jack's body and ran to him. He put his hand on his back.

Jack tried to lift his head. His vision blurred, everything moved in slow motion, and his head felt like it was glued to the front of an Astro Orbiter rocket. He fought disorientation and focused on Andy and Grace.

"K-Kendall," Jack strained to speak.

"Jack are you okay? Can you feel the rest of your body?"

"*Andy and Grace—?*" these were the only words he could get out.

"They are fine. I called Kim, and they are unharmed."

"What happened?"

"Something ignited in the Control Center, it's the only building that was hit. We have several casualties."

Jack breathed a painful sigh of relief. He tried to force himself up, but he still couldn't get his bearings.

"Jack, you need to stay put, I'll get a medic over here."

"No, Kendall, I cannot just stay here, I'm okay, I need to find Nikolai, NOW."

"Okay tough guy, you can barely get up off the floor. You need to stay put for a minute so I can make sure you don't have a spinal cord injury."

Jack ignored Kendall's request and with all his strength pushed his way to his knees. He remained on all fours for a few moments and then used his arms to get to his feet. Kendall reluctantly held him from behind. Jack turned his wrist to get a glimpse of Andy and Grace on the live video feed. It was the best thing he'd seen all day—his sweet, unharmed children.

"Tony," Jack said to Kendall, grabbing at the sharp pain in back of his neck. "He said something to me before the blast went off about a bigger plot that he'd uncovered."

"Yeah, but do you trust him Jack?"

Jack was silent, "I don't know, I don't know who to trust right now."

"He's probably on the right track because that's what I've been saying. I think your best bet is to meet with Nikolai and figure out what he wants. If there truly is a massive tunnel network under the River, our chances of finding this bomb are slim. By forcing your way through those doors, you could be sealing everyone's fate."

Jack's head throbbed and pulsated with excruciating pain. He couldn't shake off the effects from the blast. His ears rang with agonizing pain.

"Also, with the Control Center down, the little coverage we had is gone. We're totally in the dark."

"We need to talk to Tony, and figure out what he discovered." Jack attempted to walk on his own so Kendall would stop coddling him.

"Tony is unconscious, Jack, and he doesn't look good."

"Someone is working with them on the inside, Kendall. They must have someone in upper management who gave them access to The System, and the Park. I don't trust that little punk Ruddy—where is he?"

"I don't know."

"Where is Conroy?"

"I saw him on the way in here—he's unconscious with serious injuries."

Jack dialed his dad's house again out of desperation.

No answer.

He switched over to Luke.

"Luke, I need you to get someone at my dad's house on the line for me."

"Jack? Are you okay? The explosion looks like it was limited to the Control Center."

"Yes, I'm fine."

"Standby, I'm calling your dad."

THREE

August 8, 2010
El Capitan Presidential Suite
Grand Californian Hotel

Kim stared through the sliding glass door attached to the El Capitan Suite's master bedroom. Her eyes bounced between the nighttime view of Condor Flats and her phone as she desperately tried to get more information about the explosion at the Control Center. She'd been mulling through the clues that Luke had sent her earlier, trying to help decode what Jack had found. But ever since she heard the news about the blast, she frantically tried to get information about what happened to Jack, and she didn't like keeping the kids out of the loop.

Sweat streamed down her forehead, and her hand shook as she obsessively manipulated her phone.

"Are you okay Kim?" Andy could tell she was on edge.

Kim flashed a smile at him, realizing that she was sending the wrong vibe to the kids with her erratic behavior.

"Oh yes, Andy, I'm just trying to get some information to help your dad."

"Hey Kim," Grace said cheerfully as she watched old Silly Symphony cartoons, "do you like my dad?"

Kim was caught off guard.

"Um, of course I do Grace, your dad is one of the most generous men I've ever met."

"No, I mean do you *like* him."

Kim blushed, realizing what Grace was hinting at. "Oh, Gracie, not in that way, your dad is my boss."

"Oh, because sometimes you look at him like you might like him."

"I do?"

"No, she doesn't Grace," Andy said.

"Stay out of this Andrew," Grace fired back as she turned to Kim, "sometimes I wish daddy would find someone, so he wouldn't be so lonely and mad all the time. But then, I think that I don't want him to find someone else because I don't want another mom—unless she was like you, Kim."

Kim gasped, surprised and deeply touched by what Grace said.

"Gracie—that is so nice of you to say," Kim said with an adoring smile as she knelt down and held her hand. Kim's device buzzed with incoming information. She squeezed Grace's small hand affectionately, and stood up to analyze the data.

"Where's Tony?" Andy asked.

Kim stuttered, not knowing how to explain the situation with Tony, "Oh, your dad called Tony into the Park because he needed him for something down there."

Kim knew that Tony must have been in the Control Center when the explosion ignited. She was sick to her stomach not knowing what his condition was.

"I have a bad feeling about this whole thing, Kim," said Grace, "my dad usually fixes things faster than this, and we haven't heard from him at all."

"Don't worry Grace, I'm going to try to get him on the phone right now."

Kim dialed Jack.

No answer. She dialed Luke.

Luke answered, and Kim headed for the master bathroom as she whispered, "Luke, is everything okay with Jack? What happened?"

"Kim, I can't talk right now, but there was an explosion, Jack is hurt, but I think he's okay."

"What about Tony?"

"I don't have an update on Tony, but he was unconscious after the initial blast."

Kim's heart sank. Her shoulders dropped as she leaned against the wall of the bathroom.

"Look Kim, I'll call you back."

"Wait, Luke," she continued in a low voice, "those clues you sent me, they all have to do with Stan, they have his prints all over them."

"Why do you think that?"

Kim spoke rapidly, "The golden spike, Kurt Russell, it's from their wedding—the Park bench, that's where Stan proposed to Genie, Fortune Red is based on the talk Stan had with Jack about Kate. Don't you see, it? Everything has to do with Stan."

"Okay, I need to regroup and figure this out from a different perspective. Thanks Kim, let me know if you find anything else."

Kim walked out of the bathroom, and she stopped to examine herself in the mirror. She knew that she needed to pull herself together for the kids.

"Well guys, your dad is still busy, but I'll keep trying him. In the meantime, what if I send someone into the Park to get you some churros and popcorn?"

Both of their faces lit up—they were missing out on a fun summer night in the Park, but at least they would get some of their favorite treats.

Grace looked up at Kim with her big blue eyes. "So, what about Tony? Do you like him?"

Kim smiled again and sat next to her, "You know, Tony is a—" she hesitated, "he's a really good man and I have a lot of respect for him. Out of anyone I know, I think I'm the closest to Tony in that way. So, yeah, I think I do like him."

Grace opened her mouth and put her hand over it as her deep blue eyes sparkled. She glanced over at Andy, who shook his head at her.

"That would be so cool if you two got married!" Grace squealed.

Kim gave her a courtesy smile that quickly faded. She squinted her eyes and took a deep breath, and she returned her gaze to the view of the Park from the glass door. She looked out at the towering redwood trees illuminated by well placed lights surrounding Grizzly River Run, and she wished this was a normal summer night at Disneyland.

FOUR

August 8, 2010
Disneyland Park

Jack's phone buzzed, it was Kurt Russell.

"Kurt, thank you for calling me back so soon."

"Of course, Jack," Kurt said with his instantly recognizable movie star voice.

"I can't go into details, but we are in a major crisis and I need your help. Do you remember my dad's wedding inside the Castle?"

"Sure, I mean I was young, but of course I remember the wedding. It was a spur of the moment thing, but definitely something I'll never forget."

"I found your picture in an underground basement here at the Park with a group of clues starting with the golden spike."

"What? What clues?"

"A range of things—everything from Lafitte, to Fortune Red, Fowler's Harbor, the Griffith Park bench, the crypt in front of the River, and 1764—that number is attached to everything."

"Wow Jack, I honestly don't have a clue what any of that means?"

"Why did Walt write your name down, of all people, in the last few days of his life?"

"I don't know Jack, that's always been a mystery to me. The image of that piece of paper is burned in my mind, but I honestly don't know why Walt would have mentioned me like that."

"What else was written on the paper?"

"Something about Ron Miller, the Way Down Cellar, and the CIA or something like that."

"Wasn't the Way Down Cellar a live action story for the weekly TV show?"

"I think so."

Jack quickly Googled it on his device and scanned the article.

"Wait, Way Down Cellar was a story about a few kids who lost their football and discovered an entrance to a secret tunnel. They followed it to a Haunted House."

Kurt was silent on the other end.

"Did Walt ever talk to you about playing a part in this show?" Jack asked.

"Not that I can remember, but Walt always liked me, I think. After my first movie, he put me under a 10-year contract, which was unheard of at the time. He often picked my brain about movie ideas. I think he was curious to find out what I thought about things from a kid's point of view."

"Did he ever mention Jean Lafitte to you?"

"He did mention Lafitte one time, it was strange because it was a few months before he died. He was telling me a story about these *gold plates.* I thought it was a movie pitch at the time, but when I thought about it years later, I think he was trying to teach me a lesson. He talked about how Lafitte hid treasure towards the end of his life, gold plates, and other things."

Kurt continued, "I was young at the time, so I really didn't understand what he meant. Several years later, Gore Verbinski approached me about the first Pirates movie they were making, and wanted my opinion of it. I remembered the talk I had with Walt and I told Verbinski what Walt said about Lafitte. He was pumped about it—since Lafitte was someone who inspired Walt to build the attraction, he was a legendary historical figure, and a major part of Disneyland history. I thought for sure they were going to include Lafitte in the movie, but they ended up not including him at all."

"Who shut the idea down?"

"I have no idea. Jack, what's wrong?"

"I'll tell you everything next time I see you, right now I'm running out of time."

"Hey Jack, one more thing," Kurt paused, "something that has always stuck with me was the last thing Walt said after that talk. He said that he'd made the *discovery of a lifetime* and that he didn't think he'd be around for much longer."

Jack paused to think, but he couldn't figure out what Walt was referring to.

"Thank you Kurt, I appreciate it."

"You got it Jack," the legendary actor disconnected the line.

"Luke, get Johnny Depp on the line for me."

"Sure, Jack."

Jack racked his brain. Walt was obviously referring to the tunnels when he wrote the *Way Down Cellar* reference. He was trying to tell Kurt something, but what?

"Jack I have Mr. Depp on the line for you—and I haven't been able to reach anyone at your dad's house—I'm getting worried about him."

"Okay, keep trying Luke."

"Jack! How's it going my friend?" Johnny's unmistakable voice came through Jack's earpiece.

"Johnny, I need your help. Why was Lafitte excluded from the Pirates franchise?"

"Jack, did you take my advice and find that underground tunnel?"

"You don't even know the half of it, Johnny."

"Ha!" Johnny's voice was distant and cutting out, "I think your dad put an end to it. He had the final call on everything since the movie was based on the attraction."

"Why did he stop it?"

"No clue, Jack. Probably for the same reason he stopped a lot of things. If it wasn't going to be done exactly the way that Walt would've wanted it, your dad put an end to it."

Jack paused to think.

"Jack?"

"Thanks Johnny, I need to call you back."

"Wait, Jack, I do remember something. Someone in upper management at the Park lobbied hard for the inclusion of Lafitte based on something that Kurt Russell had said. I vaguely remember seeing your dad at the Studios talking to Verbinski, it looked like they were arguing and it got pretty heated. Verbinski was frustrated with the whole thing."

"Gaur." Jack said softly.

"Who?"

"Never mind, thanks Johnny, you've been a big help, I appreciate it."

FIVE

August 8, 2010
Main Street, U.S.A.
Disneyland Park

Jack limped away from what was left of the Control Center. The security nerve center of the Disneyland Resort containing millions of dollars of state of the art equipment was no more.

"Jack!" Bill Gaur appeared out of the ashes. Gaur had been in senior management overseeing attractions since the 70s.

"When did you get here? Have you been here all day?"

"I'm off today. I'm here with my wife and kids. I saw Ruddy at the front gate, and he told me what happened."

"Okay, well we're kind of busy right now, make sure no one finds out about this, we need to keep this extremely quiet."

"I can help you figure out how to get inside those doors, Jack." Gaur said.

Jack stopped in his tracks.

"Remember," Gaur continued, "I'm the one who was in charge when Sotto tried to unify the attractions, and I spent a lot of my own time and money researching the Lafitte legend. Let me go with you to examine the clues you've found, I can help you put the pieces together."

Jack wanted nothing to do with Gaur. They never got along, and he kept his distance from him when he was at the Park. At this point, however, he didn't have a choice—he needed all the help he could get.

"Okay, come with us, but do you realize how much danger you're in?"

"Yes, Jack, but there's too much at stake, I need to help."

Ruddy emerged from the dust as they were getting ready to leave. Jack bolted in his direction.

"Where have you been?" Jack's eyes locked on Ruddy.

"I've been at the front gate."

Jack glared at him suspiciously.

"Are you trying to imply that I had something to do with this?" Ruddy said as he looked around at the decimated Control Center, "Really Jack? After the information I gave you today? I can't believe that you think I would be a part of a terrorist plot against the place I love."

Jack grabbed Ruddy's shirt under his neck and brought him close.

"Someone here is working against us, and I think it's you," Jack's piercing eyes surged deep into Ruddy's as if he was penetrating his soul.

"That's ridiculous. I've never liked you, Jack, but that doesn't automatically make me a part of a terrorist plot to destroy the Park." Ruddy's eyes bulged and his face was beet red.

Jack didn't know what to think, his whole body ached, and he was confused.

Ruddy took short breaths and was helpless in the grip of one of the most dangerous men alive.

"Look Jack," Gaur interrupted, "I was with Ruddy at the front gate when the bomb went off, he brought me up to speed in hopes that I could help. I don't think Brett would be involved in something like this."

Jack looked at Gaur and back at Ruddy, who was on his tippy-toes due to the stronghold Jack had on his shirt. Jack became aware of the death grip he had on Ruddy, and let him go. He looked back at Gaur.

"Okay, Gaur let's go, we've got work to do."

Jack entered the Park through the Cast Member entrance near the Opera House in Town Square, and Gaur followed close behind heading for Main Street.

Jack brought him up to speed as they walked, "The park bench, the golden spike, Lafitte, a secret attraction under Pirates, a secret door by the Haunted Mansion, and 1764 is everywhere—what do you make of all that?"

"A secret attraction?"

"Yes, under Pirates—Lafitte's Blacksmith Shop."

Gaur stopped in front of the Magic Shop on Main Street's red-colored brick sidewalk.

"Jack, I'm almost certain the only ones who knew about this tunnel were Walt and your dad. Your dad must be the one who orchestrated these clues. We have to examine them through his eyes because they were probably meant for you. There has to be a device that unlocks those doors, and it's based on something inside your dad's head."

Luke's voice shot through Jack's earpiece, "Jack, Kim has been analyzing the clues, and she thinks they have to do with your mom and dad's wedding inside the Park."

"Their wedding?"

"Yes, Kurt Russell and the golden spike are both related to their wedding. Your dad proposed to your mom on the park bench, and Fortune Red was the basis for the talk he had with you about Kate."

"Okay, but none of this tells me how to get inside these doors?"

"I know, I'm still working on it," Luke said.

Jack focused in on Gaur.

"Why did my dad kill Sotto's unification plan in the 80s?"

"I'm not sure Jack, your dad put a stop to a lot of things, and he rarely gave reasons for them—he didn't have to."

Jack analyzed every word that came out of Gaur's mouth as he looked him square in the eyes.

"Look Jack, obviously your dad wanted to leave a way for you to gain access to these tunnels if something happened to him. Take me down there so I can help you figure this out."

Gaur was a smooth talker, which irritated Jack.

"He also might have wanted this secret to die with him." Jack said.

They continued to walk towards Pirates of the Caribbean.

Jack's phone buzzed from a blocked number.

"Jack," Nikolai's voice came through his earpiece. "Meet me at Lafitte's Blacksmith shop in one hour."

The call disconnected.

SIX

1994
Rivers of America
Disneyland Park

Stan, Jack, and Kendall stood on the top deck of the Mark Twain Riverboat as it gently pushed through the dark waters of the Rivers of America, sailing around Tom Sawyer Island.

Stan had a satisfying grin on his face as he took a deep breath and admired the mature trees on the Island. He believed the air was cleaner in this area due to the multitude of mature trees. "You know, a few days before the Park opened, Walt and Lilly had their 30th Anniversary on this boat. I remember it like it was yesterday. Walt was so stressed out getting the Park ready for the opening, he wasn't even sleeping, but he still wanted to give Lillian a memorable day on the boat. He invited 300 people, and we raced to get everything ready."

Jack and Kendall smiled at Stan as he reminisced. Listening to his stories about Walt never got old.

Stan chuckled as he put his hands on the railing of the Mark Twain.

"Admiral Fowler and I were doing everything we could to get the boat ready. I remember I was doing a final security check and I found Lillian sweeping the deck. I took the broom from her and told her that she didn't have to do that, but she grabbed it back from me and told me she wanted to help. Walt and Lillian were ordinary folks, they didn't view themselves as CEO's too big to associate with the underlings. They both pitched in to help wherever they could, no matter how famous or powerful they became."

"We really owe so much to them," Kendall said with a smile, "what a childhood we had! I can still remember running all day long through the caves on the Island with Jack. We got to play here every day in the summer. It was like an adventure that never ended."

"I seem to recall you bailing Jack out of all kinds of different situations," Stan said to Kendall. He grabbed Jack's muscular arm, "you were skinny as a rail back then, not an ounce of muscle on you. If you didn't have Kendall watching over you, I don't know if you would've made it."

Jack smiled and looked up at Kendall, "You were a giant even as a kid."

They laughed.

"Well, it's a good thing you followed him into The Teams, Kendall because Jack wouldn't be here if it wasn't for you." Stan put his arm on Kendall's lower back. Stan was shorter and hunched over in his old age. He looked like a dwarf next to Kendall.

"I was at the right place at the right time, sir, Jack would have done the same thing for me. You both have treated me like family since day one, and I've always appreciated that."

"You aren't *like* family," Stan said, "you *are* family, Son."

"Thank you, sir." Kendall said with an appreciative grin.

"Hey Dad," Jack turned to Stan, "did I ever tell you about the time when Kendall got beat up by a girl?"

Stan smiled, "No?"

"We always went to Circle Vision 360 when we needed a break from the sun—at least once a day to see the show. We spun around in circles, and it would make us dizzy—although that show made you dizzy no matter what."

Stan shook his head wondering what kind of trouble they got into while running around the Park unsupervised. There were probably so many things that he'd never heard about.

"You two are lucky the CMs have always loved you and treated you like family; otherwise you would've been banned from the Park," Stan said.

Kendall laughed in agreement.

"So we were watching American Journey's, I think," Jack said, "and I spun into this lady. She went from zero to furious in two-seconds and started screaming at the top of her lungs. I said I was sorry and tried to walk away when she grabbed my arm. Then, Kendall stepped in and said 'ma'am I'm sorry about my friend, he won't do it again, can you please let go of his arm?'"

Kendall smiled remembering how the story ended.

"The lady looked at Kendall while she still had a death grip on my arm, and she started yelling at him. She was out of control, and I was in shock—I couldn't move. So Kendall, who sounded like a cop even though he was only around eleven at the time, says 'ma'am I'm only going to ask you one more time, please release my friend's arm, you're hurting him.'"

"And I think I said, 'because he's small,'" Kendall added as he laughed.

"I think the lady thought Kendall was a lot older, because of his size. She reared back and hit him in the head with her purse with everything she had—she totally knocked him off his feet. Then she proceeded to yell at him, saying he threatened her. Everyone scattered and left the theater."

Kendall chuckled, and Stan looked shocked.

"I went to check on Kendall and he was on the ground staring at the ceiling. He was out of it, but he still said the same thing that he'd always say after he did something crazy,"

'*That was quite a ride, Jack.*'

Stan burst into laughter and Kendall followed.

"There are probably a lot of stories like that, where you stuck your neck out for Jack. You're a good man, Kendall, and I'm glad to have you as part of the family."

Kendall put his hand on Stan's shoulder and smiled.

"Walt was the same way with me," Stan continued, "in his own way. He was fiercely loyal to the people who were loyal to him—and he would go to bat for you against all odds. Walt and Lillian had a unique relationship. Lilly didn't always agree with or like the hours that Walt put into all of his endeavors, but she stuck with him no matter what to the end, and she was loyal to him. That's how your mom was with me; she would fight for me with everything she had. Life is grand when you have a loyal soul mate."

"Well, Dad, that's actually what I wanted to talk to you about, it's Kate—"

"Oh no, Jack, don't tell me you screwed things up with her again."

Jack paused and gave him a look, "No, Dad, contrary to what you might think, I don't screw up every relationship I'm in."

Kendall squinted his eyes and gave Jack a look that said, *are you sure about that?*

"Okay, whatever you two, look—ever since she was a little girl, Kate has dreamed of being proposed to on the Mark Twain."

Stan cut him off, "Wait—you're going to propose to her?"

Jack looked at Kendall, who grinned, and then back at Stan.

"Yes, Dad, she's the one, I'm going to marry her."

"That's wonderful, Son! I'm *so* proud of you!" Stan hugged Jack.

"So, Dad, I need your help, can you arrange something so I can make this happen for her?"

"Son, you have come to the right person, I can make almost anything happen in this place," Stan smiled as he squeezed Jack's arms.

Kendall and Jack chuckled, knowing that if Stan decided to resurrect the old Chicken of the Sea Pirate Ship, and drop it in the middle of the Rivers of America, Imagineering wouldn't challenge him for a second.

"I have the PERFECT thing for you, Jack," Stan said with a mischievous grin on his face, "I need a few days to make it happen, but this will blow her mind."

Jack smiled, knowing that Stan learned the art of showmanship from Walt, and had a knack for planning events.

"Okay Dad, but nothing crazy, just something simple, romantic, and memorable."

"Okay Jack, but all of the CMs at the Park have watched you grow up, they love you, and they're family. I want to invite as many of them as possible, past and present so they can be a part of this."

"Okay, Dad," Jack said hesitantly.

"You know, our wedding here was so special. It was right in the middle of the Castle entrance, on the golden spike. That circle in the ground represented our never ending love for each other," Stan got emotional as he looked into Jack's eyes. "Your mom would have loved to see you propose, Jackie." Stan's eyes welled up with tears.

"I know, Dad." Jack put his hand on Stan's shoulder and then moved in to hug him.

"I'm happy for you, brother." Kendall gave Jack a giant bear hug as the Mark Twain slowly pulled back into port.

SEVEN DAYS LATER

Anxious guests lined the Rivers of America, some who had waited hours to get a good spot for *Fantasmic!* The jazz band cruised around the River on a wooden Tom Sawyer Island barge creating a festive mood throughout New Orleans Square.

Jack told Kate tonight was a special occasion, so she wore Jack's favorite pink dress. Her deep blue eyes and her perfect smile reinforced what Jack already knew—Kate was beyond beautiful.

As Jack walked through the River esplanade, he noticed several off duty CMs, and they stopped him to say hello. This happened a lot when they were at the Park, so Kate was accustomed to it, but tonight there were an unusual amount of people approaching Jack.

Kendall appeared as they walked towards Cafe Orleans. "Well, hello there Kate, you look stunning tonight."

"Thank you Kendall," Kate said as she shook his hand, "why are you all dressed up?"

"I'm going to escort you to your seats," Kendall paused, "you will be watching the show from the balcony of Club 33."

Kate's face lit up with her mouth open as she turned to Jack.

"I'll be up there in a minute Kate," Jack said as he pulled Kendall aside, "hey, have you seen my dad?"

"Not yet, but he should be here shortly."

"Okay, because I have a sinking feeling about this, I don't know what he has planned, and you know how he can go overboard with things like this."

"Overboard is an understatement, my friend," Kendall smiled as he took Kate's arm.

Jack looked around for his dad as more CMs approached. He was second-guessing his decision to ask his dad for help. After talking to a few CMs he'd known since he was five years old, he headed down Royal Street and made a sharp right where Disney artists were drawing caricatures of guests. He opened the door behind them and headed up the stairs to the Club 33 dining room. On his way to the balcony, he looked up and froze.

"Mr. Eisner?"

"Jack!" The CEO of the Walt Disney Company stood up from his table to greet Jack with a big hug.

With each passing second, it became apparent that the biggest moment of his life was going to be blown entirely out of proportion.

"I wouldn't have missed your big night for anything," Michael Eisner said in his distinctive New York accent.

"Well, thank you sir, I appreciate that."

"So where is she? I want to meet her!"

"I think she might be on the balcony already," Jack walked Eisner out to the balcony where Kate was standing, her well-manicured hands rested lightly on the railings.

"Is this the lovely Kate that Stan can't stop talking about?" Eisner said as she turned around.

"Mr. Eisner?" Kate looked shocked as she extended her hand.

"Wow, you're even prettier than what Stan had described!"

Kate blushed and looked at Jack, smiling. "Thank you Mr. Eisner, it's an honor to meet you."

"Well, I'm going to leave you two alone so you can have a nice *quiet* night together on the balcony." Eisner winked at Jack, confirming his suspicion that Stan had something crazy planned.

"This is amazing, Jack," Kate said enthusiastically, "thank you so much for doing this. I've loved this Park since I was a kid, I have always been fascinated with Walt, and I'm so lucky to have met someone like you who shares this same passion."

"I'm the lucky one Kate—and you look amazing tonight."

"Hello Mr. Duncan," a Club 33 CM greeted them on the balcony, "we are setting up a special table for you tonight on the balcony."

Jack nodded and smiled at Kate. Looking over the railing, Jack saw his dad frantically walking down Royal Street towards the Club.

"Kate, I'll be right back." Jack headed down the stairs to meet his dad at the door since he knew he would use the same, little-known Club 33 access, across the way from the normal entrance.

"Dad?" Jack squinted his eyes at him suspiciously as he met him at the door.

Stan was caught off guard, "Hey Jack, you look great, Son!"

"Dad, what exactly do you have planned here? I'm hoping this is a quiet evening for us on the balcony, and not one of your extravagant, over-done events."

"Um, Jack, don't worry son, she'll love it. Just trust me—romantic and memorable, just like you wanted."

"And simple—remember that one, Dad?"

"She's going to love it, Jack!"

"Kendall knows about what you have planned, doesn't he?"

"Maybe—look, stop asking so many questions, I may be an old man, but I can still take you down." Stan smiled as he blew past Jack up the stairs.

"Michael!" Stan said as he approached Eisner in the dining room of Club 33.

"Stan, it's great to see you!" Eisner hugged him.

"Thank you for coming, it really means a lot."

"No problem, Stan, I wouldn't miss it for the world."

Jack smiled and walked out to the balcony where Kate was sitting at the small table, with a white tablecloth, flowers, two plates, and lavish settings.

Jack sat down at the table with a worried look on his face, "Kate, I have something very special planned for you tonight, but I have to warn you in advance, I left some of the planning up to my dad so it might get out of hand."

Kate put her hand on top of Jack's on the table, "Don't worry Jack, your dad is a gem, and he means well, don't be too hard on him."

Jack smiled, but he still didn't have a good feeling about it. He didn't like surprises.

"I'm so excited to see Fantasmic tonight!" Kate said with a big smile as she leaned over to smell the flowers on the table. Jack looked Kate in the eyes and held her hand as the head chef of Club 33 walked out on to the balcony.

"Good evening! Tonight, I have something unique planned for you that I think you will like. We are going to start with a five course meal based on your personal favorites."

Kate's eyes lit up, smiling at the head chef and Jack.

They savored the gourmet meal as they soaked up the ambiance of New Orleans Square from the Club 33 balcony. After the five-star dessert was served, the lights dimmed on the Rivers of America.

The sound of an orchestra holding one grandiose note echoed throughout the entire Land. The multitude of powerful speakers placed throughout New Orleans Square allowed guests to feel the strength of the music. The crowd applauded, floodlights pointed to the sky, and Mickey Mouse appeared on stage. Michael Eisner and his guests made their way to the balcony along with Stan and Kendall.

"Can you believe this show, Jack?" Eisner said.

"It's very impressive, sir." Jack's noticed how dry his mouth was. His mind envisioned the worse case scenario.

"This show is mind boggling, Mr. Eisner, the way the River is utilized is brilliant, and undoubtedly one of the greatest Disney shows I've ever seen."

"Well, thank you Kate, I'm glad you like it," Eisner smiled as he leaned over to whisper to Jack, "you've got a great woman here Jack, I definitely approve!"

Jack grinned as Eisner put his hand on his shoulder.

Mickey Mouse, from his stage at the front of Tom Sawyer Island, conducted inspiring music, made the water dance, and caused fireworks launch into the sky. He raised his arms, and water fanned out from the River in full color. Mickey invited the audience into his imagination as images from *Fantasia* magically appeared on the huge screens of misting water. Dancing monkeys appeared with a large alligator in the background, then Pinocchio, and after that, the Sailing Ship Columbia appeared with a lively scene featuring a boat full of pirates. Captain Hook and Peter Pan clanked swords as they fought throughout the ship.

Belle and the Beast appeared on a barge decorated with colored lights in the shape of a rose. Candles lined the edge of the floating stage.

"This is my favorite part of the show," Kate whispered in Jack's ear with a big smile.

Stan was happy to see Jack and Kate together. He kept a vigilant eye on his wristwatch. He leaned over to Kendall to get him ready for action, "Okay after this we need to escort them down to the River."

As the theme song from *Beauty and the Beast* continued to play, Ariel and Prince Eric appeared on their barge, dancing to the music. Snow White and Prince Charming also appeared while "Some Day My Prince Will Come" resonated throughout New Orleans Square.

Kate admired the beauty of the royals dancing on their magic stages. She focused on Belle who was wearing her gorgeous yellow dress as she danced in step with the Beast.

"Okay guys," Stan said anxiously to Jack and Kate, "follow me."

Jack's eyebrow rose as he looked at Kate. Kendall and Stan escorted them down the stairs and into the dimly lit New Orleans Square. Stan walked them towards the far right of the River past the Mark Twain loading dock where a few Cast Members stood waiting for them.

When they arrived, Jack figured out what was going on. He leaned into his dad and whispered softly so Kate wouldn't hear. "Dad, please tell me this isn't what I think it is."

Stan ignored him and introduced Jack and Kate to the CM tasked with getting them to the proper location on the Mark Twain.

"Mr. Duncan, come with me."

"Jack, what exactly are we doing?" Kate asked as the booming music from *Fantasmic!* continued to resound throughout the entire Land.

"I'm not sure Kate," Jack said as he held her hand; guiding her through the darkness.

The CM shuttled them on to the boat where they saw Disney characters on board preparing for the big finale. The CM led them upstairs to the top.

"Mr. Duncan, can I talk to you quickly?"

Jack moved closer to the CM as Kate waved to the nearby characters. She was clearly enjoying the backstage view of the show.

"Okay, so this is what we have setup for you," the CM said to Jack, "during the finale as the boat moves to center stage, you and Kate will be front and center here at the top."

Jack's suspicions were correct; his dad had orchestrated an event of epic proportions. Stan and Kendall stood behind them as if they were blocking Jack from making an exit. At this point, Jack had no choice, he had to go on with it. The CM gave Jack and Kate wireless microphones and pinned them to their shirts.

On the Island, Mickey appeared again as large flames hovered on the surface of water coming from the fire breathing jaws of the 45-foot animatronic dragon, otherwise known as Maleficent. To regular park goers, she was known as "Murphy" because of her recurring mechanical blunders. Mickey exercised his powers for good as he attacked Maleficent in a dazzling animated segment projected on the water screens. The villain was dismantled with a final pyrotechnic explosion as the music climaxed.

The entire area was quiet and black as thousands of people watched Tinkerbell dance across the magical water screens, ushering in the main theme song for the finale. Large spinning sparklers lit up the Mark Twain as it moved towards center stage.

Kate squeezed Jack's hand.

"Jack?"

"Just hold tight, it'll be over before you know it, and hopefully you'll still want to talk to me after this."

As the Mark Twain neared the center of the Rivers of America, the theme song escalated. An explosion erupted from the platform where Mickey, who now appeared as Steamboat Willie, was standing. The boat and the River were illuminated. Kate and Jack were below and in front of Steamboat Willie's platform, near the front rail. A spotlight made them visible to the multitudes below.

Kate remained composed looking to her left at the large sea of spectators. People from the audience noticed Jack and Kate on the boat, and they pointed with excitement.

A large number of Disney characters uniformly danced around the boat carrying sashes that they whipped in unison as the final song rang out.

Jack looked to the left as the water screens emerged from the River. The crowd went crazy when they saw Jack and Kate projected on the water screens throughout the River. Camera flashes popped throughout the crowd. It looked like a sporting event as everyone tried to capture this once in a lifetime moment.

No matter how uncomfortable Jack was, he knew he needed to get this done. He knelt to one knee as the volume level of the crowd increased. The *Fantasmic!* theme song raced towards its climax.

Kate cried as she put her hand to her mouth, the dream she'd kept in her heart as a little girl was coming true before her eyes.

"Kate, you are the love of my life, and I want to spend the rest of my life with you," Jack's voice rang out across the River, echoing throughout the entire Land. Kate giggled as she looked Jack in the eyes and then out into the crowd.

Jack paused.

"Will you marry me?"

The crowd came unglued.

The Mark Twain was center stage. The image of Jack and Kate on the water screens was larger than life, the music was in full swing, and the crowd was going wild.

After several seconds, the crowd fell silent, patiently awaiting Kate's response. Large sparklers lit up the background as the characters danced to the music.

Kate paused, tried to talk, but she was crying. She lowered her hand from her mouth and said, "YES!"

The crowd exploded. New Orleans Square sounded like The Great Western Forum at a Lakers playoff game. The camera maintained its focus on Jack and Kate so everyone could see them as the boat moved out of sight. Kate hugged Jack and the crowd continued to cheer. The water screens remained extended as explosions ignited in the background while large walls of fire lit up the River.

Mickey, now appearing as Sorcerer Mickey, materialized at the top of Lafitte's Tavern as he conducted laser beams while launching fireworks into the air. The fireworks finale ensued behind the water screens. Everyone could still see Jack and Kate's image on the screens as they hugged at the top of the Mark Twain. Mickey reappeared center stage again as the music peaked.

"Some imagination, huh?" Mickey recited his final line.

He disappeared with a flash and a bang as searchlights beamed throughout the area; the crowd continued to roar as they watched Jack and Kate on the screens. The orchestra hit the final note as the lights went black, but the screens remained. The CMs and guests in the audience let out the largest standing ovation for *Fantasmic!* in the short history of the show.

The screens went black.

Stan and Kendall hugged each other, both with tears in their eyes. Several CMs in the crowd who'd seen Jack mature from a scrawny little kid to an American war hero cried and hugged each other.

Michael Eisner wiped a tear from his eye, putting his arm around his wife as they watched from the balcony of Club 33.

Stan looked at Kendall and said, "Well, two out of three ain't bad, Kendall."

"Sir?"

"Jack wanted simple, romantic, and memorable—but I don't do simple."

Kendall let out a hearty laugh as they marveled at the standing ovation from the crowd below.

SEVEN

August 8, 2010
Pirate Wax Museum
Disneyland Park

Jack led Gaur through New Orleans Square, en route to Lafitte's Blacksmith Shop with Kendall following close behind. Jack stopped abruptly before going through the back entrance of Pirates of the Caribbean.

"Look, I'm going to be upfront with you Bill, I don't like you, I've *never* liked you—and I don't trust you—even now. If you try to mislead me in anyway, I will come after you and I will find you, and you will regret it for the rest of your life. Are we clear?"

Gaur cowered—leaning back as he distanced himself from Jack's verbal assault.

"Jack—I'm not the enemy here. You have to come to that realization, or we aren't going to get anywhere. We're running out of time."

Jack continued towards the exit of Pirates as Gaur followed.

Jack whispered to Kendall, "Check on Tony, I want to know the minute he regains consciousness."

"You got it."

Jack took a shortcut down the final Pirates of the Caribbean ramp to get to the Blacksmith Shop hatch. "Why would my dad neglect to tell me about the tunnel system, for all these years, and then leave clues to show me how to find it?"

"Not sure Jack. Your dad and Walt allegedly worked on a lot of top-secret projects together. Towards the end of Walt's life, your dad was the only one he confided in."

As they lowered into the Pirate Wax Museum, Gaur's mouth dropped in utter disbelief, and he couldn't believe his eyes.

"How could all of this be down here, for all these years, without anyone knowing about it?" Gaur asked.

"People did know about it—Nikolai knew about this place, and the tunnel."

Jack marched Gaur to the large metal doors with Kendall close behind.

"Nikolai is in here, along with the bomb," Jack said pointing to the door, "if I can get in here, I can save the Park."

Gaur ran his hand over the embossed symbols on the door, "What about this circle, Jack? It looks like it could be an unlocking mechanism?"

"We've tried everything and nothing has worked."

Gaur looked to the left, and his eyes almost popped out of his head. "Is that the Blacksmith Shop?"

Jack was in no mood to give tours, "I have reason to believe that the tunnel network is extensive, so when we get in, we might not have a clear path to the bomb."

Kendall put his mighty paw on Jack's shoulder, "Can I talk to you for a minute?"

Jack acknowledged Kendall and backed away from the door.

Kendall kept his eye on Gaur, who was examining the embossed markings, and whispered to Jack. "You have less than an hour before you meet with Nikolai, why not just meet with him and see what he wants. How's this guy going to solve this puzzle?"

"Jack," Gaur called from the door, "it's the circle, there's a key that is shaped like this that unlocks the door. The circle is the unlocking mechanism."

Jack moved towards Gaur, "How do you know that?"

"I don't know for sure, but Walt never used a circle in conjunction with his trademark D. I remember your dad using a similar unlocking mechanism in a project years ago."

Kendall pressed his finger to his ear to hear a transmission from the Team Six leader on the Island, "Jack," Kendall relayed the message, "Team Six discovered a hatch on the Island that appears to lead underground. We need to go."

Jack didn't say a word and bolted towards the exit.

EIGHT

1959
Submarine Lagoon
Disneyland Park

Walt Disney stopped in front of his brand new Submarine Lagoon and admired the mysterious depths of the legendary Seven Seas. The crystal clear water magnified the vivid colors. Hundreds of deep sea fish, sunken treasures, the lost continent of Atlantis, the graveyard of lost ships, 60-foot sea serpents, and the North polar ice cap, all resided within the impressive lagoon.

A group of sponsors crowded Walt, listening to the mastermind behind the most successful theme park in history describe his most recent creation. Representatives from Bank of America, Kodak, Carnation, Frito-Lay, Sunkist, Wurlitzer, C&H, United Airlines, and others were lucky enough to get a rare private tour from Walt himself. They could hear the excitement in his voice.

Stan followed with his hands in his pockets, nervous, hoping the tour was coming to an end so he could tell Walt about the Grusov threat.

Walt directed the attention of the sponsors to the half-submerged military-gray submarines in the sparkling lagoon.

"This, gentlemen is the largest peacetime fleet of submarines in the world," Walt said as he proudly gestured towards the real working subs that cost $80,000 each to build.

"We named them after the submarines in the nuclear program; The George Washington, Seawolf, Ethan Allen, Patrick Henry, Nautilus, Triton, Skipjack, and Skate."

The man from Frito-Lay raised his hand, "I like the real life mermaids you put in the lagoon, Walt."

The small crowd chuckled, and Walt smiled.

"These beautiful girls actually swim in the lagoon, and they can be seen from inside the submarines. They also lounge about on the rocks during the day."

"You always think of everything, Walt."

The man from United Airlines spoke up, "Walt, speaking of submarines and the nuclear program, this thing with Khrushchev hasn't given us the best publicity."

Walt's smile dissipated, and he briefly glanced at Stan.

"I know Roger, but we're trying our best to make the situation right." Walt smiled, put his hands together, and changed the subject. "Well, I think that will do it for today boys, have fun in the Park with your families, and I'll see you soon. I've got something in the works that you'll be extremely excited about—it's called Club 33 and I'll tell you more about it next time!"

Walt was a master at leaving people wanting more—always talking about the next big thing.

"Walt," Stan approached as Walt shook hands with a few of the remaining sponsors, "I need to talk to you."

Walt picked up on Stan's distressed look. He smiled at the lingering men, put his arm on Stan's shoulder, and headed the opposite direction towards Fantasyland and the Matterhorn.

"We have a problem," Stan said in a low voice, "I just received a credible threat from Nikolai Grusov, and it's quite disturbing."

Walt inched closer to Stan.

"I figured out why he hates me so much. Apparently it goes back to my days with the OSS. I interrogated a young NKVD agent in an attempt to prevent an imminent attack. It didn't go well, and the young man died." Stan gulped, tilted his head down slightly, and looked Walt in the eyes. "I found out today that he was Nikolai's son."

Walt squinted his eyes nervously.

"He's held a grudge against me for all these years, he said he wants to destroy the Park to get his revenge—and there's something else, Walt."

Walt raised his eyebrow and opened his mouth to say 'what' but he stopped to let Stan deliver the disturbing news.

"He knows about the tunnel."

Walt's face turned white, his mouth dropped, and he blinked rapidly.

"Stan, this is not good, no one can find out what is down there, especially him, we need to do something—maybe we should move everything now?"

"I don't think moving things is a good idea, there's too much to transport, and Nikolai will know what we're doing. We have too many employees here now, and there are a lot of guests here on a daily basis."

Walt paused and stroked his chin, "Okay you're right, but what should we do? How do we prevent an attack and protect what's underground?"

"I have a plan Walt, it will boost our security significantly, and it will safeguard your secret projects."

"I'm listening."

"It's complicated—and it will cost a lot of money—but I want to build a system using all available technology. This system will keep the Park safe from threats. It will be fully integrated unlike anyone has ever seen, everything from state of the art facial recognition, to the ability to cross reference relevant government databases. I want to develop an undercover team that blends in with guests. They'll walk the Park undetected, and prevent threats before they happen. This team will need to be five times the size of our uniformed security personnel."

"Okay, this will be a tough sell to Roy and the investors, but I agree. We need something like this to ensure the long term safety of our guests."

"Also, we need to build a solid defense system around the underground tunnels. We need to seal them so that no one else can get in there. I will create an intricate locking mechanism and gateway that will prevent all unauthorized access to the tunnels."

"Yes, that's extremely important, Stan."

"We have a credible threat right now," Stan said, "I think if we explain the threat to them it will demonstrate the urgency of putting a system like this into place. Disneyland will become a bigger target as time goes on, and we need to implement a strong security system to ensure our guest's safety."

"Okay, I'll get on it," Walt said, "we need to get this system in the works because I want people to feel like they are safe when they walk through those gates, I want them to forget their everyday worries and fears."

Walt looked around and started to walk with Stan to prevent anyone from overhearing them.

"I've made more progress with the gold plates I was telling you about," Walt said.

"Oh?"

"Yes, I'm obsessed with them, I've been trying to crack the code every night, and I found something intriguing that has to do with Benjamin Franklin, and even further, back to the Liberty Matrix. I think the founders outlined the elements for the perfect city in these plates. One component is energy. The city would need to be energy independent. I think Franklin figured this out and somehow embedded instructions inside the plates that reveal how to develop a super-energy source."

Walt stopped in front of the Motorboat Cruise attraction, and they could smell the exhaust from the engines in the air. He looked both ways to make sure no one was near, and moved closer to Stan.

"I think he outlined how to create a safe, nuclear, form of energy that's capable of powering large areas—similar to the size of what I have planned for EPCOT. But this source is far different from the nuclear energy that exists right now."

Stan looked shocked, and his mouth dropped.

"I can't figure this out on my own though, I need a few specialists in this area who can help me solve it. Do you have contact with any of your previous colleagues who can help me with something like this? I need someone we can trust. If this information—this code—gets in the wrong hands it could be devastating. But with the right scientific minds, we could change the world."

"Sure, Walt, I know a few people who would be perfect for this."

"Okay let's do it," pausing, he added, "and don't worry, I'll get Roy and the investors to spring for this new security system—oh, and another thing—"

Stan listened intently.

"Do you remember that short I did in 1953 called Ben and Me?"

"Yes, the mouse who inspired Benjamin Franklin and helped with the Declaration of Independence."

"Exactly, well, the fascinating thing is that I did some research on Robert Lawson, the inspiration for Ben and Me, and wouldn't you know it, he had a connection with the Lafittes. Jean, according to his memoirs and his great grandson, had an obsession with the Declaration of Independence and the founders, particularly Benjamin Franklin. I think Lafitte obtained the plates through his relationship with Andrew Jackson. Jean studied them relentlessly and tried to decrypt the message before he ditched them in the ocean. Because of this, I strongly believe there is a connection between the plates and Franklin—and it has to do with harnessing power so it can be used to benefit mankind. This type of energy could power entire cities, make us self-reliant, and it could be used to drive technology beyond anything anyone has ever seen."

Stan was flabbergasted at how Walt, with all of his daily responsibilities at the studio, Disneyland, and the company in general, had the time to focus on something of this magnitude. It was a testament to how effective Walt Disney was—he always looked to the future, trying to make things better for upcoming generations.

"Oh, and one more thing."

Stan listened even though he still hadn't caught up with Walt's previous mind-boggling concepts.

"If something happens to me, I need you to find the brightest technological mind on the planet to continue this research. I believe that by the 1980s, an innovator will appear on the scene and revolutionize technology. Over the next few decades, he will become one of the wealthiest men on the planet, and will have the power to innovate beyond all human comprehension. I need you to make him part of the team and continue my quest for the perfect city."

Walt pulled a wrinkled piece of paper out of his pocket and unfolded it, showing it to Stan.

"These plates aren't just a road map for an energy solution. They have the answer to something the founders might have used to form our country."

The sketch was hand drawn by Walt in his famous red oil pencil. It looked like a telescope of some kind.

"The forefathers of our country, the ones who came over on the Mayflower, lived in the early 1600s. The Declaration wasn't signed until 1776, and the Constitution was ratified about eleven years later. The founders somehow accessed the knowledge of the forefathers to form the most prosperous country on the planet. How was that information preserved during those times, when they had so many hardships, and limited technology? I believe they used something like this to do it."

Walt pointed to his drawing of the object that looked similar to a telescope.

"A telescope?" Stan was confused.

"No, I'm not sure exactly what it is, but it was probably invented by Franklin—I think it was a—" Walt paused, "something like a—" Walt hesitated again.

"Like what, Walt?" it wasn't normal for Walt to vacillate.

"I think it was a gateway or a…*portal* of some kind."

Stan's eyes widened. He thought that maybe Walt had gone too far—that he'd been spending too many late nights on this project.

"I know it sounds weird and impossible, and maybe it is—but I'm going to get to the bottom of this and figure it out."

NINE

August 8, 2010
Tom Sawyer Island
Disneyland Park

Jack and Kendall jumped into a black rubber SEAL boat docked next to the wooden Tom Sawyer Island raft. Bill Gaur followed, but Jack stopped him as he tried to board.

"We've got this from here Bill."

Kendall started the stealth motor, and they accelerated across the water to the Island, which was dark except for thin rays of lights poking through the trees from the search teams.

"Jack, we're probably going to see the same exact impenetrable metal door here," Kendall said.

Jack continued to glare at the Island. "I'm trying something different this time, I don't need a key," Jack pressed his earpiece, "Max, are you on the Island?"

"Yes, sir, I'm here and I'm preparing what you requested."

"Okay, patch me into the Fantasmic lead, I need to talk to him."

"Jack," Kendall looked surprised, "what's going on?"

Jack glanced at his friend and then back to the front of the Island where the SEALs were. "I'm not messing around anymore Kendall, I'm going to blow these doors off their hinges."

"Jack? Let's think this through for a minute."

"Kendall, we don't have time to think things through, we need to get inside this tunnel. It's our only chance."

"But Jack, how are you going to detonate something without everyone seeing it? The Team has already tried to blast the first set of doors you found. I thought you decided to wait for the meeting with Nikolai?"

"Do you really believe Nikolai, Kendall? We can't just sit around and put our lives in his hands. He's going to detonate that bomb no matter what I do. This is his final mission, his last chance for revenge. We need to act now, we need to be on offense—you should know that more than anyone."

"I know Jack, I but I also know that *you* want revenge more than anyone, and it's clouding your judgment."

"I NEED TO SAVE MY KIDS, KENDALL," Jack roared.

The boat stopped at the front of the Island.

Kendall backed down.

Jack realized he overreacted and shifted his attention back to the Island.

"I'm sorry Kendall, but you just have to trust me on this."

Jack and Kendall ran for the 15-foot basement at the front of the Island where Maleficent was stored. The SEALs were already down there with Max. A rectangle piece of concrete was standing on end at the bottom of the basement revealing stairs leading down into the darkness. As they climbed down the hatch, Kendall's eyes enlarged when he saw the massive explosive Max was mounting to the door.

Team Six leader walked up to Jack, "Sir if this doesn't open the door, nothing will. The only problem is the explosion will damage the entire basement, and it'll make a sound that will be heard throughout the Park."

"Okay, I've got that covered, just get it ready to blow on my command."

"Yes, sir."

A transmission came through Jack's earpiece; it was the lead CM in charge of the Fantasmic show. "Mr. Duncan, I have the pyrotechnics ready to commence on your command."

"Okay, I need the spotlight poles up for the finale, we're going to run that sequence to make it look like we're testing the end of the show. I need the water screens up as well."

"Yes, sir. I'm waiting for your orders."

Jack walked towards Kendall and studied the solid metal door, running his hand across the circle under the Disney "D".

"Okay, sir, it's ready." Max said.

"Okay, everyone out of here, I need some of the team to stay on the Island, a few at the entrance under Pirates, the Mansion, and the water pipe. If this works, we could have hostiles scrambling out of the other entrances, and we need to attack from all angles," Jack looked at Kendall, "get the CIA team and everyone else ready to roll."

Everyone moved on Jack's orders, clearing the underground tunnel. Max held the detonator in his hand as they moved to higher ground near the Lafitte's Tavern building on the Island.

Jack looked out at New Orleans Square and saw people leisurely strolling throughout the Land. He couldn't help thinking about what this area would look like in a matter of seconds if Nikolai's bomb went off—not just the destruction of the man-made beauty around him, but the human carnage that would ensue from a blast of this magnitude.

SEALs are trained to control their breathing. Three-seconds in, hold for three, release, hold for three again, and then repeat. This always calmed Jack's nerves before firing a weapon, or before jumping out of a helicopter. Jack went through this routine subconsciously as he waited for the perfect moment to make the call. He glanced down at his custom-made iOS wrist device to check on Andy and Grace. He looked at Kendall, who didn't appear confident about this move. Even so, Kendall's dedication to Jack was eternal, and he would stand by his friend no matter what, even if he didn't agree with the decision.

A transmission came through Jack's earpiece, "Sir, all teams are in place, we are a go, I repeat, we are a go."

"Standby for my command and be ready when you feel the blast," Jack ordered.

Jack put his hand on Max's shoulder and nodded.

No words were necessary because Max knew this meant to hold for Jack's call.

"Start the finale," Jack ordered through his earpiece to the Fantasmic lead.

Within seconds, the water screens blasted upwards, the immense light poles emerged from their underground storage areas, and the fireworks launched. Guests in New Orleans Square stopped with confused looks on their faces since most had already been informed that the show was canceled.

Jack waited for the perfect time, looked directly at Max, and said, "DO IT."

Max detonated the charge.

A ground shaking blast sent shockwaves throughout the Island—a large flash of light emerged from the basement hole. Everything blended perfectly with Fantasmic's pyrotechnic explosions.

CMs in the area looked at each other bewildered. They'd seen several tests before, but they knew there was nothing in the show that caused the earth to shake.

Smoke billowed out from the concrete hole in the basement at the front of the Island. Everyone strapped on their masks, readied their weapons, and headed down the hatch with their night vision goggles. Their lights focused on the door, praying that this desperate plan had succeeded.

Jack was the first one to approach and his heart plunged when he saw the door.

It was untouched—not even a dent.

He slammed his fists against the door and yelled at the top of his lungs. Team Six was behind Jack, and they all knew that the charge should have decimated the door. Hot flashes of rage ripped through Jack's body.

Why would my dad do this? Hide these doors from me, and then make them impossible to breach? Why didn't he tell me about this?

With each move, Jack was farther away from saving his kids.

"Jack, I have Melissa White waiting for you she says it's urgent," Luke said.

"Melissa?" Jack answered, in a low, defeated voice.

"Jack, is Bill Gaur with you?" Melissa asked in a soothing tone.

"Not right now, why?"

"I would keep an eye on him, I've been digging through his employment history and it seems that there's bad blood between him and your dad."

"How bad?"

"Well, in the 80s, Gaur was in line to become the next president of Disneyland, but it seems like your dad put a stop to that. After this happened, Gaur threatened your dad at a party while he was drunk, and since then he was never able to advance in the company."

"Yeah, but that doesn't make him a terrorist."

"But it gets worse, I tracked recent money transactions between him and a few individuals on our watch list in Russia. I can't tie him to Nikolai, but it's suspicious based on everything that's happened today."

"He must be the one who leaked the information to Nikolai on how to penetrate The System. Gaur has full operational knowledge and access to the Control Center."

"Exactly. I'm still looking into this, but I wanted to call you to let you know so you can keep an eye on him. How's the hunt for the bomb going?"

"Not good."

"Okay Jack, well, if there is anything you need, give me a call."

"Thank you Melissa, I appreciate it."

"Jack," Kendall rushed towards him, "the CIA unit just apprehended someone. They have Reuab questioning him now."

"Reuab is here?"

"Yes."

"Okay that's good news—he's the CIA's best interrogator, he'll get something out of him for sure."

A blocked call flashed on Jack's iPhone screen.

"Mr. Duncan, please hold for the President of the United States."

Jack's eyes shifted towards Kendall as he spoke, "Mr. President?"

"Jack, every available Special Ops team in the area is outside the Park right now ready to advance. Al-Haddad must be captured at all costs."

"Yes, Mr. President, that's why I'm trying to penetrate this tunnel, to disarm the bomb and stop Khalid."

"But Jack, that's not the order, the order is to find al-Haddad and take him out. He is the number two al-Qaeda operative in the world, and he is your number one priority. His presence has drastically altered the situation."

"Sir, what about the bomb?"

"Jack, like I said, al-Haddad is your number one target."

Jack's heart sank realizing the President and his advisors had already decided the fate of everyone at the Resort. Disarming the bomb had taken second seat to eliminating al-Haddad.

"We have reason to believe that al-Haddad could possess some form of a nuclear weapon, Jack. If he's not apprehended, it could mean the death of millions of people."

50,000 people, including Andy and Grace, were a small price to pay if al-Haddad could be prevented from detonating a nuclear device in Los Angeles.

"Mr. President," Jack argued, "I have the best operatives in the world here, we can still disarm this bomb AND stop Khalid. Please give me the opportunity to do this."

"Jack," the President paused trying to find a way to reassure him—even though he didn't have to, "I know your kids are on the property, and I can't tell you how hard this decision was for me to make, but you have to trust me. Based on the available intelligence, this is my only option. Under no circumstances can a nuclear device be detonated on our soil."

Jack clenched his mouth and looked at Kendall as he responded to the President, "Yes, sir, I understand."

"Thank you Jack."

President Hayes disconnected the line.

Jack kept his somber eyes on Kendall.

"He wants us to go after Khalid and forget about the bomb, right?" Kendall asked.

Jack lowered his head in defeat and looked towards the ground. Kendall put his arm on his shoulder. "I'm sorry Jack, I don't know what to say. But this is what we signed up for, you know that."

Jack's jaw locked, and he looked Kendall in the eyes, "We are NOT on active duty Kendall, we are private citizens."

"Jack, whoa, wait a minute, I know that, but you can't disobey direct orders from the President of the United States?"

"I'm not saying I'm going to do that."

"Then what?"

"The less you know the better Kendall, just trust me. I need to get to this meeting with Nikolai, and I need you to watch Gaur, he may be our mole."

"Gaur?"

"Yes. Keep an eye on him, don't let him out of your sight. Order all teams to make Khalid their number one priority."

"Okay," Kendall stopped and grabbed Jack's arm, "Jack—let's get the kids out of here, I'll figure out a way to make it happen."

"We can't, Nikolai is monitoring them. If we try to move them he could detonate the bomb."

"Maybe that's a chance we need to take."

Jack paused to think. Kendall had a point.

"What do you have in mind?"

"I don't know, let me think and figure it out. Do I have your permission to act if I have a good enough plan?"

Jack glanced down at the live feed of Andy and Grace on his wrist device.

Emotion swept over him as his chest heaved up and down. He looked up at Kendall.

"Do it."

TEN

August 8, 2010
Dream Suite
Disneyland Park

Jack walked towards the Dream Suite to regroup before his meeting with Nikolai. His phone flashed. It was Reuab.

"Jack," Reuab said in a low ragged voice, "I put this guy through a lot and got him to talk."

"What did he say?"

"He's saying someone named Ruddy is involved, that Nikolai is in the tunnels, but he has no clue how to get in. I think he's telling the truth—or at least what he thinks to be the truth."

Jack felt like his head was going to explode, "I'll get back to you."

He dialed Ruddy.

No answer.

"Luke, I need you to find Ruddy now, notify all teams to apprehend and bring him to me immediately."

"Yes, sir."

"I KNEW IT WAS HIM," Jack yelled out of control as he approached the Dream Suite stairs. A few guests stopped with startled looks on their faces.

"You knew it was *who?*" Gaur said as he stood at the base of the Dream Suite stairs.

Jack looked up, shocked to see Gaur standing in front of him. "Nothing, don't worry about it. Have you figured anything out yet?"

"No, but I saw that big explosion on the Island and I'm guessing it didn't work."

Jack glared at him, frustrated as he marched up the Dream Suite stairs.

Gaur followed. "Maybe it's better to meet with Nikolai instead of trying to barrel through those doors. We have access to the greatest people who've ever worked at Disney, and no one has been able to figure out the clues."

Jack stopped as he walked up the stairs, turned to Gaur, and put his finger in his face. "I don't need this kind of advice from you. If you have answers for me regarding the clues, then talk, otherwise, keep your mouth shut."

Gaur backpedaled—flinching at Jack's intimidating advance.

"Why did you stick up for Ruddy earlier?"

"I don't think he's involved in any way, Jack. I've known him for a long time."

"I need you to find him, NOW."

ELEVEN

August 8, 2010
Lafitte's Blacksmith Shop
Disneyland Park

Jack walked into Lafitte's Blacksmith Shop and glanced down at the three dead terrorists he'd shot earlier. The lights flickered. An image appeared in the room, forming a horizontal mid-air display. Nikolai's image materialized on the screen.

"Jack Duncan. You are quite resilient aren't you?"

"I knew you wouldn't meet me here in person, Nikolai, you're too much of a coward."

"Listen, Jack, this is what you need to do to save the lives of everyone here. You and your father need to meet me on Tom Sawyer Island, alone, unarmed, and the entire Island better be empty. That's all you need to do."

"I already told you Nikolai my dad is in Northern California, dying, I can't even reach him by phone, how am I supposed to get him here?"

"Oh, don't worry about that part, Jack. Since you were unable to make it happen, I picked up your father and had him delivered."

Jack's jaw dropped as the video feed panned to an image of his father, lying unconscious on a gurney.

"It's simple, Jack. Of course, you won't get what you truly want, which is revenge, but on the flip side, you'll get to be a hero again and your kids will live."

Jack cringed at the idea of putting the fate of his kids into the hands of a madman. He was angry at the thought of not getting to watch Nikolai squirm under his control—the thought of never getting revenge on the man who killed his true love made his blood boil.

"I know you want to break those doors down, and get to me in here, but you've probably realized that's impossible. Doesn't it frustrate you that your father never bothered to tell you about any of this? I thought he trusted you with Walt's secrets? Clearly he didn't."

Jack tried to hide his anger, to not let Nikolai get the best of him, but it was painful—and all he could think about was breaking his neck.

"You know Jack, you have your father to thank for all of this. If he wouldn't have brutally murdered my son, I would've never come after your family."

"What are you talking about?"

"He never told you that either? He keeps a lot from you, Jack. Your father brutally tortured and killed my son, years ago, and he's known that for quite some time now. It probably would have been good information for you to have in 2005."

"You're a liar Nikolai."

"No, I'm telling the truth. I have lied in the past, for the greater good, but this is the truth. If your father was awake he would admit it. But you are right, he is in fact dying, we haven't been able to wake him up, and we've tried everything."

Jack heard a loud electrical zap, and he saw Stan's body jerk on the screen in front of him.

"You will pay for this Nikolai if it's the last thing I do."

"Stop with the threats, Jack, they have no merit, you're powerless," Nikolai paused and grinned, "this is a fair outcome when you think about it. Your father took my only son—and now I will take his—while he watches."

"What guarantee do I have that you will not detonate the bomb?"

"You have no guarantees Jack—the only guarantee you have is that your wife is dead, and you will cause the death of everyone around you if you don't comply—that's your guarantee."

Jack came unglued when he mentioned Kate and yelled, "NIKOLAI," as the screen flickered and turned off. He sprinted out of the Blacksmith Shop towards the giant steel door. If only he could get in there to kill Nikolai and disarm the bomb. He desperately ran the palm of his hand over the embossed "D", the decorative border, and the small circle underneath. He headed back to the hatch and up to the Pirates of the Caribbean towards the Cast Member entrance to the Blue Bayou.

"Jack," Gaur questioned, "what happened, what did he say?"

"He wants my dad and I to meet him on Tom Sawyer Island."

Gaur looked worried, "Jack, you can't trust Nikolai to hold up his end of the bargain."

"I know." Jack was getting an incoming call from Ruddy.

"Jack—" Ruddy said quickly.

"Where are you?" Jack scowled.

"Listen to me very carefully, Jack, if Gaur is in front of you, just confirm it by remaining silent."

Jack looked at Gaur and continued to listen to Ruddy.

"I did some research, checked sign in logs, Bill said he was here with his family today—I checked everything, and this is not true. I made a few calls to verify, and his family is out of state right now."

"You're lying."

"No, Jack, I'm not lying, Gaur is involved somehow."

"Where are you at right now?"

"I'm near the front gate where you told me to stay."

Jack pressed his earpiece, "Luke?"

"Yes, Jack he's telling the truth."

Jack took a deep breath and glared at Gaur, who looked concerned.

"I'll call you back."

Jack moved closer to Gaur and quickly drew his SIG from his side, pointing it directly at Gaur's face. He knew this was the quickest way to get to the truth.

Gaur raised his hands and nervously uttered, "Jack?"

Jack's voice boomed, "WHY DID YOU LIE TO ME, BILL?"

"Lie to you? About what?"

"Your family was not here today—why would you lie about that? Also, why are you getting funds from the Russian mafia?"

Gaur stammered and tried to get words out, but he couldn't. A Cast Member unexpectedly walked through the Cast Member Blue Bayou entrance from Pirates and froze when she saw Jack with his gun drawn, she gasped as Jack looked over at her.

"Go back," Jack told the CM.

Gaur pulled a small knife from a concealed holster above his shoulder blades and hurled it at Jack. The knife flew end over end towards Jack and landed deep in his upper arm.

Jack felt the knife enter his flesh as a flash of pain swept through his body. His arm holding the gun lowered as Gaur pulled another knife out of an ankle holster and charged towards Jack.

The CM screamed. Jack timed a lethal roundhouse kick that landed just below Gaur's hip. The force of the kick swept Gaur off his feet as his body crashed to the ground. He writhed in pain as he squirmed on the floor. Jack drove his knee into Gaur's chest to restrict his breathing, pulled the small knife out of his arm, and plunged it through Gaur's forearm. The knife sliced through his arm and anchored in the wooden floor. Gaur's face flushed, and his mouth opened wide as he shrieked.

"Tell me how to get inside those doors, NOW!" Jack roared.

Gaur struggled to speak.

"J—ack, I—I—I don't know how to get in."

"WRONG ANSWER." Jack applied more pressure to his chest and pulled Gaur's stabbed arm towards him—splitting his flesh. Gaur's mouth shot open forming a terrified look, he tried to scream, but he couldn't.

Max arrived and moved in to help Jack.

Gaur spoke rapidly fearing for his life, "Jack—I do not know how to get in —Nikolai, and al-Haddad are in the tunnel with the bomb—that's all I know —I swear."

"You're lying," Jack gripped Gaur's other arm and applied enough pressure to remove it from its socket.

"NO, JACK! Please—stop."

"Why would you do this, why would you give terrorists access to the Resort?"

"Your dad—he took away everything from me, I was next in line for the presidency. It ruined my career, it ruined my relationship with my wife and kids—your dad blacklisted me and made it impossible to move forward."

"So that's a good enough reason to betray your country and kill thousands of people?"

"It wasn't just that, I needed the money to save my house and to pay for my wife's medical bills. Initially, they paid me for general information. Then they took my kids. I had no other choice."

"You should've known better. You need to help me get these doors open, NOW."

"Jack, I swear to you, I don't know, but I think it is something that your dad gave you. Something only you would have access to."

"That doesn't help me at all," Jack stood up, "Max, take him to Reuab, tell him to use all available techniques to get the truth out of him."

"NOOO Jack," Gaur screamed.

TWELVE

August 8, 2010
Blue Bayou
Disneyland Park

Jack charged through the bussing station of the Blue Bayou as he studied the incoming intelligence on his device. He found himself in the dimly lit dining room. Candlelight emanated from the small tables, but the room was empty. He briefly looked up, and his family's special table caught his eye—the table they'd used for years to celebrate momentous occasions. Jack's mind raced back to the last time he was there with Kate, Stan, and the kids.

2005

Stan established a long-standing tradition of celebrating his and Genie's wedding anniversary with Jack at the Blue Bayou. It began when Jack was a young boy because he wanted to make sure that Jack always remembered his mom. When Jack got married and had kids, the whole family joined the annual tradition. The Blue Bayou was Stan and Genie's favorite romantic place to eat, and they made countless memories together at the plantation style restaurant set on the shores of the most famous theme park attraction in the world.

Stan always reserved the same waterside table giving them a view of the dark water, the old rickety shack across the way, and Lafitte's Landing. Sometimes, guests on the boats would call out for a roll, and Stan would take one of the dinner rolls from the cloth-covered baskets and chuck it at the lucky people. This always made Andy and Grace giggle.

"Do you guys know how much your grandma would have loved you if she had the chance to meet you?" Stan looked into Andy and Grace's eyes, "She always wanted to have kids, and it was her dream to have grandkids someday."

Andy and Grace smiled at their grandpa. Jack looked into Kate's eyes as they held hands under the table.

Stan had gone through several phases of his life, from a deadly assassin, to a government spy. He was selfish and ambitious and didn't care about anyone who got in his way. He turned from his selfish life when he met Genie, and he regretted the hurtful things he'd done. He was a new man. He tried to shed his old baggage and become a better person.

"Kate, you look beautiful tonight," Stan smiled at Kate as she blushed.

"Thank you Dad," Kate put her hand on his, "and you look quite handsome yourself!"

Stan grinned and looked at the kids, "You know Andrew and Gracie, your mom and dad have a relationship similar to what your grandma and I had. We loved each other and were committed to each other through good times and bad. Always remember: there's one person out there that God made for you, be patient and don't settle for lesser treasure. You will not regret it—just ask your dad."

The kids giggled.

"I always want to celebrate our anniversary here together, as a family, for as long as I can."

"Definitely, Dad," Jack said as he reached under the table for a box. "We have something for you."

Stan's old and seasoned face formed a smile as he eyed the box. "You guys didn't have to do that," he smiled at Kate and leaned over towards her, "I know you probably put this together, knowing that my son has zero thoughtfulness when it comes to gifts."

Jack scrunched his eyebrows and gave Stan a dirty look.

"You deserve it Dad," Kate said, laughing at Jack.

Stan slowly opened the crisp white paper around the box and removed the red bow. He found a beautifully framed picture of Genie and himself on their wedding day. They were standing on each side of the golden spike at the entrance of Sleeping Beauty Castle. Walt Disney, Stan's best man was on his left and Kurt Russell stood next to Walt. On the other side was Genie's sister. It was a classic picture, in a fairy tale setting, capturing their unending love.

Stan smiled as he gazed at Genie's image, and a tear trickled down his cheek.

"This means so much to me, thank you very much," Stan got up to hug Kate. He put his hand on Jack's shoulder and then sat back down to address the family, "Listen, I don't know how much longer I have on this planet, but I have a special gift for you, son."

"Dad, please," Jack whispered to Stan, "let's not do the *end of life* speech in front of the kids?"

Stan continued, "Our wedding day was the best day of my life, the second best day was when Jackie was born," the kids chuckled when they heard their grandpa call their dad "Jackie".

"We've celebrated this day together ever since Jack was a kid," Stan continued, "and now that Jack has his own family, I want to continue to celebrate this day for as long as I live, with all of you. And I expect you to continue the tradition when I'm gone."

Everyone smiled in agreement.

"I still have some pull in this place, so I've reserved this table for us here at the Bayou indefinitely, every year on this day, so please promise me you will honor this tradition."

"Sure Dad," Jack smiled at him.

"I want our love to be an example to all of you, for generations, and I hope you can use it as a guide for your own lives."

Stan turned to Jack, "I want you to have this, son, something I hope you will keep on you at all times. Cherish it like I have for all these years." Stan pulled a box out of his pocket and handed it to Jack.

Jack held the box in his hand, glanced over at Kate, and grinned. Kate flashed an excited smile at Jack because gift giving thrilled her.

He slowly opened the box to reveal a golden wedding band. Jack looked at it and was shocked. He looked back up at Stan.

"Dad, is this—"

"Yes, it is son. It's your mom's wedding band, I had it restored just for you, I want you to have it. Keep it on you for good luck, and always remember your mom."

A small tear formed in the corner of his eye, but he tried to fight it off so the kids wouldn't see him cry.

"Dad, I don't know what to say?"

"You don't need to say anything, Jack. Just don't ever lose it or I will find you, and beat you down—you know I'm still capable of taking you out."

Jack laughed and handed the white box to Kate who was elated. She knew how significant this family heirloom would be to her kids.

Engraved on the white box was Stan and Genie's wedding date.

1-7-64

PRESENT DAY

Jack's body jolted as he stood in front of their family table.

His mom and dad's anniversary was January 7, 1964.

That was it.

He unzipped his tactical vest and pulled up his shirt to access his hidden money belt. Jack kept his valuables on him along with a wad of cash in a money belt he rarely opened. He opened a secret compartment and pulled out his mom's gold band.

Their wedding day.

January 7, 1964.

1-7-64

1764

It's the ring.

The ring is the key.

THIRTEEN

August 8, 2010
Pirate Wax Museum
Disneyland Park

Jack sprinted for the underground Pirate Wax Museum. He dodged the wax pirates as he eyed the metal door. He arrived at the door and set his sights on the engraved Disney "D". He held the wedding band in his hand. With his thumb and index finger, he placed the ring in the embossed circle under the "D".

His hand trembled—he could taste victory.

At the same time, he thought about what Kendall and Tony had said. It didn't matter at this point—he was too close to the prize. Jack never failed on any mission, and this would be no different. He would get his revenge—and he would save the Park.

The pure gold wedding band made contact with the circle on the heavy metal door. The ring fit perfectly, and it locked into place.

Jack waited.

He frantically scanned side-to-side.

Nothing happened.

Jack let out his pent up frustration, "NO!"

The door didn't open. For the first time in his life, he felt the sting of defeat. There was nothing else he could do, no way to stop the bomb, and no way to beat Nikolai and al-Haddad in time. They would win—he would lose.

He slapped both hands on the door in frustration and slid down to stare at the ring that was nestled perfectly in the circle indentation of the door.

He desperately stared into the circle, hoping that something else would come to him, perhaps another clue. He needed a quick solution.

CLANK

Jack froze, wide eyed, and backed away from the door. It was the sound of a massive deadbolt retracting. The ring, which was securely fastened popped out and fell to the ground as the giant metal doors opened inward. A surge of adrenaline pumped through his body as he watched the doors open. He went from utter sorrow, to ecstatic joy. He gripped his SIG and his tactical light as he moved towards the door, ready for a confrontation. He bent down to retrieve the ring and put it in his pocket.

He moved cautiously into the tunnel. It was bigger than he'd thought, and it had the same nineteenth century theme, the red bricks, and the sloppy mortar. It resembled the catacombs of Paris.

It was dead silent.

He took a few more steps and stopped. He knew he needed reinforcements if he was going to move through the tunnels, especially if there were hundreds of hostiles down there. A swift attack with overwhelming force was the only way to put an end to this.

Jack backed out of the tunnel and into the Pirate Wax Museum. His radio wasn't working, so he headed for the treasure room hatch to get above-ground.

"Kendall," Jack called out through his earpiece.

"Jack, where are you?"

"Get Team Six down here NOW and send the CIA unit to the Haunted Mansion door, I need all available resources down here immediately."

"Okay Jack, we're headed that way," Kendall paused, "Jack—did you do what I think you did?"

"Just get down here Kendall."

"Jack, I think I've found a way to do what we talked about earlier—a way to get the kids out of here."

"Just get down here, I need you. We can put an end to this now, with the team we have here, but I need your help to make it happen."

A blocked call came through Jack's phone, and he answered quickly.

"Jack, this is Director Camden, did you just get one of the doors open and order all units to assemble on your command?"

Jack hesitated, "Yes, sir."

"Jack, the President gave you specific instructions. By entering the tunnel, you could jeopardize the entire mission."

"Sir, I think Nikolai, al-Haddad, and the bomb are in these tunnels. I have the best Special Forces operatives in the world with me now. If we take these tunnels immediately, we can find al-Haddad AND disarm the bomb."

"You might be right Jack, but those are not your orders."

"Sir, I cannot risk the lives of 50,000 people when this option is available. I don't care what you guys have decided from your ivory tower, this is the best solution for the innocent people here at the Park."

"Not if it accelerates the detonation of the bomb and it allows Khalid to escape. Khalid could be in possession of a nuke on American soil—do you understand the implications of that?"

"Yes, sir, but the correct call is to raid this tunnel with everything we've got. If I'm right, we'll solve all of our problems in one sweep. We don't have any other choice, this is the best way to stop the threat."

The Director paused to think, "Let me call the President."

"How long will that take?"

"I'm not sure, but you need to hold your position until I get back to you."

"Yes, sir." Jack called out over the secure radio to the CIA unit, Team Six, and the other SEALs on site. "All units be ready to storm the tunnel on my call."

Kendall arrived with Max in their full assault kits. They handed Jack his gear.

"I'm just waiting for word from the Director. Show the teams the schematics of the tunnels when they get here."

Kendall nodded at Jack with a lingering look. Jack had finally gone off the deep end, and he was going to directly disobey the orders of the President of the United States.

Team Six arrived and started their weapons checks. The CIA unit was behind them, and more SEALs followed. The deadliest fighters in American history were assembled in one place, at one time, ready to enter the tunnel. Masters of close quarters combat, each person had been through hundreds of similar missions, they knew how to communicate without saying a word. They were the most accomplished operatives in the history of Special Forces.

"What's taking them so long?" Jack uttered under his breath as he checked his sights and readied his weapons. Max glanced at Kendall who looked worried.

"Gentlemen," Jack addressed the elite group, "we could be facing over one hundred hostiles in these tunnels. These tunnels are unknown to us so we could be walking into a maze. Our target is al-Haddad, and the bomb."

The men nodded, ready for action. This is what they lived for. Each man wanted to be the one to put the bullet in al-Haddad's head. It was biggest mission of their careers and failure was not an option.

Suddenly, their headsets went fuzzy, and no one could hear anything through their closed circuit devices.

"Are you guys hearing this?"

"Yes, sir," the Team Six leader responded, "our secure coms appear to be failing."

Jack pulled his earpiece out and checked the transmitter on his belt.

He looked at Kendall, then back at the team who was eagerly awaiting his command.

"Kendall, we need to go, we are out of time. I know you don't agree with this, but it's our best shot right now, and we need to take it."

Kendall paused for a second and looked Jack in the eyes, "I'm with you Jack, let's do it."

Jack addressed the group, "GENTLEMEN, we are a go, follow my lead, and execute on my orders."

The mechanical clicks of high-powered assault rifles filled the cavernous underground attraction as they prepared for battle. The men lowered their night vision goggles and crept into the mysterious tunnel.

FOURTEEN

August 8, 2010
El Capitan Presidential Suite
Grand Californian

"Hey Kim," Andy smiled, "have you heard from my dad?"

"Not yet, Andy."

Grace looked tired, "Can we go to the Lounge and get some dessert before they close, Kim?"

"No, Gracie, we can't leave right now, but I'll have some sent over for you, okay?"

The kids were getting antsy.

Kim had been monitoring the events and knew the situation was not looking good. The kids could see the worry on her face.

"You know, Kim," Andy interjected, "we're lucky to have you, I don't know what we'd do without you."

Kim smiled at Andy, but her smile faded as she analyzed the chatter coming in from the field teams.

"Look you guys, no matter what happens, you'll be okay. Your dad will be okay, everything will work out in the end."

"I don't know about that," Andy said, "things didn't really work out for us with our mom. I thought she would be okay too, and she wasn't."

"I know what you mean Andy, and I can't explain why that happened. You two are the best kids in the world, and you deserve better. You deserve to be happy."

Kim's phone rang. She looked down and put her finger up signaling that she had to take the call. She scurried over to the massive master bathroom to answer the call from the blocked number.

"Kim,"

"Yes."

"I need you to bring the kids to me, now."

"Now?"

"Yes."

Kim's face turned pale, and her hands shook. She closed the door to the bathroom and took a deep breath.

She lowered her voice to a deep whisper and said, "You promise they will not be harmed, right?"

"Yes, Kim, it's like I told you—do what I say, and I will let your mom and sister live."

"Give me proof that they are okay."

A live video image appeared on Kim's phone revealing her mom and sister tied to a chair with gags in their mouths.

Kim injected anger into her whisper, "You better live up to your deal, or I will slit your throat, and these kids better not be harmed—you know what I'm capable of."

"I do not want to bring harm to the children that's not my game. But let me also advise you that if you do not come through, your mom and sister will die—they will suffer tremendously, and it will be your fault."

Kim listened as her lip trembled; trying to hold back tears.

The voice continued, "You will have to live with that for the rest of your life."

Kim grit her teeth and couldn't stop her hand from trembling.

"I'm on my way."

Kim lowered the phone from her ear, covered her mouth, and sank to the bathroom floor as she suppressed her urge to scream.

JACK DUNCAN

IS

THE DEADLIEST CAST MEMBER

SEASON ONE

EPISODE FIVE

ONE

1995
Jack and Kate's Wedding
Disneyland Park

"Jack, this is a dream come true," Kate said smiling as they exited the Tomorrowland Monorail Station. The Disney Store Trivia Showdown was in progress directly in front of them on the Tomorrowland Terrace stage.

"With all of our friends and family staying at the hotel, it's like one big celebration!" Kate said as she put her arm around Jack.

Jack beamed at Kate as he brought her in close. The sun was setting on Tomorrowland, and the temperature dropped. Summer nights at Disneyland were exhilarating, and everyone always had renewed energy at this time of day.

The *40 Years of Adventure* signs were visible throughout the Park commemorating Disneyland's 40th Anniversary celebration.

"So who are we meeting next?"

"Everyone!" Jack said, "Your mom is en route from the airport and the entire group wants to ride Space Mountain together. After that, we'll head back to the hotel to get ready for the rehearsal dinner."

Kate squealed with excitement. Their fairy-tale whirlwind romance over the last twelve months was like a dream, and to top it off, both of their families got along so well. It was as if they'd been friends for years, and they had fun at the Park together.

Stan took care of everyone's room and most of their expenses including food for the entire weekend.

Kate's family seized every opportunity to be around Stan at Disneyland since they admired Stan's role in Disney history, and loved hearing his stories about Walt.

Best of all, Kate's mom had become close with Jack.

"After the Park closes, we're going to do the rehearsal in front of the Castle." Jack said as Kate looked up at him with a big smile. The sunset intensified her striking features, which left Jack in awe of her.

Kate could barely contain herself as she greeted the good-sized group waiting in front of Space Mountain.

"BOBBY!"

"Kate!" Bobby said as he ran to her and gave her a loving hug and kiss.

"I'm so glad to see you little brother! You made it just in time!"

"I wouldn't miss this for the world," Bobby said as he turned to Jack.

"Jack, how've you been?"

"Great Bobby, I'm glad you made it." Jack gave him a hug.

"So is everyone here now? Are we just waiting on Mom?"

"Yep the entire family is here! Isn't it amazing? It's like a huge family reunion at Disneyland!"

Bobby grinned at Jack, "This is fantastic Jack, thank you for doing this for us. I have to be honest, that day at the French Market, I never thought you and Kate would get married. You weren't her type!"

Jack chuckled, "It truly was meant to be. I didn't believe my dad when he tried to tell me that, but he was right."

"You actually have Stan to thank, Bobby, he's the one who's paying for all of this."

"Where is Stan?" Bobby asked Jack.

"He's running around making sure the wedding planner has everything ready. It's his new passion, he loves planning—or should I say over-planning."

"So we get to play in the Park today, eat at the Blue Bayou tonight, do the rehearsal, and then hang out at the hotel?"

"Yep, little brother," Kate said, "we've got a lot of fun stuff planned for the entire weekend, even after we leave for our honeymoon, your hotel is covered, so you can hang out and have fun!"

Disneyland was designed for large events and big groups. There was nothing else like the child-like anticipation of the entire family coming together and having fun inside the "bubble" that Walt created.

"Kate," Jack pulled her aside, "things are going to get crazy over the next few days, and I need to tell you something."

"Sure, Jack." Kate's glowing smile faded.

"I've decided to quit The Teams. I'm done. We're going to start our own business like we've always talked about—I'm going to start a new life with you."

Kate was speechless, and her mouth dropped.

"Jack—are you sure about this? Remember what we talked about, I don't want you to give up on something you love to do."

"Kate, I am not giving up anything—I have you, and that's all I need. You're more than enough for me."

She smiled and took his hands. "How will we start the business?"

"Well, Dad has been friends with Steve Jobs for years, they've worked on several projects together, and his closest friend wants to work with me and financially back our business."

"Wow, Jack that is great news!"

"Yeah, it's crazy when you think about it. My dad said that Walt told him to form a partnership with a man like Steve to help him perpetuate his dream of advancing technology to a new level. Apparently they've worked on other projects together for years, and now they want to work with me."

"Jack! That's amazing, I am so proud of you, this is going to be wonderful!" Kate hugged him, "this weekend keeps getting better and better!"

"That's why I wanted to tell you ahead of the wedding, to put your mind at ease," Jack glanced up over Kate's shoulder and smiled.

Kate looked at Jack and then turned around to see her mom standing behind them.

"MOM!"

"Oh my Kate, you look beautiful my little princess!" she said giving Kate a big hug. She looked over at Jack. "And you look handsome as ever Jack."

"Hello Mom! You look lovely, and I'm so glad you made it." Jack hugged her.

"I wouldn't miss this for the world," she said, "so where's that big hunk Kendall?"

Jack laughed, "He's around here somewhere. He's been running around with my dad, he's the *assistant* to the assistant wedding planner."

"An Ex-CIA veteran, and an active duty Navy SEAL planning weddings?"

"I know," Jack laughed at how ridiculous it sounded.

"Oh Jack, I think that's so sweet that your dad and your best friend would want to play such a big role in your wedding. You're a lucky man!"

BLUE BAYOU REHEARSAL DINNER

The exquisite lighting of the Blue Bayou set the tone for a magical rehearsal dinner. The Royal Street Bachelors played on the balcony of the plantation-style house—the backdrop for the Blue Bayou. The wedding party guests looked up at the Bachelors as their subtle jazz, the lingering smell of the Pirates of the Caribbean water, the stars above them on the ceiling of the attraction, and the candlelit tables created the ultimate romantic celebration for Jack and Kate.

The entire dining room was full of people from the wedding party, laughing, taking pictures, and eating. Energy permeated the room as excitement and anticipation flowed throughout the party. Stan made his way to his special table near the water, which he'd left empty with a setting for two, in honor of Genie. He turned around to address the wedding party.

"Welcome everyone to the Blue Bayou, I am so glad you could make it from all over the country for this special event. This is the biggest day of my son's life," Stan looked at Kate and smiled, "I couldn't have asked for a better woman for my son, Kate is beautiful on the inside and out, and I'm so blessed to have her as part of our family."

Everyone applauded as Kate blushed and smiled at Stan with tears in her eyes.

"There's a gift on your table, just a little something from me to express my gratitude. Go ahead and open it."

The guests eagerly opened the small envelopes on their tables to find a small certificate with the Disney logo on it.

Kate's mom put her hand over her mouth—gasps spread like a wave throughout the restaurant.

"These certificates are valid for a five-year Disneyland Annual Pass. God-willing, we can all gather together again right here and celebrate Jack and Kate's five year anniversary."

Everyone applauded and thanked Stan.

"And now, I have a treat for everyone—a special guest. The heart of the Walt Disney Company. He reminds me so much of his Uncle, who I loved very much. Ladies and Gentlemen, I am honored to have Mr. Roy E. Disney here tonight."

Everyone in the dining room gasped as they stood to applaud the legendary Disney executive.

"Thank you everyone," Roy said, "and thank you Stan," he looked in Stan's direction, "you know my Uncle loved this man right here," he said pointing at Stan, "they were like two peas in a pod, Walt trusted him with everything, and Stan has played a significant role in the success of this Park. He kept Walt safe for all those years, and he's kept millions of guests safe since opening day."

Everyone clapped to acknowledge Stan.

"That's why I was honored when he invited me to this wedding celebration. I watched Jack grow up at the Park, he's been a part of the Disneyland family for a long time—Cast Members love him. Jack, I just want to tell you that we appreciate your service to our country, and for what you've done to protect the American dream, which is so eloquently preserved here at the Park. Walt Disney was a patriot. He respected people in our military, and he appreciated their sacrifice. He put a high value on people who serve our country. Maybe one day, you'll follow in your dad's footsteps and come to work here with us."

Stan interrupted, "Now that would be something!"

"So, again, thank you for joining us for this special event, I hope you enjoy your time at Disneyland celebrating Jack and Kate—whose love began here at the magical Park that Walt built." Roy looked at Jack, "Walt would've been proud of you Jack, and I know your mom would've been proud as well."

The guests stood to their feet with a roar of applause, showing their appreciation for Roy and Stan.

SLEEPING BEAUTY CASTLE

Stan's original plan was to close the Park early for the sunset wedding, but Jack didn't want that. He wanted the Park to stay open so guests would not have to exit prematurely.

Orange-tinged streaky clouds appeared in the clear light blue sky as the complexion of the Castle, and the entire Park began to change. Jack stood in his tuxedo in front of the Castle as he looked to the sky—remembering the romantic sunset Skyway trips with Kate. They had so many memorable moments in the Park while the sun was setting.

Kendall stood next to Jack, looked down, and smiled at him.

"This is it, Bro, are you ready?"

Jack grinned at him. It was what Kendall always said to him before they jumped out of a helicopter or a plane.

White folding chairs lined the front of the Castle. Special bows decorated the Castle lanterns, the water shimmered, and excitement for the much-anticipated fairy-tale wedding was in the air. The dynamism of Disneyland along with the sentimental fragrance of popcorn filled the air. A large crowd formed on both sides of the Castle to catch a glimpse of the big event. Most people had never seen an in-Park wedding take place, and this extravaganza felt like a Royal Wedding. Cast Members who'd known Jack throughout the years were in attendance. There weren't enough seats, so most of them stood around the front of the Castle and helped the on-duty CMs with the crowds.

Jack leaned over to Kendall and whispered, "You know before I met Kate, I was fine on my own, I didn't need anyone. But now, I can't imagine my life without her. I was so independent, but now I'm completely dependent on her, it's kind of scary knowing that I could be attached to someone this much."

Kendall beamed, "That's cause you were meant to be together, nothing wrong with that little brother."

The music throughout The Hub area lowered and "Here Comes the Bride" reverberated throughout Main Street. Everyone stopped to watch and take pictures. Women cried as Cinderella's Crystal Coach made its fairy-tale entrance in Town Square at the beginning of Main Street. White roses covered the silvery pumpkin shaped carriage—it mesmerized onlookers. A magnificent white horse pulled the carriage guided by a coachman in full white Royal attire. Kate and Bobby were inside the Crystal Coach as they waved to the people who lined Main Street. Everyone clapped and tried to take pictures as fast as they could.

Jack could see the carriage in the distance, and he could hear the crowd reacting to it. He raised his head to get a glimpse of Kate. She was beautiful in everyday attire—he couldn't imagine what she'd look like in her wedding dress.

The carriage continued down Main Street with the Castle ahead of them on the horizon. Kate waved to people on both sides of the street as she soaked up the ambiance of the sunset—her favorite time of the day at Disneyland. The Crystal Coach veered to the right and parked on the Tomorrowland side of The Hub in front of Sleeping Beauty Castle. Bobby jumped out of the carriage and offered his hand to Kate. Onlookers wowed in awe of her breathtaking dress. Her stunning appearance, elegance, and natural beauty put Royal brides to shame.

Jack moved side-to-side to try to get a glimpse of Kate, but he still couldn't see her.

Bobby escorted Kate to the center of the aisle lined with a red carpet leading up the drawbridge of the Castle.

When she turned the corner, Jack's eyes locked on to her.

Chills ran through his body. He was captivated by her blonde hair streaming from her white veil, her sun-kissed arms and shoulders against the white lace wedding dress. The ambient lighting of the setting sun ignited her dazzling blue eyes. She almost didn't look real—her features were flawless.

Kate was the only person Jack could see, everyone around her became a blur, it was as if she was the only one in the Park.

Jack had no doubts, no reservations. He only regretted that he hadn't met her sooner. All he could think about was spending the rest of his life with her, growing old with her, and finally getting the chance to have a family of his own.

They read their vows and were pronounced man and wife.

They kissed.

Fireworks launched behind them over the Castle.

The crowd in front of the Castle, the people in The Hub and Main Street went wild as Jack and Kate faced them looking towards the Main Street Train Station.

Jack looked at Kate's sparkling smile and excited eyes. His life was complete; he'd found the woman of his dreams. He smiled and kissed Kate again. He looked down Main Street at the thousands of cheering people. He caught a glimpse of his dad who was bawling.

He glanced at the empty seat next to his dad that was reserved for his mom.

Kendall flashed a reassuring smile as he patted Jack on the back.

The newlyweds strolled down the red carpet on the Castle bridge to board the Crystal Coach for their celebratory journey down Main Street.

TWO

August 8, 2010
Underground Tunnels
Disneyland Park

Jack and the SEALs activated their state-of-the-art night vision goggles revealing the details of the pitch-black tunnel. Lafitte's Blacksmith Shop blended seamlessly with the underground tunnel leading to "Barataria" Island, Lafitte's smuggling hideout. The nineteenth century New Orleans Square theme permeated the underground attraction.

The SEALs crept into the tunnel with confidence. They moved strategically with eye contact. Jack was at point, Kendall and Max were by his side. Their weapons shifted left to right as they caught glimpses of Disney-esque storytelling spread throughout the tunnel. The stories Jack had told for years about Lafitte were coming to life before his eyes.

Archaic signs on the walls pointed to "*Barataria*". Skeletons hung from iron shackles, others were hunched over on the ground, remnants of treasure littered the walkway, and cobwebs were everywhere. The tunnel told the story of Lafitte's smuggling operation—the stronghold he built on the islands off the coast of Louisiana. A large painting of a well-dressed Lafitte hoisting the American flag over his head had an inscription that read: "*Attack an American ship and die!*" This was a quote from Lafitte's memoirs.

The silence throughout the tunnel was unnerving—not a peep came from any direction. The air was damp, and the dust was thick. The tunnel was larger than Jack thought it would be, with no corners or turns, it was a straight shot, leaving no place to hide. If hostiles were headed their way, they'd be coming straight for them.

Jack noticed something ahead on the each side of the walls. He put his hand up to stop the Team from proceeding. He saw a large brick archway on each side of the tunnel, similar to the small redbrick archway in New Orleans Square and the structure surrounding the large metal doors. There were no metal doors in these archways though; instead there were bricks exactly like the ones on the small River esplanade crypt.

With his left hand, Jack pushed on the bricks to find a way in. He let his gun rest at his side motioning for Kendall and Max to cover him. He pushed again with both hands—the bricks moved slightly. He pushed harder, and the entire mass of bricks shifted inward. Kendall and Max provided cover for Jack as the other SEALs took their spots watching both sides of the tunnel.

They entered the spacious room, and quickly scanned it to make sure it was clear. A large table was in the middle. An oversized mirror covered most of the wall on the other side. Old-style chairs were scattered throughout, presumably for guests, and Disney memorabilia from the 60s covered the tables. Old park maps, vintage attraction posters, E-ticket books, and pirate artifacts were everywhere. Pictures on the walls from opening day, Walt with Shirley Temple, dignitaries, and other rare memorabilia lined the walls. It was a private lounge of some sort that didn't appear to coincide with the story in the tunnels.

Jack exited the room and pushed his way through the matching redbrick archway on the other side. This room was identical in shape and design. It had different pictures on the wall, and distinctive memorabilia on the table, but it had the same oversized mirror.

He needed to get the team further down the tunnel, so he left the private lounge and proceeded, stepping over gold coins and skeletons. Portraits of Lafitte hung on the wall with the words "*Gentleman Pirate*" above them.

The team deliberately moved, pointing their weapons strategically, silent and calm as they proceeded—eager to engage with their first target.

They approached a massive metal door on the right side of the tunnel. Jack assumed this was the door they tried to blow inside the 15-foot basement at the front of the Island. He opened the large metal door with the ring to confirm. He was correct; they were at the front edge of the Island. He ordered one of the SEALs to remain there to keep watch.

The tunnel continued towards Pirate's Lair on Tom Sawyer Island as the Lafitte smuggling theme thickened. They approached a massive wooden door covering the width of the tunnel. An image of Lafitte was painted on the wooden door, and above the image read: "*Lafitte's Tavern*".

Jack gently nudged the door with his right hand, and it moved forward. He motioned to Max and Kendall who got in position to cover him as he entered the room. Jack got low, pushed through the door, and immediately spotted human shaped figures throughout the tavern.

He gently squeezed the trigger of his H&K MP7 and waited for movement. Kendall and Max entered the room and did the same thing.

Jack's finger was millimeters from firing a round when he realized the figures were not moving. He removed his finger from the trigger and moved forward.

"These are pirates from the wax museum, animatronics, or something like that," Jack whispered to Max and Kendall as the rest of the SEAL team entered the room.

They were inside an early nineteenth century tavern—Lafitte's Tavern with pirates sitting at the tables, eating and drinking. Vintage maritime maps of New Orleans hung on the walls, pictures of Lafitte and his crew, swords, evidence of smuggling activity, fake drinking glasses with simulated liquid, and pirate artifacts were scattered throughout the Tavern.

"Jack," Kendall whispered, "we're directly under Lafitte's Tavern—this must be the *real* Tavern."

Jack didn't say a word but acknowledged Kendall's assessment. Wooden tables were everywhere, large barrels of rum rested near the walls—it was a replica of a nineteenth century pirate hangout. A large portrait of Lafitte raising a glass to his patrons hung on the wall.

They examined everything in the room but found no trace of hostiles. Jack inspected the large wooden table in the center of the Tavern—big enough to hold twenty-five or more people on its benches. He ran his hand across the top middle of the table removing a thick layer of dust. A carved "*1764*" was revealed.

"Are we getting any trace of the bomb in here Kendall?"

Kendall motioned back to the bomb specialist, who shook his head after looking at his device.

"No, he's not picking up anything," Kendall said.

Jack noticed a picture of Andrew Jackson on the wall, a replica of the Constitution, a map showing the island of Barataria off the coast of New Orleans, miscellaneous treasure maps, and swords.

"Okay, let's keep moving."

They exited through the other set of wooden doors on the far side of the Tavern as they prepared for a confrontation. The tunnel resumed, leading towards Pirates Lair on Tom Sawyer Island.

The odd silence was disconcerting, there was no place to hide, and they were sitting ducks to anyone who came around the corner.

The story on the tunnel walls continued. Jack noticed another portrait of Lafitte, this time leading his troops in battle, with this inscription:

"*The greatest and most sacred documents ever composed and written by men, the great Declaration of Independence, and the great Constitution of the United States, would have been erased from the face of the earth.*"

Another sign read "*Jackson's Island*" with an arrow pointing up towards the surface. This was a reference to the island used as a hideaway by Lafitte in Mark Twain's books.

There was another painting of Lafitte shaking hands with Andrew Jackson. Further ahead there were a series of paintings that appeared to tell the story of Lafitte hiding his treasure. Jack glanced at a picture of a New Orleans estuary with silver and gold buried in it. He saw another intriguing image of Lafitte throwing gold plates and silver ingots overboard at Largo.

Jack noticed the strange telescope looking device he'd seen earlier in another picture. No caption on this one, but Lafitte stood to the left next to Benjamin Franklin and on the right was none other than—*Walt Disney*.

Jack didn't know what to make of all of this, and he didn't have the time to figure it out.

"This tunnel ends and turns to the left," Jack whispered to Kendall and Max, "it probably leads back to the Mansion. I assume we're directly under Pirates Lair. Watch this corner."

The front row of the team knelt down so the men behind them had a shot at anyone who came around the corner. The team silently arranged their strategy with hand motions.

The bomb expert tapped Kendall on the back to let him know he was picking up small traces of something.

"Jack, the bomb must be in this area," Kendall said.

Jack silently gave the order to check every crevice in the tunnel. The SEAL team moved into position, performing without speaking a word.

They searched every square inch of the area but found nothing.

As they crept through the tunnel towards the sharp turn, they noticed an old-style spiral staircase to the right. Jack moved quickly with Kendall and Max towards the left wall of the tunnel so they could approach the sharp turn. The team followed.

Jack peeked around the corner with his night vision goggles. It was clear. Others took his place on the wall as he headed for the spiral staircase.

"This must lead up to Pirate's Lair," Jack whispered. He ordered another SEAL to stand guard by the staircase.

They made the left turn and headed towards the Mansion. This leg of the tunnel was uniform in appearance resembling the catacombs of France, with a nineteenth century New Orleans feel to it. Jack noticed a difference in theming though, everything in this leg of the tunnel referenced the Haunted Mansion. He saw a picture of Lafitte shaking hands with a man in front of the Mansion. Another portrait showed Lafitte fighting the British Army with this caption: "*The best moment of my life was when I decided to chase the brutish English from American soil. The United States would have been crushed.*"

Jack spotted the full April-December portrait from the Haunted Mansion, portraits of Benjamin Franklin, and several Andrew Jackson props that looked as if they were from the old Fort Wilderness.

About halfway through the tunnel, Jack noticed the same redbrick crypts on each side, just as they'd seen before.

"Jack, the trace of the bomb is fading."

Jack moved towards the familiar looking entrances. He opened the one on the left to find the same type of private lounge as they'd been in earlier, complete with the same oversized mirror. The other SEALs cleared the room on the opposite side of the tunnel.

Several other pictures and props lined the tunnel, telling the story of Jean

Lafitte and the role of the Mansion in the 1815 Battle of New Orleans, which resulted in an American victory—largely because of help from Lafitte and his Baratarian crew.

Another grandiose image lined the walls of the tunnel—it was Lafitte standing with several signers of the Constitution including George Washington, Benjamin Franklin, James Madison, Alexander Hamilton, and others. The inscription read: "*I sacrificed almost all that I possessed because I wanted to spare the Constitution from being trampled.*"

They continued through the tunnel until they reached the end.

"This is the door we found in the hidden pet cemetery," Jack said to Max. The tunnel turned sharply to the left. Jack opened the metal door and put another member of the team on guard.

As they made the sharp left, Jack figured this leg of the tunnel would take them back to Lafitte's Blacksmith Shop and the Pirate Wax museum, where they entered. He didn't remember another door though, at the entrance near the Blacksmith Shop.

The silence was maddening. The SEALs were itching for a confrontation. Everyone knew they were out of time, and they needed to make something to happen. They noticed that this leg of the tunnel appeared unfinished. Old wood beams emerged from the walls, the floor wasn't complete, and it wasn't themed like the other sections of the underground network.

They moved slowly through the tunnel, inspecting every inch along the way, glancing back at the bomb expert, becoming more and more desperate with each step.

A set of solid metal doors appeared out of the darkness. These doors were much different from the other ones.

Jack approached the doors and realized they were bound with an old, heavy chain lock. He motioned to one of the SEALs who came forward with over-sized bolt cutters. The SEAL struggled for a few minutes due to the thickness of the chain, but then it finally snapped. Jack opened the doors, and the team followed.

They entered a room much smaller than Lafitte's Tavern. The team quickly cleared the area. Jack realized they were in an office of some sort. At the far end of the room, there was a thick regular sized metal door. It had the familiar D on it with the ring shaped unlocking system.

He examined the desk covered with paper, documents, and pictures. "This was someone's office—someone who hasn't been down here in a long time." Jack said to Kendall. He went through a few of the papers, old sketches, handwritten notes, and small trinkets from the 60s. A script for the *Way Down Cellar* was on the right side of the desk, next to another stack of papers labeled "*Project X*". A thick layer of dust covered everything.

Jack knew he needed to keep moving. He put the gold ring in the metal door. The team covered Jack as he opened it. Nothing was visible until he moved forward a few feet and saw what looked like an underground hub—it was horseshoe shaped with several small passageways. On the wall next to each entrance were makeshift signs with abbreviations. One said "FS", another said "FG", "TL", "FL", and "SKYWAY FL". On the far right, there was a staircase going up that said "33" next to it. Jack looked at Kendall.

"The Club is directly above us—and these tunnels lead to every major location in the Park."

Kendall looked at the signs, "FL must be Fantasy Land, TL Tomorrowland, and Skyway Fantasy Land. Walt must've built tunnels leading everywhere."

Jack looked to the right, and used his hand to dust off the sign that read: *West Street.* "They dug an underground exit leading to the street."

Kendall read the West Street sign over Jack's shoulder and immediately knew what it was referring to.

THREE

1962
New Orleans Square Construction Site
Disneyland Resort

"Stan, follow me," worry covered Walt's face as he accelerated down Main Street.

Stan followed without question.

"This whole Cuban Missile Crisis thing," Walt said as his breathing quickened. "If this continues to escalate, I need to get Lilly and the girls underground."

"Khrushchev worries me Walt, he has the potential to inflate this issue into a full blown war."

Walt glanced back at Stan with his eyebrow raised. They headed towards the New Orleans Square construction site and entered through the security gate.

"Let's go to my office," Walt said.

Locked chain link fences surrounded the construction site. Each one had a dedicated security guard. It was unlike any construction project in the history of Disneyland. Security was extremely tight, it was hard for the construction workers to gain access, and people complained the extra measures were slowing down the work.

Stan didn't care. They were protecting top-secret information, and structures that needed to be kept hidden.

Walt and Stan entered the gate surrounding the area that would later become the Blue Bayou—and above that, Club 33.

Stan and Walt both pushed a large scaffold to the side, revealing a hatch in the ground. Stan quickly unlocked the entrance and descended towards the underground office.

They submerged into a quaint office similar to Walt's other offices at the Studio and at the Park. He had pictures of his girls and grandkids on his desk, memorabilia on the wall, ambient lighting, and other things that made him feel at home.

Walt sat in a large chair behind his desk, unbuttoned his suit, and grabbed a stack of papers labeled *Project X*. Stan stood in front of Walt's desk catching up on the latest Park security briefing.

"What's the plan?" Walt asked as he leaned forward in his chair.

"Well, Walt, if you want to take preventative action, it would be best to get your family, and whoever else you want to protect down here as soon as possible."

Walt listened as he looked off to his right.

"The entire underground system is complete," Stan continued, "*The System* is mostly complete, making this the safest place on the West Coast, outside of maybe a government facility. The tunnel from your office goes towards the Haunted Mansion, turns right and leads under the River to the Island. That tunnel comes back to Pirates, and another one leads back to the Mansion. We can protect a large number of people in the underground system."

"Yes, but we can only use these tunnels as a last resort because I don't want anyone to see them, I don't want people near the vault or to know about this underground network."

"Maybe we can utilize the other tunnel system," Stan motioned towards the locked metal door leading to a horseshoe shaped hub with multiple tunnel entrances, "that tunnel system allows you to quickly reach all vital locations in the Park."

"And the tunnel leading outside is fully functional?" Walt asked.

"Yes, that tunnel leads to a secret hatch on the other side of West Street."

"And what about the strength of the tunnels," Walt paused and looked down at the *Project X* packet, "for example if a nuclear bomb was detonated?"

"They are impenetrable, but it depends on where the nuke detonates—you would need to stay underground for a long time to be protected from the radiation—that's why we made the tunnel system self-sustaining, with access to fresh underground water, and we have years of supplies stored in case of a disaster."

"Okay Stan, I have my life's work stored in the vault, inventions that no one else can access—everything must be protected no matter what."

"Yes, Walt, the vault is the most secure room I've ever seen, the metal we used from floor to ceiling is similar to the metal we used in here, it's impenetrable. Also, since we built it under Lafitte's Tavern, it's disguised extremely well."

Walt frowned, "I really wanted to make this underground attraction available to guests, that was my original intention—to join the Mansion, the Island, and Pirates together. Tunnels are fascinating, and kids love them. I wanted to link everything to real US History, along with the intrigue of pirates, how Lafitte occupied Barataria, and how he helped the United States win the Battle of New Orleans—which was an integral part of our history that most are unaware of. It's an incredible concept with threads of history running through it, mixed with the intrigue of underground tunnels that transport you to new places—like the *Way Down Cellar* show. This would make New Orleans Square the most unique and wondrous experience in theme park history."

Stan listened to Walt as he nervously looked down at the security briefings in his hands. Even during stressful situations, Walt always talked about making things better, and the possibilities of the future.

"We've successfully utilized the tunnel concept throughout the Park to transport people to other worlds, and different time periods. From the tunnels at the front gate, to the tunnel we'll have before the first drop on Pirates."

Walt paused and stared at a black and white aerial picture of Disneyland on the wall.

"But what I have in the vault is just too valuable, and potentially dangerous, I don't think we can ever open up these tunnels to the public even though the vault is well-hidden."

"I agree Walt."

"The power source is nearly complete, it will be a scientific triumph, and it will power Project X in Florida. But I still wake up in the middle of the night worrying about it getting into the wrong hands."

"My thoughts exactly, Walt. That's why it's better if we limit access to the tunnels for now."

"And, there's something else, Stan—something I haven't told you, but something you need to know."

Stan tilted his head and put his security briefing down. Walt told him everything, what could he be keeping from him?

"The telescope-looking instrument I've been working on, I think I've figured it out—the code on the gold plates, and the information I unlocked inside the plates. It's the instrument that Benjamin Franklin wrote about—I haven't used it yet, but I've finally cracked the code and it's going to change our world."

"Okay..." Stan didn't know what to say, his mind was racing—preoccupied with the current crisis.

"It's a portal—a gateway—it's what the founders used to gain information beyond themselves, to form the greatest country on earth. It's why the Declaration of Independence fascinated Lafitte, he discovered the power of the machine too. The founders were able to reach beyond their existing knowledge, and access knowledge from people in the past to do extraordinary things. I can use the same discovery to make this Park, and my other projects live beyond my years. It will allow me to innovate like never before, to create the dream city, and to foster a safe feeling here at the Park. Disneyland will continue to flourish because I'll be able to set things into motion that will keep imagination overflowing for decades after I'm gone."

"Walt, are you serious?"

"Stan, do you realize what this will allow me to do? If I can make it work and advance this secret technology, I can bring the less fortunate to Disneyland, kids with terminal diseases, people who'd never get the opportunity to come here otherwise—I can bring them here to experience the magic. I can tap into the most brilliant minds of the past and learn from their wisdom. Our underground system will be like the Grand Central Station of the ages, we can keep everything hidden and do what we need to do without anyone finding out."

Walt opened a secret safe mounted under his desk and pulled out a stack of drawings and diagrams.

"I call it…the *Multiplaner*. The documents I found inside the gold plates outlined a theory explaining that the current moment is the sum of events from the past and these layers of time can be accessed with the proper technology. Similar to my multiplane camera, how it creates the illusion of depth by having several layers of artwork moving at different speeds. The depth of our current reality is comprised of several layers of time. The documents explained that the current moment is the closest representation of eternity—the present moment is when time actually touches eternity. Wisdom from the past, events from the past, ideas from the past—they're all contained in the present moment. The greatest innovators and thinkers have always had access to past ideas and wisdom through books, artwork, and other methods of documentation. But the code I found demonstrates how to physically access the other layers from the past. It's not a perfect system, but it was how the founders were able to gain so much wisdom, how they were able to defeat a British army that was one hundred times more powerful, and how they led us to becoming the most powerful country on the planet."

Stan stood in front of Walt Disney wide-eyed; he didn't know what to say. If anyone else had told him this, he would've thought they were crazy.

"Walt, this would be the greatest invention in history if it actually worked."

"I know! That's why it is so exciting!" Walt threw both of his hands in the air with a huge smile on his face, "I could use this technology for so many things! I could give people a feeling of safety in the Park so when they walk through the front gate tunnels, they'll feel as if they've been transported to another world—not just because of the atmosphere we've created, but maybe because they *have* been transported to a certain extent." Walt stopped. "Well, okay I don't know if that is possible or not. But we're the first people with this technology who have the resources, the land, and the facilities to make it work. Disneyland is our workshop; we can use the portal to access brilliant minds of the past—we can harness their wisdom to benefit humanity. The Multiplaner will open a portal to different time periods, and it can also be used as a transportation device. I can bring people here and make their dreams come true, manage Project X in Florida, my studio work, and Disneyland all at the same time. I can integrate history into the Park to allow people to learn the true history of our nation—parts of Disneyland will be like an outdoor museum."

"Walt, I don't know what to say, other than I can see why you wouldn't want anyone to know about this. Can you imagine what our government would do with this technology, or worse, our enemies?"

"I know, that's the scary part."

"And what about the energy source, it's dangerous as well. If the wrong people found out about it, they could use it to destroy everything. If the CIA found out about it, they would confiscate it."

Walt nervously scratched his chin, "I know Stan, that's why the highest level of secrecy and protection is imperative, only a select few can know about it. When I pass, I need you to protect it at all cost, and find a successor."

"And what about this current crisis, with Khrushchev?"

"Monitor it for me, hopefully Kennedy will diffuse it, but in the meantime let's get a list of people, and the different places we can utilize in case there's an emergency. Our basement under Fowler's Harbor would be a good start."

"Okay, and about the *Multiplaner*," Stan hesitated as a wave of emotion swept over him, "are you saying this could be some sort of time travel device?"

Walt grinned at Stan with a look of youthful adventure, "Anything is possible with this technology. With the information we've decoded, and the brilliant minds we'll have on our team, we can discover uncharted territory, we could change the world—and Disneyland will the place where the magic happens."

FOUR

August 8, 2010
Underground Tunnel Network
Disneyland Park

"Jack," Kendall said, "this tunnel is labeled Dark Water System, it probably leads to the first tunnels you found at the front of the River."

Jack approached the wooden sign next to the tunnel entrance and nodded to Kendall. He motioned to the rest of the team to follow him.

"Let's keep two men here, this is a central hub, and Khalid's guys could be in this tunnel system."

Two of the SEALs took their positions at the underground hub as the rest of the team proceeded through the small dark tunnel leading to the water system. These tunnels were significantly smaller than the others—raw and unpolished, not designed for the general public. Jack, Kendall, and Max led the way. Only two could fit side-by-side, so they moved quickly knowing they had to reach cover. They arrived at the first metal door, which Jack quickly opened. The team prepared for a shootout.

It was clear. They entered the room that Jack had discovered earlier, with the large pipe and another steel door heading in the direction of the Jungle Cruise. Jack darted for the second door and opened it—revealing a ramp leading downwards into a much larger tunnel.

"These tunnels must have been built early on, it was probably easier to build them while they were digging the underground water system," Jack whispered to Kendall and Max.

Everyone proceeded with caution into the bigger tunnel as they neared the Jungle Cruise. They approached a small stairway leading to a hatch labeled "Jungle Cruise" that was locked with a safe-like dial.

"Walt must have used these hatches to get above-ground at discreet locations throughout the Park." Kendall said.

"This is big enough to be a bomb shelter, sir, they could've protected hundreds of people down here in an emergency," Max said.

"We're under the Jungle Cruise right now, let's proceed." Jack ordered.

They walked the length of the Jungle Cruise attraction, under the water lagoon until they reached another familiar-looking massive metal door. The door was on the far wall directly in front of them. Jack noticed the tunnel, turned left, and he was parallel with Main Street leading towards Frontierland and the Castle entrance. He cautiously approached the large metal door in front of him.

"We must be somewhere near Town Square," Jack said as he put the gold ring to the door. Kendall and Max covered him. The thick door sluggishly opened. A few of the SEALs kept guard outside as the others moved in to clear the room. This room was enormous. Jack could see furniture and other things throughout; it looked like a large apartment, much bigger than the Dream Suite. As they searched, Max hit a switch on the wall, and the room lit up. The team removed their night vision goggles, squinting as their eyes adjusted. This apartment or living space was designed after Walt's Fire House apartment. The interior, the upholstery, everything was decorated exactly the same—even down to the rose-themed fabric on the chairs and sofas. At the far right corner of the room, Kendall noticed a gold-railed spiral staircase.

"Jack, this place is under the Fire Station Apartment." Kendall said.

Jack looked up and agreed, "It looks like Walt could've gotten down here from the Apartment."

The room had all of the amenities you would need to live for months—shower, running water, and a full kitchen. On the left side of the room, there was another large mirror on the wall; similar to the ones they'd seen in the tunnels under the River. To the right of the mirror was a control panel of some sort. Jack looked in the mirror, confused.

"It's like they used these rooms to entertain people," Jack said as he examined items on the tables. He found an old leather book sitting on one of the tables near a couch. With his free hand he flipped open the book and saw that it was a guest book of some sort. He saw names like Art Linkletter, Ronald Reagan, John F. Kennedy, and several other famous people. As he thumbed further he stopped.

Mark Twain? Andrew Jackson?

"What's wrong Jack?" Kendall asked.

"This is a guest book, but it has Mark Twain's signature, Andrew Jackson's, and others?"

"Maybe it's just a prop?"

"This doesn't look like an attraction though, it looks like Walt's private suite."

"Well, Jack, I don't think Mark Twain was here if that's what you mean."

Jack stared at the book, disillusioned.

"Okay, let's keep moving, we've been through a lot of this underground system so far, and no sign of hostiles—not one, we need to figure out where they're hiding, the bomb has to be somewhere in these tunnels."

The team moved out of the apartment and headed down the long corridor. There were several staircases and hatches as they'd seen before, probably entrances to locations on the left side of Main Street. The tunnel began to curve to the right when they saw a sign for Frontierland. A sign appeared for the Carnation Plaza Gardens, then the Castle.

Jack was expecting to find something elaborate when they approached the Castle, but there wasn't anything, not even a sign or hatch. Probably because the Castle was a high traffic area. The tunnel narrowed and angled off to the right towards the old Motorboat Lagoon.

They kept moving forward. Jack noticed a makeshift sign that said "*Matterhorn-Top*". He looked back at Kendall, "Has anyone checked the basketball court yet?"

"Not that I know of, Jack."

Max confirmed Kendall's statement and the Team Six leader nodded.

"Okay, we're going up," Jack said to the Team Six leader as Kendall headed up the stairs. Max got into position on the ground as Kendall opened the hatch. It was clear. Kendall went up through the hatch and gestured to Max. Jack went up the stairs next with Max close behind. They crawled up a narrow access that followed the contour of the mountain. Built for normal sized individuals, Max and Kendall had a hard time squeezing through with their assault kits.

They finally made it to the top of Matterhorn Mountain and entered a small area. It was a hidden storage space attached to the basketball court at the top of the tallest structure at Disneyland. CMs could access the half-court from the normal entrance, but not the hidden room. There were several machines that looked like antiques in the hidden room. Jack found drawings of the machines which showed them pointing towards the top of the Matterhorn—towards incoming Skyway gondolas. Jack studied the sketches of the old-style telescopes.

"Kendall, look at these concept drawings, the telescopes are pointing at the oncoming gondolas, have you ever seen anything like this?"

"No, I thought this was just a storage area up here, or a place for the mountain climbers to take a break."

"It almost looks as if these instruments were transporting people into another time?" Max said.

"Well, that would make sense because from the Fantasyland Station, the tunnels in the middle of the Matterhorn transported people into Tomorrowland," Kendall said.

Jack looked up at Kendall and then back down at the drawings. "Yeah, you're right, that's probably what it was." Jack approached the door with a safe-style lock on it and entered the same combination he'd used for the other doors. The door was seamless on the wall, the edges were invisible, which is probably how it remained hidden for so long. The door creaked open as they prepared for action. They entered the basketball court area of the Matterhorn and quickly scanned the room, it was clear.

"Okay. Let's head back down," Jack said.

They made their way back down the hidden Matterhorn corridor to meet with the rest of the team. Back in the underground tunnel, they proceeded towards the Motorboat Lagoon. They found a few more hatches along the way, but no hostiles. They made a sharp left towards Storybook Land.

Jack froze in his tracks. He dusted off the sign on the wall directly in front of him—"*FL Skyway*".

He looked back at Kendall, "This goes up to the old Skyway station." A wave of emotion came over him; all he could do was think of Kate.

"I'm going up," Jack said as he darted up the staircase.

"Jack, maybe we should keep going until we get to the end, we're almost to the backside of the River," Kendall said.

Jack ignored Kendall and went up the hatch. Max and Kendall followed. They entered a large room the size of the Skyway platform.

"We must be directly below the Skyway platform," Jack said.

Kendall searched the room with his night vision goggles, everything was clear, but he noticed vintage equipment everywhere, it was a workshop of some kind. Large mirrors lined the walls, and there were more telescope-looking devices in the room.

"There must be a reason why they never got rid of this Skyway chalet." Jack said.

"Well, yeah, your dad kept it here because he knew how much it meant to you."

"No, but there's something else to this." Jack frantically scanned the rest of the workshop. He knew they were running out of time, but something was drawing him to this place.

Jack grabbed a handful of papers from one of the tables, "More drawings of these telescope-like devices in the Matterhorn pointing to the Skyway Station. This was more than just an attraction, this was an experiment that Walt was working on, maybe an invention of some kind."

"It may be Jack, but we don't have time to figure it out right now."

Jack knew Kendall was right, but his emotions were getting the best of him. He'd spent so much time directly above this room, on the abandoned Skyway platform, reminiscing about Kate. This location meant so much to him.

What if this invention is what Khalid is after? What if Walt invented some type of time travel device, or portal? What if I could go back in time and save Kate?

Jack shook his head and snapped out of his delusional state. He realized how stupid and selfish this was. He was holding the team up for his own sentimental reasons.

"Okay, let's head back down," Jack ordered.

They climbed down from the hidden Skyway workshop to the underground tunnel where the SEALs were waiting.

"We're almost to the River—get ready," Kendall said. They passed a sign with a hatch above it that read "Pope" but they kept going, eager to get to the end of the tunnel. The Team tightened up and prepared for battle as they anxiously approached what looked to be the end.

"This is it, Jack, this is the end," Kendall said.

Jack had a look of despair and defeat on his face. Everything was quiet, and most of the team released their grip on their weapons. Jack walked back towards the Pope hatch, "This must be the Pope House, backstage."

Max and Kendall looked at each other, concerned about the look of desperation on Jack's face.

Jack shot up the stairs and opened the hatch.

The unmistakable sound of automatic gunfire erupted from above, Jack grabbed his arm, fell down the stairs, and slammed to the ground. Kendall ran to Jack, scooped him up like a baby, extracting him from the shower of bullets. Max stood strong and fired on the hatch with the SEALs behind him.

Two hostiles dropped through the opening and onto the tunnel ground.

The overhead assault stopped.

Without hesitation, Max charged up the stairs with the other SEALs on his tail. They emerged into the Pope House, located backstage behind Big Thunder Ranch. It was one of the original orange grove houses left 'as is' on Disney property since the beginning. The room was partially lit, and no other hostiles were in view.

CRACK—CRACK

Bullets zoomed towards Max and the other SEALs, narrowly missing. They returned fire, and two more hostiles dropped to the tunnel floor.

FIVE

1962
Fantasyland Skyway Station
Disneyland Park

"Watch this, Stan!" Walt said like an excited little boy.

Stan stood dumbfounded with Walt on the Fantasyland Skyway station platform, looking across at the Matterhorn. It was a clear Southern California night, stars glimmered in the sky, and very few employees were in the Park. Walt and Stan had Fantasyland to themselves.

"If this works as planned, these test-dummies, once they hit the Matterhorn, will be transported to a different place in the Park." Walt pointed to the human shaped "dummies" that were frequently used to test attractions.

"Transported where?" Stan asked, not knowing what to think about this.

"To the secret workshop we built under the Skyway platform. There are certain places in the Park where I've been able to transport objects. It requires the Multiplaner to be at a certain height, so I positioned it in the secret Matterhorn room. The object has to be traveling above ground, at a certain speed. That's why I had them change the speed of the gondolas."

Walt hit the button on the podium that directed the Skyway gondolas. The overhead cables yanked the empty buckets out of the station. They watched the silhouettes of the test-dummies in the moonlight as they traveled over Fantasyland towards the Matterhorn.

Walt and Stan jumped down to the end of the platform to get a better view as they waited with eager anticipation. They were like grade school kids testing a science project.

The gondola approached the Matterhorn. As it entered the giant hole in the middle of the mountain, there was a quick flash of light.

"Okay, let's go downstairs, and check it out," Walt said.

Stan followed him to the backside of the Skyway queue platform, through a door, and into a closet-like room. Walt quickly removed a rug on the floor revealing a hatch with a dial on it. He spun the combination quickly, and it opened. They both descended into the workshop under the Skyway platform.

The test dummies were on the floor. Walt's face lit up when he saw them.

"HA! HAHA! STAN, CAN YOU BELIEVE THIS?"

Stan cautiously approached the test-dummies. *How could this be? How could this have happened?*

He touched them, and they were in perfect condition. "Walt, I don't know what to say, this is unbelievable—how in the world did you pull this off?"

Walt was elated, with a whopping smile on his aged face. He coughed a few times putting his hand to his mouth, "I've figured out how to transport things to different locations with the Multiplaner! It's taken me forever to figure it out, but with the right height, speed, and location, it works!" Walt pointed to the large mirror on the wall of the workshop. "I've designed several portal gateways like this one. They allow me to transport things. I also designed a mobile version of the portal so I can transport things from different locations—anywhere in the world. The only problem is that it takes a large amount of power to make it work each time, so I can't do it a lot, it's expensive, and it requires the power source."

Stan squinted his eyes in disbelief, looking at the test dummies, then back at Walt.

"Stan, I am very close to figuring out the other part as well—stepping into another time period. I'm within a few weeks of doing a test run. This test gives me a lot of confidence that it'll actually work. I can't jump to the future, but I think it'll work for journeying to the past. If it works, I'll be able to access knowledge from Benjamin Franklin, the founding fathers, *Abraham Lincoln*, and other prominent historical figures."

"But Walt, wouldn't that disrupt the fabric of time or something like that? You meeting Benjamin Franklin?"

The moment he finished saying that he realized Walt had probably already thought this through.

"I don't think so, because it has been done before, the more I analyzed the contents of the gold plates, the more I realized that this type of thing has existed for centuries. The technology has always gone missing for a period of time, then someone from a newer generation picks it up and moves forward with it. Franklin didn't invent this, he stumbled upon it and advanced the technology. He tried to pass the information forward through the golden plates that Lafitte obtained. There's so much from the past that I can integrate into Disneyland and the Florida project. I'll take the wisdom from these legendary figures and build the perfect city in Florida while giving the next generation the keys to the city. Then, I will teach people how to gain wisdom from the past, just like all great innovators have done."

Stan looked around their hidden Skyway workshop, in awe of Walt's discovery. He was in the presence of the most brilliant man of his era.

"Walt," Stan hesitated, "if you have the ability to go back into the past, could you…" He paused again.

"Yes, Stan?"

"I mean…could you go back and make things right…you know, things that you did wrong?"

"Whoa," Walt put his hands up, "no, you can't do that because if you were to do anything besides learn and gain wisdom from other great minds, if you altered past events, you could create major problems."

"Oh, sure, that's what I thought," Stan agreed.

"But, if something like this were to work, I could ensure the long term success of the Park, I could reveal the discovery to a select group of people, a secret society, who could watch over the Park after we're gone, to make sure it stays true to my original intentions."

Stan's mind spun as he imagined all of the different possibilities.

"This will change the world, Stan. I need you to protect it—or shut it down if it gets out of hand. If something happens to me, you have to make sure the power source and the Multiplaner will not get into the wrong hands."

"Sure, Walt."

"One more thing, Stan," Walt stopped what he was doing and sat on one of the wooden workshop benches. "If for some reason my health deteriorates, I'm going to use this portal to move to another dimension, so I can continue my work."

Stan was concerned, "Walt, are you sure you're okay? Is that why you are so focused on this project?"

"Yeah, don't worry Stan, I'm fine. I'm focused on this project because it's the greatest discovery of our time, and it's my responsibility to advance it."

SIX

August 8, 2010
Underground Tunnel Network
Disneyland Park

"Jack," Kendall said as he kneeled next to him, "are you okay?"

Jack held his arm and looked up at Kendall, "Yeah, I think it just grazed my arm."

"You're bleeding everywhere, hold on," Kendall wrapped a cloth tightly around Jack's arm to stop the bleeding.

Jack was dazed after falling ten feet from the Pope House hatch. His vision blurred as he tried to get to his feet.

"The room is clear," Max yelled down the stairs. "Four hostiles down." It had been years since Max was on active duty, but his skills never faded, his aggressiveness and expert marksmanship made him extremely effective. He ran to Jack to help him up. "Are you okay, Jack?"

"Yeah, I'm fine, who was up there?"

"Looks like a few of Khalid's men set up shop in the Pope House, we found a large cache of weapons, and two CMs tied up."

"Any sign of the bomb? Are any of them alive?"

"No bomb and the four hostiles are dead."

"Have someone stay here, we need to go back through the tunnels, they might try to ambush us from the other side."

Jack struggled with his first few steps as he tried to maintain his balance. He was light headed, and his sixty-five pound assault kit didn't help.

"Let's go," Jack said as he motioned towards the Matterhorn. The SEALs moved through the tunnel under Storybook Land, then under the Motorboat Lagoon as they approached the right turn where the tunnel bent towards the Matterhorn. Jack sensed something was wrong—he took the lead at the corner, ready for an assault. The size of their team had dwindled. He cautiously peeked around the corner.

BANG-BANG-BANG-BANG

Bullets whizzed by Jack's head. Gunfire erupted. He jerked his head back, switched his Heckler & Koch 416 assault rifle to his left hand, and fired blind around the corner. The hostile gunfire came to a halt as Jack pulled his rifle back. He gestured to Kendall and Max, who in turn relayed the message to the rest of the team.

Jack took a deep breath; he could hear footsteps approaching. He waited another second and extended his 416 around the corner and opened fire again with his left hand. At the same time, Kendall, Max, and the rest of the team dove to the ground getting a better view of the hostiles.

Kendall picked them up first—BANG—BANG—BANG—three shots, three terrorists down. Max took out another two, and within seconds the gunfire ceased. Jack turned the corner with his assault rifle poised to shoot as he scanned the tunnel with his night vision goggles. All hostiles were down, and none were moving, Jack moved forward as the team followed. He heard a moan from someone on the ground. Jack sprinted towards the man, and rolled him over—the terrorist struggled to breathe.

"WHERE IS THE BOMB?" Jack yelled in his face.

The hostile tried to speak as blood trickled out of his mouth. "It—it's—under the Island—the Tavern."

Jack glanced up at Kendall and turned to race down the tunnel. "LET'S GO." He yelled.

"Luke, do you read me?" Jack said as he pressed on his earpiece. No response. Just static. They were still in the dark without *The System*.

The team moved at a quick pace through the tunnel, under the Castle, the Frontierland entrance, and down the long corridor towards Walt's hidden underground Fire Station Apartment. As they reached the corner, they moved to the right towards the underground Jungle Cruise tunnel.

"Get ready," Jack said as he looked back. He motioned to the men who stayed behind at the apartment to follow him. Jack took the lead again and slowly peeked around the corner.

It was clear.

He got low, and moved his entire body around the corner so he could get a good look. The team followed as they headed for the underground hub near Walt's secret office. They arrived at the hub where the other SEALs were waiting, and moved towards the Haunted Mansion connector. Jack spotted a man down—near the section that turned right heading towards the Island.

"Oh, no," Jack said as he ran to the SEAL and checked his pulse.

He was dead.

The stutter of automatic fire showered the tunnel walls with bullets as Jack dove to the ground for cover.

Kendall helped Jack up as they took their positions from behind the wall. The rest of the team seethed as they eyed their fallen brother, they were ready to explode, and light up whoever came around the corner. Jack caught his breath and looked at the team, "Same thing—on my call."

Jack went left-handed again using his MP7 this time to blindly hurl suppressed ammunition around the corner. The rest of the team charged ahead of Max and Kendall and didn't bother diving to the ground, they stood up and opened fire as they moved forward. With rage in their hearts, they controlled their emotions and hit targets with miraculous precision—they cleared the tunnel within seconds, leaving ten hostiles dead. Jack checked the terrorists on the ground to see if there were any who could give him information. They were all dead, each one from a SEAL team headshot.

Jack led the team forward towards Pirate's Lair so they could make the final turn towards the Tavern. He peered around the corner again and pulled back.

He took a longer glance—no one there.

He saw the wooden doors leading to the Tavern in the distance as he turned the corner. The team moved slowly, trying to not make a sound. Jack abruptly paused and put his arm up, turning to the other men.

"We have to assume they've taken our men we left in the Tavern," he whispered, "we need to spread out, and take this room at all cost."

They nodded.

The team crept towards the wooden door.

Jack's earpiece buzzed.

It seemed as if he was getting reception. Jack stopped the men as he pressed on his earpiece.

"Luke?" he whispered.

Static continued in his ear.

Unexpectedly, a voice came through.

"*Jack Duncan*."

"Who is this?"

"This is Khalid al-Haddad. I need you to have your team stand down immediately."

"Why would I do that?" Jack said as he kept his eyes on the door. Kendall, Max, and the team listened to every word Jack uttered keeping their weapons focused on the door.

"Because I am the one in control of this bomb. I am the one who can end this nightmare for you. I can guarantee you that the bomb will not detonate."

"And I'm supposed to trust you? You're crazy Khalid. You're about to meet *your* worst nightmare, the most skilled fighters on the planet. They want blood—and they know you've already killed some of our brothers."

"It's not that easy, and you know it Jack. The bomb is underground, and if anything happens to me it will automatically detonate. This entire park will be leveled—everyone will die. I only want you. If you help me get what I want, then I will help you get what *you* want."

"What do you want, Khalid?"

"Tell your team to stand down, come in here unarmed and alone, and I will tell you."

"How would you know what I want?"

"You want Nikolai, I know that. You want revenge. I can show you how to get your revenge while saving everyone here."

Jack glanced over to Kendall, and then to Max.

"Jack, you have no other choice," Khalid continued, "you've been through all the tunnels and you're no closer to finding the bomb—let alone disarming it. You'll never find it in time. I'm giving you a way out, a way to save lives. I have bigger plans than this amusement park—if you help me, I will help you."

Jack tried to catch a glimpse of Andy and Grace on his wrist device, but the feed was scrambled.

He looked back at the team, "Everyone fall back, I'm going in."

"Sir?" the SEAL Team Six team leader looked confused.

"Do what he says," said Kendall looking back at Jack, who was already dropping his weapons to the ground.

"Tell them they need to go all the way back to Lafitte's Blacksmith Shop," ordered al-Haddad, "stay there, no outside transmissions."

Jack relayed the message to the team, and they retreated. Kendall turned towards Jack and put his hand on his shoulder. "I'm going with you, Jack."

Jack half-smiled at Kendall, "No, brother, not this time, I need to finish this one on my own."

Jack embraced Kendall's arm.

"Sir, if anyone can handle this, you can," Max said as he shook Jack's hand.

"Thanks Max."

Kendall, Max, and the team retreated back down the tunnel towards the Blacksmith Shop.

Jack was on his own against the number two al-Qaeda terrorist in the world.

He took a deep breath as he approached the wooden doors of Lafitte's Tavern.

SEVEN

August 8, 2010
Lafitte's Underground Tavern
Disneyland Park

The massive wooden door of Lafitte's underground Tavern creaked opened.

"Put your hands on your head and turn around," Jack reluctantly complied.

A man approached him and patted him down.

"Walk backwards until I tell you to stop," said the voice from the other side of the room.

Jack inched backwards with his hands on his head.

"Stop."

"Khalid, show yourself you coward. I don't have time for games."

"Jack Duncan," Khalid emerged from the far end of the room. "We finally meet." Khalid motioned to his underling, "Tie his hands together."

Jack turned around to see four hostiles with Khalid in the Tavern. He looked Khalid dead in the eyes with a piercing stare.

Khalid smiled.

"Where is Nikolai? And where's my father?" Jack asked.

"You'll soon find out Jack, in the meantime, I need your help."

Jack glared at him without blinking or making a single movement. "Prove that you can deliver Nikolai to me."

"Jack, I have that old man in the palm of my hand. Sure, he's the one who gave us all the info about the tunnel network, he's been watching your father and Walt Disney since the inception of this park. I have no need for him now, he's taken me the distance—I just need to get inside the vault."

"What vault?"

"There's a vault under this room, and there's something in there that I need."

"What?"

"You don't need to be concerned with details, Jack, you just need to do what I say."

Jack leaned forward and yelled, "I WILL STICK MY FIST DOWN YOUR THROAT AND—"

"I believe you, I've seen what you've done to my men in Afghanistan. But you are in no position to threaten me. You open the vault, I get what I need, and then I will stop the detonation sequence. Get me off the property, undetected, and you will have saved the day…again."

"And when do I get Nikolai?"

"I'll turn him over once I'm off the property, and you can do whatever you want with him."

Jack's eyes were full of rage; they locked on to Khalid's like heat seeking missiles.

He broke his stare and his eyes shifted.

"No."

"No? What do you mean no, Jack?"

"The President of the United States wants your head, I cannot let you walk away from here."

"I'm getting out of here anyway, Jack. Don't you realize that? If you don't get me what I want, I will exit, and detonate the bomb, it's that simple. You can either help me, and save thousands of lives, or you can decline my offer, and you will die with everyone else. Like I said, Disneyland isn't my ideal target, but I will take it if things don't work out."

Jack grit his teeth.

"WHERE IS THE BOMB KHALID?"

Khalid chuckled, "Jack, I'm not the one tied up unarmed, I'm the one making the deals."

"How am I supposed to open a vault that I know nothing about? I've never even seen this room until today."

"I know Jack, but your dad has," Khalid removed his backpack and pulled out what looked like a journal. "Untie him," Khalid ordered one of his men. "Have a seat Jack."

Khalid tossed the journal on the large wooden nineteenth century-style table in the middle of the room as a plume of dust scattered into the air. Jack sat down with four automatic weapons aimed at him.

"What is this?"

"It's from your father, I think he wanted you to find all of this someday, eventually, but he didn't think you were ready, or at least that's what it seems from reading his journal. We don't have time to read it all, so I just want you to focus on this right here."

Khalid opened the book to a page that showed a diagram of the Tavern. On the page, it showed the large wooden table with *1764* etched into it, then a picture of the ring.

Jack looked up at Khalid, "It's under this table, help me move it."

Khalid nodded at two of his men as he kept his weapon focused on Jack. They helped Jack move the massive table, and then he got down on his hands and knees to search the ground. He moved thick layers of dust. He noticed a familiar circle etched into the ground.

"It's right here," Jack said as he looked up at Khalid, "grab that metal bar over there so I can pry this open."

One of the men grabbed the thick bar from the table on the far side of the room and handed it to Jack while keeping their weapons on him. "Help me hold this down while I try to get it open," Jack said. Two of the men looked at Khalid for permission and got down next to Jack.

Jack attempted to pry the hatch open with the bar.

CLANK-CLANK

Jack cracked the skulls of the two men next to him, knocking them flat on their backs. He immediately dove at Khalid, grabbed his hand and forced his gun on the two other men, killing them instantly. He elbowed Khalid in the face sending him reeling to the floor. Jack grabbed the gun and pointed it at Khalid.

"WHERE IS THE BOMB, KHALID? TELL ME NOW OR YOU DIE."

"Jack, I would rather die than tell you. Go ahead and kill me, but if you kill me, that bomb will explode," Khalid said as he looked at the lifeless bodies of his men on the ground. "Like I said, I am the only one who can help you."

"I *will* find the bomb Khalid, I've got the best team in the world here, so you either tell me now, or die."

Jack flipped Khalid face down on the ground forcing both of his hands behind his back. He drove his knee into Khalid's spine and jerked his head back by grabbing a handful of his hair.

"Do you feel that Khalid? I am going to snap your vertebrae one by one until you tell me where the bomb is."

"Jack—" Khalid was suffocating, he couldn't breathe with the way Jack was manipulating him. "There's something you need to see, Jack, in my backpack."

"What are you talking about?"

"Pull out my tablet and turn it on."

"I don't trust you—tell me where this bomb is, NOW." Jack applied more pressure to Khalid's neck.

Khalid yelled in excruciating pain, struggling for air and unable to take the pressure on his neck.

"JACK, THERE IS NO BOMB, LOOK ON MY TABLET."

Jack was confused, he kept him pinned down as he unzipped the backpack and grabbed Khalid's tablet.

Khalid gasped for air.

Jack turned the tablet around and hit the home button—nothing happened.

"What are you talking about, we've already detected a bomb, don't lie to me Khalid—"

Jack froze as the tablet lit up.

The bright light from the screen was blinding at first, and then his eyes began to focus.

A fuzzy image of three people appeared on the screen.

Jack squinted his eyes.

The image became clearer.

Jack's heart stopped.

His throat constricted.

His arms went numb.

It felt as if someone ripped his stomach out.

NO, NO—NO, this can't be?

It was a live video feed of Andy and Grace.

Jack could see their frightened faces come into focus.

They were tied up and gagged.

Even worse, he saw the evil ragged face that had haunted his dreams for so many years.

It was Nikolai.

He was holding Andy and Grace at gunpoint.

"WHERE IS THIS?" Jack yelled at Khalid, "This can't be real." Jack tried to activate his wrist device, but it wouldn't work.

Khalid was face down on the ground with Jack on top of him. "Like I said Jack, I am the only one who can help you. There is no bomb, we knew that your desire for revenge would lead us here. We couldn't have gotten inside these tunnels without you, we knew they were here, but we couldn't get in. We knew you would get in at all cost if you thought Nikolai was here, and if you thought you could diffuse the bomb."

Jack continued to stare at the live feed in disbelief, "No, no, no this can't be happening," Jack gripped Khalid's tablet with both hands—shaking uncontrollably, "WHERE ARE THEY?" he yelled at Khalid striking the back of his head with the palm of his hand.

Khalid's head slammed against the floor as blood from his nose shot through the air. His head came to rest on the floor with his eyes closed.

"They are above-ground, on the Island, with other hostages. Your kids don't need to be harmed, Jack. I want to get in the vault, get what I need, and get out of here."

Jack jumped up and ran for the door.

"Not so quick, Jack." Khalid pointed an assault rifle at him.

Jack turned around and yelled in Khalid's face, completely ignoring the gun pointing at his chest. "Nikolai will kill my kids, that's what he wants, revenge for his son's death, that's what this is all about."

"Like I said, Jack, I have full control over Nikolai, he will not harm your kids if you do what I say. All you need to do is open the vault. I have a helicopter that should be landing on the River now. After I get what I need out of the vault, you'll take me upstairs to the helicopter."

"They'll never allow that chopper leave this airspace."

"Yes, I realize that. It's a diversion. I want them to think I'm on board, but in reality I will slip into the River, and then exit through the West Street tunnel. Your government will believe they killed me in the helicopter. You will look like a hero, and your kids will be saved."

"What could possibly be in this vault that you would go to all this trouble for?"

"It's better if you don't know Jack, trust me, you've already served your miserable country, you are a hero, haven't you sacrificed enough? Is it really worth losing your kids over this? I mean you've already lost your wife—"

Jack dove at Khalid and knocked him to the ground.

Khalid's rifle slid across the wooden floor.

Jack quickly put him in a suffocating headlock lifting him off his feet.

"Jack—" Khalid struggled to talk as his feet dangled off the ground, "if I die, or do not answer Nikolai in the next few minutes, he will kill your kids. You have to keep me alive and stay on schedule, or it's over for you."

Jack increased the pressure. Everything in him wanted to snap his neck and hunt Nikolai down on his own terms.

He released his grip and yelled in Khalid's ear, "This is about a nuclear weapon isn't it? That's the only reason why you'd go to all this trouble."

"Yes, it is, but Jack, I am not going to detonate it here, it will be in another city, and that's only if we can make it work, so there's a chance it might not even happen."

"I can't let you leave here with nuclear capability on American soil, are you insane?"

"Jack Duncan—the deadliest soldier in US history wouldn't allow that, but Jack Duncan—Andy and Grace's dad—will."

Jack paused.

"No one will ever know, this is out of your hands, you've given enough to your country, it's time to think about your own family now—your kids."

Jack took a deep breath. He realized that his desire for revenge had caused this situation. His inability to keep his emotions in check had put him in this predicament. There was no bomb, he didn't have to open the tunnel doors, he could've listened to Kendall and got the kids off property, and none of this would have happened—his kids would be safe if it weren't for him.

It was his fault.

Getting final revenge on Nikolai blinded him.

The stinging realization of his culpability in this disaster sliced him to the core.

He released Khalid.

Jack's hands trembled as he watched the haunting images of Andy and Grace on the tablet. He was losing control.

He focused on Grace's terrified little face.

Fear.

It was never a part of his psyche, but it was overtaking him.

He stared at the images while his chest heaved.

His body shook involuntarily.

His mind flashed back to the day Grace was born.

EIGHT

2000
The Birth of Grace

"She's beautiful!" Jack said with an ear-to-ear smile. He took baby Grace into his arms as Kate looked on from her hospital bed. Jack knelt down next to Kate.

"She looks just like you," Jack said with an awe-struck expression on his face. Watching Kate birth their babies made Jack respect her even more. The pain, the struggle, the twenty-five hours of labor, and watching his baby girl come into the world was an unparalleled miracle. Kate's soft face glowed; she looked beautiful, even though she was exhausted.

"I can't believe we have a baby girl!" Jack said.

"Knock, Knock." Kendall was at the door with a giant balloon and flowers. The nurse took one look at Kendall and couldn't believe how big he was; he barely fit through the door.

"Kendall," Jack smiled at Kendall as he approached.

"I brought something for little Gracie," Kendall bent down to look in her eyes with a smile on his face.

"It's your Uncle Kendall, Gracie," Kate said as she smiled at baby Grace.

"Can I hold her?"

"Sure, you can," Jack carefully handed Grace over to Kendall. She looked like a miniature doll in his arms.

Kendall grinned at Grace as he rocked her in his arms.

A lady's voice came from the doorway, "The boys will have a tough time getting by Uncle Kendall."

"Mom!" Kate said.

"Honey, I am so proud of you," she said as she rushed towards the baby. Kendall handed Grace to her.

"Oh, my, she's beautiful, Kate."

"I'm so glad you made it mom!"

"I wouldn't miss it for the world, although I almost did due to snow on the runway at JFK."

"Hey, Mom," Jack said as he leaned in to kiss her cheek.

"Jackie, I am so glad to see your handsome face. You two make beautiful babies, that's for sure!"

Jack hugged her. Over the years, she'd taken a liking to Jack, and they'd become extremely close. In many ways, she was like the mom he never had.

"Look who I have here!" Stan was at the doorway with Andy. "Someone wants to meet his little sister!"

"Andy!" Kate was thrilled to see him, "Come here, baby, I've missed you so much!"

Stan lived for moments like this, he adored babies, and he couldn't think of anything better than being at the hospital when his grandkids were born.

"I can't believe I have another grandchild!" Stan said with a giant grin on his face.

Andy grinned, and his eyes lit up as he approached baby Grace, he had a gift for her. He giggled when he saw her squished little face topped off with a striped hospital cap.

"Hi Gracie, I'm your big brother!"

Kate's mom rapidly snapped pictures as Stan fiddled with his camera trying to get it to work. Kate smiled with tears in her eyes as she watched Andy meet his sister for the first time.

The nurse cut in, "Okay, let's take Grace over to the weighing station."

Jack remained near Kate's bed as everyone else went over to the baby station to watch the nurse record Grace's vitals.

"Kate," Jack looked into her eyes as his eyes welled up with tears, "I am so proud of you, and I just don't know what I'd do without you. I can't imagine life without you. It's so rare, what we have, and I am so grateful for you. I'll always protect you and the kids no matter what."

"Oh, Jack, I know you will. Hey, I'm married to the most decorated Navy SEAL in history, I've got nothing to worry about!"

He framed Kate's face with both hands and kissed her forehead.

"I love you, Kate Duncan."

"I love you too, Jack."

NINE

August 8, 2010
Lafitte's Underground Tavern
Disneyland Park

Jack continued to glare at the tablet, in a psychotic daze, paralyzed with fear. He could see that Andy was distressed; his eyes were scrunched, rapidly shifting back and forth.

He could see Nikolai's wretched face, and all he could think about was strangling him.

He looked up at Khalid, "I'll open the vault, but I want Kendall on the Island with my kids."

"Jack, I can't do that, Kendall will take out Nikolai."

"He won't, I'll give him direct orders, he'll listen to me. You already have other men on the Island, if Kendall tried anything, they would take him out."

"You don't think I realize that Kendall could slaughter dozens of my men before they'd be able to kill him?"

"He'll listen to my orders, that's the only way I'm going along with this. Otherwise, I'm going up there right now and taking my chances."

Khalid paused for a second; he was a master decision maker, which is one of the reasons why he'd moved up the ranks of al-Qaeda.

"Okay Jack—deal."

"Open my communications up to Kendall, now."

Khalid switched his tablet to a control panel app and pressed a button.

Jack put his finger on his earpiece, looking at Khalid. "Kendall? Do you read?"

"Jack? What's going on?"

"I can't explain everything right now, but I need you to go to the Island, Nikolai has the kids—"

"WHAT JACK? HOW?" Kendall's voice came roaring through his earpiece.

"Kendall, I just need you to go there, don't do anything unless I give you a direct order, the hostiles on the Island know you're heading their way. Don't engage, I repeat, do not do anything under ANY circumstance, without my approval, are we clear?"

"Yes, Jack."

The transmission ended, and Jack turned to Khalid. "Okay, let's go."

Jack got down on the floor and pulled out the ring. He stood over the door as he put the ring in place.

Nothing happened.

"Nikolai said these doors are retina scan equipped, you need to put your eyes in the right place for it to open."

Jack looked cautiously at Khalid and then aligned his eyes at the proper location on the hatch.

Silence filled the room.

After a few seconds, something clicked, and the hatch slightly opened. Jack pulled the underground door up revealing a stairway leading down into darkness. He glanced at Khalid and headed down the stairs. Khalid followed.

The vault was the same size as the Tavern, and it had equipment everywhere. He noticed the same type of telescope looking machines that they saw in the Matterhorn, stacks of drawings, blueprints, file cabinets, and framed artwork.

"It's over here," Khalid said as he walked to the far end of the room to what looked like a bank safe.

Jack approached the safe door and noticed the familiar ring sized etched cavity. He paused for a minute. His mind raced through every possible alternative, there had to be another way.

The images of Andy and Grace haunted him. He had to save them at all cost; he couldn't live with himself if something happened to them—especially if it was his fault.

He put the ring to the door and put his face in the vicinity of the ring hole. Everything was quiet for a few moments, then CLANK—the safe opened and the heavy door creaked towards them.

Khalid grabbed the safe door and entered immediately. He frantically searched through the items in the vault until he found what he needed.

"This is it! Okay, Jack, it's time to go," Khalid walked out of the vault, and Jack put his arm out to stop him.

"You said you would turn Nikolai over to me, how is this going to work, and how do I know my kids will be safe?"

"In a few minutes, you will transmit to your CIA director and tell him that I have you at gunpoint and that I'm boarding the helicopter. They'll assume that once I get on that chopper they'll be able to blow it out of the sky. Tell them if something goes wrong, you'll give them the order to "TAKE THE ISLAND"—which gives them the signal to attack the Island to prevent me from leaving."

"Then what?"

"We go up to the Island, you get me to the helicopter, I will slip through the bottom compartment into the water so I can get to the hatch that will lead me to West Street. Once I am clear, I will confirm with Nikolai, and he will release your kids."

"Why would he release my kids? He wants to kill them?"

"Actually, he doesn't, he wants to kill you and your father, he doesn't want your kids—they are for insurance. I will tell Nikolai that you've agreed to surrender once I am clear. Once he releases your kids, you can do whatever you want with him, I don't care."

"I don't believe you Khalid, there is no way I can trust you to follow through with all of this."

"But you can trust me, Jack because I need you to make this whole thing work—I need you to keep this secret, which is why I'll deliver your kids unharmed, that way I know you'll keep this whole thing quiet and under the radar."

Jack's stomach turned, he habitually grabbed the back of his neck to nurse the constant pain he felt, but there was no pain this time, he was numb.

His mind spun as he came to the realization that he was making a deal with the devil himself.

"Make the call." Khalid pointed to Jack's earpiece as he tapped a few commands on his tablet. "And you better sell this, Jack."

Jack squinted his eyes, pressed the earpiece, and listened for the Director's voice.

"Jack, what's going on, can you hear me?" Director Camden said frantically.

"Sir, you need to listen to me," Jack spoke quickly in a low tone, "Khalid has me, and he's going to take me by gunpoint to the chopper that landed on the River. Let him board the chopper, and once he gets out of range you can track and destroy it. If something goes wrong, I'll give another command, for all units in the vicinity to take the Island, which means to launch a full scale attack."

"But Jack, your kids are on the Island?"

"I have to go—wait for my transmission, get all teams ready to act on my orders."

Khalid cut the transmission, "Very good Jack—let's head out." Khalid put the items he retrieved from the vault and his tablet in his backpack. "There's a secret hatch directly above this Tavern that opens inside the fake Tavern building on the Island, let's go through there."

They went up through the hatch and entered the Tavern building at the front of Tom Sawyer Island.

"We need to hold here, Jack." Khalid said as he kept his gun on him.

"Sit here for a minute, I need to get some final things ready."

Jack stared straight ahead, trying to get his anger under control. His rage was different now, it was directed towards himself instead of Nikolai. He knew that he could've easily prevented this. Everyone had been right for all of these years. His desire for revenge had stolen his joy, it had robbed Andy and Grace of their father, and now it had put him in a situation where his kids could be killed in front of his own eyes within minutes. His only other choice was to put the lives of millions of people at risk by letting Khalid go while harboring a lie.

Anything sounded better than losing his kids. Maybe he could stop both things from happening. But he needed to save his kids no matter what.

Jack closed his eyes, hoping this was just another one of his vivid nightmares.

With his eyes closed, he could see Kate and the kids posing for a picture with the glimmering Rivers of America behind them. The brilliant rays of sunlight illuminated Kate with a divine glow, Andy and Grace beamed with excitement and anticipation. The Mark Twain sailed by, and the aroma of Pommes Frites from Café Orleans was carried by the cool breeze. The smiles on their faces revealed the feeling that everything was okay—they had nothing to worry about, and so much to look forward to in their future life at Disneyland.

TEN

September 11, 2001
Disneyland Park

Jack glanced at his phone and answered it once he saw it was Kate.

"Hold on a second, gentlemen," Jack said to the team following him along the Rivers of America.

"Hi, sweetheart, what's up?"

"JACK—are you seeing this? Something just crashed into the World Trade Center, and it's on fire."

"WHAT?" the men following Jack stopped talking and stared at him, Kendall approached him to find out what was wrong.

"My mom is in there," Kate said frantically over the phone, "I know she is, she always goes in early. I can't get a hold of her, she's not answering her phone."

"It's okay, don't panic, maybe she isn't there today. Hold on, Kate." Jack lowered his phone, "We need to get to the Control Center now—Kendall, get NYPD on the line for me."

Everyone headed for the Control Center. Jack held the phone to his ear as he ran. Kate was crying.

"Jack hold on—" Kate's call dropped.

Jack raced for the Control Center making calls to Park executives.

They arrived at the Control Center just in time to watch the second plane hit in real-time. Everyone in the room gasped, not believing what they were seeing.

"This is no accident," Jack said, "get everyone on high alert. Contact all of our security personnel. Kendall, have you gotten through to anyone?"

"No, Jack, all of the lines are down in the city, I can't get through."

Jack dialed Kate again, no answer.

All they could do was stare at the overhead monitors listening to the reporters trying to put the pieces together.

Suddenly, to their horror, the South Tower fell to the ground. Seasoned professionals in the room had horror on their faces and couldn't speak; they just held their hands to their mouths.

Jack watched in terror, thinking that Kate's mom might have been in that tower. At the same time, rage overwhelmed him. He didn't need confirmation from anyone, he knew exactly who did this, it was al-Qaeda—this was a deliberate attack on the United States. His blood boiled, he instinctively wanted to avenge the deaths of the innocent and the first responders who were in the building.

"Yes," Jack said to someone on his phone, "we're not opening the Park today, this is an act of terror, this is no accident, and we must be on high alert, we're a high-value target."

Jack hung up the phone and continued to watch the screens with his hands clenched.

Jack looked at Kendall, who knew exactly what he was thinking. Their chests heaved with anger.

Jack tried Kate again—no answer.

He jumped on a computer terminal to scan the perimeter of the Park. He flipped through prior alerts checking for any connection to the attacks. He scanned every aspect of *The System* to make sure the Park was safe.

A woman screamed.

Jack looked up at the monitors to see the horrifying image of the North Tower crashing to the ground. His heart fell through his stomach as he bent over and put both hands on the desk. The massive plumes of smoke, people running down the streets of New York, and the realization that thousands of people were probably dead, triggered fury inside of him that he hadn't felt for years.

Everyone in the room looked at Jack, they knew Kate's mom worked in the South Tower.

His phone rang, it was Kate.

"Kate?"

All he could hear was sobbing on the other end. Kate tried to talk, but Jack couldn't make out what she was saying.

"JACK—my mom—she called me from the tower—the heat—it was too much—NO!!!"

Tears came to Jack's eyes, his throat knotted up, and his stomach twisted. She was like a mother to him; she took him in as her own child, and treated him like her own son.

Kate, who'd already lost her dad, was now without her mom—and was forced to experience her mom's horrifying last moments.

He tried to stay strong for her.

"Kate, honey—" he stopped talking because he couldn't hold back the tears, he cried like a baby as Kendall put his hand on his shoulder to comfort him.

Then he caught himself and immediately choked back the tears.

He had that look on his face again, something Kendall recognized instantly. Jack's expression of crazed determination was something that even Kendall feared.

ELEVEN

August 8, 2010
Tom Sawyer Island
Disneyland Park

Jack opened his eyes. A small tear formed on the right corner. He turned around to see Khalid working on his tablet. He squinted his eyes with hate towards Khalid, and everything al-Qaeda stood for. This unfortunately wasn't one of his reoccurring nightmares, it was real.

In 2001, Jack's rage turned into a desire to avenge the death of Kate's mom, and the thousands of people who died on September 11—leading him back to The Teams.

Kate begged him not to go, but he wouldn't listen. He wanted blood and justice. He felt that he'd chickened out by leaving The Teams early. Kendall tried to talk him out of returning to active duty, but Jack wouldn't listen.

He went on countless missions on the hunt for Osama Bin Laden, killing most of the top 100 al-Qaeda leaders.

After all of the killing, the sacrifice, the lonely nights in far away deserts, and the time away from his family—he was now cooperating with one of the architects of 9/11.

Jack was confused and disoriented.

This went against everything he'd ever fought for, everything that he believed in.

2004

"Jack, please, we need you to come home," Kate pleaded over the phone, "my mom wouldn't have wanted this. You've done enough."

"Kate, I need to finish this, I set out to get the man responsible for your mom's death, and I can't quit until I get him."

"But what about the kids, Jack? They miss you, they've been without their father for the last three years."

Jack was silent, blinded by his rage, and hate-fueled tunnel vision.

"And what about me Jack? What about us? I know you did this for my mom, our mom, but I am telling you, Jack, I knew her better than anyone, she wouldn't have wanted you to do this. There are so many other capable people who can fight this war, you don't need to be there, you've done enough for your country."

Jack stared at the picture he carried with him of Kate, Andy, and Grace on the Rivers of America.

"Jack, revenge is *not yours*, don't you realize that? The hate that runs through your veins will not bring my mom back, it will poison you, smother you, it will ruin your life. You could lose your kids, and me."

Suddenly it hit him. Jack realized how blinded he'd become. He started to weep.

"I'm sorry Kate, you're right."

PRESENT DAY - TOM SAWYER ISLAND

"What's taking so long?" Jack asked Khalid, who was still typing away on his tablet.

"I have a lot to prepare before we go out there, and my connection is horrible right now."

"Hurry up, let's get this done before I change my mind."

"Almost there, Jack," Khalid paused as he analyzed something on his tablet. "Your military has a lot of firepower in the air right now surrounding the Island, they aren't messing around, are they?"

Jack glared at Khalid and paced back and forth.

"We're set, let's head out. Act like your hands are tied behind your back."

They exited the above-ground shell of Lafitte's Tavern. Jack looked out at an empty New Orleans Square. They turned down to the dirt path and walked through the dense Island foliage until they reached the sign pointing right towards Pirate's Den, directly across the River from Splash Mountain on the left. Khalid pointed his handgun to Jack's back as they turned right and approached the wooden-rope Pontoon Bridge that spanned over the edge of the River. Across the way, traces of the old Nature's Wonderland were visible. Jack could hear the helicopter's rotors as he and Khalid turned left in front of the Pontoon Bridge.

"Where are my kids, Khalid?"

"They are near the helicopter."

Jack could hear the familiar sound of Navy helicopters in the distance. He had unlimited firepower at his disposal, but he was powerless, he couldn't use it.

Jack's earpiece crackled, and his head turned reflexively. He looked forward, not wanting Khalid to notice.

"Jack?" the voice broke up. Jack couldn't determine who it was.

"Jack," this time the voice was crystal clear, "The System is back, I got it back, the lights are on, Jack!" Luke frequently used this phrase when *The System* came back online from maintenance mode.

Jack looked to his left and right to see if one of the cameras would catch a glimpse of him and Khalid.

"Jack, I see you on the continuous video feed now, and I see Khalid. I will give you info, ask questions, and you can just nod or make signs to communicate."

Jack looked back at Khalid whose gun was lazily pointed in his direction. Khalid was preoccupied with his tablet.

"There are approximately eighty hostiles on the Island, the kids are with Nikolai by the helicopter. We have four helicopters hovering right now, two that can strike from the air and the other two are ready to insert two Mark V SOC's full of SEALs, who will attack from the water. We have snipers setup across the River from all angles."

Jack inconspicuously scanned the area to confirm what Luke was saying.

"We have a clear shot right now on Khalid, do you want me to take it?"

Jack immediately shook his head no.

"Kendall is on the Island, and he's unarmed, they confiscated his weapons. We do NOT have a clear shot on Nikolai, he's well hidden and using the kids as a shield. Jack—I've run diagnostics on what Khalid has in his possession, there's an extremely good chance, I'd say a 95% chance that what he just obtained underground will give him nuclear capability on US soil. I'm sure you understand that we have no choice, we have to take him out."

Jack knew Luke was right, he knew Khalid wouldn't go to all this trouble unless there was a monumental upside. However, the only way to keep Andy and Grace safe was to go along with Khalid. He had more than enough manpower to take him out along with all of his men, but the chance of his kids getting hurt in the process was extremely high.

Dirt crunched under Jack's boots as everything moved in slow motion.

I have no other choice? No one will know if I let Khalid escape, I've already lost so much, I cannot lose them. They're innocent, they didn't do anything, they depend on me, they think that I'll protect them. I already failed to protect Kate, I am NOT going to fail them again.

"Oh and Jack," Luke hesitated, "I thought you should know…Kim is with the kids." Jack's eyes shifted erratically trying to figure out what Luke meant, "It appears that she had something to do with Nikolai getting the kids."

Jack grunted and grit his teeth so hard it felt as if he crushed his molars.

He continued down the narrow dirt path with the water on his right. Thick, aged tree branches hung over the pathway, man-made rock structures created an overhead barrier. After passing under the rock structure, the helicopter came into view, floating on the water directly ahead of him. They passed the old wooden pirate boat on the left and approached a small landing directly across from Fort Wilderness. The landing was roped off where the helicopter sat on the water.

Four men greeted Khalid with a hug. He quickly took off his backpack and gave them a glimpse of the device. The looks on their faces confirmed what Jack was thinking—they had nuclear capability.

"Jack," Luke said through his ear bud, "the one embracing Khalid right now is Amir Ahmad, a leading al-Qaeda weapons expert, he's verifying the device."

Jack looked beyond the landing, his mouth dropped, and his eyes widened.

He made eye contact with Andy and Grace.

They were gagged with their hands tied behind their back. Kim stood with them with her hands tied. Nikolai's pale white face emerged from the darkness with a cynical grin.

Jack locked eyes with Nikolai momentarily. He felt a surge of adrenaline rush through him. Everything in him wanted to rush Nikolai, but he was equally, if not more, furious with Kim and her unforgivable betrayal.

Jack snapped.

He darted towards Nikolai.

Something struck him in the back of his legs. He landed flat on his back in front of the men who hit him—getting nowhere.

"Jack?" Khalid looked over. "Let's stick with the plan."

Jack tried to pull himself together. Everything was black, and blurry as he looked straight into the starry heavens.

He turned on his side and tried to prop himself up when he noticed several assault rifles pointing in his direction.

Khalid shook hands with the scientist as they embraced again, smiling.

"Jack, are you okay?" Luke said, "The scientist just confirmed with Khalid. Jack I know this is an impossible situation for you, but right now you are the only one who can make the call to Director Camden. If you let Khalid go, he'll most likely detonate a nuclear bomb on US soil. No matter what he's told you, don't believe it—millions of people will die—certain areas will be uninhabitable for decades. There's only a small window of time to make a decision, we need to take him out, and we need to do it now."

Jack's vision came back into focus. He saw his beautiful kids and their frightened faces. He knew Luke was right. He'd be signing the death certificate of millions of people if he didn't order the strike right now.

The CIA director watched via the live feed from Virginia, the President and his entire staff watched from the situation room at the White House.

Everyone was on the edge of their seats.

They all knew the impact the next few moments would have on millions of people's lives, the United States, and the rest of the world. They knew

Khalid had to be stopped at all cost. He could not be allowed to get the device off property. At the same time, they knew a strike would probably kill innocents, including Jack's kids.

"The President just ordered an attack on the Island, they don't believe Khalid is getting on that chopper," Luke said frantically, "I just jammed all transmissions, so you are the only person the team leader can hear. It's your call, Jack."

Jack looked around, knowing full well what the right choice was, but the line between right and wrong was grey. He knew how these raids worked—civilian casualties were guaranteed—and Nikolai would most likely harm Andy and Grace once the bullets started to fly.

All of the teams on site knew the President was desperate to take out Khalid, and no one would stop until he was dead—collateral damage would be accepted.

He looked at his kids, then at Nikolai, and then back at Khalid.

TWELVE

2005
Main Street, USA
Disneyland Park

"Jack, I'm so glad you are back, and we have our life again here at the Resort." Kate said with a huge smile as she held hands with Andy and Grace. They walked down Main Street towards the Castle with the thrill of anticipation for what they had ahead of them. A life of living at Disneyland, being together 24/7, no more goodbyes, no more missing each other, no worries about money, or anything else. They had the ideal life, a dream life, a life inside the magical gates that Walt invented.

"I needed you to talk some sense into me as usual," Jack said as he looked down and smiled at Kate.

She smiled back and kissed him.

"So where do you guys want to go first?" Jack asked the kids.

"Let's go to the place where you and mom met so you can tell us that goofy story again, then let's go on Pirates!" Andy said with a huge smile.

"You got it Andy."

Kate stopped Jack in the middle of Main Street, "You know what Jack Duncan? I love you, more than anything, and I know you can protect us from anything. But you've got to remember that at some point, it's our time to go, and there's nothing you or anyone can do about it. Stop obsessing over your security measures, your weapons, because your desire for revenge will always lead you the wrong way. Sometimes the right decision is the one that benefits the most people in the end; the decision that you know is right in your gut. You did an honorable thing, fighting for my mom, and avenging her death. You removed a lot of bad people from this planet. But if it was fueled solely by your desire for revenge, then was it the right thing to do? You could've lost so much. Just know that we'll always be together, our entire family, even after death. You are a powerful man, and you can make almost anything happen, but please promise me that you'll use that power for good, and you won't use it for revenge or other selfish things. Promise me that you'll use your power to benefit everyone, not just our family. I believe that's what you're called to do."

Jack grinned realizing how lucky he was to have someone who could always put things into perspective for him. "What would I ever do without you, Kate?"

Kate smiled, and they kissed in front of the Castle, the same place where they became man and wife at their fairy-tale wedding ten years ago.

"Hey kids, how would you like to live at Disneyland?" Jack asked Andy and Grace.

"Yeah!!!" the kids exclaimed, excited for this new chapter in their life. They all held hands as they walked through the Castle into Fantasyland.

THIRTEEN

August 8, 2010
Tom Sawyer Island
Disneyland Park

"CAMDEN," President Hayes shouted, "why haven't you ordered the attack?"

"Mr. President, something is wrong, I've lost communication with the entire unit."

"What do you mean you've lost communication?" President Hayes looked up at the monitor as the camera zoomed into Jack's face. The President's mouth dropped as he realized what Jack had done.

"Sir," the Chairman of the Joint Chiefs said to the President, "Mr. Duncan's system has resumed, I believe they've jammed communications, and he's the only one who can make the call right now."

The President lowered the phone from his ear as he watched. Director Camden watched the same feed from the CIA situation room. Everyone watched helplessly realizing their fate, the fate of the United States of America, and the whole world for that matter, was in the hands of Jack Duncan.

Jack had been beaten at his own game of revenge; he had no one to blame but himself at this point.

He glared at Khalid—powerless.

He looked over at Andy and Grace as his bottom lip quivered uncontrollably, the look on his face said *I'm sorry*.

Khalid boarded the chopper, preparing to exit underneath into the water. He gave one final mocking salute as he smirked at Jack.

Jack's head lowered focusing in on Khalid. He put his finger to his earpiece, "This is Jack Duncan, hold for my orders." Jack's raspy voice echoed throughout all teams who were monitoring the feed, the helicopter pilots, the teams on the ground, the SEALs, Director Camden, and the President.

The President glanced nervously at his cabinet members as they watched the live feed with dire anticipation, not knowing what Jack was going to do. A close-up of Jack's image dominated the video monitors—the President gazed into his eyes. The most powerful man in the world was helpless. The Commander in Chief could not make the call, he only could hope that Jack would make the correct call.

Director Camden lowered his head with his hands over his eyes, realizing the magnitude of this pending disaster.

The video feed switched to Andy, Grace, and Nikolai.

For a split second, the President, Director Camden and the others watching the feed understood what Jack was about to do. They were parents. They would probably save their kids too, especially if they were the only people they had left—if they'd lived through Jack's unbearable grief.

"Jack, this is President Hayes, I know you can hear me. Listen, I know you're in an impossible situation, but you have to trust me and allow us to take the Island. If Khalid leaves the property, millions of people will die. Please Jack, issue the order—tell the teams to take the Island before it's too late. Khalid must be stopped."

The live video feed switched back to Jack. Everyone watched as his eyebrows lowered and he switched into attack mode.

The Joint Chiefs and the cabinet members noticed a fearful look on the President's face. They put their hands to their heads—praying that Jack would make the right decision.

—Silence fell over the Rivers of America—

Nikolai scooped Andy and Grace closer to him.

Navy helicopters hummed in the distance.

Snipers zeroed in on their targets.

Boats full of SEALs waited patiently.

Kendall zeroed his focus on Nikolai.

The President, his cabinet, and Director Camden held their breath.

Jack gazed into the heavens and could see Kate's beautiful face and reassuring smile.

He opened his mouth but could not speak.

He took one more look at Andy and Grace.

He put his finger to his earpiece and locked his sights on Khalid.

Sweat dripped from his forehead, and his breathing intensified.

His eyes drilled through Khalid—who tilted his head and squinted, noticing a change in Jack's body language.

He forced his voice through the secure channel.

Jack Duncan's command rang out across the River, the Island, CIA headquarters, the White House, and to everyone else who was listening.

"GENTLEMEN..."

"*TAKE THE ISLAND.*"

JACK DUNCAN

IS

THE DEADLIEST CAST MEMBER

SEASON ONE

EPISODE SIX

ONE

"Jack."

"Jack—"

"Honey, wake up."

Jack's eyes shot open. Sweat streamed down his face. He gasped for air with a look of terror on his face.

"Kate," Her face came into focus, and he recognized her beautiful smile. A white haze surrounded her, he could only see her face, but he knew it was her. Everything was blurry behind her.

"Jack, are you okay? You were shaking and talking in your sleep?"

He was able to focus a little more. He lifted his head and tried to sit up in bed—recognizing the posh surroundings of the majestic El Capitan Suite, the sun blasting through the balcony window, the sound of Grizzly River Run in the distance and the early morning crowd moseying through the Park.

He was confused.

He looked into Kate's caring eyes, the woman of his dreams—her gorgeous face was the best thing he'd seen in a long time. He instantly felt at ease, as if everything was okay.

"Kate—it felt so real, it was—horrible. The kids, they were taken from me, and I was trying to get them back—and you—" Jack froze and stared into Kate's eyes as he caressed the side of her face with his hand. "You were—"

"Jack," Kate's smile and her naturally sensual voice was like a sedative to Jack; her smile lit up the room. "It was just a dream, don't worry, everything is okay."

Jack had never been more grateful to have Kate next to him, something that he'd missed for such a long time. Seeing her face was like heaven after waking up from a nightmare. Realizing he was in the El Capitan Suite, made it even better.

"Andy and Grace—"

"They're asleep, honey, don't worry, we have all day to play with them in the Park. Let's get something to eat, and then we'll take the kids to Screamin'."

Jack relaxed and laid back in bed. His chest heaved. He wiped the sweat from his forehead trying to figure out how the dream felt so real. Recurring nightmares were an everyday reality for him, but he never had a dream that felt *this* real, it shook him to the core.

"I can't believe how real it was, Kate. It was horrible," Jack paused, looking at Kate, and beamed at her as he looked in her eyes. "I can't tell you how good it is to see you here, to have you with me, it feels like I haven't seen you in years."

"Oh, Jack," Kate's deep affection for him was evident by her caring gaze, "you're so sweet, I love you so much." She kissed him softly on the lips, and Jack felt as if they were kissing for the first time.

Suddenly the master bedroom doors burst open.

Jack jumped up and scrambled for his SIG.

It was Andy and Grace.

"Dad!" Grace yelled with glee, "let's go, we're ready, let's go to the Park!"

They both ran to the bed and jumped on Jack. Kate smiled, happy to see them reunited with their dad.

Jack hugged them and brought them close, taking a deep breath. He loved the way they smelled, "You two scared me, but I am so glad to see your faces!"

"Dad," Andy said, "I have to tell you. I love this suite, I can't believe how big it is, it's totally awesome."

"I'm glad you like it Andrew."

Jack hugged Andy and Grace and kissed Kate. Everything was perfect, he was at home with his favorite people in the world, no one was in danger, and he was ready to begin his life at Disneyland with them.

Jack crawled out of bed and saw the USA Today on his nightstand. On the front page, there were images of mangled red buses with large black LONDON SUICIDE BOMBING headlines.

"When did this happen?"

"I think it happened late last night," Kate said.

Jack searched the front page for the date:

July 7, 2005

TWO

August 9, 2010
Rivers of America

Jack took a shallow breath after the "Take the Island" command—wondering for a split second if he'd made the right call.

Within seconds, suppressed sniper fire erupted from the old Nature's Wonderland side of the River. Bullets sliced through the thick Tom Sawyer Island foliage. Several al-Qaeda members, including the scientist who was with Khalid, dropped to the dirt pathway near the River.

Andy and Grace were the only ones in Jack's sights.

He sprinted in their direction as bullets whizzed in front and behind him. He felt streaks of air blasting in front of him as he anticipated taking a bullet. Nikolai rushed into the Fort Wilderness complex with Kim, the kids, and a group of armed terrorists—locking the tall wooden doors.

Jack recognized the familiar sound of a Hellfire anti-tank missile heading his way.

BOOOOOM—BAAAANG

Fire lit up the River, the heat was intense, the initial flash from the blast was blinding. The helicopter exploded knocking him off his feet and sending him soaring through the air.

Kendall was launched into the air as well.

Jack's right shoulder hit the ground first as he rolled across the dirt walkway—his head hit a rock on the ground.

Nikolai had already made it into the Fort Wilderness compound, and the large wooden walls protected them from the blast.

The Stealth Blackhawk helicopters previously in a holding pattern approached; each one holding a SOC-R boat full of Special Warfare Combatant-craft Crewman under them—the most highly trained operatives on the water. They lowered the boats into the water as the engines kicked on and the special boat team prepared their arsenal of weapons. The iron war boats splashed into each side of the Rivers of the America—surrounding Tom Sawyer Island.

The terrorists on the Island caught a glimpse of the SOC-Rs dropping into the water, and they scrambled, knowing their chances of survival were slim.

A high buzzing chainsaw-like sound echoed throughout the River as the GAU-17/A miniguns attached to the boat hurled 7.62mm bullets at their targets at over 6000 rounds per minute. M240B machine guns rattled, as the most heavily armed boats in the world assaulted Tom Sawyer Island. The thumping of the M2HB .50 caliber machine guns echoed through the River sounding like an extended fireworks finale. They repeatedly fired on the decimated helicopter ensuring there were no survivors. Hostiles dropped to the ground.

Empty brass shell casings ejected, hundreds at a time as a fog of smoke covered the River.

More SEALs approached on rubber boats from New Orleans Square with their assault rifles aimed at predetermined targets.

The Raven, under Luke's control, flew over the Island giving him an electrifying view of the bullets flying across the Island from all directions. It was a full scale, relentless attack from all sides of the Island.

Max and his team started at the front of Tom Sawyer Island. Another SEAL team converged from the back of the Island as the long-range snipers surgically removed Khalid's men from their hiding places in the caves and trees. Max proceeded with his H&K 416, shooting several hostiles on the roof of Lafitte's Tavern. He communicated with the SEALs on the other side of the Island as well as the SWCCs on the SOC-R boats, to prevent friendly fire deaths, and to strategically sweep the Island. Max continued to the left, down the gravel path of Tom Sawyer Island scanning up and down for hostiles.

Bullets littered the pathway in front of them. Max dove into the planter. Within seconds, snipers on the New Orleans Square side took out the perpetrators.

On the other side of the Island, the SEALs moved in—taking hostile fire. Snipers from the Nature's Wonderland side took out several men hiding in the trees and caves.

"Jack—Jack can you hear me?" Luke tried to get his attention.

Jack opened his eyes. Everything was dark. He heard men screaming, and the familiar zipping bursts of the GAU miniguns. His mouth was full of dirt. He rolled over to get a better idea of what was happening.

"Luke."

"Jack, Nikolai took the kids into Fort Wilderness, he's holed up in there. The Fort is protecting them from the incoming assault."

Jack jumped to his feet heading for the Fort. He saw Kendall on the ground.

"Kendall, are you okay?"

Kendall groaned and rolled over.

"Come on let's go." Jack helped him up.

Kendall got to his feet and followed Jack.

"Everyone hold your fire," Jack called out over the secure com.

The onslaught continued.

"Sir," the Team Leader answered back, "we're under direct orders from the President to continue the assault until al-Haddad is confirmed dead—we cannot take any chances."

"There are hostages in Fort Wilderness. I repeat DO NOT fire on the Fort."

Hostiles fired automatic rounds from the Island at the SOC-R boats. When the SWCCs on the boats saw the orange flashes coming from hostile weapons, they aimed and blasted everything in sight. If they missed, the snipers finished the job.

The fire from the helicopter raged over twenty feet high.

"Give me your SIG," Jack told Kendall.

Jack wasn't going to let the wooden walls of the retired Fort Wilderness attraction keep him from his kids. He sprinted up the stairs and leaped onto the wooden gate. Adrenaline pumped through every vein in his body allowing him to defy gravity and the laws of physics gaining traction on the slick gate. The gate was a little over ten feet tall, but there was nothing to hold on to.

Jack leaped high enough to catch one of the diagonal wood slats on the gate with his foot. He used this thin piece of wood to gain traction so he could prop himself to the top of the gate. He extended his arm as far as he could—his tendons felt like they were going to pop. The tips of his fingers barely made it over the top of the gate. He held there for a second trying to get a better grip. His assault kit weighed approximately thirty pounds without his weapons, and at this point nothing but his fingertips were holding all 225 pounds of his weight. When Jack was in battle mode, his strength mysteriously increased no matter how badly he was beat up. He peeked his head over the gate making a final push while extending his arms, which allowed him to get his waist over the top. He straddled the top of the gate—

BAM

A bullet entered his left upper arm and knocked him off balance, he struggled to maintain his position but he couldn't hold on and plummeted down the wall. Kendall stood under him and broke his fall, slamming both of them to the ground.

Jack grabbed his arm to try to stop the bleeding. He couldn't feel any pain with all of the adrenaline. He tried to climb the wall again but fell to his knees.

"Jack, hold on, you need to stop that bleeding," Kendall grabbed supplies from his kit and wrapped Jack's arm.

Jack's phone buzzed.

"Jack, if you try to enter this fort again, your kids will die. Do you understand that?"

"Nikolai, you can have me, let my kids go."

"That sounds like a deal Jack, but you need to stand down while I figure out how this is going to happen." Nikolai yelled over the phone over the deafening machine gun fire, "DO NOT TRY TO BE A HERO. If you or your men try to come in here again, I will kill your kids."

The call ended.

Bullets continued to fly. The iron SOC-R war boats picked up speed as they circled the Island taking out any recognizable enemy combatant. They shouted back and forth over the com with the SEALs on the Island, and they knew exactly who to shoot at.

A team tried to extinguish the large helicopter fire while others frantically searched for Khalid's body. Another SEAL team raced to the helicopter in a boat to search the surrounding water.

The gunfire ceased as the Team Six Leader's voice rang out over the com.

"Hostiles are contained, search all caves and hiding places, and converge on the fort."

Jack called out over the com, "Do not enter the Fort, I repeat do not enter. Hostages are being held by Nikolai Grusov."

"Jack," Luke said, "I'm picking up traces of the device Khalid had under the water—towards the front of the River, where you went through that metal grate."

"Team Six, what's your location," Jack called out.

"We're all on the Island, sir."

"Get to the underground hub, Khalid is going to try to exit to West Street."

"Yes, sir."

"Luke have Anaheim PD set up a perimeter around the entire Resort so Khalid can't get away."

"They've already set a thick perimeter Jack."

"Jack," Kendall said showing him his iOS wrist device with a live feed from the Raven overlooking Fort Wilderness, "it looks like there's around fifteen hostiles in here. Nikolai has the kids in this area."

"We need to wait, he wants me, I will turn myself over to him, but I need you to make sure he releases the kids."

"Jack, we own the airspace, we can have one of the snipers take him out from the Blackhawk."

"It's too dangerous, Kendall."

"Jack, they do this all the time, it's a routine shot."

"Yeah but there are fifteen others in there, we won't be able to get in there fast enough."

Kendall paused, "Hey do you remember that secret tunnel leading to Fort Wilderness—the one we used when we were kids?"

Jack looked at Kendall with hope in his eyes, "Yes, the one that led to the crack in the rocks by the River, we would go from the River's edge and end up at the old storage door inside the Fort—I think they closed that up a long time ago?"

Kendall gave Jack a look. Anything was possible after all of the underground tunnels they'd been in today.

"Let's go check out the old rock."

They scurried towards the location of the old rock that they played in as kids. It was in the vicinity of where the current caves were located.

"It's sealed up Jack."

"Let's blow the inside of this rock, how much do you wanna bet that tunnel is still here, but it's covered by these new rock caves."

Kendall pulled explosives out of his assault kit and got them ready.

Jack pointed his device at the face of the rock and called out to Luke, "Can you see through this? I need to know if there's still a tunnel here that leads to the inside of the Fort."

"Standby Jack, I will use your view and a few others to check."

"Okay Jack," Kendall said, "we're ready."

"Let me see what Luke says before we do this."

"Jack I'm not getting a good signal, it is hard for me to tell if there's a tunnel there."

"Blow it, Kendall."

Kendall backed up and held the detonator, he ignited the charge and a small blast resonated across the River.

The smoke cleared as Jack put his night vision goggles on with his mounted light and entered the small tunnel.

"Wait here Kendall."

The crawlspace was small, but Jack pushed through it. From what he could see, the tunnel was still intact. He continued until he reached the end. A wood panel covered the top of the tunnel, probably the current floor of the storage closet. He saw a padlock on the right side, and he barely fit his bolt cutters through the narrow slot.

He gently clipped the lock, trying not to make any noise. He pushed the wood panel up and climbed into the locked storage closet. He peered through a crack in the door and caught a glimpse of Nikolai, the kids, and the other hostiles.

Fort Wilderness was closed to the public. It served as a storage area and a place for Fantasmic CMs to relax. The wide range of objects inside the Fort from Fantasmic prevented him from getting a clear shot.

He briefly considered breaking through the door, shooting Nikolai in the head, and taking out as many terrorists as he could, but he knew that if he didn't take out all of them within seconds, the kids would be harmed.

He had an idea.

He walked back down the tunnel towards the River to talk to Kendall.

"Kendall, that tunnel is still there, it leads to the old storage shed. If you lead a team through that tunnel, I can go through the front, make sure the kids are safe, take out Nikolai, and then your team can clear the rest of the hostiles."

"Let's do it." Kendall called for a team of SEALs on the Island.

"Jack," the Team Six leader called out, "we're at the underground hub, and we have guys out by the West Street tunnel exit—there's no sign of Khalid."

"He knew better than to go where he told me—Luke can you see where he is?"

"No, Jack, I can't get a fix on him, I'm still trying."

"Check the tunnel that goes under the Jungle Cruise towards Walt's Apartment, he could be heading that way."

THREE

July 24, 1966
New Orleans Square Dedication

Walt Disney stood in front of the cameras with Victor Schiro, the real mayor of New Orleans as they dedicated the newly opened New Orleans Square. Walt spent a whopping $15 million on his version of New Orleans and opened it with a southern style jubilee.

Dixieland Jazz filled the air as members of the press floated down the River on the Mark Twain, getting a unique glimpse of the opening ceremony. A Tom Sawyer Island barge filled with excited guests led the way.

Walt had captured the original architecture and atmosphere of the old New Orleans of the 1850s. The design was flawless.

Stan leaned over to Walt smiling, "You didn't miss a detail, Walt—the narrow winding streets, the intimate courtyards, and the iron laced balconies."

Walt smiled as he looked up at a Jazz band on the second story balcony dressed in their white hats, candy striped jackets, and white pants playing their authentic riffs.

Performers strummed banjos for onlookers below on Royal Street. Guests enjoyed the flower marts that added color to the streets, the quaint shops offered treasures from all over the world. Skilled craftsmen made stain glass treasures on the spot. Marching bands made their way down the streets with their light blue vests and their striped pants, tambourines in hand. They marched with trombones, drums, and trumpets throughout New Orleans Square.

Walt leaned into the two microphones positioned in front of the cameras. He'd gained some weight but was still a handsome man with his famous, contagious smile. His greying hair was slicked back, his precisely trimmed mustache made him instantly recognizable, he had a dark grey suit on with a dark blue tie, and a crisp white dress shirt. He laughed as he joked with the mayor.

The crowd applauded.

Walt Disney thrived from the excitement of his guests. He posed for the media, then talked with a few reporters explaining his plans to make this area even better by adding new attractions.

He suddenly started to cough and couldn't stop.

Stan put his arm on Walt's back and addressed the press, "Thank you everyone for coming today, Mr. Disney has a few things to attend to."

Stan shuttled him towards the green Club 33 door. The Club was completed, but not ready for the public. They climbed the wooden staircase in the Club's lobby and made a right through the private door leading to the balcony overlooking the Blue Bayou dining area and the beginning of the Pirates of the Caribbean attraction; both were not open to the public. They walked to the right and entered a locked door at the end of the Blue Bayou balcony. It opened into what looked like closet. Stan knelt down and removed a rug that revealed a hatch underneath that he quickly unlocked. They descended nearly four stories down until they reached another hatch that opened into Walt's secret office.

Walt continued to cough violently as he sat down in his chair. Stan poured him a cup of water.

"Walt, are you okay?"

Walt swallowed the water and paused. "Yes, I'm fine, it's just this nasty cough of mine."

"It sounds like it's getting worse, Walt."

"Ah, maybe, but I'll be alright."

"I'm worried about you, Walt, let me take you to the doctor."

"No, it's okay Stan, I appreciate it, but I'm okay."

"Walt, you trust me with your life, and I love you like a brother, let me take care of you, let me get you the help you need. I know you don't like going to the doctor, but you really need to get in there to be checked."

"Stan, you are a great friend, but there's nothing they can do for me, I need to put my head down and get the Multiplaner fully functional."

Stan frowned.

"How's Genie doing with little Jack?" Walt asked.

"She's doing well, she's a natural—she was born to be a mom and she loves him so much."

Walt grinned, "That's great to hear, Stan. I have a lot of hope for your boy —I never had the privilege of having a boy of my own," Walt paused, "Jack is going to be *the one* Stan. He will succeed our plans and take over what we started."

Stan smiled, "I'm looking forward to that Walt, but he will only takeover if he meets your guidelines, even though he's my son, I will honor your wishes."

"I know you will, Stan. It makes me feel better knowing that I have you to fill in for me when I'm gone."

"Why are you talking like this, Walt? Are you not telling me something?"

Walt smiled and gazed at the back wall of his office. "No, but it's like I've said, I don't think I have much more time left here on this planet, so I need to make the most of every minute."

"Walt, I know you've laid out your plans for me to follow, but the bottom line is that this company depends on you, I don't know how you think it's possible for it to continue without your vision. Nobody has your passion or vision for the future?"

"I agree, Stan, but I need you to do your best. The Multiplaner is going to allow me, among other things, to form a secret group of people who'll protect my interest in the Park. You'll be in charge of this top-secret program."

"Sure, Walt."

"Also," Walt paused with a disappointed look on his face, "I have a feeling the company isn't going to follow through with EPCOT. We aren't going to get the funding we need, and they're going to scrap the project." Walt paused with a disappointed look, then he raised his eyebrow and leaned towards Stan, "I've discovered a way to make the gateway work—with the Multiplaner I can use this gateway to pass into a new 'Land', this other dimension I was telling you about. I'm going to build EPCOT there instead, with the help of some of the greatest minds in history. We'll create more than just a Dream City, we'll create something that will change the world. I won't be limited by time, or resources. This is where my true creativity will flourish."

"Is this the type of place where you'll be able to live…forever?"

"Not really, when this old body ceases to exist, I'll physically be gone from this earth. I'm limited to my natural lifespan. However, the Multiplaner opens up the possibility of moving through time, and if I can access this new dimension, I won't be subject to time. This new Land I've discovered is outside of our time continuum so I won't be limited by normal time constraints."

"So far what you've been able to do is phenomenal, Walt. You've secretly transported so many less fortunate kids, dying children, and made their dreams come true. You've done so much to help people and the world. If you truly think your days are numbered why don't you just take some time off and spend it with Lillian, the girls, and your grandkids?"

"I have to get this done, Stan. It's important, not just for me, but for the entire world. This discovery will benefit your kids, grandkids, and future generations. I must sacrifice my time to make this work—and if I get it to work, I'll have all the time I need with my family. It's risky because I could end up working on this project day and night without it coming to fruition—losing precious time with my family. But I'm so close to figuring it out, Stan."

"I will do whatever you need, Walt."

"I want to record the television show about EPCOT, I want my ideas to be out there for the world to see so that people will remember them, I want my vision to be public so people will learn of my true intentions for the Florida project."

"Sure, I will get that done."

"I need our underground tunnel system to be secured. No one besides us can get down here, especially into the vault and my underground Fire Station Apartment."

"Yes, Walt."

"They mock my vision of EPCOT, about the climate controlled bubble over the city, the underground transportation system, the city-wide monorail and PeopleMovers, but the technology and the innovation that will come from people living in an ideal environment will change the world. Someday, people will have computers that are smaller than a penny, computers in their eye glasses, computers in their telephones—I'm talking about phones that people will carry in their pocket. This technology will sprout from an ideal environment for innovation. I will build EPCOT in this new Land, this other dimension, then I will transport the greatest minds to this perfect environment to allow them to innovate for the good of mankind."

"How close are you to opening the gateway to this new Land?"

"Very close. You've already seen how we can transport things through the gateway. Well, by tweaking the Multiplaner, I've been able to use our large mirrors to view other dimensions. Now, if I can just perfect the time travel aspect of the Multiplaner, I can go backwards—and possibly forward—to obtain the proper technology to enter this gateway to the new Land. I'm missing a key ingredient that I need from future technology to make it work."

Walt coughed again, but this time he couldn't stop.

Stan put his arm around Walt to comfort him.

FOUR

August 9, 2010
Fort Wilderness

"Jack," Luke said, "no sign of Khalid yet."

A SEAL team assembled on the Island at Kendall's command near the cave entrance by the River.

Jack addressed them, "I'm going to surrender myself to Nikolai. Your team will go through this tunnel and end up on the right side of the Fort. All you need to do is take out the fifteen hostiles on my call—and I'll take care of Nikolai and Kim."

"Jack, it sounds like Kim may have been forced into this so maybe we can reach her somehow to see if she can help."

"She's a traitor Kendall."

"I don't think she is," Kendall said with confidence.

Jack normally would have made up his mind without wavering. This time he stopped to consider what Kendall was saying, knowing it was time to listen to other options since he'd been wrong so many times.

"Luke," Jack called out, "is there any way you can get a message to Kim?"

"I will try, but I can't ping any of her devices right now for some reason."

Jack turned to the SEAL team, "Okay, you guys head into the tunnel and await my orders, do you see a problem with taking out all fifteen hostiles at the same time?"

Kendall grinned at the SEAL team leader.

"I don't think so, sir." The team leader said to Jack.

"Kendall has a live feed from The Raven that will give you an aerial view of their positions in the Fort. We need simultaneous kills for this to work."

"Yes, sir, we'll hit our targets."

Jack took a deep breath realizing he was finally within reach of resolving this disastrous situation; soon he would have Andy and Grace in his arms, and Nikolai would finally be dead. It wasn't about revenge anymore; it was about saving his kids and making this situation right. It was about making good on his promise to keep them safe, to rebuild their lives at Disneyland, and to give his kids hope and a great future after all they'd been through.

"Jack," Director Camden's voice shot through his ear bud, "I need all teams in pursuit of Khalid, immediately."

"Sir, there are several teams in pursuit of him as we speak, I have ten SEALs here on the Island who are going to help me free my kids."

"Jack, I said ALL teams, the President has given direct orders, those men are not under your command."

Jack grit his teeth and looked at Kendall. The SEAL team leader put his finger to his ear.

"Mr. Duncan, I'm sorry, but we have to go."

Jack cracked at Camden, "Listen, Camden, the perimeter of the entire property is blockaded, you have tons of Special Forces, Anaheim PD, SWAT teams, everything at your disposal, and you can't give me ten SEALs to save my kids?"

"No, YOU listen to me Jack—unless you want to be taken into custody, you will follow the direct orders of the President of the United States—you need to find Khalid. If he gets nuclear capability, the blood of millions of Americans will be on your hands."

"I'd like to see you *try* to take me into custody, Camden."

Jack cut the line and switched to Luke.

"Luke, block him from contacting me."

"Um, okay Jack." Luke paused and seemed concerned about Jack's interaction with Camden. "I think I can get a message to Kim through her iWatch—I'll try to flash a message via Morse code, she knows it well and will be able to recognize it."

"Tell her that when I dip my head, she needs to take out Nikolai from behind, and see if you can get a reaction from her."

"Got it."

The SEAL team headed for their boats. Jack and Kendall stood on the dirt path next to the Fort. The Island was dark.

"Jack, I can still make this happen, I can blast through the back of the fort from the tunnel and take out as many as I can—probably all of them." Kendall said.

"That's a suicide mission Kendall, I won't let you do that."

"Jack it's our only chance; otherwise you'll be at the mercy of Nikolai—you can't trust him to hand over Andy and Grace."

FIVE

August 9, 2010
Disneyland Front Gate

Anaheim PD, Special Forces, the CIA, FBI, and every other available law enforcement agency were camped out at the front gates of Disneyland—in the esplanade between Disneyland and California Adventure. The entire perimeter was covered by hundreds of officers. Streets were closed and surrounding hotels and homes were evacuated.

"Mr. Ruddy," an officer said, "approximately how many Cast Members are still inside the Park?"

"I'm getting that number for you now, officer."

Ruddy checked his tablet as his hand shook; he was flustered, and fought to get himself under control.

He glanced up for a second and noticed a CM in a custodial outfit with his hat low trying to exit through the Newsstand that shared an inside-the-Park storefront.

He headed over in that direction to get a better look at the CM.

—BOOOOM—

A loud explosion erupted on the Harbor Blvd side of the entrance. Law enforcement officers and others in the esplanade ran towards that direction.

Ruddy slowly approached the CM at the souvenir stand.

"Excuse me, what is your name."

The man grabbed Ruddy by the neck and yanked him into the Newsstand, forcing him to the ground so no one could see.

"You're going to get me out of here, if you want to live," the man said with a Middle Eastern accent.

Ruddy realized this had to be one of the terrorists.

"Okay, I will help you," Ruddy was terrified as he looked into the eyes of a man who was most likely a member of al-Qaeda. Ruddy never had any contact with criminals in his line of work. He'd only heard about what al-Qaeda was capable of on the news—never thinking he would come face to face with one of them.

"You must act like you are talking to me as if we are friends—guiding me towards somewhere you need help."

"Okay." Ruddy said with a shaky voice.

"Escort me to the Innoventions loading dock so I can get to Harbor Blvd. If you get me there, you will live. If someone stops us, you will die."

Ruddy couldn't speak, he couldn't stop his teeth from chattering, and he was shivering as if he stepped into a freezer.

"Let's go," the man commanded. "Give me your phone and any other device you have, if I find you trying to send a message to anyone, you are a dead man."

They walked out towards Main Street heading to Tomorrowland.

"Talk to me like you are giving me instructions," he said.

Ruddy talked to the man with phony instructions, using his hands, and pointing. He mumbled and felt like throwing up. His stomach turned, and he was sweating profusely.

They passed several Special Ops teams dressed in black who were rushing in the direction of the blast. They passed them without taking a second look at Ruddy; most of them had already seen him at the front gate. Ruddy despised Jack for so many years, he thought he was arrogant and too big-headed for his own good. But at this moment, he would've given anything to see Jack walk around that corner.

The man kept his hat low, and his head down to prevent people from recognizing him.

They reached the Tomorrowland Cast Member backstage entrance, and they headed towards the loading dock behind Innoventions. It was dark, and most CMs had been sent home. The terrorist pulled out his tablet and began to type rapidly.

They proceeded through the backstage area behind Innoventions until they reached the tall fence on Harbor Blvd. The man looked left and right—it was clear. He glanced down at his tablet and smiled.

"My ride is here," he said.

Ruddy noticed a police car on the other side of the gate that had stopped on the road.

"Get on your knees," the man commanded Ruddy.

Ruddy looked at him sheepishly and realized he had no other choice. He wanted to run, but he knew he couldn't outrun him, being so out of shape. He remembered having nightmares where he'd try to outrun someone who was chasing him, but he couldn't move fast enough. He knew he needed to make a move, but he didn't have the confidence to do so.

Ruddy went to his knees in utter despair, staring into the backstage darkness. He closed his eyes and thought of his wife and young kids as he waited for the impact of the bullet in his head. Would he feel the bullet entering his skull? Would he die immediately? Would it hurt?

Questions raced through his head as his heart thumped in his chest, it felt like it was going to burst.

"Khalid," a quiet voice came through the darkness. "Drop your weapon."

It was Tony.

He stepped directly behind Khalid with his gun pointed at the back of his head. White bandages covered Tony's face, blood stained his clothes, and the slightest move caused a look of pain.

Ruddy trembled with fear on his knees—realizing he was not just dealing with any al-Qaeda member, he was dealing with Khalid al-Haddad, one of the most feared terrorists in the world.

Ruddy recognized Tony's voice.

Khalid put his hands up in the air and dropped his gun.

"Get on your knees Khalid and put your hands on your head."

He knelt and obeyed Tony.

"Ruddy, give me your radio." Tony had no way of communicating since everything was confiscated before the blast in the Control Center.

"He has it."

"Give it to me slowly, Khalid."

Khalid reached in his jacket to pull out Ruddy's radio, and held it up in the air.

Tony reached for the radio.

Khalid spun around and sliced Tony's arm with a blade. Tony grabbed his bloody arm, and his weapon slipped out of his hand.

Khalid turned around and struck Tony in the face, knocking him to the ground.

The men dressed as police officers called Khalid through the fence. He realized that he needed to go, and fired a suppressed shot into Tony's chest. He took another step towards Tony to shoot him in the head.

—BAM—

Ruddy fired a shot with Tony's gun, hitting Khalid in his left arm. Khalid grabbed his arm in shock and turned to Ruddy.

Ruddy fired again, and again—trying desperately to hit Khalid.

Khalid grinned at Ruddy and fired multiple suppressed shots.

Ruddy's body hit the ground with a thump.

SIX

August 9, 2010
Fort Wilderness

Kim's hands were tied in front of her, and her mouth gagged. She watched from inside Fort Wilderness as Nikolai kept Andy and Grace close to him. Five of Khalid's men watched her, making sure she didn't try anything.

Her iWatch began to blink rapidly.

She turned her arm so the men watching her wouldn't see the blinking light. It was hard to decipher the message because she couldn't stare at her watch with the men hovering over her—but she knew it was coming from Luke.

The advanced iOS watch stopped blinking.

She yelled as loud as she could—trying to talk through the gag in her mouth. One of the terrorists bent down in front of her and slapped her in the face as hard as he could—knocking her to the ground. She looked up at the other men and tried to get their attention.

Nikolai paced back and forth nervously. He stopped and noticed Kim squirming on the ground.

"Remove the gag," Nikolai said in his thick Russian accent.

One of the terrorists bent down and removed the gag from her mouth.

She was still on the ground.

"What, Kim?"

"Nikolai, I can help you—I know how Jack thinks—I know what he'll do next. You don't have a chance right now, and you know it, you're a sitting duck in here. He will sneak in, you won't even realize it, and he'll slit your throat. You will die unless you listen to me."

She looked at the other men who were standing over her.

"All of you—you're going to die, don't you realize that? Khalid has abandoned you—every single one of you will have a bullet in your head within the hour unless you listen to me—or if Jack decides to torture you, you'll die a slow, horrifying death. He's fuming right now, plotting the death of each and every one of you idiots—and you know full well that you don't have a chance once he gets a hold of you."

Khalid's men looked at each other with fear on their faces, knowing that Kim was right.

Nikolai paused—his hesitation confirmed his fear. He wasn't afraid to die, he was afraid to die without getting final revenge.

"What do you have in mind, Kim?"

"He's trying to message me right now, through this watch," she lifted her arms to show him the watch. "I will act like I'm on his side, and then you'll know what their plan is. Jack is going to try to kill me, he thinks I betrayed him; my only chance of staying alive is to fight. I will get him for you, Nikolai."

Kim caught Andy glaring at her out of the corner of her eye—it broke her heart.

She glanced back at Nikolai, "Untie me so I can decipher this message."

Nikolai motioned to one of the men to untie her.

A man bent down, with his assault rifle strapped around his shoulder and began to unravel the restraints on her hands.

Her hands were free.

Kim kicked the man in his groin with lightning speed. At the same time, she grabbed his rifle and rapidly shot five times killing five of the men near her instantly.

She elbowed the man who was hunched over in the head and turned her sights to Nikolai.

CLICK

The gun jammed.

She dropped it and sprinted towards Nikolai, wanting to strangle him with her own hands—to free Andy and Grace—that was her only concern at the moment.

She was within a few feet of him when…

—BANG—

Kim felt the bullet enter her from behind, she lost her balance, but her momentum still carried her into Nikolai, she tried to tackle him and put him in a headlock.

Her strength was fading; she could feel the blood pouring from her body.

Her grip on Nikolai's neck weakened.

She began to slip off of his back.

She looked at Andy and Grace trying to say, "*I'm sorry.*"

She slid down Nikolai's back trying to maintain her grip on him.

She felt something on his chest. She pulled his coat away, and her eyes widened.

A Claymore mine was strapped to him. She recognized the FRONT TOWARDS ENEMY words on the device as she gasped, wide-eyed.

Nikolai grinned at Kim as he yanked her hands from his coat.

She fell to the ground.

Her vision faded, but she tried to send a signal to Luke through her watch to let Jack know about the Claymore mine that Nikolai had fastened to him.

She started to type, but her vision deteriorated. She couldn't keep her eyes focused.

She looked back up at Andy and Grace who were both crying hysterically. She closed her eyes, and everything went black.

SEVEN

August 9, 2010
Fort Wilderness

Jack heard the shots and terror swept over his face.

Kendall dashed for the cave entrance to the Fort.

Jack charged the Fort again, trying to break through the large door in but it wouldn't budge.

His phone buzzed.

"Jack, your kids are alive, that was your friend Kim. She tried to take us all out, and her plan didn't work."

"Let me talk to my kids Nikolai."

"Standby."

"Dad?" Andy's shaky voice came through Jack's phone, he was crying.

"Andy—are you okay?"

"Yes, we are fine, but Kim—I think she's…she's…?"

"Okay buddy, just sit tight and take care of your sister, I will get you out of there, I give you my word. Just take care your sister."

Nikolai pulled the phone back.

"Okay Jack, this is the deal. We make an even trade. You come in here unarmed and surrender. Then, I will let your kids out. It's as simple as that."

"How can I trust you Nikolai?"

"You don't really have a choice Jack. Like I said, I want revenge, that's it. Khalid has abandoned me. He left me here and didn't hold up his end of the bargain. He used me," his voice lowered to a whisper, "I have all of his plans on my device. This was my insurance plan. I know where he's going with the nuke and where he plans to detonate it. I will give this to you, your guys can upload the information, and you will be able to stop him. I never supported his idea to detonate the nuke—I only wanted you and your father."

"So you'll give me my kids, information on Khalid, and all I need to do is let you kill me."

"And your father, I want him here too, I want him to watch."

"Where is he?"

"He's below the Pope House, in a small basement."

"I'll send someone to get him."

"No, you need to get him, and come back alone. If you try anything Jack, your kids will die, I promise you that. There's only one thing you can do to save them tonight—and that's by doing things MY WAY."

Nikolai disconnected the call.

Jack radioed Kendall, "Kendall did you hear that?"

"Yes, Jack."

"I'm going to get my dad."

"Roger that Jack, I will stay here."

Kendall radioed Luke, "Luke, how many hostiles are left?"

"From what I can tell, Kim killed five of them, so that leaves ten." Luke said.

"I can take out all ten of them—no problem," said Kendall.

"How fast?" Jack asked.

"As fast as I can pull the trigger."

EIGHT

August 9, 2010
Pope House
Disneyland Park

Jack jumped in one of the SEAL team's black rubber boats and sped across the water towards the Big Thunder Ranch area. He jumped off the boat and landed on the riverbank while the boat was still running—it slid up onto the side of the River. He pushed through the thick foliage on the riverbank, heading for the Pope House.

As he neared the old house, his phone buzzed from a blocked number.

"Mr. Duncan, standby for the President of the United States."

Jack's shoulders dropped, this was not what he needed right now.

"Jack," President Hayes said, "you need to stop what you're doing and pursue Khalid. He's unaccounted for, and we can't find him—he must be stopped immediately."

"Mr. President. With all due respect, sir, my kids are being held hostage on the Island, and I need to save them. You have the top operatives in the world on this property right now—there isn't anything I can do that would be more than what they're doing."

"Jack, I realize your situation, however, I'm giving you a direct order. Khalid will escape, and if that happens, he'll detonate a nuclear device on our soil."

"Sir, Nikolai told me that he has evidence of Khalid's plans, all I need to do is trade him for myself and my father, and he will give me that information."

"I'm sorry Jack, but I don't believe Nikolai, he's lying to you, and I can't allow millions of lives to depend on his word. You are likely the only one who can track Khalid down, and I need *you* to do it. THAT IS AN ORDER."

Jack paused. He looked up at the Pope House, he was so close to getting Andy and Grace back. Maybe he just wanted to believe that Nikolai had the information on Khalid, so he could justify his actions. Finding Khalid right now would be virtually impossible; he knew he had a better chance making the deal with Nikolai. The quickest way to find Khalid was to make this deal.

"I'm sorry sir, but I don't work for you anymore." Jack hung up his phone and pushed towards the Pope House.

"Luke how do I get to the basement?"

"Go to the back of the house and there is a door in the ground," Luke hesitated, "um, Jack I heard what you said to the President, this could get us all in a lot of trouble."

"Don't worry Luke, I will handle this, I'll save the kids *and* get Khalid, but I have to do it my way."

Jack opened the wooden doors in the ground and went down the stairs into the Pope House basement. It was dark. He activated his tactical light and saw his dad lying on a table with his arms strapped.

"Dad!"

Stan didn't move, he was unconscious.

Jack broke the restraints and put Stan over his shoulder, heading up the stairs.

He reached the top of the stairs and four CIA agents stopped him with their guns drawn.

"Jack. Put your dad down, you need to come with us. We're under the President's direct orders."

Jack put Stan on the ground and put his arms up. He noticed the man who addressed him was mildly confident, but the others looked extremely nervous.

"Listen," Jack said softly, "you have to trust me on this, I will handle this situation, but I need to do it my way. I know how Nikolai and Khalid think—no one else does. I need to make a trade with Nikolai, and then I'll get information that will help me find Khalid."

The point man hesitated, glanced at the other agents, then back at Jack. "I'm sorry Jack, I need to take you into custody, I don't have a choice. Don't make this any harder than it needs to be—just come with us and no one will get hurt."

With his hands up, Jack inched towards the four CIA agents, "Look, guys, I don't want to have to go this route, but I can tell you this—I'm doing this *my* way and NO ONE will stop me, do you understand that?"

The agents retreated a few steps, with their weapons extended. Jack's tone was convincing, and his piercing stare rattled them. They were aware of Jack's ballistic chest plates. Shooting him might not stop him. They were also aware of the damage Jack could do in a matter of seconds.

"You guys know that you can't stop me, so let me handle this without anyone getting hurt."

"Jack, do not come a step closer, I am warning you…"

Taser darts shot from behind Jack and penetrated his back—instantly dropping him to his knees. The CIA agents approached him, but Jack swung at them from his knees, knocking two of them out. The Taser charges continued to send thousands of volts through Jack, but he resisted. The CIA agents had looks of horror on their faces—they'd never seen anyone overcome this kind of an assault, especially after being hit with this many volts of electricity.

Jack managed to rise from his knees, reached around his back and yanked out the metal darts. He immediately attacked the point man, kicking him in the solar plexus, and striking the remaining agent. The men who hit him with the Tasers took off.

Shaken, he regained his focus and picked up his dad, heading for the rubber boat through the trees. He put Stan in the boat, turned it around, and jumped in.

He zoomed towards Fort Wilderness, exited the rubber boat with Stan, and headed for the entrance.

"Luke make sure no one can pick up our communications."

"Got it, Jack."

"NIKOLAI," Jack roared at the Fort Wilderness gate, "my dad is here, let's finish this."

Jack's phone buzzed.

"Jack, I will open the door, you and your father surrender to me, I will let your kids out of the fort. Understood?"

"And you'll give me the device that shows us where to find Khalid?"

"Yes."

"Open the door, I'm unarmed."

Jack stripped himself of all weapons and put his dad on his shoulder.

NINE

August 9, 2010
Fort Wilderness

The tall wooden doors of the defunct Fort Wilderness creaked open. Jack anxiously stood outside the door waiting to go in. He could sense that Nikolai was on edge, so he moved carefully so he wouldn't startle him.

Four men greeted Jack at the gate with automatic weapons pointed at his face.

"One step at a time, walk towards us, no sudden movements," said one of the terrorists in a mild Middle Eastern accent.

Jack obeyed and inched forward until he was inside the Fort. They quickly closed the gate.

Max arrived and met Kendall at the cave entrance.

"Max, boy am I glad to see you, buddy!" Kendall said.

"I've searched the Island sir, and all hostiles are down." Max said.

"Okay, here's the deal, just stay behind me and follow my lead."

Max nodded.

Kendall snuck through the cave near the River until he reached the closet inside Fort Wilderness where he camped out, watching all movement through his night vision goggles as he readied his weapons. Max followed.

More guns pointed at Jack. Behind these men, he could see Andy and Grace's feet—Nikolai held them close to prevent any separation. Jack could hear them whimpering.

The terrorists inched backwards. Their stiff arms shook, and their fingers twitched on the triggers of their automatic weapons. They knew what Jack could do, even if he was unarmed, and they were not taking any chances—especially after what just happened with Kim.

Jack scanned the area to see if there were any other options. There were too many of them to take out. If he tried anything, the kids would be harmed.

"Nikolai," he called out, "we don't have a lot of time, let's make the trade, my own people are after me now."

Nikolai inched forward as Khalid's men moved aside. His handgun pointed at Andy and Grace keeping them in a loose headlock to maintain control.

Jack seethed when he saw the way Nikolai was handling them, his blood boiled and he felt himself shifting into killing mode. It took everything for him to contain himself. Blood pumped through his body, his confidence rose, and he felt as if his strength was increasing.

"Put your father down, Jack."

Jack gently put Stan on the ground in front of him.

Nikolai cracked an uncharacteristic smile as he reminisced, "You know, my son, he was a beautiful boy—like your boy. I had done a lot of bad things in my life, but my boy always listened to me, he always followed directions, he was obedient—*he was perfect*."

Jack didn't like where this conversation was headed.

"Nikolai, your beef is with me, not my kids, let's make the trade and send my kids outside."

Nikolai screamed at Jack and shook his arms violently, "LISTEN TO ME DUNCAN!"

Jack stepped back, recognizing Nikolai's instability.

"You don't know what it's like to lose a child, you are CLUELESS about that kind of pain."

"Okay, Nikolai, but I had nothing to do with your son's death, and my kids had nothing to do with it."

"Don't try to talk me down, Jack, get on your knees, NOW!"

"Wait a minute, the deal is that you let my kids go and give me the device you promised."

Two of the terrorists turned their heads while holding their positions.

"I will keep my end of the deal Jack, get on your knees now."

Jack dropped to his knees.

"Tie his hands behind his back."

Two men approached Jack to tie his hands.

Nikolai loosened his grip on the kids after Jack was securely bound. He put his gun in his belt and walked towards Jack, glaring at him. He reared back and slapped Jack across the face. Andy and Grace cried as they watched.

Nikolai pulled a small device out of his pocket and put it into Jack's pocket.

"Tell your friend Luke he can access the device through port 1010—access code 917658."

"I'm on it Jack," Luke said through his earpiece.

"He should be able to authenticate the information in a matter of minutes."

"What is this Nikolai?" one of Khalid's men asked.

"Don't worry about it, if you want to get out of here alive then keep your mouth shut. Khalid has left all of us here to die—including you."

Nikolai got behind Andy and Grace and nudged them forward towards Jack. "Now it's time to let them go."

They walked towards Jack, with the gags still in their mouths.

"Andy. Gracie," Jack choked back tears as he tried to remain strong for them. "Don't worry, you're safe now. I love you two more than anything in the world. I'm sorry you had to go through this. Just know that I will always be with you, no matter what happens, and you'll always be taken care of."

Andy started to cry uncontrollably which triggered Grace to break out in tears.

Jack pushed his burly chest out while kneeling, his head was up, and he showed strength. "Hey guys, don't worry, everything will be okay," he said in a soft reassuring voice.

Nikolai continued to push them towards the gate. Two terrorists slowly opened the Fort Wilderness gate.

The kids didn't want to leave Jack's side, and they grabbed on to him as Nikolai stood in front of them.

"Kids, go to the gate, now," Nikolai said.

They cried. Jack could tell they knew what was going to happen to him.

Jack glared at Nikolai, who was expressionless—focused on the one thing he came to do.

Jack heard something slice through the air—the familiar sound of a suppressed sniper bullet flying at 3000 feet per second.

He looked up at Nikolai and heard a thud.

Nikolai's body didn't move, he slowly put his hand up to his chest and looked at Jack as blood began to trickle out.

Andy and Grace were still latched on to Jack. Khalid's men looked at Nikolai and couldn't figure out what was going on, they didn't even hear the shot.

Nikolai dropped to his knees.

The terrorists knew something was wrong and blindly opened fire outside the fort. Jack lunged towards the kids from his knees knocking them to the ground, trying to stay on top of them.

Nikolai had a confused look on his face as he held his chest, saw the blood, and realized what had happened.

Kendall exploded from the backside of the Fort firing strategically placed shots. Five shots in three-seconds as Khalid's men dropped. The remaining hostiles turned their fire towards Kendall.

They landed a few shots on his ballistic chest plate, jerking his body back —but it didn't phase Kendall. He took the blows and kept advancing.

Three bullets hit Max on his chest plates, sending him to the ground.

Kendall continued to fire.

Another five shots—five more men dropped as he continued towards Jack.

Jack looked up at Nikolai's pale white face as blood flowed from his chest. Nikolai moved his coat aside, and Jack saw the fateful words on the Claymore mine—FRONT TOWARDS ENEMY. He saw something in his hand.

It was the detonator.

"KENDALL!" Jack yelled.

Kendall looked over at Nikolai and recognized the Claymore mine.

His eyes widened.

Nikolai gripped the detonator—trying to ignite the device.

Nikolai looked solemnly at Jack as his thumb lowered on the button.

Kendall dropped his rifle and charged at Nikolai. He leaped in the air and soared with his hands extended.

The impact of Kendall's massive body slammed Nikolai to the ground.

Kendall smothered Nikolai as they slid across the dirt floor. His enormous frame overwhelmed Nikolai—completely covering him.

—BOOOOOM—

A muted explosion rocked the Fort.

Jack put his head down and covered the kids with his body—his hands still tied behind his back.

He looked up and saw Kendall's body lift off the ground and come crashing to the floor.

Smoke and dust filled the Fort.

Jack looked at Andy and Grace and then examined himself, they were unharmed.

Kendall's body restricted the explosion.

"NO!!!" Jack cried out.

He struggled to get out of the restraints but couldn't. He got back up to his knees, checked the kids again and went to Kendall's side.

One of Khalid's men on the ground lifted his automatic weapon and pointed it at Jack.

—BAM—

Jack looked to his right to see what had happened.

The terrorist's head exploded from the incoming shot.

"Jack."

He turned his head.

It was Tony.

"Tony?"

Tony rushed to Jack and cut the restraints.

With his hands free, Jack scooped up Andy and Grace and took them outside of the Fort. He sprinted back into the Fort to check on Kendall.

Tony and Jack both turned Kendall over, he was bleeding bad.

"Kendall, buddy, hang on for me, stay awake."

"Jack." Kendall tried to talk.

“You saved us brother, you saved us all.”

Kendall smiled as blood trickled from his mouth.

“You would’ve done the same for me, brother.”

Jack started to cry, remembering all the time they had spent together inside of the Fort, all of the times Kendall stood up for him and protected him.

“You hold on, we’ll get you through this.” Jack frantically examined Kendall’s chest. It didn’t look good, and he knew it. Even with the ballistic chest plates, the blast was too strong.

Jack looked up at Tony, helpless.

Even with all of his resources, there was nothing he could do to save his best friend.

Kendall mustered the strength to look Jack in the eyes, “Hey brother, I just want to tell you that *this has been quite a ride*.”

"No, Kendall listen to me all you need to do is hang on for a few more minutes—we have the facilities on site to save you, I will airlift you out of here with my helicopter—I will spend every last dollar I have to make you better."

“I wouldn't have done it any other way. I love you Jack. I’ll see you on the other side."

Kendall smiled at Jack, closed his eyes, and his head dropped into Tony's hands.

Tony looked at Jack, stunned.

"NO!"

Jacks voice echoed throughout the River as the Navy hospital Corpsmen raced into the Fort.

Stan’s body squirmed on the ground.

"Dad?"

"Jack? What happened?"

"Dad—are you okay?”

"I don't know son, I can't see anything."

Luke’s voice came through, “Jack the information Nikolai gave you was authentic, we tracked Khalid and we have him cornered on the five freeway right now. I've notified the President’s Chief of Staff."

“Thank you Luke.”

"Jack I am sorry about Kendall, I truly am, I know how much he meant to you. I watched this happen from the Raven, and I’ve never seen a more heroic act in all of my life."

Jack took a deep breath and looked up into the sky. He looked at Kendall's lifeless body and was so grateful to him for what he did.

Kendall was always willing to lay down his life to protect others. The impact of his sacrifice cut Jack to the core.

Andy and Grace were finally safe.
Nikolai was dead.
Khalid had been stopped.
And his best friend just gave his life for everyone.
Jack put his head in his hands and dropped to his knees as he wept.

TEN

1976
Tom Sawyer Island

"Jack check this out!"

Kendall and Jack stepped off the wooden Tom Sawyer Island raft and on to the dirt path. Kendall sprinted ahead.

Jack followed, speed walking as fast as he could—he didn't want to run and get in trouble. If his dad got word from a CM that he was breaking the rules, he would be in a world of hurt.

"Kendall slow down!" Jack yelled as he watched Kendall disappear at the right turn towards the rope bridge.

Jack's speed walking turned into a slow jog; Kendall's excitement piqued his interest.

He made a left in front of the bridge, and he saw Kendall way out ahead of him. Kendall stopped, turned around, and waved his hands at Jack.

"C'mon, Jack hurry up!"

Kendall was in front of the crack in the rock at the River bank. It was the secret entrance leading into Fort Wilderness.

"What's up Kendall, what are you so excited about?"

"Follow me."

Kendall slipped through the crack in the rock and headed into the tunnel. Jack followed.

Kendall talked as he bent over walking through the tunnel.

"I was digging in here, and I found something, but I need your help."

"You were digging in here again, Kendall? You can't do that you're going to get us in trouble."

Kendall didn't respond. He stopped at the spot and moved the dirt around with his big hands.

"Look," Kendall said over his shoulder, "it's some kind of a black box buried under here."

Jack's eyes widened, he'd never seen anything like this, and they'd spent hundreds of hours on the Island exploring every square inch of it for years.

Kendall knocked on the black box, and it sounded hollow.

"Is that crazy or what, Bro?"

"What is it?"

"No clue. Help me get it open before someone comes through here."

They both got on their knees and tried everything to pry it open. Kendall dug deeper into the dirt. He felt a latch on the right side of the box buried several inches in the ground.

He dug his fingers deeper until he got deep enough to pop the latch. He smiled at Jack and slowly opened the box. A gold-looking circular instrument was in the box.

"What in the world?" Jack asked.

"Ha! I told you Jack! Walt probably put this here!"

"Why would Walt bury things in the dirt, he didn't have time for things like that?"

"Well, I don't know, but this is cool, huh?"

"We need to show this to my dad, he'll know what it is."

"Here take it and wait for me by the River, I'm going to bury this box."

Jack walked back towards the River entrance to keep people from entering through the secret crack in the rock while Kendall was hiding the box. He emerged from the dark cave to a view of the sparkling water of the Rivers of America. He looked both ways and admired the beauty of the greenery, mixed with the rugged Island terrain.

He noticed a few kids from school approaching.

"Hey Duncan, what are you doing you little dweeb?"

Jack looked down, hunched over and crossed his scrawny arms; he was intimidated by these boys who always chastised him at school.

"Oh hey guys, nothing, just hanging out." Jack looked the other way.

"What do you mean nothing, you look like you're hiding something?"

Jack looked up at the boys and then down at the ground. "No, I'm not hiding anything," he said timidly.

The boys approached Jack with smirks on their faces. They surrounded him and looked back and forth to make sure no one was around.

"Look guys, I don't want to cause any problems, I'm not hiding anything, I swear. Please just leave me alone." Jack had a defeated look on his face, keeping his head down.

"Oh, are you sad, you little pathetic baby? You get to be at Disneyland every day don't you? You're spoiled because your mom died. You get to do whatever you want because of that, and you think you're special."

Jack squeezed his fists together when they mentioned his mom, and a tear began to form in the right corner of his eye.

"Oh, what are you going to do, little Jackie, are you going to fight us?"

Jack unclenched his fists and looked away. He glanced at the rock, hoping that Kendall would emerge.

One of the boys pushed Jack and knocked him to the ground.

"Come on you little punk. Wasn't your dad a spy or something, how did you turn out to be such a little weakling?"

Another boy kicked dirt in his face. Jack put his hands to his eyes in agonizing pain. The dirt in his eyes made him double over on the ground, the pain was unbearable. The powdery dirt and small bits of gravel shot up his nose and mouth. Jack coughed and squirmed.

One of the boys whispered to the main boy, "Hey there's no one around right now, let's teach him a lesson and get out of here."

The boy smiled, took a step towards Jack, and reared back to kick him in the stomach. He thrust his leg forward, aiming for Jack's belly, when *BAM*, it was as if his leg hit a brick wall.

A giant hand gripped his shin and rotated his leg sending the boy reeling to the ground.

Kendall was furious and glared at the other boys.

They were amazed by his strength, realizing he was much bigger than they were. Kendall looked at Jack on the ground with dirt in his face—he squinted his eyes and pursed his lips in anger.

Kendall charged after the boys, and they quickly retreated like scared dogs.

The main bully was still on the ground in shock. Kendall towered over him and stuck his finger in his face, "If you EVER touch my friend again, I will beat you into an unrecognizable state. Do you understand?"

The boy nodded rapidly, jumped to his feet and took off.

Kendall extended his beefy arm to help Jack up.

"Thanks Kendall."

"No problem, those guys are jerks, don't listen to them." Kendall could tell that Jack was about to cry.

Kendall dusted him off and helped him to his feet.

"Hey Kendall, don't tell my dad about this, I don't want him to do anything that will cause more problems at school."

"Sure—okay check this out, is this cool or what!" Kendall showed Jack a close up of the golden-brass instrument. He was thrilled about the discovery he'd made.

"It looks old."

"I think this is something from that secret society I told you about—you know the group of time travelers who work for Walt and live above the shops on Main Street."

"Kendall, that's not real, we've been over this before."

"I'm telling you Jack, that's why they never let us go up there—think about it, we can go wherever we want—except there. I think there's something your dad isn't telling us."

"Well, let's go ask him."

They headed for the rafts that would take them back to New Orleans Square.

"Do I still have dirt in my face?" Jack asked.

Kendall scanned Jack's face and brushed a little dirt from his cheek. "There ya go buddy, good as new."

They gazed across the waters of the Rivers of America.

"Hey let's go to the Chicken of the Sea Ship, I've been meaning to try this new stunt and the Park is dead today, no one's here."

They crossed the River on the rafts and bolted to the left heading for The Hub. They could see a massive pirate boat through the Castle entrance behind King Arthur's Carrousel. The bottom was blue with gold trim, and the top was painted a glossy red. It had four masts with one angling out over the water. Kendall eyed one of these as they approached.

"You aren't thinking what I think you're thinking, are you?"

Kendall smiled and headed for the wooden pier entrance to the boat.

"See, I told you Jack, there's no one here today!"

He darted for the long wooden pole that slanted off the boat and over the water. He looked both ways and headed for the back of the boat towards the wooden pole. He jumped on it and shimmied himself out to the small wooden lookout at the end of the pole.

Jack put his hands over his eyes, and then looked up out of curiosity.

"Kendall, this is not—" he paused, realizing no matter what he said, Kendall would do it regardless. He always did—he couldn't help himself, he was a shameless thrill-seeker.

Kendall reached the end of the wooden pole, removed his leather belt, and draped it around the pole. He gripped both ends of his belt as he lifted his leg over the pole, inching himself down until he was hanging by his belt.

"Kendall, this will not end well for you. What are you thinking?"

Hanging from his belt, he flung his body forward and started to move down the slanted pole. He started off slow, and the picked up speed as momentum kicked in.

"Whooohooo!" Kendall yelled as he accelerated towards the end of the boat.

"Uh oh."

That was all Jack heard until—

BAM!

He slammed against the end of the boat, lost his grip on the belt, slid down the side of the vessel, and splashed into the water.

"Oh no." Jack jumped into the waist-high water after him, but he couldn't figure out where he was. The water was calm, and Jack frantically searched for any sign of Kendall.

Suddenly, he emerged out of the water.

"Whoohooo! *That was quite a ride, Jack*!" Kendall yelled.

"Kendall, are you okay? You hit that boat hard?"

"Nah, I'm fine Jack, I've been wanting to try that for awhile now."

"Jack?" A voice called from above.

They glanced up in terror from the water—it was Stan with his mouth wide open. His hot tuna pie dropped to the ground with a big *splat*.

"JACK!" Stan yelled. He lowered his voice, "What are you guys doing in there? Get out of that water now!" he looked back and forth, hoping no one else saw them in the water.

Jack and Kendall got out of the water as fast as they could.

"I'm sorry sir," Kendall said.

"Oh Dad, sorry, Kendall was just showing me something."

"I allow you guys to run the Park unsupervised, but you have to obey the rules or I'm going to make you work the jail in the afternoons to teach you a lesson." Stan paused and looked at Jack's face. "What happened to your face, why is there dirt in your mouth?"

"Oh," Jack wiped his mouth, "it's nothing, I just fell."

"Fell?" Stan said in disbelief, "Are those boys from school bothering you again?"

"No, Dad, I mean…well."

"Jack, you can't let them push you around like that, you have to defend yourself." Stan looked over at Kendall who was dripping wet from head to toe. "Kendall helped you again, didn't he?"

Kendall looked down. Jack opened his mouth to talk and then stopped.

"Kendall?"

"Um, yes sir, I helped a little, but Jack had it under control."

"Thank you for standing up for him, Kendall, I appreciate that."

"Oh it was nothing, sir, Jack handled it, I just stepped in because he was outnumbered."

Stan frowned and looked at Jack.

"If you let people push you around your entire life, Jack, you're going to have a tough time."

Jack looked down at the wooden slats on the pier below him.

"Sir," Kendall asked timidly, "I found something in the hidden cave on the Island, do you know what this is?"

Stan's eyes almost bulged out of his head when he saw the brass-looking instrument Kendall held in his hand.

"Where did you find that Kendall?"

"It was in the cave, well, underground slightly, I had to dig it out and open up a box to get it."

Stan snatched the device out of Kendall's hand and examined it, then quickly shoved it in one of his pockets.

"Boys, I can't have you digging around in the Park, this is not a school playground."

"But Dad, what is it? Why was it buried in the cave?"

"It's an artifact that's very important to the Park."

"What kind of artifact."

"Well, it's kind of hard to explain, I'll tell you more about it later."

"You always say that, Dad, just tell us."

"No. I have an important meeting to get to. You two behave, I don't want to hear about you guys getting in trouble again."

"Sir, does it have something to do with that secret society of time travelers who work for Walt Disney?"

Stan looked shocked, "What? Kendall where'd you hear that from?"

"Oh, I talk to everyone around here, and they tell me all kinds of cool stories."

"No, that's a legend Kendall, don't worry about it."

Stan looked flustered as he headed off the pirate ship dock.

"Kendall, did you see his face when you asked him that? He's hiding something."

"Well, I don't think your dad would lie to us Jack. Hey let's go hit Circle Vision, Inner Space, and America Sings, we haven't been over there yet."

"Okay, Kendall." Jack grabbed Kendall's arm as he was heading off towards Tomorrowland, "Hey, thanks for sticking up for me today."

"No problem little buddy. You guys are like family to me, and now I get to play at Disneyland every day after school. You guys rescued me!"

Jack smiled at Kendall, realizing how lucky he was to have a friend like him.

"Don't worry Jack—I've always got your back! I was just a foster kid stuck in the system, and you guys helped me out, I'll always remember that."

Kendall put his arm around him as they headed towards Tomorrowland.

ELEVEN

August 9, 2010
Fort Wilderness

On his knees, hunched over with his hands on Kendall's chest—blood covered him as he cried. Jack remembered all the good times they had together as kids with free rein of the Park. He remembered all the times Kendall stuck up for him. He remembered when he saved his life when they were SEALs.

Through Kendall's death, he and his kids would live. Jack realized Kendall had been right the entire time. He told him over and over again that his vicious desire for revenge was killing him. Looking at Kendall's body was another reminder for him to never go down that path again.

Jack wept over him as the morning sky gave the first sign of the looming sunrise.

The River was calm.

Jack felt relief because he knew Andy and Grace were safe.

He felt mercy—he was given life, which he didn't deserve.

He felt gratitude for Kendall's sacrifice.

But most of all he felt unspeakable sorrow—he knew that it was because of his mistakes, because of his actions—*he* was the reason why Kendall died.

He wept.

TWELVE

December 1966
Walt Disney's Underground Fire Station Apartment

Walt sat on the large rose-colored couch in his underground Fire Station Apartment, dressed in one of his nicer suits. He used the same upholstery that Lillian picked out for their original apartment upstairs. Everything in the underground apartment was patterned after Emile Kuri's original Fire Station Apartment decorations, except the furnishings were much bigger due to the sheer size of the room.

This apartment was directly below the firehouse and was much bigger. They'd built simulated windows into this apartment with special lighting, giving the impression of real sunlight coming through. He could live for weeks in this apartment—it had everything he needed. Walt had a grilled cheese machine, a pantry stocked with his favorite canned chili, and his very own fresh orange juice machine.

The underground apartment gave him easy access to the tunnels that led under the Jungle Cruise allowing him expedited access to his office under Club 33. He could get anywhere in the Park from this residence.

"Stan, the progress I've made on the Dream City is astonishing. I can't even explain it with words, it's unlike anything I've ever experienced."

Stan smiled as he sipped his coffee.

"I mean it's everything I ever imagined it would be, and more! We've been able to tap great minds from the past—Benjamin Franklin, Andrew Jackson, Mark Twain, and *even Abraham Lincoln*. I've also been able to access the knowledge of innovators from the future—I found a technology pioneer who's helped me use the power of computers to access this other dimension."

"Walt, you don't look well."

Walt's smile faded, and he looked towards the ground.

"Yes, that's why I brought you down here, Stan. You know, you've been one of my greatest friends. Over the years, you've selflessly looked after me and protected my interests over your own, defended me until the end, and you've always had my back. I just wanted you to know how much your friendship has meant to me."

Stan knew something was wrong. Walt was never one to lavish so much praise on him or anyone else.

"It's cancer, Stan—and I don't think I have much longer to live."

Stan's mouth dropped, and he spilled his coffee on the rose-colored upholstery.

"What? Walt?"

"I know, Stan, it's quite a surprise, although I think I've known it all along."

Stan's eyes welled up. Walt meant so much to him, he was like a brother, a mentor, and he was his inspiration. Walt instilled in him a child-like excitement that made him want to get out of bed in the morning.

"I don't know what to say, Walt."

"Don't be sad, Stan. The Multiplaner will give me the ability to travel through time, and this new Land I've discovered allows me to create and innovate outside of this time continuum."

"But what happens when you…you…"

"When I die?"

Stan nodded as he leaned over to look into Walt's aged eyes.

"When I die, my physical body will cease to exist, there's nothing I can do about that. But that doesn't stop me from building the Dream City now. The more I learn in this perfect environment, the more I can advance the Multiplaner. The time travel aspect is exceedingly difficult, and I'm not sure if I can fully crack it. The gateway I've built is not perfect—and each time I pass through it, it's risky—life threatening. That's why I don't want to take you through it. Not until it's ready."

"Walt, if it's life threatening, then maybe…" Stan paused.

Walt smiled, "Ah, your natural instinct is to protect me, I know that Stan. But it really doesn't matter now. It's a risk I need to take for the better of humanity—for future generations."

"But Walt, if you can go back in time, and build and discover things in this other dimension, can't you find a treatment for your cancer and solve your health problems?"

Walt grinned with compassion.

"Stan, I can't change my appointed time to pass from this earth. But I can do everything possible within my lifetime to discover things that will change the world."

"But Walt, this world needs you, it needs your vision, you're too young to go."

"But maybe not, Stan, maybe I'm leaving at the perfect time. I might not have pushed as hard if I thought I had another forty years to live."

Stan dropped his head, trying to process the devastating news. It wasn't just about losing his dear friend; this was about losing the catalyst behind everything he was familiar with—his entire reality and way of life. Walt's death would directly affect tens of thousands of people associated with the company. These people depended on Walt—their entire existence depended on Walt's vision, his excitement, and his passion.

"What do you need me to do, Walt?"

"I need you to see our plan through, and find our successor." Walt handed Stan an antique handheld device.

"Here, take this. This is a mobile version of the Multiplaner, it's not as powerful, but you should be able to communicate with me to a certain extent through it."

"What will I do, Walt? Without you the company won't take risks, their focus will turn to profit, and they won't keep your vision alive."

"Maybe so, Stan, it'll be tough, and we won't win all the battles, but through the technology of the Multiplaner, we will do what we can to keep the dream alive."

"Yes, Walt."

"They aren't going to build Project X in Florida, Stan. They think it's a crazy idea, and they're going to turn the Florida property into something else. I'm okay with that now since the gateway opened by the Multiplaner will allow me to build my original vision of EPCOT."

"But how will I be able to keep your dream alive?"

"We'll need help. I've become fond of the foster kids we've helped. Their hearts are pure even though their entire young lives have been filled with adversity. They're not spoiled kids, they're grateful for everything they have. Kids like this who have a true love for the Park can help us in our journey."

"How will these kids help us?" Stan asked.

"We'll find a way to choose the right ones, and we'll give them access to the Multiplaner, so they can travel through time and keep things on track."

Stan didn't fully understand what Walt was referring to, but he was accustomed to not always grasping Walt's brilliant ideas.

"What about our tunnel system, the vault, everything that's down here?"

"I don't think people are ready to see what's down here yet, Stan. I don't think they'll be ready for a long time. The power source is still too dangerous to expose. The Multiplaner can't be trusted in anyone else's hands. It needs to be kept behind the scenes and revealed only to people we can fully trust."

"Walt this is a lot to hide down here. I'm surprised we've kept it hidden for this long. As we have more and more employees and other people in the Park, it will be tough to conceal."

"I know, but that's why I have you Stan. I'm going to leave you some money—you won't need to worry about finances. Jack's future will be secure. I'm also going to secure your position and authority in the company so you'll have the appropriate power necessary to carry out my plans. I need you to vet your successor. I have a lot of hope for your son, Stan, but if he's not ready, don't bring him into this. It will hurt him more than it will help him. If you can't find a viable successor in your lifetime, then keep these things hidden. It's better for them to be buried instead of falling into the wrong hands."

"Okay, Walt."

"One day Stan, I want to take you to this new Land, you will love it. We'll play like little kids, invent whatever we want, and share our results with the world. *Wouldn't that be fun*?"

Stan smiled, realizing it could be his last time hearing Walt's famous tag line that he added to everything he was excited about.

"Yes, it would Walt."

"Also, I don't care what it takes, we need to make people feel like they've entered another world when they come to Disneyland. It hit me the first time I went through the Multiplaner gateway. I passed from a dark, underground tunnel, into a Land of enchantment with no earthly parallel. That's what I want guests to feel when they walk through our front gates and under the railroad tunnels. I want them to feel as if they've been transported to another time, into another world, another dimension."

Stan smiled at Walt, savoring the moment, wishing that he could sit here and listen to him talk forever.

"When we built the Magic Skyway for the World's Fair, it made me focus on the phenomenon of time travel. I'm going to use our Skyway as a gateway, like we've done in the past, it will be the 'Magic' Skyway that I envisioned, and we'll use it as a vehicle to travel back in time."

Walt paused, glancing at the full size aerial picture of Disneyland on the wall, and talked with a sentimental tone, "You know, I'm going to miss this place. This Park is my baby, I love it so much. I still remember opening day, in my apartment upstairs. When the gates opened, and I saw all of the people come flooding in, I shed a tear, it was beautiful. My dream of creating another world for people to enjoy had come true. I will never forget that day. I will never forget this Park. Disneyland will always hold a special place in my heart, it has made me so happy to see people enjoy and appreciate something I've created. This is the environment that allowed my creativity to flourish, without Disneyland, nothing else would have been possible."

Stan's eyes watered as he listened to Walt's love for the place that had such a colossal impact on his life.

Walt's face shifted from a sentimental look to a determined gaze.

"I will always be here, Stan, and I'll find a way to come back to Disneyland one day."

Stan smiled big, knowing that if anyone could figure out how to avoid a final goodbye, it was Walt.

"This new Land is phenomenal," Walt continued, "it's so difficult to explain—almost like trying to explain our magnificent earth to a baby in the womb. Can you imagine trying to explain to an unborn child that they are about to enter a world that has mountains that are thousands of feet tall, huge waterfalls, amazing sunsets, and a place like Disneyland? That's how this new Land is, it's like the earth remade in its perfect form, no blemishes, no errors."

"That's amazing Walt."

"You know, scientists have known about the existence of other dimensions for quite some time. Franklin knew it. The challenge has always been how to access them. That's what the Multiplaner has allowed us to do."

Stan leaned back on the couch, admiring Walt as he did so many times in the past—grateful for his one-on-one discussions with the greatest mind of his generation. He knew there would never be another Walt Disney.

"Well my friend," Walt said softly, "it's time for me to go. I get a little nervous when I use the Multiplaner—so many things can go wrong. Let's just hope I can make it through to the other side. Otherwise, you're going to have to tell everyone I died of a heart attack."

Stan was flabbergasted by Walt's comment and just stared at him, confused, not knowing what to say.

Walt put his coffee down on the table, stood up, straightened his suit, and walked towards the big mirror on the wall. He analyzed himself in the mirror, his face showed dissatisfaction with his physical appearance. He turned back to Stan and gave him a big hug.

"Walt," Stan's voice broke up as he fought back the tears, "I just want to tell you what an impact you've had on my life. I was a bitter man before I met you and you've taught me to dream, you taught me to forgive and forget, if it weren't for you I wouldn't have Genie. I owe you so much, Walt, and I can't tell you how much I'm going to miss talking with you while you sip your orange juice, listening to your dreams and visions, or strolling down Main Street with you."

Walt smiled affectionately, "Someday, we'll walk down Main Street again. But it will be the *perfect* version of Main Street, and we'll be able to soak up its splendor and beauty without having to worry about time. We'll be able to fully enjoy it, worry-free, without feeling as if there's somewhere else we need to be."

Stan smiled as Walt put his hands together and turned towards the mirror. He pushed a few buttons on the wall, and Stan felt a low hum throughout the room.

Walt cautiously approached the mirror as it illuminated with a bright liquid light.

He turned back one last time with a confident grin.

His famous mustache curled.

His eyes twinkled.

The child-like look of anticipation returned to Walt's face—the look Stan had seen so many times.

A blinding flash of light filled the room as Walt walked through. He was gone.

THIRTEEN

El Capitan Presidential Suite
Grand Californian Hotel

Jack walked into the El Capitan Suite with his arm in a sling. He showered and cleaned up in the Dream Suite to prepare to see Andy and Grace. He didn't want them to see him in the state he was in on the Island.

"Dad!" Andy and Grace ran to him. They looked tired, and sad, but they were happy to see Jack.

He hugged them and relished their innocent childlike scent, their soft skin. He was so grateful to be able to hold them in his arms again.

"I'm so glad you guys are okay."

"What happened to Uncle Kendall?" Andy asked.

"Well," Jack paused and got choked up as he looked into Andy's wet, bloodshot eyes. "Kendall saved us. He died for us. He jumped on that man and shielded the blast so it wouldn't hurt us. Your Uncle Kendall is a hero."

Andy and Grace wept.

"And Kim?" Grace hesitantly asked as she cried.

"I'm sorry, Gracie, she's gone—she died while trying to free you guys in the Fort."

Tony stood behind the kids, and his eyes welled up. He wiped the tears away so they wouldn't see.

Grace whimpered, "You know, Tony, Kim said that she liked you yesterday, like in a boyfriend way."

Tony looked at Grace and then up at Jack, "She did?"

"Yep, she told us both last night."

Tony paused and tried to maintain his composure, "Just remember guys, Kim was forced into an impossible situation. Her mom and sister are okay now. They were being held hostage, and she was trying to save them."

"Sorry I doubted you, Tony." Jack said.

"It's okay Jack, I was trying to find information to prove that there was another motive behind the threat, but I just couldn't get the info in time."

"What about Ruddy?"

"Brett was the last person who I ever thought would be a hero. But he was. He saved my life—he took a shot at Khalid and hit him in his arm. Then he continued to fire at him, which distracted Khalid from finishing me off. He displayed incredible bravery. We certainly underestimated him all these years."

"Luke," Jack called out over his earpiece, "let me know when I can talk to my dad, I need to talk to him as soon as possible."

"Will do Jack, the doctors are still looking him over, he's in critical condition."

Max opened the door of the suite, "Sir, Ms. White is here to see you."

Jack smiled, glanced at Andy and Grace, and then at Max.

"Send her in Max."

Melissa walked through the doors. She had aged well, and Jack was surprised at how radiant she was after all these years. She was dressed in her rugged black spec ops gear. She removed her LAPD hat, and her hair fell over her shoulders.

"Jack!" Melissa walked in and gave him a hug. She looked down at the kids and knelt in front of them. "How are you guys doing, are you okay?"

Andy smiled, but Grace would not look at her.

"Yes ma'am," Andy said.

Melissa stood up and looked Jack in the eyes. "I'm sorry about Kendall, Jack, I know how much he meant to you and what a huge loss this must be for you."

"Thank you Melissa, and thank you for your help through all of this."

"Anything for you Jack, I know you would've done the same for me. I was just doing my job."

Grace gave her a dirty look. Andy noticed this and elbowed her.

Jack noticed Grace's scorn and bent down in front of her.

"Hey Gracie, what would make you happy right now?"

She looked back and forth with tears in her eyes. "I want to go to our spot at the French Market, the place where you and mom met, and I want to hear *the story*."

"Honey, I don't know if that's possible right now." Jack paused while Max jumped on his radio. Max nodded at Jack letting him know they could go to New Orleans Square if they wanted.

"Sure, okay let's do it." Jack said.

"Melissa, you can come with us if you want," Andy said with a smile.

Jack hesitated and looked at Melissa, and then at Grace. "Andy, I don't know what Ms. White has going right now, I think she's working."

"I would be happy to go with you guys," Melissa said smiling.

Jack's life had been drastically altered in the past several hours. From being consumed with revenge and living in the past—to being free of that bondage. He was lucky to be alive—his kids were lucky to be alive. He felt as if he needed to move forward and make significant changes—he didn't want Kendall's death to be in vain.

"Sir, our Spec Ops team will escort us," Max said.

They walked through the foyer of the El Capitan Suite, and Jack caught a glimpse of Gracie. She was a beautiful miniature version of Kate. She'd suffered through too many losses in her short little life, and Jack could see the hurt in her face.

He stopped at the door.

"Melissa, actually, I think it might be better if we do this on our own."

Melissa stopped, "Oh, sure, Jack, I completely understand. Just call me if you need me—anytime."

Jack smiled at her, looked into her eyes, and left.

Jack's phone buzzed from a blocked number, and his heart dropped.

"Yes."

"Jack, this is President Hayes."

Jack stopped, "Yes, Mr. President."

Melissa appeared to be surprised and impressed to hear Jack talking to the President.

"Is that the President of the United States?" Grace whispered to Max.

"Yes, Gracie, it sure is."

"Jack," The President continued, "I want to thank you for your help, we couldn't have done it without you. I'm going to forget some of the things that happened because I know you were under a lot of pressure."

"Thank you sir, I'm sorry, it was just—"

"No need for apologies, Jack. I was deeply saddened to hear about Kendall, he's a true American hero. My staff will be in touch to make arrangements to accept something on Kendall's behalf. I'll be awarding him the Medal of Honor."

"Oh, Mr. President, that's extremely generous of you."

"He earned it. Thank you again Jack." The President hung up.

Jack put his phone back in his pocket, "He's going to award the Medal of Honor to Kendall," he said to Max.

"Sir, I am very happy to hear this, Kendall deserves the highest honor for his sacrifice."

"What's the Medal of Honor?" Andy asked.

"It's the highest military honor, something that's awarded by the President of the United States in the name of Congress."

"Wow," Andy said with a smile on his face.

They headed out of the El Capitan Suite, down the Cast Member elevator and took the underground passageway towards New Orleans Square.

Everything around the River looked normal with the exception of several large instant walls surrounding the entire Island where frantic repairs were being made.

Andy and Grace walked hand and hand with Jack as they approached the table where Jack and Kate first met.

"Hey Gracie, do you like Melissa?"

"No," she said without hesitating.

"I think she's nice," Andy said.

Jack kneeled down in front of them, "I just want you two to know that at this point in my life, I don't need anyone else, I only need you. No one will ever take the place of your mom—and I have no plans of replacing her."

"But won't you be lonely, Dad?" Andy asked.

Jack smiled. "No, Andy, these events have changed me, seeing what your Uncle Kendall did for us, realizing that I've been holding on to bad feelings for way too long. I've witnessed a sacrificial love that's greater than life itself—you two are my life, our life begins again here at Disneyland, the right way this time."

Andy and Grace both smiled big at Jack.

He knew how much their love story meant to Andy and Grace, it was therapeutic for them to talk about it and it made them feel as if Kate was still with them. Jack mentally removed everything on his mind, the death of Kendall, the extremely close call with the kids—everything—so he could give the kids what they needed.

Jack smiled and journeyed back in time to one of the most memorable days of his life.

"So, I was walking with my head down, looking at something your grandpa gave me, when I looked up—" Jack stopped in front of the small exit gate of the French Market veranda, with the detailed French Market sign directly above. He looked at the table facing the walkway just past the exit. "I saw the most beautiful woman I'd ever seen in my life, I was dumbfounded and didn't know what to say, I had a lump in my throat, but I kept staring at her anyway because I couldn't take my eyes off of her."

Grace giggled.

Jack became more animated, "Suddenly, she looked up at me, and her deep blue eyes pulled me in like a tractor beam," he smiled big and looked down at Grace. "I was stunned and taken back by her beauty, and with the way the sunlight made her face glow. Her long blonde hair flowed with the gentle breeze—she looked like an angel, something that was not of this world."

At that moment, all three of them stared at the table, and it was as if Kate gloriously appeared in front of their eyes. Her beautiful face beamed at them as she leaned forward on the small French Market table. Her blue eyes sparkled, and the cool breeze tossed her hair. She lifted her hand, smiled big, and daintily waved her fingers at them.

Jack took a deep breath and smiled. Andy had a giant grin on his face, and Gracie looked excited. They waved back at her.

"Hi Mommy!" Grace said softly.

FOURTEEN

Club 33
Disneyland Park

"Jack, meet me at The Club."

"Dad, you sound horrible?"

"I know, but there are things I need to tell you in case I don't make it."

"I'm heading there now," Jack raced towards the Club. He was angry. He had so many questions for Stan, so many things that he needed answered.

Jack hit the buzzer to the left of the green Club 33 door, and it opened. The hostess greeted him, "Mr. Duncan, your father is in the Trophy Room."

Jack ran up the stairs to find Stan in a wheelchair staring out the windows of the Trophy Room overlooking Royal Street. His caretaker was with him monitoring his vitals.

"Dad."

Stan looked like he'd been crying. "You know, Walt and I ate here a lot. Most people think he never got a chance to dine in Club 33, but we spent a lot of time here before it opened. We hosted luncheons and other things." Stan chuckled, "We used those microphones to listen in on key discussions with city officials." Stan pointed to the hidden microphones in the chandeliers. "So many important decisions were made in this room."

Stan coughed, he didn't sound good at all.

"Jack," Stan said in a soft weak voice, "I'm so sorry about Kendall." He started to cry, "I can't believe he's gone, he was like a son to me."

Jack wanted to rip into his dad the moment he saw him, but after seeing him and realizing his condition, he held back.

"I know Dad, he loved and respected you very much."

"I can still remember you two running through the Park together, you getting beat up, and Kendall always stepping in to help you out. He always had your back."

"Yes, he did. He saved us. He saved me—and the kids. He never once thought about himself."

"That was Kendall. A true gem. A true American hero. He was a handsome boy." Stan looked down into his lap as tears dropped.

Jack chuckled through his tears, "Guess what he said to me right before he died?"

Stan knew the answer, "*That was quite a ride*?"

"Yeah, then he told me he loved me and that he'd see me on the other side."

Stan gazed through the windows, looking at the ornate iron Club 33 balcony on the other side of Royal Street.

"I remember planning yours and Kate's engagement that night at the Club. Kendall was like a big kid, he had as much fun as I did planning that whole fiasco."

Jack smiled.

"He was the same way at your wedding. He was so proud of you and how you'd grown. Going from that scrawny little kid getting beat up on Tom Sawyer Island, to the most feared SEAL in military history."

"Dad, why did you keep so many secrets from me? About Nikolai's son, the tunnels, the vault…why?"

"Jack, I didn't have a choice."

"What do you mean you didn't have a choice? That information would've been good for me to know, it could've saved lives?"

"Son, your temper, your thirst for revenge, it was too much—you'd do anything to get revenge for what happened to Kate and it made you a dark person for many years. Even before that happened, your arrogance after you left the SEALs mixed with your wealth was a dangerous combination. This information would've hurt you more than helped you."

"That is *your* opinion, you should have trusted me—I can't understand how you could've kept all of this from me for so many years?"

"Like I said, son, I didn't have a choice. Let's go down to the vault, I need to show you something."

"How are you going to get down there, it's too difficult in your condition?"

"Not the way we're going."

Stan's caretaker pushed him out of the Trophy Room, they made a left and went for the Cast Member door that led to the balcony of the Blue Bayou facade. They turned right and stopped at the end.

"I'll take it from here, Bob."

"Yes, sir," said his caretaker who exited the balcony.

Stan typed in a code to open the door, they both entered, and Stan keyed another code. Suddenly, the platform they were on lowered. Jack looked up as they descended.

"What is this?"

"You'll see Jack."

They lowered into Walt's underground office, and the lights clicked on. Jack looked around in amazement at how everything looked with the lights on.

"I still can't believe you guys built this entire underground network without anyone knowing."

Stan looked around the office nostalgically, "We had to Jack—there were too many valuable things to protect. Walt was working on projects that would change the world—things that were out of this world."

"What do you mean by that?"

"Let's go to the vault." Stan paused momentarily to look around Walt's office. "I remember Walt would sit in his chair, and he'd tell me about the crazy things he was working on. That man had more vision and creativity than anyone I'd ever met—even to this day, there hasn't been a greater innovator. No one dreamed as big as him, and he had such a love for this Park."

Jack stared at Walt's chair, imagining what it would be like to sit across the desk from him and chat about the future, and the possibilities of tomorrow.

Jack wheeled Stan through the tunnels, heading for Lafitte's underground Tavern.

"How are you going to get into the vault?" Jack asked as they moved through the large wooden doors of the Tavern.

"There's another entrance over here." Stan pointed to the barrels on the left side of the Tavern. "Move those aside."

Jack moved them to find a dusty hatch on the floor with a familiar etched circle in it. Jack pulled out the ring and placed it on the thick iron hatch.

"If you thought I wasn't ready," Jack said, "why did you leave all of these clues for me to find. If I wouldn't have opened the doors, none of this would have happened."

"In my condition, I had to leave a path for you to get in because no one else knew about it, and I wanted you to be the successor. I hoped that you would somehow come around, but I didn't know when it would happen."

The large hatch opened. An elevator platform emerged that was large enough to fit Stan's wheelchair. Jack stood on the edge next to Stan, and it lowered into the vault.

Stan turned on the lights.

Jack was astounded at the contents of the vault. It was a treasure room, there were so many things piled in there—the strange looking telescope devices, gold bars, gold plates, and hundreds of other antique devices and contraptions.

"What are these things?" Jack asked, pointing to the Multiplaner.

"That, Jack, is Walt's greatest invention. He called it the Multiplaner."

"Multiplaner? What does it do?"

"Well, that's complicated. It does several different things including transporting things to different locations, different dimensions, and different points in history."

"What? Are you talking about a time machine?"

"To a certain extent," Stan explained, "although it isn't time travel like you've seen in the movies or read about in books. It's very complicated."

"If Khalid would've known about this, it could've been disastrous, worse than a nuke, he could've used it to erase key points in American history."

"Yes, thank God he was only focused on nuclear capability."

"Are you saying this machine can send me back in time? Visit people in the past? Alter past events?"

"Oh, no—you wouldn't want to do that Jack, it would cause major problems. Walt was adamantly against that sort of thing. His main goal was to pull wisdom from the past, and the future, he wanted to create the Dream City—a city with the perfect environment for innovation and the advancement of technology."

"Dad, if this thing can take me back in time to see Kate—to *save* Kate, you had better tell me."

"Jack, it's extremely risky, you could die in the process, and there's no guarantee you'd ever get to see her. You could make things infinitely worse."

Jack's mind was racing as he touched the Multiplaner.

"Walt never built the Dream City—why?" Jack asked.

"That's kind of hard to explain."

"What do you mean Dad?" Jack was at his end, frustrated that Stan had kept so many secrets from him. "People died, my best friend died, my kids almost died because of all this. Why didn't you tell me about this stuff? Sure, I wasn't in my right mind at the time, but you should have trusted me. Bad things happened because you hid things from me."

"Not necessarily, Jack. You see, Walt had high hopes for you. He wanted you to be our successor, he wanted you to take this technology to the next level." Stan struggled to lift his arm, "The greatest inventions of our time are right here in this vault. Walt needed someone to continue his work after he was gone, and after I was gone."

"But what? He changed his mind? He died the year I was born? It was *your* decision to keep this information from me, not Walt's."

"Jack, this technology had to be protected at all cost—it was too important. Only someone who met Walt's exact criteria could learn of it—I had to honor Walt's wishes."

"I still don't understand Dad. If you didn't think I was ready, great, don't put me in charge. But my job was to oversee the security of this Resort, I put millions of dollars of my own money into *The System*, I lived here with Andy and Grace, don't you think I should have known about all of this so I could've watched for people who might be after it? I can't believe you would've been so selfish, that you wouldn't think of this. Why Dad?" Jack's frustration mounted as his voice grew louder, "Why would you do this to me? Why would you keep me in the dark when I had so much to lose?"

Stan broke eye contact with Jack, peering over his shoulder.

Jack glared at Stan, wanting answers.

Stan looked at Jack and then beyond him. Jack was irritated by his evasiveness. He leaned into Stan trying to get him to focus on his eyes.

"Dad?"

Stan took a deep breath and grinned.

"*It was me, Jack.*"

Chills ran up Jack's spine.

It was the most recognizable voice he'd ever heard.

Anyone would've recognized it.

Jack's eyes widened as he looked at Stan.

He slowly turned his head to see who it was.

He saw a man in the shadows, wearing a suit, standing in a dark corner of the vault.

The man stepped forward.

The light revealed his slicked back hair, friendly eyes, famous grin, and a mustache only *one* man could wear.

It was Walt Disney.

By Kelly Ryan Johns

If you loved Season One, please leave positive feedback on Amazon. This helps us gain more readers and will keep the possibility of future Seasons alive!

Like *Deadliest Cast Member* on Facebook for real-time updates and behind the scenes info!

Go to www.DeadliestCastMember.com to join our Priority Email List and to get notifications via Facebook and Google+!

August 9, 2010
Rivers of America

Khalid heard the explosions and the gunfire while he swam through the dark water of the Rivers of America. His breathing apparatus and night vision goggles allowed him to move quickly towards the pipe at the front of the River. The helicopter explosion was a close call—too close.

He reached the pipe at the front of the Rivers of America and quickly swam to the top hatch. He exited the pipe and landed in the dry, empty tunnel.

A man emerged from the shadows. He was the spitting image of Khalid.

They embraced.

"Brother, I knew you would make it."

"I told you that I would never fail you Khalid."

"We don't have much time, take my backpack, the device is inside."

His brother nodded.

"You know what this means, my brother—because of what we did to your DNA, they will think you are me. They will torture you, and eventually kill you."

"I know, Khalid, I am ready to die for our cause, you know that."

Khalid smiled, "You are a true hero."

Khalid pulled a small brass instrument from the backpack with an evil grin on his face.

"I have the ability to travel through time now, to change history, to ERASE the United States from the face of this planet."

Khalid's brother smiled, "I knew you could do it Khalid. Now go—change history—make all things right for our people."

"Your sacrifice will not be forgotten, my brother—"

Khalid embraced him.

"But I will do *everything* in my power to come back for you."

"Jack's Favorites"

The following was transcribed from an audio interview with Jack Duncan and Giada De Laurentiis. It was intended as the basis for an article in *Food Network Magazine*. The interview was never published...until now.

Giada: Jack! It is so nice to finally meet you! I've read so much about you and your family and I just wanted to personally thank you for your service to our country! Thanks for taking the time to do this interview; I think our readers are going to love it!

Jack: Thank you Giada, it's nice meeting you too, the kids and I have watched your show for a long time and I'm a big fan.

Giada: Maybe one day I can get you to do a cameo on the show?

Jack: Oh, I don't know about that, I don't think I'm very good on camera.

Giada: You'd do great, Jack. By the way, this suite is breathtaking! These windows overlooking California Adventure are so extravagant; it feels like a luxury penthouse suite but at the same time a cozy residence. The cool thing is that is overlooks California Adventure! It must be incredible for you and your kids to live here.

Jack: The kids love this suite, we've had so many great memories here as a family and the sheer size of it makes our extended stays possible.

Giada: How big is this suite?

Jack: It's just under 2000 square feet, we can fit around 75 people in here for a meeting if we have to. This is the main living room that we're sitting in, to the left is a dining room, to the right a private office and then the master bedroom which has a private balcony. We spend a lot of our time on the main balcony though, it's a spectacular view, and as you can see it spans almost the entire width of the suite.

Giada: Wow! How much does this cost a night?

Jack: I think they charge around $5500 per night depending on the season.

Giada: I want to say, off the record that I am sorry about your wife Jack, I can't imagine what you and your kids have had to endure.

Jack: Thank you Giada, it's been tough, especially on the kids.

Giada: I know you have a good-sized staff that helps, but how do you manage to keep tabs on everything? I know after what happened in 2005 that it must have been tough to come back here and live with the kids.

Jack: It was tough, but the bottom line is that they are safer here, I have the most advanced security system in the world monitoring the Resort, along with an elite security force watching the kids 24/7. This is where they want to be, so I've done everything possible to make it happen for them.

Giada: That's awesome, Jack that you've done this for them. And I've seen your security detail, it's more intimidating than the Secret Service!

Jack: In many ways, our detail rivals the President's protection.

Giada: Well, let's get into it. You're at the Disneyland Resort most of the year with Andy and Grace, and I know you love great food. We figured you could give us the inside scoop on what to eat. What's your favorite place to eat at the Resort?

Jack: We love to eat, no doubt about that, and when you stay here over 300 days a year, you naturally learn where to find the best food. You would think we'd get tired of eating here, but we don't, there's such a wide variety, and the quality has improved a great deal over the years. I'd have to say Napa Rose is my favorite purely because of the quality. It's one of the more expensive places to eat, but it's worth it, especially if you're celebrating a special occasion.

Giada: What do you normally eat there?

Jack: I like to try everything, but my go-to dinner is their Slowly Braised Angus Beef Short Rib. It's out of this world, you can cut the meat with your fork and it tastes like butter. They change the sauce seasonally, but all of their sauces are magic, and they perfectly compliment the main ingredients. It's a nice chunk of premium beef, and you can split it with someone—they don't charge a split plate fee. This Short Rib is comfort food for me.

Giada: What about Andy and Grace? What's their favorite at Napa?

Jack: They love the wood fired pizzas. We can smell the wood fired oven scent on our balcony all day long. Chef Sutton always puts a different culinary spin on their pizzas. They could eat Napa pizzas every day and not get tired of them. They're reasonably priced when you consider the quality—I think they're around fifteen bucks. The atmosphere at the Napa Rose is second to none, the architecture and the interior design are remarkable. We usually get a table on the far patio, which gives us a view of Condor Flats. The movie music plays in the background, the tall redwoods and pine trees are everywhere, and we can watch people strolling through the Park. Sometimes we'll sit out there for hours.

Giada: Any other favorites from Napa?

Jack: Pretty much everything at Napa is out of this world. They can make anything taste good. They carefully craft tons of layers of flavor into every dish. I'd recommend the Chef's table for anyone who wants to sample their creations and get a front row view of the open kitchen. You would enjoy this, Giada. They usually serve 4-5 courses, and then you get dessert. All you do is tell them your likes and dislikes and then let the chef surprise you. The Warm Dark Chocolate Truffle Cake with Bailey's ice cream is a must. It's hard to explain how delicious it is because the Truffle appears to be thick when it's served, but when you take a bite, it disappears in your mouth—I've never had anything else like it.

Giada: Ooooh, that sounds wonderful, I'm going to have to give that a try! Okay, so what would you recommend for a family on a budget.

Jack: There are a lot of different options, one being the Plaza Inn Chicken Dinner. The plates are big enough to split , and the fried chicken is delicious. You can order extra pieces of chicken a la carte, extra mashed potatoes, green beans, and things like that.

Giada: What's your absolute favorite in Disneyland?

Jack: That's a tough one, we have a lot of family history at the Blue Bayou, so we're partial to that place. The food is excellent, and the ambiance is unmatched. I always order the Cajun Pan-seared Salmon. Another one of our favorites is Carnation Café, mostly because of Chef Oscar, and it's a blast eating right on Main Street with the parade going by. There's nothing better than eating lunch or dinner right in the middle of Main Street, USA.

Giada: What about a romantic place to eat in Disneyland?

[Silence for several seconds on the audio]

Giada: I'm sorry Jack, I didn't know if I should even ask this question if you don't want to answer we can skip it.

Jack: It's okay, it's hard to talk about it but it's good for me to talk about her. It's therapeutic to a certain extent—it helps me control my rage, I guess.

Giada: I can totally understand and appreciate that, Jack, don't feel bad about it.

Jack: It eats away at me to be honest.

Giada: Have you ever thought about forgiving the people who were responsible?

Jack: No, not for a second, I only wish they could have suffered more.

[Another pause in the audio]

Giada: But maybe by not forgiving them, you are actually hurting yourself?

Jack: You're probably right, but I just function better this way, it sort of eases the pain.

Giada: I totally understand Jack, you have every right to deal with it in your own way.

Jack: Sorry Giada, I didn't mean to get into all of that. Back to the question, the Bengal Barbecue was a romantic place to eat for Kate and I when we first met. You wouldn't think of this as a romantic spot, but we loved the chicken and vegetable skewers, and we loved the Adventureland ambiance. When you're by the Tiki Room, surrounded by the Hawaiian theme, and you smell the barbecue in the background, it's like heaven. We always enjoyed sitting on the patio of Cafe Orleans so we could be in the middle of the action in New Orleans Square. We ate a lot at the old Big Thunder Barbecue, back when you used to line up to get your food, and they'd serve it on those old-style cowboy metal plates. They had ovens right there where they would slow cook, and smoke the meat for hours—it was so good. Then, of course, there's the French

Market, where we'd always sit and watch the Royal Street Bachelors play.

Giada: Wow, Jack, it's so great to hear your memories with Kate in the Park. You light up when you talk about her. Is it hard for you to go to those places now when there are so many memories like this everywhere you look?

Jack: No, it actually makes it easier when we visit places she liked. The kids love it, and they always like going to these restaurants and hearing the stories.

Giada: What are Andy and Grace's favorite place to eat?

Jack: Andy loves White Water Snacks at the Grand Californian. He could eat their chicken nachos every day. We usually order them to go because they give you more food. Grace loves the bread bowls from the Pacific Wharf Café in California Adventure. We love that entire Pacific Wharf area, I think it's because it reminds them of their grandpa.

Giada: Speaking of Stan Duncan, there was probably no one closer to Walt Disney, especially towards the end of his life. What were his favorites over the years?

Jack: Well, Dad and Walt were very simple. Walt liked chili out of the can. He'd make my dad grilled cheese sandwiches in his apartment. My dad loved Aunt Jemima's Pancake House. In his later days, he loved anything Chef Oscar would make him from the Carnation Cafe.

Giada: And what about Kendall? We've had a lot of requests, especially from our female audience, asking about his favorites.

Jack: [Laughter] Kendall has always had a big appetite. This guy will clear out a buffet. When he goes to the Big Thunder Ranch Barbecue, the servers know to keep the food coming. At Storytellers, they actually make more food when they realize Kendall is there. His favorite though is the Sunday brunch at Club 33. He loves the Club, and of course he loves buffets, so the brunch is the best of both worlds for him. He eats around ten pounds of lobster claws when he's there.

Giada: What about your favorite breakfast?

Jack: We are partial to Storytellers Café because it's a short walk from the suite, and the ambiance is phenomenal. They have a character breakfast, which is a brunch buffet, that's fun for the kids, and the food is good. Goofy's Kitchen is another favorite, their buffet has more of a variety, and there's a lot of characters. We really love the breakfast burritos at White Water Snacks, and I love their salsa. La Brea Bakery in Downtown Disney is one of our favorite breakfast spots, their patio near the front gate is fun to sit on and the people there are very nice. Other options are the Pacific Wharf Café—breakfast on the Wharf is always nice, and Taste Pilot's Grill.

Giada: What about your favorite lunch?

Jack: The flatbread pizza at the Boardwalk Pizza and Pasta is pretty good and filling if you're looking for something quick. The Lucky Fortune cookery makes tasty Chinese food, we like the Coconut Curry Sauce. The Clam Chowder Bread Bowls at the Pacific Wharf Café are always a favorite. The bread is fresh baked in the Boudin Sourdough Factory. You can order the soup on the side, and you can save your bread for later if you want. You can also order a big loaf of bread there, and they'll cut it up for you—makes for a great snack. On the Disneyland side, Grace loves the Little Red Corn Dog Cart, and sometimes we'll get a burrito at Rancho del Zocalo so we can watch the Big Thunder Mountain trains come into Rainbow Ridge—the kids love that.

Giada: What about snacks?

Jack: The corn on the cob is good, with butter and chili powder. When I'm craving chicken late at night, I'll get a chicken breast a la carte from the Plaza Inn—that's one of the best snacks at the Park when you consider they are only like $3.50 each. We like to grab cupcakes at the Hungry Bear and sit on the second deck overlooking the River, it's a phenomenal view, and it makes you feel as if you're in another world. If you like onion rings, go to Taste Pilot's Grill, they are fried in a delicate batter, and they're not greasy at all. They have a great barbecue sauce there too.

Giada: How about your favorite dessert?

Jack: Oh, we have so many favorite desserts, everything from the soft ice cream on Paradise Pier to the Bread Pudding at the Storytellers Café buffet that tastes like gourmet French Toast. If you want something extravagant, you have to go to the Napa Rose. You can sit in the Lounge side of the restaurant if you want, with no reservations, and order dessert. Get the Dark Chocolate Truffle I mentioned—or try any of the desserts because they're all good. On your birthday, they actually give you a free dessert. Most people don't know this, but you can get the dessert portion of the Storytellers Café Buffet for around $9—all you can eat dessert including our favorite Bread Pudding. In Disneyland, we always get a mint and chip waffle cone sundae from the Gibson Girl. We also love the treats they make at Candy Palace like the dark chocolate pineapple spears. The dark chocolate and caramel marshmallow wands are like magic in your mouth, and of course the kids always want one of those huge Candy Canes they make at Christmas time. I think Guy did a special on those not too long ago.

Giada: Well, Jack, I think that gives us plenty to work with, thank you for sharing with our Food Network readers, I know they will appreciate this the next time they are at the Disneyland Resort.

Jack: No problem Giada, it was great meeting you.

Giada: Out of curiosity Jack, what's a normal day like for you here?

Jack: Well, it depends, usually we'll wake up and the kids will head to the Craftsman Club Concierge Lounge down the hall to eat breakfast with the security detail. I usually order in to the suite. I also have a private chef who cooks here for us. After that, if my schedule allows, we'll head into the Park for a few hours and just hang out. Then the kids will come back to the suite and get their school work done. We usually do most of our roaming around the Park at night for obvious reasons. A lot of times we'll either eat dinner at the Club—

Giada: Club 33?

Jack: Yes, or we'll just go there for dessert. The great thing is that we've got a security system and strategy that works extremely well at the Resort so nothing like what happened in 2005 could ever happen here again. It's the safest place on the West Coast.

[Noise from people entering the suite.]

Andy: No way, it's Giada!

Giada: Well hello there kids, you must be Andy and Grace!

Grace: Yes, we love your show!

Giada: Well thank you!

Kim: Oh my gosh, I can't believe it's you!

Jack: Giada, this is Kim.

Giada: Nice to meet you Kim!

Kendall: No way, is this Giada De Laurentiis, sitting right here in the El Capitan Suite? Come here and give me a hug!

Giada: Kendall! It is so good to see you, I've been wanting to meet you for a long time!

Jack: Excuse me for a second, everyone, I need to take this call.

[End of audio]

Get more ideas about what to eat at Disneyland from the MouseWait Real-Time Food Blog http://www.MouseWait.com/disneyland/tag/food

Author's Note Continued

Walking through the front gates of Disneyland transports you to another time. There's nothing else in the world that compares. Walt Disney designed Disneyland to make people feel as if they were in an enchanted, storybook world—and since 1955 it has been an enormous success.

When you walk down Main Street, the only thing that reminds you of Anaheim is the weather. Other than that, you feel as if you're in a charming, turn of the century town, with unlimited possibilities. The enticing aroma of fried chicken, popcorn, and freshly made sweets transports you to your childhood when things were simple and exciting. Disneyland is a special place for our family, and we have so many fantastic memories there.

My grandpa, Kelly Uno, took me to Disneyland when I was three years old, and I've loved it ever since. He was like Walt Disney. He invented things, had an entrepreneurial spirit, and a patriotic love for the United States. My grandpa and I had a unique relationship. The excitement in his voice when we talked over the phone is still burned into my memory. I'd always kiss him on the forehead and give him a big hug when we'd say goodbye, and it feels like only yesterday that I hugged him for the last time—even though he's been gone for twelve years.

He loved me unconditionally. He built a go-cart so I could act like I was on Autopia, he landscaped his yard in a style similar to Disneyland, and he always believed that I could do anything. When I was little, I told him my dream was to work as a street sweeper at Disneyland so he made a replica dust sweep and I would clean his driveway with it. I miss him dearly, and I look forward to the day when I'll see him again.

When I think of Walt, I always think of my grandpa because of their similarities.

My parents continued the Disneyland tradition in our lives by taking us at least once a year. It was always an open to close visit. I still don't know how they were able endure those long, hot summer days with us!

My wife and I went on our first date at Disneyland on August 13, 1993. A few years later we were married in the Rose Garden Gazebo at the Disneyland Hotel. Our six kids have grown up at the Parks, and they love it just as much as we do. We've been annual pass holders for twenty years consecutively, and the Resort is like a second home to us.

This love and admiration for Disneyland inspired me to build MouseWait, a free iPhone/iPad/Android/Windows Phone App that connects Disney fans from all over the world showing them real-time images from the Parks on a daily basis. My goal was to share the magic of the Disneyland with everyone no matter where they were so they could view live images, videos, wait times, and live vicariously through others at Disneyland.

I've learned so much from the 100,000+ people in the MouseWait community. My appreciation for the Parks has increased tremendously by meeting and talking with people who have great admiration for Disneyland and Walt's dream. I am extremely grateful to the wonderful members of MouseWait for their support and friendship over the years. Watch the MouseWait Story on YouTube and you'll see what I mean.

To my beautiful wife of eighteen years, Chelsea, who's been with me through good times and bad. She's seen me at my best and at my worst, yet she loves me the same. She is the most loyal person I've ever known, and I'm so grateful that she's the mother of our six children. She is more beautiful today than when I first met her. Without her support, MouseWait would not exist, and this book would not have materialized. She spent many hours helping me work out storyline challenges. She's the one I was destined to be with, and she inspires me daily—I hope I can still walk down Main Street with her when we're in our nineties and watch our great grandkids enjoy the place where our love began.

Thank you to my wonderful kids who have always been there for me helping with all of my crazy ventures; Ryan, McKenna, Kyrsten, Luke, Jack, and Andrew. They love Disneyland just as much as I do and it brings me joy to share it with them.

Thank you to my parents, Doug and Janet Johns who have always believed in me and have supported me in everything I've ever tried. They've always done everything in their power to help me with anything I set out to do. My Dad is a thirty-year Air Force veteran, and through my upbringing I developed a strong respect for people who serve our country in our Armed Forces.

Thank you to Bonnie Lawley and Dr. Tom Macready, two incredibly gracious people who have always been there for us. Thank you to Lynda Martin-Lawley who has been a tremendous source of encouragement and inspiration to me. She has blessed our family with her presence and overwhelming generosity for so many years.

I would like to extend a special thank you to the great people at the Hojo Anaheim, Jonathan Whitehead, Willie Simpson, and Tommy Sison, who've all been strong supporters of MouseWait over the years.

Thank you to BCC (Brendon), Sean Robison (Experiment818), and especially BaseballMickey for your help with this book. These Disney Cast Members helped tremendously with this Series, and they've also done a great deal to help MouseWait. They spread the magic of Disney to everyone they're in contact with, and the Walt Disney Company is lucky to have them on their team.

Thank you to Alan Cranford who helped me improve the military accuracy of the story. He gently corrected me on several tactical errors while sending volumes of relevant research to give the book a higher level of authenticity. Thank you, Alan, for your service to our country.

Thank you to the author of the "Long forgotten Haunted Mansion" blog for providing such an in depth investigation into the legend of Lafitte. This article inspired me to dig further historically and implement this incredible backstory in to *Deadliest Cast Member*.

Thank you to Shelly Wutke for lending her Disney expertise to this project and for being so gracious with her time and talent. Her editing skills and suggestions helped shape this novel. Thank you to Todd Barselow for editing and reviewing countless drafts with me.

This book is dedicated to two people who have since gone to Heaven; my grandpa, and my father-in-law, Lloyd Lawley. Lloyd always encouraged me and was one of our biggest cheerleaders. I can still hear his strong, deep voice over the phone saying, "I am SO proud of you." It's astounding how a short phrase like that, conveyed from a genuine heart, can influence a life. He recently lost his battle with cancer at only 59 years old and I miss him daily. Someone who genuinely encourages you, while putting their ego aside, is such a rare thing these days, and I never could've known how difficult it would be to lose him. I will always be grateful to him for treating me like his own son instead of a son-in-law. He would have been so proud to see this book completed, and he would have bragged about it to all his friends (no matter how it turned out)! He was the perfect example of a loving and accepting father-in-law, and I hope I can be half of what he was to my future sons-in-law (although frankly I'm not looking forward to it).

Most importantly I want to thank my Lord and Savior Jesus Christ, for dying so that I might live, for being the ultimate sacrifice and forgiving me of my sins so I can be reunited with my family one day in Heaven and on the New Earth where there will be no more death, mourning, crying or pain and everything will be made new again. (John 5:24)

I hope you've enjoyed reading *Deadliest Cast Member* as much as I enjoyed writing it. It's been a lot of fun exploring the rich history and the intricate details that have been embedded in the Parks for us to discover and enjoy.

Thank you for your support,

Kelly Johns

VOYAGEERS
KELLY RYAN JOHNS
VOYAGEERS
MAIN STREET
THE MULTIPLANER

The following is an excerpt from our brand new Disneyland Adventure Saga:

VOYAGEERS
THE MULTIPLANER

"Disneyland is like a time machine. You want to go back and have a glass of lemonade on a day that's been lost for a long time? Walt will do it for you."
RAY BRADBURY

"DO YOU REALIZE WHAT THIS MEANS?"

"We never have to leave Disneyland!"

"WE GET TO LIVE HERE!!!"

Christa was ecstatic.

Thomas looked confused and highly skeptical, "I still don't see how this is possible?"

"It's exactly what the Cast Member told us!" Christa said with glee. "We've been selected to be a part of a special program," she held the hotel-like keycard they were given to his face.

They stopped in the middle of Main Street, U.S.A.

Jubilant guests passed them on their way to The Hub, "Aviation Rag" cheerfully rang out in rhythm with the clopping of the horses' hooves in the background as they carried passengers down Main Street, and the smell of fresh caramel cooking in the Candy Palace wafted throughout the magical turn-of-the-century town. Normally, they walked slowly down Main Street, taking it all in, never knowing if they'd get the chance to come back again. They were lucky enough to visit one time per year because of the Smiths, but future visits were never guaranteed.

The sounds, the wonderful smells, and the carefully crafted buildings of Main Street surrounded them—but at this moment, everything was just a blur.

"This is what we've been praying for," Christa continued in her effort to convince Thomas, who thought it was too good to be true. "This is our way out—no more holding centers, *no more Fred*."

"I just think..." Thomas paused. He'd been trying to figure out a way for years to get his sister away from Fred and his mental abuse.

"I just think it might be a trick or something, Chrissy. Look, we've had bad luck our entire lives, and suddenly we're offered this? *Out of nowhere?*"

"Yes, but that's how this kind of stuff happens," she argued. "You know, like in Cinderella: one day, she's a servant; the next day, she's a princess. I think we're due—long overdue—to have something good happen!"

Thomas scrunched his eyebrows and looked down at the keycard. He looked back at Christa. He flashed a rare smile, and then quickly erased it from his face, not wanting to give her false hope.

"Okay, let's try this out and see if it works. I don't think it will; I think someone is playing a joke on us."

They walked towards the Main Street Magic Shop. The inviting doors to the quaint little shop were wide open. Striped awnings topped the first level windows. Above the door was the majestic classic MAGIC sign lined with oversized light bulbs. Two stories of petite windows with green awnings and laced curtains sat atop the Magic Shop. Patriotic red, white, and blue banners hung from the top of the building, giving it an old-fashioned turn-of-the-century feel.

They cautiously walked into the famous Magic Shop, the same place where Steve Martin worked when Disneyland opened, and looked for the old wooden phone on the wall. They were told to voice their code into this antique device. Two Cast Members, working behind the old-fashioned counter of the Magic Shop, watched them as they went straight for the phone.

Christa put her mouth in front of the black mouthpiece and discreetly voiced the code, "V1764."

There was no sound on the other end.

"See, Chrissy, I told you," Thomas said. "C'mon, let's get out of here and catch up with the Smiths."

One of the Cast Members behind the counter looked at Christa, "Excuse me, miss, can you come with me?"

"Um, sure," she said as the Cast Member walked out from behind the counter.

"Your code has been authenticated," he said with a smile as he took them through the red curtain near the old telephone. "Can I see your cards?"

Not saying a word, Thomas and Christa pulled out the gold cards they were given. "VOYAGEERS" was written in black across the top. The Cast Member took them to the back of the 20th Century Music Shop and opened the frosted glass door. He closed it behind them and swiped their cards on another door directly in front of them. It made a clanking sound.

"Ok, please put your eyes up to the viewfinder."

Christa smiled and did it without hesitation, but Thomas was reluctant to blindly follow directions.

She saw old Mickey Mouse cartoons playing in the viewfinder.

A light turned green.

"Ok, miss, you are clear. You're next, young man."

"I don't think this is a good idea, sir; we need to go."

"Thomas," Christa whispered while jabbing him, "just do it; we're at Disneyland—this is a chance of a lifetime."

Thomas frowned and reluctantly complied. He put his eyes up to the viewfinder and the light turned green.

"Okay, you're both set; wait a few seconds and this door will unlock."

"What's on the other side?" Thomas asked.

"You'll find out soon enough," the Magic Shop Cast Member said as he winked.

The deadbolt on the door released. The man opened it for them and motioned for them to enter.

They found themselves in a small, dark room with another door in front of them.

"You need to swipe one more time," the Cast Member said as he closed the door on his side.

The small room went pitch black, except for the red light on the second door's card scanner.

They looked at each other and swiped their cards.

The door opened, and their mouths dropped.

"Oh my goodness! Can you believe this, Tommy? What in the world?"

Thomas was wide-eyed and couldn't speak. They were in awe as the brilliant light from the room in front of them poured in. It was breathtaking, like something out of a movie. The room resembled an early 1900s hotel lobby. The floors were shiny with inset designs, and an antique Victorian golden-colored circular sofa was in the middle. The lobby was circular, in the form of a hub, and it was massive. Cream and light brown beech and maple accentuated the rich wood throughout the lobby. They could see the second level through the elegant wrought iron railings as people walked down the halls, stopping in front of the rich wood doors. A grand staircase was in the middle of everything. To the right of the staircase was what looked like a check-in desk, and to the left was a bellboy station. An elegant antique chandelier hung directly above them. Kids their age walked back and forth through the central hub of this turn-of-the-century lobby as Cast Members sat behind the front desk and counters dressed in early-American clothing.

There were comfy seating areas everywhere; it was like a big hangout—

the kids were sitting together talking, eating, and having fun. A large fireplace dominated the wall at one end with rocking chairs around it; at the other end a long ice cream bar stood out with old-fashioned stools and soda jerks serving sundaes—everywhere they looked, there were intimate little areas to sit, relax, and talk.

Thomas and Christa looked at each other and didn't say a word. The room buzzed with the excited talk of all the kids visiting, and no one noticed them enter. They walked up to the Cast Member at the front desk who was dressed in turn-of-the-century clothing with round rimless spectacles. He had his head bent down, busy with paperwork.

"Umm, excuse us, sir," said Christa.

"Can I help you?" the man said without lifting his head.

"Ummm," Thomas said, "I think we're supposed to show you these." They put their Voyageers cards on the desk in front of them.

The man was preoccupied with his work and didn't bother to look at their cards.

Thomas and Christa looked at each other and then gazed at their impressive surroundings. It was as if they'd been transported to another time —but the cool thing was that it seemed to be a hidden community of some kind, with kids mostly their age. Other than the Cast Members, there were no adults around.

Without looking at them, the man took their cards and swiped them in his machine.

Thomas noticed the sign on his desk.

Welcome to the Main Street Hotel.

They'd always seen the Main Street Hotel sign above the Magic Shop, but never thought it was an actual place.

The man finally looked up. "Well, hello, Thomas and Christa," he said in a monotone voice, "we're glad to have you stay with us." He sounded less than thrilled.

"Main Street Hotel?" Thomas said in disbelief.

The man stared at him with a blank look.

Christa interjected, "Sorry, my brother…well, actually both of us are a little confused right now. Is this actually a hotel above Main Street?"

"Yes, of course," the man said curtly with an irritated look as he pointed to the sign, "we've been here for a long time; I'm sure you've seen our sign on Main Street."

"Well, yes," Thomas said, "but we thought these were just empty rooms and this wasn't a real hotel."

"Well, you were wrong!" the man said sarcastically. "Do you think Walt Disney built things just for show? Everything he designed had a distinct purpose. Every second-story room on Main Street and throughout the Park, for that matter, is unique and functional."

Christa looked at Thomas with her mouth open.

"Your guide should be here in a minute, and he'll fill you in on the details."

Christa had a giant smile on her face. Thomas was skeptical.

A tall, handsome man came fumbling down the stairs, missing a step as he tried to read one of the papers on his clipboard. He had wavy blond hair, blue eyes, and a charming smile.

"Well, hello, you two; you must be Thomas and Christa!"

"Yes, sir," Thomas said.

"Welcome aboard; my name is Franklin," he smiled as he extended his hand to shake theirs. In the process, he dropped his papers all over the floor.

Thomas and Christa got down to help him.

"Oh, I am sorry about that," Franklin said as the man behind the desk shook his head. Frazzled, he reshuffled his papers trying to find the right ones for Thomas and Christa.

"So, you guys are from…Michigan?"

"No, California," Thomas said.

"Oh, California, sure, that's right; now I remember!"

"And your name is…" He looked blankly at Thomas. He already forgot his name, even though he had said it just a few minutes ago.

"It's Thomas."

"Oh, yes, of course, you'll have to forgive me; I have so many things happening today."

The Cast Member at the desk shook his head again, and Franklin caught him, "Okay, well, other guides might have bigger workloads, but this is a lot for me."

"Sir," Christa asked, "is this for real? Do we really get to live above Main Street?"

"Yes, I'll show you to your room. Come this way, um…" Franklin shuffled through his papers trying to find Christa's name.

"It's Christa."

"Sure, Christa, follow me."

Franklin led them up the grand staircase—the focal point of the dramatic two-story lobby. As they reached the second floor, he led them down the hall a bit until they arrived at a door.

"Here it is. This is where you'll be staying for now…" Franklin paused. "Are you guys ready for this?"

He opened the dark polished wooden door.

Christa gasped and put her hand over her mouth.

The room was beautiful; everything was decorated in an early-1900s small-town hotel theme. White laced fabric adorned the windows; the same fabric was used on tabletops and other furnishings throughout the room. It had two beds, a bathroom, and a beautiful little window. Christa ran to the window.

"Tommy, look at this view of Main Street!"

The Emporium was directly across the street from them. Town Square was to the left. She could see the flag pole, the train station, City Hall, and Walt's Fire Station Apartment. The jubilant Main Street music was audible through the closed window.

"Are you serious? We get to stay here?" Christa squealed, thrilled out of her mind.

"Yes, this is where you start out in the Voyageers program—the Main Street Hotel. We will assign you each a job as a Cast Member, and then we'll determine if you have what it takes to join our program."

"But what about our normal life? What about going home and school?" Thomas asked.

"Well that's the interesting part—you see, we have control of…well, how do I put it…we have control over *time* to a certain extent."

"What?" Thomas grabbed Christa's hand and prepared to walk out of the door.

"Thomas, wait," Christa said, pushing his hand aside. "Sir, what do you mean by 'control over time'?"

Franklin paused, "Think of it like this. Who are you with today?"

"The Smith family," Christa said quickly.

"Oh, yes, right, the Smiths." Franklin continued to fumble with the paperwork. "The Smiths will never realize you're gone. If this doesn't work out, you'll end up going home with them when your work is done here, and they'll never know the difference."

"What do you mean 'they'll never know'? Is this some kind of a joke?" Thomas was becoming frustrated, "I'm not going to let my sister get her hopes up only to be disappointed by some kind of elaborate scam."

Franklin paused, looking up confidently from his papers right into Thomas's eyes and stated, "This is no joke or scam. I can guarantee you that."

"How can we get jobs as Cast Members, train, and things like that without anyone knowing we're gone?" Christa asked.

"You two better sit down," Franklin said, motioning to the bed.

Thomas reluctantly sat next to Christa, as she gazed out the hotel window in awe.

"First of all, there are a few rules that need to be followed. You are not to tell anyone about what you see or hear in the Voyageers' Realm. It's top secret and not open to the public. Only a few select Cast Members have access to this community. It's hidden, and we need to keep it that way."

"How in the world can you keep all of this hidden?" Thomas asked skeptically.

"We have an elaborate system that we're tied into; it's too complicated to explain, and frankly, I don't fully understand it. All I know is that it works."

"So you just let random people in here who pass your test and answer a few trivia questions?" Thomas said sarcastically.

"No," Franklin opened a file folder on his clipboard as he talked, "you and your sister were chosen for this program years ago, shortly after your parents died."

Thomas got up from the bed, shocked by what Franklin said, "What? How do you know about our parents? This is too weird, Chrissy; we need to go." Thomas grabbed her hand and headed for the door.

Franklin watched them as they walked to the door and waited for the right moment. Then he spoke softly, "But Thomas, haven't you been looking for a way out of your current situation for a long time?"

Thomas stopped at the door with his back to Franklin.

"You've tried everything," Franklin continued, "every scheme you could come up with to make enough money to create a better life for your sister. You've trusted people to help you out, and they've failed you. You have made so many valiant attempts, but they've all failed. You've done everything in your power to get away from…*Fred*."

Thomas froze. He turned around as a tear formed in the corner of his eye. "How do you know everything about us? Have you been spying on us? Are we in trouble or something? How do you know about Fred? Does he have something to do with this?"

"No, Thomas," Franklin said with a soft, reassuring voice, "I'm here to offer you the opportunity of a lifetime, a chance to finally be free of your miserable situation, a chance to live inside the gates of the Park you love, and to make a significant impact on the world. Walt Disney had a special place in his heart for orphans who possessed a love for Disneyland. He had a desire to help the underprivileged. We found you because of your love for Disneyland, and we want to set both of you free from the abusive situation you're in."

A single tear streamed down Thomas's cheek, and he wiped it as fast as he could so no one would notice. *Could this be real?* After all of these years of trying everything to find a better life for his sister, he had almost given up hope. So many hurtful things had happened to them—the abuse, the neglect, the abandonment, moving from house to house, not being able to make friends, and rarely finding anyone who truly cared about them.

Could this be their way out?

Franklin waited until they both looked him in the eyes, then he spoke with authority, "Thomas and Christa Hart—you've been invited to join a secret society created by Walt Disney, the greatest innovator of our time. You've been selected to be part of an extraordinary group of people tasked with keeping his dream alive—an alliance that fights for the good of mankind..."

Franklin paused and flashed a confident smile at Thomas and Christa. "*You* have been selected to join *Walt Disney's Voyageers*."

Credits

I sincerely thank each one of you for your feedback throughout the Series! Some of the entries only contained email addresses, so I naturally excluded those from this list.

EPISODE ONE

Amanda (HadMatter)
Daniel John
Nickelnorm
Scott Loudon
Sallyg
Carl Greco
Mariah
Ann Franklin
Amanda Bennett
Faser Cohen
Frmky
Teresa
Jeff
Shari Kenyon
Mike Frankovich
Keala76
Boundin
Elizabeth Olivas
Brandie Lynn
Cathy Chavez
Nick White
Sandy Sullivan
Sallen
Robyn Eggleston
Amanda Hiteshew
Jrabbit
Sandy

EPISODE TWO

Cynnamon Curtis

Tony
Nick White
Tracy Ojeda
Sallyzero13
Jrabbit
Ned Canepa
Stacy
Scott Loudon
Jackie Griffith
Cathy Chavez
Daniel Shahidzadeh
Joanne Yensidtoo
SallyG
Suzy
Amanda Hiteshew
Gina Spina
Sandy Abernathy
Nate Clark

EPISODE THREE

C. Oliver
Kelly Bonne
Phillip Mendez
Deanna
Dawn H.
Sallyg
Robyn Eggleston
Suzanne
Debra Gamreiter
Ned Canepa
Cathy Chavez
Nate Clark
Gothamgal
Carol
Cynnamon Curtis
Sara Murphy

Amanda Hiteshew
Teresa
Stacy Wilke
Glitter
Terry Halverson
Sandy Abernathy
Alan Cranford
Daniel Shahidzadeh
Jrabbit
Alan Cranford

EPISODE FOUR

Alan Cranford
Jackie Griffith
Dan John
Sallyg
Nathan Clarke
Dawn Hopkins
Ned Canepa
Kim
Daniel Shahidzadeh
Fraser Cohen
Liliosdog
Bev
Jay Turley

EPISODE FIVE

Alicia Ellis
Kim Prentice
Kelly Rice
Alan Cranford
Doreen Carney
Jennifer Halstead
Judy Balmer
Belinda Turnbow
Andrea Butler

Teresa P.
Dawn Hopkins
Jay Turley
Carol
Daniel Shahidzadeh
Nathan Clarke
Bethany Woodard Thomas
Cindy Myers
Sheila Auberzinsky
HadMatter

Made in the USA
San Bernardino, CA
27 August 2014